## INTO THE DARKNESS

We descended down a short, dark passage. As the side d
shut behind me, the dank smell of the exercise pool was imm...
ately cut off and replaced by the smell of old wood
the dusty scent of bedding chaff. The salty odor
and the leathery reek of dragon hide, laced with the tang of
venom, overlay everything.

The short passageway leveled, abruptly turned. A row of stalls,
all empty save the last one, stood directly before me. In the last
stall, an old destrier stood, her wings folded along either flank.

The dragonmaster stopped at the first empty stall. He set his
lantern on the ground, turned to face me, and waited for me to
stand before him. I did so stiffly.

"She's old, this dragon," he murmured. "Been long in my service,
mine and mine alone. She's practiced on many a reluctant apprentice that I've drugged and gagged and tormented into submitting to
her tongue, apprentices who're no longer alive to tell the tale. But
you don't need such persuasion, do you, Skykeeper's Daughter? Because you've done this sort of thing before."

His fingers closed on my chin. "Ah, yes. You can't hide them
from one who knows. I saw it the day we met at Mombe Taro:
You've got dragon eyes."

His own eyes glittered brightly, and his shoulders twitched.

"You're hungry for it, aren't you?" he breathed. "You want the
venom."

"No," I whispered, but he only grinned madly at the lie.

"You know what I expect from you, after you lie with the old destrier, hey?"

I refused to answer. His fingers tightened on my chin.

"You'll tell me what you heard, Skykeeper's Daughter. You'll reveal the dragons' mystery to me. . . ."

# SHADOWED

## by

# WINGS

BOOK TWO OF THE
### Dragon Temple
### Saga

## JANINE CROSS

A ROC BOOK

ROC
Published by New American Library, a division of
Penguin Group (USA) Inc., 375 Hudson Street,
New York, New York 10014, USA
Penguin Group (Canada), 90 Eglinton Avenue East, Suite 700, Toronto
Ontario M4P 2Y3, Canada (a division of Pearson Penguin Canada Inc.)
Penguin Books Ltd., 80 Strand, London WC2R 0RL, England
Penguin Ireland, 25 St. Stephen's Green, Dublin 2,
Ireland (a division of Penguin Books Ltd.)
Penguin Group (Australia), 250 Camberwell Road, Camberwell, Victoria 3124,
Australia (a division of Pearson Australia Group Pty. Ltd.)
Penguin Books India Pvt. Ltd., 11 Community Centre, Panchsheel Park,
New Delhi - 110 017, India
Penguin Group (NZ), cnr Airborne and Rosedale Roads, Albany,
Auckland 1310, New Zealand (a division of Pearson New Zealand Ltd.)
Penguin Books (South Africa) (Pty.) Ltd., 24 Sturdee Avenue,
Rosebank, Johannesburg 2196, South Africa

Penguin Books Ltd., Registered Offices:
80 Strand, London WC2R 0RL, England

First published by Roc, an imprint of New American Library,
a division of Penguin Group (USA) Inc.

First Printing, August 2006
10  9  8  7  6  5  4  3  2  1

RoC  REGISTERED TRADEMARK—MARCA REGISTRADA

LIBRARY OF CONGRESS CATALOGING-IN-PUBLICATION DATA:
Cross, Janine.
Shadowed by wings / Janine Cross.
p. cm. — (The Dragon Temple saga ; bk. 2)
ISBN 0-451-46089-8 (pbk.)
I. Title.
PS3603.R674S53 2006
813'.6—dc22          2005035629

Set in Weiss
Designed by Ginger Legato

Printed in the United States of America

*To mothers and children everywhere.*

# SHADOWED
## by
# WINGS

# ONE

The massive carrion bird plummeted groundward, casting a cool shadow that rapidly engulfed the entire Lashing Lane.

The spectators who had intended on stoning me moments before paused a half moment as the reality of what they were seeing sank in: A legendary creature with a fifty-foot wingspan was descending upon them, its razor-lined beak gaping, its scimitar claws grasping, its elliptical body shimmering with blue light.

They were staring at a Skykeeper, a creature who, as a guardian of the Celestial Realm, held dominion over life and death for mortal humans and divine dragons alike.

A creature who was, unbeknownst to them, my mother's haunt.

She would not allow them to stone me to death for the crime of daring to join the dragonmaster's apprenticeship. No. The haunt wanted me alive, to serve its own mad purpose.

The Skykeeper screeched, rattling hearts within rib cages and the timbers of the nearby stables with its reverberating skirl. As one, the spectators broke for cover, screaming.

I was seated upon a dragon on the lane, held there by Waikar Re Kratt, First Son of the warrior-lord of Clutch Re. For reasons as yet unknown to me, Kratt had galloped into my stoning and hoisted me atop his destrier. As the Skykeeper screeched, the dragon we rode reared, trumpeting; I was unsaddled and landed heavily on the ground. The dragon's wicked talons slashed the air above me. I scrambled away, back, the rocks that littered the ground biting into my bare buttocks and legs.

The Skykeeper rushed earthward with terrifying speed. Twenty feet above ground, it pulled up sharply and skimmed over the lane, dust and the stench of carrion whirling in its wake, the air preternaturally chill.

The dragons harnessed to the parade of satin-and-silver-decked carriages that lined the lane trumpeted and tried to bolt. Talons the color of newly minted steel and dewlaps glittering with milky opalescence flashed in the sunlight as dragons reared and bucked against their harnesses. Carriages overturned or became entangled with one another, spilling screaming bayen women and children onto the dusty lane.

Great wingspan shuddering, the luminous Skykeeper banked away from the lane and rose into the sky. It skirled again—a harrowing, earsplitting shriek—and flapped ponderously toward the lone cloud high in the hard blue sky.

My mother was leaving me yet again.

Grief overwhelmed me as I watched the Skykeeper shrink into a zircon marble and disappear into the cloud far above.

The dragon I'd been seated upon bucked and clawed the ground, snorting, eyes rolling, foam falling in venom-scented clouds from her muzzle. Waikar Re Kratt fought to rein her in, struggling to stay in his saddle. His blue satin cape flashed behind him like the wings of a giant, livid raven.

I scrambled farther back from his panicked beast and looked about me, disbelieving.

The crowd was gone. Dragonmaster apprentices, monks, spectators, and attending eminent Holy Wardens alike had all run for cover. Mother—the Skykeeper—had saved my life.

"Get up, girl."

My eyes jerked toward the flushed face of the dragonmaster of Clutch Re. Unlike everyone else, he had not run for cover from the

Skykeeper. No. He'd remained on the lane. And as he walked toward me, his green-whorled brown skin gleaming in the sunlight and the glass bead at the end of his chin braid swinging to and fro, he grinned dementedly, as if the appearance of the creature had pleased him immensely. He glanced at Waikar Re Kratt, still struggling with his beast, then looked back at me.

"Get up!"

I scrambled to my feet, legs unsteady, breath thready and cold. I looked about the ground, seeking the tunic the dragonmaster had demanded I shuck, so I could be inducted into his apprenticeship through ritual whipping. It was that which had spurred the crowd into murderous indignation, see: my nakedness, and my female gender.

The garment was nowhere in sight.

"Walk over to the bar," the dragonmaster barked.

I gaped at him.

He meant to whip me, to continue with the annual ritual of Mombe Taro whether or not he had spectators and apprentices, with or without the pageantry and ritual. He still meant to induct me into his apprenticeship.

Fear and triumph shot through me in equal measures.

It wasn't too late to back out, to flee. After all, women did *not* enter the apprenticeship of a dragonmaster, and as a woman of seventeen years, I would be defying centuries of tradition by allowing myself to be inducted into dragonmaster Re's apprenticeship.

But if I fled, I would never again experience the heady splendor of dragon venom, would never again taste its licorice-and-lime effervescence. Would never get another chance to share myself with a dragon and hear divine dragonsong.

So, of course, I wouldn't flee.

Trembling, mouth so dry I couldn't swallow, I walked over to the whipping bar. I was intensely aware of my nakedness and felt exposed and highly vulnerable. As I walked, my bare feet raised clouds of the red dust unique to my birth Clutch. It was warm, that dust, and powdery. A caress, almost. I pictured myself clothed in it.

Behind me, I heard Waikar Re Kratt exchange words with the dragonmaster.

An epiphany struck me: Custom dictated that a dragonmaster's apprentice could not be inducted or reinstated into his apprenticeship by the dragonmaster himself, and that the ritual whipping had to be done by other hands. It would therefore be Kratt who would lay leather against my back.

Nausea rushed over me, and I stumbled and would have fallen if not for the whipping bar that ran, hip high, down the median of the Lashing Lane. I gripped the smooth wood of the bar tightly and forced myself to breathe in, breathe out.

The whipping bar was the color of wild honey, and it was slick with consecrated oil yet furred here and there with red dust. It had been carved to resemble a sinuous, impossibly long dragon, and amongst the bar's labyrinthine wooden scales, contorted human shapes leered at me. From the corner of one eye, I saw Kratt ride over to a section farther along the whipping bar and tether his lathered, exhausted beast.

I was going to get what I wanted most now.

Venom.

Yet that venom would be imparted by a whip, a whip wielded by someone I had vowed to kill, someone I feared and hated, someone who had murdered my father, sent my mother down the spiraling path of insanity, and destroyed my childhood.

"Mo Fa Cinai, wabaten ris balu," I murmured. *Purest Dragon, become my strength.*

I closed my eyes.

The dragons entangled in the smashed carriages farther down the lane lowed in fear and pain. I heard wood splinter and chain clank, smelled the burning-oil stench of agitated dragon. Women and children were crying. Some distance away, a pack of feral dogs howled, their syncopated yelps and yowls eerie.

I heard footsteps approaching me from behind. Steady. Soft. They moved without hurry.

My pulse sped up.

The footsteps stopped.

I heard a slithering, raspy sound: a whip uncoiling.

My fingers tightened on the bar. I could not breathe properly. I started panting. My bare back and buttocks crawled with dread anticipation; I could feel every muscle clenching tighter, tighter.

The waiting stretched on. And on.

Mo Fa Cinai, wabaten ris balu, I repeated in my mind. Mo Fa Cinai, wabaten ris balu.

Then a near-silent whisper flicked over the air, and leather cracked near my ear. I jumped, eyes flying open, and a scream escaped me.

Another long pause. I grew giddy.

Crack!

Leather snapped near my other ear, without touching, though my hair wafted a little in the breeze the whip made. Again I jumped and screamed, couldn't help it, and suddenly I was filled with fury, for I was being toyed with by a sadist who'd once smashed my mother's jaw, over and over, beneath his boot heel, and I would *not* play his vicious game; I would *not*.

As always, I didn't hold my tongue when I should have.

"You dragon-sucking screw!" I shrieked as I whirled about. "Don't you feel man enough to whip me properly? Don't you feel strong enough, brave enough, unless I've pissed myself in fear first?"

For one volcanic moment, we stared at each other, Kratt and I, his cold blue eyes boring into my brown ones. Then his whip moved, and a breathtaking pain sliced the skin below my left breast, and then another gashed me between the legs, reaching up under my sex and cracking against my tailbone so hard that I swore bone fractured. I screamed and spun away from the whip, lurched into the whipping bar, which I'd forgotten about, almost fell over it.

And still that whip fell.

It stung, it burned, and my breath came ragged and fast as my chest rose and fell, rose and fell, beneath my head, which I instinctively covered with my arms. Eight times only a dragonmaster's apprentice should be whipped during induction. Eight times. But Kratt's whip fell far, far more often than that upon my naked body.

With each whip fall, my screams intensified, till they burst from my mouth like shrieking birds, and the whip no longer stung or thudded but landed like a shard of ice, the sensation like that of being splashed with boiling oil: that moment when it feels not hot, but intensely cold, and then not cold or hot but another sensation entirely, one that can be described only as keen agony.

The whip falls smashed against me like fists, bit as deep as hurled knives. Each strike jerked my entire body and burned iced flame into the marrow of my bones.

Suddenly, the world tipped. Hardpan slammed against my knees. My forehead thudded slowly, slowly against dirt, and I was confused and felt poised on the lip of complete vertigo. Grit coated my tongue. A salty, metallic fluid filled my mouth.

"Stop, please stop."

Not me, choking the words out from a throat so raw that each word tasted of blood. Surely not me. I was stronger than that, would never beg for mercy from this man, of all men.

For an answer: silence.

Stillness.

Then.

Black boots coated in fine red dust floated before my face. Fad-

ing. Oscillating. Beneath my cheek hot earth pulsed. A thready
whine filled my ears. A hand caught my hair, jerked my face off the
ground.

Blue glistened before me: the sky. No. An eye. Two eyes. *His*
eyes. The eyes of Kratt. Above those eyes, hair the color of sun-
blanched almonds, dusted with golden cane sugar.

The hand released me. My head plunged groundward, down-
ward, tumbling and spinning, falling forever.

*Thud!* My cheek struck earth.

Darkness, with a pinpoint of blinding light at its center.

The point of light grew, pulsing. The darkness receded. From
the center of the light grew a face. Not Kratt's face, no. This one
was deeply lined, was the piebald color of dried herbs and bark.
Gray eyebrows as thin as desiccated millipedes furrowed at me beneath a bald, scarred head. I stared into the eyes of that face; they
were marbled with blood.

The face slewed sideways. Blinding light again, and sensation returned in excruciating swiftness to my body.

Agony across my flayed back, across my calves and rump.
Agony as I lay belly down in the dust, one cheek pressed against
hot ground, the sun's angry eye glaring directly into mine as I continued the agonizing process of returning to consciousness.

That blood-eyed face loomed again into the light; it grinned at
me. It was a knowing grin, a grin possessing the wisdom of the insane. The drawn lips exposed listing and rotted teeth, gums speckled with bruises. Below that leer dangled a chin braid garnished
with a green toggle.

"Bite," said the face.

Sunlight shone on something wet and black: a whip. The whip's
handle was shoved crosswise into my mouth. And then . . .

Oh, then.

A slow effervescence on my tongue, tasting like licorice and
limes. A subsequent burning, so beautiful and complete it set my

mouth and throat aflame, sent pain-dulling heat roaring through my nose, my eyes, my ears.

Dragon venom. Sweet, forbidden dragon venom.

The agony of my flayed back and calves guttered as the analgesic hallucinogen filtered through my blood.

But no, I should not taste venom! I had forsworn the illicit drug in my quest to seek vengeance against Kratt. Yet I could no more prevent myself from swallowing the venom than I had been able to prevent myself from begging for mercy from the whip. Some things are greater than noble aspirations, more powerful than determination. Some would call it instinct. Some, magic.

Others, addiction.

So I did what I had to do to end the overwhelming agony, and as I sucked, my pain-induced dizziness cleared and I recognized the piebald green-and-brown face leering at me: the dragonmaster.

He patted my head as though I were a dog, took the whip from my mouth, and stood.

"Who is she?" Kratt said. He stood above me, a whip's length away, panting from the exertion of flailing me.

" 'Who is she?' " the dragonmaster parroted. "You've whipped her on the lane during Mombe Taro. She is, therefore, my apprentice—"

"Don't dissemble, old man."

"She's the one I told you about," the dragonmaster grunted. "The Dirwalan Babu."

Dirwalan Babu. The Skykeeper's Daughter, in the ancient Malacarite tongue.

"What proof have you?" Kratt growled.

"Other than the holy will of Re, which directs me?"

"Yes."

"Other than that which you witnessed just now?"

A momentary silence from Kratt as he glanced up to where the Skykeeper had disappeared.

He looked down at me again. His eyes were cold and penetrating, made of turquoise and quartz. I closed my lids against them.

"She knows venom," Kratt said slowly. "Knows it well, to have sucked the whip so."

"You suppose?" the dragonmaster said dryly; then he roared with laughter. Behind my closed lids, I saw the laughter as a rainfall of jewels, sharp and multicolored, tasting of iron and coal. I felt a flicker of fear, quickly soothed by the venom coursing through me. The dragonmaster's laughter bespoke years of exposure to venom and his inner battle to retain his sanity. Any who'd oft imbibed the dragons' liquid fire would recognize the sound.

"She'll die for this travesty, Komikon," Kratt said, his voice low and dark. "No woman can serve the bull, and no one should know venom as well as she."

"Not even one of my apprentices?"

"Don't play me for a fool. Temple will scythe her down before the sun sets on this day."

"You'll stay the execution," the dragonmaster said angrily.

"Will I?"

"By all that is sacred, you *must* stay her execution; we agreed upon it!"

"You would have me defy Temple over a myth that no one but you knows."

"It is a prophecy as real as the creature that just flew over us. Few know of it."

I could smell the tension between the two men, the clash of wills as pungent as the musk male mongooses emit in combat. I lifted my cheek from the ground a little, head numb with venom, and squinted into the sunlight. The two men stood facing each other, inches apart. Waikar Re Kratt still breathed heavily from having whipped me, his flaxen hair a brilliant crown in the sun, his eyes polished beryls, his high cheekbones and chiseled nose the essence of power and calculating might. The dragonmaster stood half-crouched as if to spring at him, was naked save for a stained leather loincloth, every inch of his sinewy, mottle-colored body crisscrossed with white scars.

Kratt turned away from the dragonmaster and walked the few paces to me, his leather boots falling softly upon dusty hardpan. With the languid ease of a jungle cat, he squatted on his haunches and regarded me.

"Her mouth should be blistered from that venom," he murmured. "She should be choking to death. Frothing. Spewing blood."

"She knows venom," the dragonmaster said simply, repeating the very words Kratt had used moments before.

"Who are you, rishi whelp?" Kratt cocked his head to the side. His were the dulcet tones used to sing a child to sleep, but those piercing blue eyes belied the temperate sound. "Who are you, that you know venom so well?"

I tried to summon enough saliva to spit in his face but could not. Neither could I find the courage, not with the wounds on my back so fresh and the memory of pain so immediate.

"I asked you a question, rishi whelp. Answer it."

"Zarq," I croaked. "I am Zarq."

"Is that so? A woman bearing the name of Malacar's legendary warrior. An unusual piece of refuse, then." Amusement curled his lips, but his eyes did not join the mirth. "Can you summon that bird at will, hmm? That Skykeeper?"

"Yes," I lied, my eyes never wavering from his.

"Summon it now."

"Can't." Venom lent me the inspiration to fabricate. "The effort would kill me, in this state."

"What state?"

He wanted to hear how fiercely he'd wounded me, was poised for such. I would not give him that satisfaction.

From the stable end of the Lashing Lane, where lay the wreckage of overturned carriages, came voices and the answering snorts and bellows from the entrapped dragons. People were beginning to emerge whence they'd hidden in stable and doorway, and I could hear them approaching the smashed carriages, calling out to the wounded.

Kratt's eyes did not flicker from my face.

"Could you summon that Skykeeper in Arena, rishi whelp, were you to survive the apprenticeship long enough to make it there?"

"I'll survive long enough," I said, with more conviction than I felt. "And the Skykeeper obeys my will."

"Does it." He looked away from me and stared down the lane, as if he might descry the future from its dusty length.

I heard crying. A woman crying, a child wailing. Someone calling for help, over and over. Kratt had chosen to whip me rather than aid them. I wondered whether he had sisters, daughters, claimed women in those crippled carriages.

I licked my lips but could not swallow for the dryness.

He looked back at me, eyes cool, appraising. "Why?"

I didn't understand the question.

"What motivates you, that you defy Temple by joining the dragonmaster's apprenticeship? If you are the prophesied get of a Guardian of the Celestial Realm, what need have you to serve me and my bull dragon?"

I borrowed a phrase of the dragonmaster's. "The will of Re directs me."

"Does it, now."

"Yes."

"The holy will of my bull dragon bids you serve him."

"Yes."

"Indeed."

I forced myself to meet his beryl eyes for all of several heartbeats.

"Well, then," he murmured, mockery lacing his words. "We must obey the will of Re, mustn't we?"

He rose, unclasped the cape from his neck, and dropped it over me with a swirl of silk. He became brisk, impatient. "Get her out of here, Komikon. Get her out of here before everyone returns. I'll deal with Temple."

# TWO

The dragonmaster draped me over his shoulders as if I were a slaughtered young doe and carried me behind the stable domain's imposing sandstone walls, into the world he ruled. He deposited me belly down upon a hammock, brusquely clasped about my neck the cape Kratt had dropped upon me, and adjusted the cloth as best he could to cover my appalling nakedness from the eyes of his apprentices. I was aware of the apprentices only vaguely; eruptive fevers assailed me, in the manner that only venom, its effects intensified by pain, can.

Belly down and awash in a sea of venom drink, I slept that entire day, right through to the night. As night descended, as thick and smothering as a slurry of coal dissolved in water, I remained in venom's grip, alone upon that hammock, which hung from the rafters of but one of the hundreds of stalls in the dragon stables of Roshu-Lupini Re, the warrior-lord of my birth Clutch.

I say I slept, but I use the term loosely, for pain, fear, and hallucinations foster little in the way of sleep.

The night stretched long, impossibly long. It undulated onward with no sign of ending, like an ebony serpent slowly being disgorged from the maw of some vast, timeless sky-beast.

Middle-night came and went, and seemed to come again, and I hated that darkness, so relentlessly present each time I shifted in my sleep, each shifting rousing me with the pain it caused. At some point the dragonmaster appeared, as silent as an apparition at my head, and slid the cold steel of a drinking pipette between my dry lips.

"Drink, drink," he hissed, his breath tinged by the citric tang of venom.

"What is it?" I asked, though my words came out venom slurred and incomprehensible. I didn't need an answer, though. I knew full well what liquid floated cold and viscous in the hairy gourd the dragonmaster held cupped in his palms.

So I drank.

Racked by pain, chattering with cold, burning with thirst, I drank his dreadful draft, with each swallow both loathing and craving the venom within.

Loathing it, for how dependent I'd once been upon the poison, for how reckless it could make me, for how it saturated my limbs with bestial lust and my mind with vivid hallucinations.

Craving it, for how the venom created a shield against my mother's haunt, the Skykeeper, who would have me abandon my current course of action and whittle away my life searching for Waivia, my lost, and most likely dead, half sister.

The consequences would be severe should any find out that the dragonmaster was giving me venom. Its use was strictly governed by Ranon ki Cinai, the Temple of the Dragon, and never was it wasted on a rishi, a Clutch serf such as I. Never. Yet it wasn't fear of Temple that made me tremble each time I swallowed the dragonmaster's draft.

When would dawn come?

Never.

I would be locked in that cycle of pain and giddiness, desire and loathing, reality and frost blue hallucinations, forever.

Those hallucinations. Harrowing, accusatory images, they were. Of my sister, Waivia, forced by cruel men to commit acts of sexual degradation. Of emaciated holy women tortured with scalding oil, then decapitated beneath an Auditor's scimitar. Over and over I heard the melon-fat thunk of blade upon neck; the wet, bubbly exhalation that followed; the gristly thud and sudden stop of blade buried in bone, withdrawn by the Auditor with a twisting wrench from half-hewn neck; his grunt of exertion as he again swung his blade.

A bitter night that was as I lay there, alternately plagued by hallucinations and racked with pain.

But morning did come at last. Pale and watery, the dawn's light seeped into the stall where I lay facedown on the hammock and stained the flagstones beneath me light gray. Nourished by that light, the muscles in my body eased a little.

Real sleep would come at last.

"Sa Gikiro," a voice cackled in my ear, and my heart stuttered, then galloped, and at once I was painfully awake again. "Time for me to gather more inductees, hey-o. Fresh fodder for our bull dragon."

I turned my head and stared into the bloodshot eyes of the dragonmaster. The green bead at the end of his chin braid swung before me as he lifted yet another gourd of venom before my face.

"Drink, Babu. Drink."

Enough of the poison still burned through my veins from the last draft I'd consumed to lend me sufficient courage to refuse. "No."

"You'll rue that decision soon enough! There's not an inch on your back and rump that isn't bloody or bruised."

"I don't need your poison," I said, with more conviction and less fear than I felt.

The dragonmaster leaned nearer my face. "So you won't drink, hey-o?"

He cackled. I closed my eyes against the sour blast of his breath.

"I'll do so, then."

My eyes flew open. He tipped the gourd to his lips; the steel drinking pipette fell to the ground and clattered against flagstone. *Glug, glug, glug!* His larynx punched up and down as he drained the gourd, and fury rushed over me, for that had been *my* venom.

No sooner did the thought sweep over me than I hated myself for it and the dragonmaster for provoking it.

The dragonmaster drained the gourd, threw it aside, and smirked at me, beads of venom glistening upon his goatee braid. Triumph blazed in his eyes as he saw my clashing emotions.

"I'll be back this eve, with fresh fodder for Re and more venom for you. I dare you to refuse it then, girl. Ha!"

He turned and loped out of the stall.

Seething with resentment and regret, I watched him cross the courtyard. The dragonmaster moved like a simian, stooped a little, arms hanging low, his lithe, scarred form taut with coiled muscle. I half expected him to spring to the stable's tetrahedral rooftops and swing himself along the upturned eaves.

But he did not.

He merely entered a long, whitewashed, wattle-and-daub hovel backed against part of the sandstone wall that surrounded the entire stable domain, and disappeared inside the hovel through a doorway of hanging skins.

It was then that I released my breath and the pain that had seemed so manageable moments before swelled, became a fire blazing up my calves, raking across my buttocks and back.

What had I done, refusing venom in that state?

But surely I could overcome the pain without aid of the dragon's poison. Surely, after all I'd suffered in my life, I was stronger than that.

Eyes clenched shut, I faced away from the courtyard, turning my back, as it were, upon the dragonmaster's departure, and lay as still as possible, belly down, breathing shallowly, carefully, riding the swell and ebb of pain. Desperately awaiting nightfall and the return of the dragonmaster and his evil, irresistible draft.

The shuffle and lowing of the stable's hungry dragons heralded the new day. A flock of pigeons landed in the courtyard, cooing, then burst into flight again with a brisk, staccato flutter of wings. Beyond the stable walls, a cur barked, joined by another. From the hovel into which the dragonmaster had disappeared came voices raised in brief argument.

The sun crested the ridge of mountains that surrounded the valley of Clutch Re. I felt the dawn's light reflecting from the courtyard onto my flayed back. My bladder, distended with all the liquid I'd consumed during the night, gradually became a pulsing thing in desperate need of voiding.

But what to do? Get up? Impossible, in my condition. And pointless, for where to go in the male-exclusive dragonmaster's domain? There would be no Temple-authorized place where a woman might rid herself of dirty waters without tainting dragon-blessed soil.

But I was no ordinary woman, yes? I had been circumcised years ago, while at Convent Tieron, cleansed by a holy knife. Could I therefore not piss where the male apprentices pissed?

I was near frantic with the need to urinate. I rose onto my elbows; agony flared across my back. I gasped. My eyes leaked tears.

Holding my breath, I slowly sat up and swung my legs over the hammock's edge. Kratt's cape hung askew from my neck, covering my torso down to my thighs. My bladder threatened to loose itself as the shift in position heightened the sensation of urgency.

But no, I couldn't urinate here, on stable floor! For whilst *all* the soil of a Clutch is dragon blessed and not to be sullied by a woman's secretions, the ground of the dragon stables, where a Clutch holy bull resides, is by far the most consecrated of earth, and however much I might justify my actions by arguing that my womanhood had been cut from me by a convent holy knife, I would still be violating a fundamental principle of Temple law.

I had to find the dragonmaster, had to have direction on where I might relieve myself.

Ignoring the rasp of coarse twine against my raw buttocks, I slid off the hammock, lightheaded from pain and drug and urgency all. Flinching from the dawn's light, I staggered toward the hovel at the far right of the courtyard, the hovel into which the dragonmaster had disappeared.

Each footfall felt like a whiplash across my back as I crossed the courtyard's dusty hardpan. Each footstep reverberated across the bruise-heavy tenderness of my buttocks like the aftershock of a cudgel's blow. The whitewashed hovel swam drunkenly before my eyes, growing closer with agonizing slowness.

The smell of the hovel: a fug of ash from the primitive cooking pit outside, and the stench of old blood that had soaked into the butchering table beside it.

The feel of the gharial hides hanging askew over the hovel's entrance as I pulled them aside: as hard as bark, furred with dust, speckled with guano.

I ducked into the dark hovel and tripped, clumsy with frantic need. I sprawled full-length across hardpan; my bladder loosed. I shuddered with shameful release.

I lay there several moments, loathing myself for defiling sacred soil, then muttered the Good Woman's Prayer into the rank earth beneath me.

"Ris shiwenna gindwari, mo Fa Cinai." *Purest Dragon, punish and forgive me.*

Something moved near my head.

I rose swiftly to my elbows, looked about. Saw only blackness and shadow; smelled dank earth and rancid tallow.

Then.

Movement. Whispers of air flowing about me, around me. The smell of unwashed bodies.

I was being surrounded.

I launched myself toward the door I'd just staggered through, scramble-crawling through the disgraceful puddle I'd just made. I bumped into hairy shins and reared away from them with a cry, then held myself still, not daring to breathe.

Slowly, my eyes adjusted.

I was ringed by men.

Boys and men, all staring at me, where I knelt, frozen with fear, upon the floor. Their eyes were wet and white and unwavering in the light slinking around the hanging doorway hides.

Outside, a hungry dragon lowed; I started. No one else inside the hovel moved.

A mighty shudder racked me head to toe. My teeth clacked hard together, then again, then again. The noise sounded like a stick running over wooden lathes. I clenched my jaw, but it did no good. *Clatter-clack, clatter-clack.* Paralyzed by fear, I could not rise to my feet from where I knelt on the ground.

"You're a *girl*."

My eyes swung around the faces, back and forth, round and round.

"Aren't you, hey?" The voice, although that of a mature male, held all the innocence of youth. The words were slightly slurred, as though flapped between loose lips. Someone shifted in the crowd. My eyes latched onto the movement.

A meaty, broad-shouldered young man stepped forward and wrinkled his thick nose at me in great puzzlement. His brawny arms hung past his thighs. He stood stooped.

He gestured at me. "Girls can't 'prentice."

"I've served bulls before." I licked my lips, wanted water.

"Where?"

"Tieron. Convent Tieron. I was an onai."

"So?"

Another voice answered for me, one from the back of the hovel, deep in shadow. "She thinks she can serve because she's been cut, Egg. Gelded. Circumcised. Rendered clean as a holy woman."

Someone snickered. A few of the youngest exchanged uncertain looks.

The oaf's eyes widened and he stared in the direction of my groin. Lust flared across his overlarge face. My paralysis shattered and I scrabbled to my feet, heart in my throat, and drew Kratt's cape as best I could about myself, ignoring the pain caused by the touch of fabric upon my wounded back.

"So you *are* a girl," the oaf breathed, not looking away from my groin. "What's it look like, where you've been cut?"

"Why don't you go see, hey-o?" the same voice suggested from the shadows. "Go on, Egg."

Imperceptibly, the apprentices drew closer to one another, forming a tighter circle. Grins broke out onto faces. Expectant, unfriendly grins.

"Don't touch me," I said hoarsely.

"Why not?" the shadow-voice said. "Go on, Egg, spread her legs. Show us what she looks like."

"Yeah, go on, Egg," someone else said. "Mount her while you're at it."

Snickers, jostling, an exchange of tight grins.

The brawny oaf stepped toward me: "Show me," he said, voice thickening. "Let me see."

"Stay back!"

"C'mon, I just wanna see. Don't make me hurtcha. Come on."

"Go on, Egg," someone called out. "We'll hold her down if she gets too much for you."

Laughter.

"Come on, Egg! Spread her legs!"

"Mount her, Egg, mount her!"

"No!" I cried. "No one touches me. I've got pustules, hear?"

The oaf stopped in his tracks and frowned mightily. "Pox?"

"Why else would I throw my life away defying Temple?" I croaked the lie with credible conviction. "I'm dying. Any who lie with me will soon join me in death."

The expressions around me changed and the youngest boys unconsciously backed up a pace or two.

The oaf made a noise of disgust. *"I'm* not gonna touch her."

"She's lying, Egg. She doesn't have pox."

I turned toward that voice, still hidden in shadow. Half maddened by fear and intoxicated by the dregs of venom still lacing my blood, I gasped, "What manner of coward are you, that you hide in shadow and goad others to do ill?"

The room itself drew a breath and held it.

A shifting of bodies as the owner of the voice pushed forward, and I cursed my impetuous nature that had, yet again, only furthered my trouble.

I recognized him then, the lean, muscled youth that came toward me. I recognized his face, even though it was pocked and healed over from adolescent acne, and I recognized the manner in which the brown hair half hid the familiar quick, shrewd eyes set above an equally familiar aquiline nose. That face, now prickly with unshaven stubble and weathered by a hard adolescence, had once nursed alongside me from my mother's breast.

Before me stood Yeli's Dono.

Dono: an orphan of danku Re, the pottery clan in which I'd been born. Dono: a playmate of my youth. Dono: the would-be lover of my ill-sold sister.

"Dono," I said, nonplussed.

He stood before me, as beautiful as a lost ruby discovered, chipped and filthy, upon a forsaken road.

"I know you," he said, eyes narrowing. "What's your clan?"

It was then that I realized that Dono had mastered his speech impediment, so obvious in his youth. As a seven-year-old, he'd claimed his manhood by yanking out the remainder of his milk teeth. The subsequent infection had rotted his budding adult teeth and had all but killed him, and marked his speech with an obvious lisp. I could envisage him grimly practicing words each night in the early days of his apprenticeship, forcing himself to enunciate clearly and eradicate his lisp while hiding somewhere in the dark stables.

Irrationally, the knowledge that he had succeeded heartened me.

"It's me: Zarq. Danku Re Darquel's Zarq. We grew up together."

The apprentices about us exchanged startled looks at this revelation.

Dono stared, incredulous. "Zarq? What in the name of Re are you playing at?"

"I've joined the dragonmaster's apprenticeship. Like you."

"You're a woman."

"I'm circumcised."

He frowned. "You *can't*."

"I've served the bulls already in a convent—"

"A holy woman serving a retired bull is completely different than an unclaimed girl serving a fertile bull. You know it."

"I don't see the difference at all."

"You can't serve Re." He clenched his hands into fists; veins protruded on his forearms. "If you turn Temple against the dragonmaster, they'll revoke his title. All the apprentices under him will lose their status then. I'll be thrown out of here. We *all* will."

His fellow apprentices muttered amongst themselves; a few swore and flicked their earlobes to ward off bad luck and evil. One spat in my direction. His spittle landed at my feet. "Dono, listen. There's a scroll that says one such as I can serve—"

"Get out of here, Zarq." Dono's anger was feeding off the unease he'd created amongst his peers. "Get out of here *now*."

"The dragonmaster chose me to serve!"

"You ruined my plans once before, Zarq; I'll be ass-screwed before I let you ruin them again. *Now, get out.*"

"Ruined your . . . ? What are you talking about?" I cried. "I haven't seen you since we were nine. I've done nothing to you."

"Out!" he bellowed.

I looked again at the faces gathered about me. Some were poised on the brink of physical violence; others flushed with angry unease. Biting back futile argument, I pushed my way through the mob and staggered from the hovel.

Despite my oozing whip welts and a fever provoked by venom's ebb, I didn't return to the empty dragon stall designated as mine, lest Dono incite the apprentices into bodily forcing me from the dragonmaster's domain. Instead, I staggered across the courtyard and disappeared into the next, then the next, rapidly losing myself in the maze of adjoined stable yards. I moved as the wounded boar does when it crashes and staggers through the jungle, seeking blindly to escape the very pain of the spear embedded deep in its side, yet carrying the pain with it wherever it goes.

My pain was not just from the ragged welts across my back, understand.

As the venom dissipated in my blood, a maelstrom of emotion clashed and howled within me, unleashed not just by the retreat of the dragons' fire but also by Dono's hostility and the pulsating, persistent memory of Kratt's pleasure in whipping me senseless the day previous.

Both were equally unsettling.

It burned that I had allowed Kratt to injure me, see. It smarted that I had so readily *submitted* to him, he whom I had been about to murder. I had planned it so carefully, had schemed for years over how I might exact vengeance upon the man who'd ruined my clan and my childhood. Up until the moment when the dragonmaster had singled me out from the crowd lining the Mombe Taro lane, I had been resigned to execution for killing Waikar Re Kratt.

Now the madness that had gripped me upon receiving that outrageous hope from the dragonmaster seemed just that: madness. Here I was, suffering excruciating pain when I could have been plunged into the nether-blackness of the One Dragon's Essence. Instead of enfolded in the numb oblivion of death, here I was, horribly alive and reeling from the shocking hostility of a milk-brother who had no desire to realize that I had joined the dragonmaster's apprenticeship, defied convention, and allowed my sworn enemy to live, all so that those such as Dono and myself might one day be free from the tyranny of Temple, aristocrat, and Emperor all.

I collapsed onto my knees on the cool dust behind a grain silo.

I knelt there, swaying in the meager shade, buffeted by pain both physical and emotional, as the bloated sun rose hot and pulsing into the sky.

I thirsted. I dreamed.

I dreamed of a carrion bird, the carbuncles on its wattles obscenely red. It stood before me, its narrow gray head cocked to one side. How brilliant and cruel those glass-bright eyes as they stared at me!

"I can stop it, hey-o," the buzzard cackled. "I can stop your pain."

I ignored the hallucination, concentrated on breathing, on not toppling face-first onto the ground.

"A bargain, yes?" the bird croaked. It lifted a wing the length of my arm. *Flick-flick,* its beak darted in and out of its bedraggled plumage, snapping at lice and dust motes. The bird looked at me again and tucked its wing back into place. It held a feather in its beak. A blue feather.

Of course. No fever-dream was this, and no ordinary carrion bird. This was my mother's haunt. I hated and feared the thing almost as fiercely as I was glad to see it.

"Mother," I gasped.

The haunt placed the feather on the ground, carefully.

"A bargain," it croaked. "Health for service."

I stared at the feather that shimmered in the heat, and I reminded myself that this was *not* my mother, but Mother's obsession with finding Waivia made manifest. Whatever dregs of my mother that remained within the creature were sunk deep beneath layers of madness, magic, and dire intent.

"You know this can heal you, yes?" The bird's scaled claw shifted the blue feather slightly in the dust.

Yes, I knew the feather could heal me. It had done so once before. And I needed to be healed to not only survive the enmity of Dono and his peers but also tackle the daunting task of living life as an apprentice.

"If you take it, you agree to leave here and find Waivia," the bird croaked. "Health for service."

"Agreed," I said, and I lurched for the feather, as swift as an adder's strike. With a squawk, the buzzard jumped into the air, wings beating clouds of dust into my eyes and mouth. My hand closed around the feather; it burst into an effervescing cloud that settled over me as soft as mist, as tender as a mother's caress. A moist scent delicately laced the air, that dainty fragrance that bespeaks dew sliding slowly down an orchid's petal, moisture adorning spider silk.

My head was at once clear, my senses sharp. While the wounds upon my back still pulsed, the pain was vastly muted and quite bearable.

The buzzard alighted upon the ground again, several feet away. It regarded me with wary defiance.

*You will leave here now,* the creature said, its voice embedded in my skull. *You will keep your part of the bargain.*

I hesitated, envisioning a life of fruitlessly wandering Clutch Re in search of my long-dead sister.

The buzzard clacked its beak at me. *You won't throw your life away over a madman's vision! No. A mere fantasy, that is, one you scarcely believe yourself.*

It rankled, that she could so swiftly, so facilely, pinpoint my weakness and doubt. As is the case with all daughters of the age I was then—seventeen, and immensely world-wise, or so I believed—

I was immediately determined to deny the truth of my mother's words, just because she had had the gall to notice the obvious about me.

"I believe what I saw in his eyes!" I cried. "I can do it. I must, I will!"

*To follow the dragonmaster is to set yourself on a course of slow suicide.*

"And what would you instead have me do? Throw my life away seeking a sister most likely dead."

*Cheat! Liar!*

"No! I'll keep my word; I'll leave here." I took a quavering breath. "But not now. You didn't stipulate when I should leave, and I'm not ready to leave yet. I'm good with dragons; maybe I *can* do this thing that I saw in the dragonmaster's eyes."

The buzzard shrieked at me, both wings widespread.

I clapped my hands over my ears, though that didn't prevent the bird's angry cries from ricocheting around the inside of my head.

*Never again! You won't ever receive one of my feathers again.*

"Leave me, then. Begone!"

With one last angry squawk, the enraged bird sprang into the air, flapped ponderously into the sky, and disappeared over the stable rooftops. Trembling, I sank back into the shade of the silo.

I had sorely angered the haunt. What repercussions might I suffer?

I did not know, and the not knowing worried me.

Exacerbating the worry was a twinge of guilt at my use of sly trickery to obtain the healing feather from the creature that had been, in another form, my mother. After all, was not that very lack of compassion exactly what goaded the haunt into its relentless, deplorable stalking of me? Re prevent me from turning blind to empathy and grace in my quest to obtain that which I desired. Re prevent me from turning into a mirror-image of my mother as she was in her last mad years of life.

But what *was* it that I desired most now?

Muddled not by pain and fever but by twisting thought only, I dozed.

Susurration laced my sleep, much the way the lapping of waves against the hull of a boat insinuates itself into your slumber without really rousing you. The noises I heard provoked no instinct to bolt upright, no desire to run, hide, or pray for deliverance.

Womb noises, they were. The sound of industry, of others hard at honest work. Rasp of rake, chink of pitchfork upon stone. Burble of water, trundle of wheel, squeak of axle. Bantering voices, answering voices, voices directing and organizing. Soothing sounds. Combined with the heat of the day and whatever magics imparted by the feather that had dissolved into my skin, those sounds cradled me in convalescent sleep.

Magics. Yes.

Make no mistake, something unearthly occurred when that luminescing feather exploded into mist and lit upon my skin, for when I woke at twilight, neither hungry nor thirsting, neither stiff nor sore, the bloody ribbons on my back were the slightest of weals, itching fiercely from the healing process.

I dared roll my back carefully against the silo behind me: No flare of pain, no agony when my skin connected with the silo's sun-warmed wood.

A chortle, though.

My head snapped round to where the dragonmaster was crouched in shadow, precisely where the buzzard had stood many hours before at noon. He rubbed his hands together and his eyes gleamed in the dusk.

"Clever little rishi whelp, hey-o?" he cackled. "Well done."

The unnatural healing of my body felt tainted, then, sullied by his pleasure in it.

"Where do I piss?" I snapped.

His smug leer vanished, replaced with a scowl. He rose. "That's not my concern."

"It will be, if I start urinating all over the place. How much do you want Temple angered?"

He leapt toward me, slapped my cheek. My head snapped back and thudded against the silo, and the stinging ring of the blow, so instant, so unanticipated, clouded my ears and vibrated like a hornet in my head.

His raised hand clenched into a fist, as if he were struggling with himself not to strike me again, and his eyes rolled briefly in their sockets.

I stared at him and held my breath.

"You are mortal, Skykeeper's Daughter," he finally gasped, chest heaving. He dropped his hand to his side. "Never forget that. Mortal *and* subject to my authority."

I touched my burning cheek gingerly, tears from his blow blurring my vision.

His face twisted and, as if of its own accord, his hand sprang up to strike me again.

"Your response is 'Yes, Komikon'!"

"Yes, Komikon," I gasped. *Yes, Master.*

He leaned down into my face, his chin braid like a rat's tail upon my throat, his breath as foul as bile. "You can be hurt, rishi whelp. You bleed. Never forget that."

I swallowed.

"I won't, Komikon."

"You'll build yourself a latrine, understand? You'll pay to have it monthly purified, as you'll pay to have the apprentices' quarters cleansed."

He waited, then tensed.

"Yes, Komikon," I said hastily.

"Good." With a snort, he turned to leave.

"How?" I dared ask. "How will I pay? Komikon."

He paused, then turned back to me. He gave a tight, venomous grin.

"You'll do my bidding, girl. That's how you'll pay. Now, get back to your hammock."

And I had not the heart to ask, then, what his bidding would be.

# THREE

As the dragonmaster had bid me, I returned to the empty stall designated as mine.

It was well past middle-night, and the dark was chill and dew-laden. The stars were as hostile as a thousand eyes, all glaring at me from the silken sheets of night's bed, as if, by my very passage, I'd woken them from carefree sleep. It was a night of cloaking black, as airy and dark as watered silk, with the merest bowed splinter for a moon; the darkness reminded me of a clan's pidi-nos, the treasured strips of black silk used to tie a woman's wrists to the chancobie, the throne of submission and apology upon which a woman sits during a Claiming Ceremony.

Each stable yard I crossed looked much like the last: rows of stone stalls, all ringed about a square court, each stall housing, behind an iron gate, a sleeping dragon. The scaled beasts slept without care, secure in the dragonmaster's domain, their snouts settled like roosting birds upon dewlapped throats or their necks stretched long between foreclaws, muzzles prone upon the ground. Some dragons slept with neck curled over spine, head thrust under one wing; others stood on all fours, head drooped low, firm lips almost brushing the ground. Ribs rose and fell. The occasional limb dream-twitched. A stomach rumbled here, a tail thwacked stone there.

I knew that no such restful sleep awaited me, for I feared the animosity of my stable peers and wondered whether they'd dare oust me from the dragonmaster's domain this very night, even with the Komikon somewhere present within the stable yard walls.

I therefore didn't lay upon my coarse twine hammock at first, but paced about my stall, bedding chaff shushing round my ankles like wood shavings falling leaflike from a carpenter's lathe. The slate beneath the bedding was cold and damp on my soles.

Sometime toward dawn, exhaustion wore me down. I found a good-sized stone, and, clutching it to my chest, clambered onto my hammock. The old twine creaked beneath my weight.

I stared at the stars as they faded to the color of rain in the gray murk of the oncoming dawn, vowing not to let my heavy lids close.

I jerked violently awake much later, when the rock I held thudded to the ground. Heart pounding, I blinked and squinted against the brightness of the sun. Muddleheaded, I listened tensely to the very sounds of industry that had, the day previous, lulled me to sleep near the grain silo.

The day was well on its way toward noon. The dragonmaster apprentices of Komikon Re were hard at work. I had slept, ignored and untouched by them, since dawn.

I sat up carefully, conscious of the weals on my back. Of the ribbons of ruined flesh, only a crisscross of ridged skin remained. I ran my fingers cautiously over the snakes of scar tissue. No pain. Slowly, I climbed off my hammock and stretched. Healthy muscle pulled beneath feather-healed skin.

Well.

I stood there, sound in body but not in mind, and stared blankly at the day before me.

What to do now?

Attack the monumental task I'd set before myself, of not only surviving the wrath of Temple for joining the dragonmaster's apprenticeship but also becoming a dragonmaster, with the aim of using the influence and power a Cinai Komikon commanded to alter the very fabric of an entire nation.

Great Re. Is it any wonder that the prospect exhausted me, that I felt rooted to the spot with defeat?

Once again, I had the brief, sharp realization that, had I followed my original intentions of killing Kratt at Mombe Taro, my head would have long been separated from my neck by an executioner's blade. I shivered with brief longing for the escape death would have afforded me.

Clutching my elbows to myself, I closed my eyes and took an unsteady breath to clear the dark thought from my mind.

The seductive scent of venom lay as heavy as lead over the stables, and as I inhaled, the fragrance flowed down my nostrils and set my heart glowing like a live coal. The acrid yet honeyed scent danced on my tongue, pimpled the skin on my arms anew, sang through my veins, swelled my heart, soared through my soul.

Yes. Oh, yes. That most desired scent, reminiscent of limes and licorice both: venom. I could not breathe enough of it, ached for it, trembled for it, was dizzy and aroused and consumed by need because of it. I could not help it; I opened my mouth wide and inhaled deeply, repeatedly, savoring the warm, malleable scent as a nebulous substitute for liquid venom.

A feverish flood of memories surged over me: crumbling convent rotunda; ancient, infertile bull dragons. The rasp of scaled hide against my thighs; a dragon tongue leaching black venom upon my belly.

This, then, was a reason to forge into the day: the possibility of imbibing venom. A despicable reason, yes, and a crutch I reached too readily to lean upon. But even as I realized that my fondness for the dragons' poison provided a stronger impetus to confront the day than the mere desire to live had, I dismissed the dreadful revelation.

I inhaled again and again through an open mouth, drunk on the odor of the dragons' fire, and when my head reeled from too-quickly sucked-in air, I finally stopped and opened my eyes. Vision unsteady, pulse racing, I took stock of my surroundings.

A massive courtyard sprawled before me, ringed by stalls made of granite blocks quarried from who-knew-where. Half the stalls stood empty save for youths who frantically shoveled manure, and the stalls that were occupied were occupied magnificently by Roshu-Lupini Re's uncut dragons, yearlings and satons both, females either too young or too hard-worked to lay eggs.

Lean and nervy, trained to spring into the air upon the slightest spur touch and lock talons with other dragons, these were fighting beasts. Unlike the dull hides of the wing-amputated brooders prevalent throughout Clutch Re, or the faded, flaking hides of the dying bulls I had cared for while in Convent Tieron, the scaled hides of the Roshu-Lupini's destriers fairly shone with vitality and color.

Whereas a brooder's hide is dappled rust and moss, the hides of the Roshu-Lupini's dragons shone chestnut and the green of wet jungle foliage. Whereas a brooder stands with head hanging, indifferent to all and sundry, the destriers snorted in their stalls, their long, forked tongues flicking out, black as tar with venom. They rumbled, they tossed their heads, they threw their weight against the heavy iron gates that barred them within their stalls. They rasped their deadly talons against stone.

I loved those dragons, I did.

With my body miraculously healed and the scent of venom effervescing through my blood, I loved those dragons. Exhilaration swelled through me and I felt I could spread my arms and fly.

The courtyard was a-clatter with motion. Pitchforks flashed in the early morning sunlight as apprentices mucked stalls, carted away manure, and wheeled in fresh bedding and fodder. In a shadowy corner, two scrawny boys worked the rusty handle of a pump; water gushed out, splashing into what appeared to be an open aqueduct running through the far side of every stall. Curses rang to and fro; bellows echoed about. Snake poles and muzzle hooks glinted from the cool shadows, the tools wielded by boys either astraddle a dragon or attempting to immobilize one for grooming.

At the far end of the courtyard leaned two dilapidated, narrow structures: the apprentices' latrines. A pile of lumber and a stack of bricks sat to one side of them. Ah. I understood at once. Those were the materials the dragonmaster wanted me to fashion into a latrine, and the tools I'd require to do so.

I flared my nostrils, piqued by the flagrant challenge he'd set before me. Like any other man, he'd assumed that, as a woman, I'd have no idea how to build a latrine. Such a simple task would not confound me, hey-o! I lifted my chin. I would show him that I was no ordinary woman.

I started across the courtyard, the red, sunbaked earth as warm as fresh blood upon the soles of my bare feet.

At the same far end of the courtyard as the latrines and pile of lumber, an immense sandstone archway led to yet another stable courtyard, and beyond that, another. A line of apprentices was just starting to walk beneath that sandstone archway, each apprentice leading a muzzled, wing-pinioned dragon by means of a hook notched firmly in one of the dragon's nares. They were taking them somewhere, perhaps for exercise.

I stopped a moment, halfway across the yard, and watched the apprentices and their winged charges disappear through the archway into the courtyard beyond.

How big *were* the Roshu-Lupini's stables? There was no way I could tell, standing there, though from my fevered rambling the day previous, I knew the ochre sandstone walls enclosed the entire stable domain, however large. Those walls were twice my height and topped by ceramic shards, necessary to prevent rishi and bayen alike from pestering the dragons and holy Re, our illustrious Clutch bull, with petitions for good luck, fertile wombs, and plentiful food.

Dragons were divine. By mere dint of their intact wings and venom sacs, the Roshu-Lupini's dragons were regarded as especially divine and most likely to answer the prayers of the devout. There was no real logic in that supposition, but superstition and myth run strong amongst rishi.

I continued across the courtyard, toward the building supplies stacked beside the apprentices' latrines. The lumber was new and freshly treated with hagi, a Malacarite pitch used to protect wood from the elements, and as I approached the stack of wood, the tar-and-vinegar reek of the hagi combined pleasantly with the stables' peppery tang of venom.

The planks were straight, the tawny color of heartwood, and bore few knots. Never before had I worked with such fine wood, for during my years in Convent Tieron, the lumber we'd used to mend our mill wheel had been roughly hewn and weathered, castoffs grudgingly sent our way by the Ranreeb, who, as Temple's Overseer of the Jungle Crown, was responsible for the Tieron sanctuary.

A wooden crate stained blue and decorated with a rendering of a dragon's head sat atop the lumber. I crouched on my haunches and cracked the crate open.

"Hey-o," I murmured in wonder. "What have we here?"

The array of tools within was a treasure. Reverently, I touched one of the sharp teeth of a saw, then picked up a hammer. As a woman, I should have had little knowledge of how to use such tools. But I'd had an unusual life, in Convent Tieron.

I stood, said the customary quendi cinai farkta, the request to the Dragon that the chosen site meet with the bull's favor, and looked about for a shovel to begin digging the latrine pit.

One of the young apprentices mucking stalls spotted me and hailed another apprentice, a brawny fellow who stood atop a cart loaded with fresh fodder. The brawny fellow lumbered down from the cart and stalked toward me. I recognized him immediately: Egg, the oaf Dono had tried to goad into mounting me.

I fumbled to cover my front with Kratt's cape, which hung askew from my neck.

With a scowl upon his massive face, Egg lurched toward me. A shadow crossed over him when he was but several feet away. He abruptly stopped and glanced at the sky. I likewise looked up.

A carrion bird glided not far above our heads, swooping toward the great sandstone wall that surrounded the stable domain. Egg shuddered with relief at the buzzard's deceptively nondescript appearance, then turned his scowl back on me. The bird looked at me from its perch and shook its feathers.

" 'Bout time you woke up," Egg grumbled petulantly. "You can't do that, y'know, sleep late while the rest of us work. You can't. And you can't walk around like that, neither." He gestured at me as color burned up his swarthy neck. "Y' have to wear somethin' that covers *all* of you—"

He cut himself short and his far-spaced eyes widened.

"What happened to your cuts?" he squealed, no longer sounding the bear but a cornered wild pig. "Turn 'round, turn 'round!"

I did so uneasily.

A strangled noise gargled from his throat and he back-stepped several paces. "Where'd they go? How'd they disappear?"

I gauged his reaction and calculated the possibilities. From the corner of my eye, I saw the carrion bird perched on the sandstone wall.

I said, deliberately, "I'm the Dirwalan Babu."

"The *what?*"

"The Skykeeper's Daughter."

Sure enough, his eyes shot skyward again and he involuntarily flinched, remembering the dreadful appearance of the Skykeeper at the Lashing Lane.

"I heal like this sometimes," I said with great certainty. "I have that power."

Egg's eyes skittered over me like a bead of water dropped upon a hot pan. Slowly, his overlarge face folded in on itself. "Why do inductees have to be assigned to me?" he whined; then he flapped his hands as though shaking out wet laundry. "We got work to do, hey-o. We'll get no food tonight if our work ain't done, an' he'll flog us after without venom on the whips."

"I have a latrine to build."

"You've been assigned to me; didn't you hear what I said?"

"I heard."

He stared at me, fat lips quivering. I refused to drop my gaze as a woman should before a man.

He grabbed his oily curls and pulled. "You ain't a veteran, y'know. You can't do what you like. You ain't even a servitor. You're an *inductee*. So you do what I say, an' I'm tellin' you: Muck stalls."

"No."

His face suffused with the color of crushed pomegranates, and for a moment I thought he'd tuck his great chin to his chest and charge at me, bearlike. But instead, he shuddered, glanced again at the sky, and gurgled, "We'll all be whipped."

He turned and lumbered back to the young boys mucking stalls.

"Faster!" he bellowed at them, snatching a pitchfork from a flaxen stack of clean bedding chaff. "You're too slow; work faster!"

At his cry, a flock of roosting pigeons burst into flight. The carrion bird, perched upon the wall, shook her feathers at me and cackled angrily.

I picked up the shovel and set to work building my latrine.

I worked hard, familiar with the labor that had oft been my lot during my years in Convent Tieron, for of the two sorry latrines we'd boasted in the convent, either one at any given time had needed extensive structural repairs; as the youngest holy woman, I'd always been assigned the task.

By late noon, I'd dug the latrine hole and clumsily framed up two of the latrine's four walls. Kratt's cape was my only piece of clothing, and this I wore knotted shut in several places. The garment, however, offered poor protection against the sun. Heat dizzy, famished, and parched, I staggered toward the courtyard's rusted pump.

Egg and my fellow inductees—the motley assortment of young boys he'd been screaming at all morn while they mucked out stalls—had long since moved into the adjacent courtyard. I was alone, though even now I could hear Egg in the distance, relentlessly badgering the inductees to work faster.

I was alone, that is, save for the dragons the veterans had returned from exercising some time ago; they now stood quietly in their clean stalls, either chewing maht, regurgitated crop food, or eating the fresh fodder in their mangers. A few preened, one membranous wing spread as best it might be in the stall while a scaly muzzle worked under and over the thin leather, rubbing away insects and the omnipresent red dust of our Clutch.

Other than the dragons, one more presence kept me from being alone: my mother's haunt.

The wretched bird lofted soundlessly into the air and glided after me as I crossed the courtyard to the pump for a drink. I could feel her baleful eyes boring into my back, could feel her will pulsing behind my temples like a headache. She wanted me out of the stable domain, oh, yes. She wanted me to forget all this apprenticeship nonsense and spend my days searching for Waivia, whom I was certain was dead. Kiyu, sex slaves, didn't oft live long, and Waivia had been sold into such slavery ten years previous.

I stumbled as I approached the pump, as if a gamy hand were trying to turn my feet in a direction different from the one I desired. I hunched my shoulders and resolutely walked on. As I neared the pump I stumbled again, harder, and I staggered the last few paces forward and caught hold of the pump's cool iron to stop my fall. Behind me, the haunt perched upon the upswept corner eave above a stall.

Her will continued to throb feverishly behind my eyes. *Leave here. Find her.*

My knuckles turned pink as I gripped the pump. I squeezed my eyes shut, as if in doing so I could squeeze out her voice.

*Leave here and find her.* Her will was more insistent now, as sharp and invasive as grit stabbing into an abscessed tooth.

With teeth clenched, I wrenched the pump's handle up and down, then plunged my head under the cool water that gushed forth.

I kept my head under the water, hoping the cascading splash could shield her off, block out her insidious words. But it couldn't. Of course it couldn't. Her presence was an unwanted, unseen visitor trickling into my body, occupying me, threatening to entrap me in limbo and suspend me in nothingness.

"No!" I cried, and I flung my soaked head up from the pump. Water droplets arced into the air and scintillated in the sunlight like the shards of a shattered rainbow, flying higher than gravity should have permitted. They splattered against the perched vulture and sizzled like beads of lard dropped on live coals.

The vulture opened its beak and hissed at me.

"Leave me," I hissed back as water ran from my drenched hair and soaked the neck of Kratt's cape.

*Leave here,* the haunt countered, and its will fell like a hammer blow against my head. I gripped my ears and staggered away from her and the water pump. I didn't get far before collapsing against the iron gate of a stall.

"Re help me," I gasped.

I needed venom to stave off the haunt.

I felt new eyes upon me then, and I raised my head and met the gaze of a dragon in her stall. Her horizontally slitted eyes blazed with a feral sentience; I caught my breath. Suspended in amber irises that seemed backlit by flame, her pupils widened, then swiftly contracted. The forked tip of her tongue slid out between her firm, ivy green gums. A droplet of venom fell from her tongue to the flaxen bedding chaff. It sat there, at the periphery of my gaze, like a nugget of wet obsidian.

The dragon's opalescent dewlaps began to inflate. Her sienna wings, folded along her flanks, shuddered. The black claws at the tips of her wings twitched once, twice, thrice, clacking together like wooden needles.

If I stayed much longer draped over the gate to her stall, she'd lash out at me with her venom-coated tongue.

The craving that followed that thought thrilled, then horrified, me.

I hurled myself from her stall and staggered backward, away from the dragon. The buzzard perched on the eaves clacked its beak at me.

With a savage cry, I began scooping up rocks, pebbles, and handfuls of grit from the courtyard ground.

"Get out of here; go!" I shrieked, and I hurled the rocks and pebbles at the haunt. "Go, go; leave me!"

One of my rocks hit the bird square on the breast. She shrieked and shook her head at me. Another struck the roof tiles just behind her. With another cry, she launched into flight.

I ran after her, hurling expletives and rocks. She rose higher into the air, slowly. Unhurried. She lazily flapped beyond the confines of the stable domain and glided from sight.

I stood there, panting, one fist clenched around a remaining rock.

I had to eat. Surely that would fortify me somewhat and help me ignore my mother's relentless will.

Surely.

*Something* had to help, and it couldn't be venom. I couldn't descend into those beguiling, debilitating depths as I had only a short year ago.

Shuddering, I returned to the pump, to where a pile of fresh fodder sat. I began sifting through it, frantically looking for nuts to eat.

# FOUR

Sundown.

A hot, earthen scent hung in the air, as if a huge loaf of mud, wreathed by jungle bracken, was baking in an enormous clay oven. That smell is, understand, peculiar to a Clutch Re twilight during the Fire Season.

I was precariously balanced atop two of the braced walls I'd constructed during the day, hammering in a rim cap to give my latrine more stability during monsoon gales. As red streaked the gloaming, a lithe, somewhat effeminate servitor returned to the courtyard. I paused in my work to watch him kneel before the battered cauldron that sat in the primitive cooking pit outside the apprentices' hovel, not far from a great butchering table and a line of hutches, the latter of which were filled with grunting renimgars. Cupping his palms about his mouth, the lithe servitor blew the embers beneath the cauldron to life. My empty stomach torqued at the mere thought of food. I wearily turned back to my work.

Sometime later, the inductees staggered wordlessly into the courtyard.

They all crossed the court through its center, keeping a goodly distance between themselves and where I worked. One inductee in particular slunk by as if I were a kwano snake poised to strike. I'd earlier snatched the boy from Egg's service, without Egg's knowledge, when I'd needed a pair of hands to hold up the crooked little walls of my latrine while I hammered temporary braces into place. I'd had to press the young inductee into aiding me through use of hissed curses and threats. Only his fear of the Skykeeper had overcome both his fear of Egg and his outrage at obeying a woman, and a deviant one at that.

As the inductees shuffled toward their hovel, the servitors and veterans likewise returned from their work elsewhere in the stable domain. I felt their eyes upon me as I worked, and I drove in the nails I was pounding harder, ignoring the trembling in my exhausted arms and legs, ignoring the stiffness of aching neck muscles. As my hammer blows rang assertively around the stables, the young men's astonishment that a woman could possess even my paltry skill with tool and wood tingled against my back like stinging nettles.

The faggots beneath the great cauldron began to glow as red as the twilight sky, and the broth scent of gruel wafted from its depths. The young man designated as cook stirred the pot vigorously with a great wooden ladle and ordered an inductee to fetch water for him, another to fetch more faggots from the pile stacked under the thatched eaves of the hovel, a third to feed the caged renimgars.

The veterans eased their scarred, muscled bodies down to the ground while the servitors crouched on their haunches not far from them. Although I wasn't looking for him, I was acutely aware of where Dono sat, sprawled long-limbed upon the ground.

Despite his hostility toward me yesterday, part of me was glad to see him, for he was familiar. He was clan.

Though in truth, I and my mother had been pronounced nas rishi poakin ku when I was but nine, when we were ousted from the pottery clan for her crimes against Temple in her efforts to buy back Waivia. Even if I *had* been declared an unstable, violent person unable to form kin bonds, neither Dono nor my heart knew it, and I longed for a simple look, a small sign of support, from my former milk-brother.

Neither was forthcoming.

Realizing that I was only delaying joining my fellow apprentices for the evening meal, I reluctantly quit my work. I gingerly lowered myself from my perch, praying the while that the walls wouldn't collapse upon me during my descent; then I stiffly gathered up the tools and replaced them in the crate. My every muscle felt set in mortar.

As I joined the apprentices, I tried to walk as if I weren't tired, tried to act as if it were the most natural thing in the world for a woman to be present in the dragonmaster's stables. Try as I might, I could not ignore the stiff silence that fell upon the crowd of youths at my approach.

The dregs of crimson from the setting sun melted into the star-speckled sky. The lithe servitor designated as cook banged his ladle upon the great butchering table, and the stacks of wooden bowls upon the table wobbled.

"S'ready," he announced, and a two-clawful or so of youths sprang up from the ground, grabbed the wooden bowls from the table, and jostled into a queue before the cauldron. I assumed these industrious youths were all servitors, for the scars upon their backs bespoke previous years' participation in Mombe Taro, but their ages were too young to mark them as veteran apprentices. The cook ladled gruel into their outstretched bowls, which were then taken to the eldest of the apprentices, clearly the veterans, seated and reclined about the ground. With all the pomp of placing an offering upon a Temple altar, the servitors placed the bowls of food before the veterans.

I noticed that not one but two servitors vied for the privilege of serving Dono his meal.

The veterans ate without hurry or grace, demanding that their bowls be filled over and over while the rest of us watched. As a woman, I was accustomed to waiting until men had eaten their fill before partaking of food, but to the new inductees, such subservient attendance was new and awful. Few of them could contain their hunger without shifting about or chewing their nails in agitation.

At last, the veterans had filled their stomachs.

"Servitors," the lithe cook called out, and while the veterans swatted mosquitoes and picked their teeth with sticks, the servitors lined up before the cauldron.

We inductees waited, slavering like curs, stomachs roiling, eyes riveted on the cauldron. Night encroached on the courtyard. Hands scooped into wooden bowls; gruel was licked slowly from fingers. The sated veterans and servitors began spilling destiny wheels and dice from worn leather sacks carried at their waists. Egg, who'd eaten when the veterans had, finally took the ladle from the cook.

"Hey-o, inductees," he growled, standing before the cauldron, poised to ladle out gruel. "Grab a bowl an' line up."

We all scrambled for the bowls that had been dropped with deliberate negligence to the ground when each servitor had finished eating. There were far more inductees than bowls.

I espied a recently used bowl near the thigh of a veteran and went quickly toward it, wending my way through the sprawled boys and young men. Those I passed stiffened, and all eyes turned upon me, one by one.

I feared that the veteran beside the bowl would pick it up, would refuse me its use. The same thought must have crossed everyone else's mind, for the air grew rife with tension the closer I got to the bowl.

I forced myself not to clench my hands into fists, to walk with chin up.

The veteran I approached sat rigidly and refused to acknowledge my approach by glancing in my direction. I stopped before him, breath held.

Stiffly, I bent to pick up the bowl.

The muscles of his closest forearm twitched.

I dove, made faster than he by desperation and hunger, and snatched up the bowl before he could knock it out of my reach. I clutched the bowl to my stomach as if it were precious and stepped somewhat smartly away from him.

Hostile eyes surrounded me. Swallowing hard, I walked to the cauldron, fingers clasped tight about the bowl, looking neither left nor right. A chill sweat broke out on my skin. Behind me, I heard the veteran spit, imagined him flicking his ears with his thumb to ward off the taint of a deviant.

By the time I stood at the rear of the queue before the cauldron, I felt drained and limp, as if I'd fought a skirmish.

The queue moved forward with agonizing slowness. My nervous sweat began cooling in a thin line down my spine. The twilight darkened toward night.

A young man with an empty bowl approached. I moved aside; a woman always eats after a man has partaken of what has been cooked.

Another servitor stepped forward, empty bowl in hand. Again I moved aside. A third apprentice, then a fourth, came to have his bowl filled. Each time, I moved aside, though my tension mounted unbearably.

Finally, it was my turn at the pot.

Egg smirked at me. "None left."

"What?"

He shrugged his thick shoulders, a little uncertainty creeping into his smirk. "None left."

I stared into the blackened cauldron. Nothing but a film of gruel sat hardening about the inside of the dented kettle.

Sniggers erupted amongst the apprentices.

My cheeks burned.

How foolish of me, how utterly stupid, to have stood aside as others ate their fill. By joining the dragonmaster's apprenticeship, I was defying one of the most time-honored beliefs about what a woman could and could not do. I would have to be aware of the other customs that ruled women's lives and decisively flout them if I wanted to survive the apprenticeship.

Furious at myself, I stared into the empty pot as the sliver of waxing moon rose into the black sky.

And, as is too often the case when in trouble, I let my temper get the better of me. I decided that I would *not* go hungry that night. No.

I slammed my bowl down onto the butchering table and stalked over to the renimgar hutches. I fiddled with a latch, wrenched the door open, and snatched at one of the lizardlike mammals within. It writhed and kicked with its back legs, trying to bury its hind claws in me, but I clung to its leathery nape and dragged it out. I slammed the cage door shut again and latched it.

At Convent Tieron, I'd slaughtered many a renimgar for eating, and snakes, voles, rats, and monkeys, too. Anything that moved had been deemed edible at Tieron.

I slammed the renimgar down on the table hard enough to stun it, picked up the rusted machete that sat nearby, and drew it across the renimgar's neck. The squeal of the little animal cut through the night air like a scimitar through the skin of a baby. It was a horrible noise that violated the soul.

Always was.

I swiftly moved the writhing animal above the cauldron so it would bleed into the pot.

"What're you doin', hey?" Egg bellowed in front of me. "You can't help yourself to meat whenever you want!"

"I'm hungry." I glared at him, disturbed by the fear of the animal dying beneath my hands and annoyed at myself for letting others eat before me.

My response to Egg was wholly inappropriate, for a woman should never publicly display anger to a man, and Egg *was* a man, albeit a yolk-brained one. I felt the crowd stare at my back in astonishment.

"But you can't," Egg spluttered, and with an aggrieved expression, he looked toward the veterans for help.

A pause. Then:

"If she wants to cook, she can cook," a voice said from the gloom. I looked in the direction of the voice: Dono.

Joy leapt like a tongue of fire through me, for here was the kin support I'd so longed for.

"That'll be her job from now on, not Ringus's," Dono continued. "Every night, she can cook the meal."

The lithe servitor who had heated the slop pursed his lips. He, obviously, was Ringus.

"Oh?" said a bearded young man reclined on the ground near Ringus. He had shoulder-length brown hair shot with streaks of red, and his thighs were as muscled as a dragon's, and though there was no anger in his voice, the tone he used was fraught with tension. "And what'll Ringus do now instead?"

A moment's silence from Dono. "Why, he'll serve you, Eidon. 'Cause that's what you like. Service from Ringus."

Snickers peppered the air, hastily snuffed. Ringus glanced at the ground. Eidon's shoulders twitched.

Egg, either oblivious to the tension between the two or too concerned about himself to care, tugged on a curled lock. "But she's not gonna quit work early just so's she can cook, right? She's gonna have to do it when she's finished, 'cause I ain't losin' her work time just so's she can do Ringus's job."

Dono tossed the dice he was holding onto the ground, making a show of continuing casually with his game. "She'll do both. That'll be the price the deviant pays for thinking she can help herself to meat whenever she's hungry."

My heart sank. No support was this, but a punishment for my audacity.

Eidon rose into a sitting position and draped his arms loosely over his knees. The muscles in his great thighs bulged out, clear even in the rising moon's weak light. "I don't recall the Komikon choosing you to speak on behalf of the rest of us, Dono."

"Should we put it to a vote, then, Eidon?" Dono said quietly. "Is that what you want, a vote? There are others here who like the way Ringus does what he does best, and I'm sure they'll be glad he's got some free time to serve their needs as well as yours. A vote, then?"

"I think a vote is a good idea," Eidon replied. "A vote between eating food made by a deviant, or Ringus, who's been cooking for over a year and not a one of us poisoned by his feed."

"She won't poison us," Dono said, anger audible through his poise. "Temple would execute her immediately."

"They're going to execute her regardless. It's just a matter of days."

My heart beat faster.

Dono looked around at the apprentices. "The more work we give her, the quicker she falls. The longer she stays, the more reason Temple'll have for revoking the Komikon's status. We're all out of here then."

"You don't know that for certain, Dono, my friend," Eidon said. "If they revoke the Komikon's title, one of us could just as soon be elected Komikon by Temple."

"You're deluded," Dono snorted. "Temple would purge these stables. If they question the Komikon's choice of one apprentice, they'll question his choice of all of us. We'd *all* be out of here then."

Dono stabbed a digit at the inductees clustered together some distance from the veterans. "You know who'll be first to go when they revoke the Komikon's title? All of you. You'll be executed, sure as the sun rises at dawn, because the Komikon chose you the day after he chose *her*."

Fearful looks were exchanged amongst the inductees.

"Are you saying the Komikon shouldn't have chosen her, Dono?" Eidon murmured. "Are you questioning the Komikon's judgment?"

"Are you protecting the deviant, Eidon?"

"A vote, hey-o?"

"A vote." Dono raised his voice. "All for giving the deviant the extra work of cooking, raise a hand. The sooner she's out of here, the safer we all are."

"Remember what you're voting for, if you raise a hand," Eidon interjected. "The risk of poisoned food."

Uncertainty rife in the air. More looks exchanged amongst the inductees. Slowly, uneasily, hands went up. Dono counted them silently, as did we all, then he swore under his breath.

"Looks like you lose, Dono," Eidon said.

Dono lurched to his feet. "She'll be the death of us if she stays."

He shot me a malice-honed look, then strode into the darkness, crossing the courtyard and disappearing into the next. One by one, the eyes of every apprentice turned toward me, where I stood holding the lifeless body of the renimgar.

"Ringus, watch over the deviant while she prepares tomorrow's meal," Eidon said in the same voice he'd used on Dono. "I don't want that meat wasted, and she sure isn't eating a whole renimgar herself. She'll cook this once, and that's it, and don't you pull this stunt again, girl, hear? Or there'll be consequences. Your Skykeeper be damned."

I soon learned what a favor Eidon had inadvertently done me by blocking Dono's move to have me cook, for by the time I had the vast cauldron filled with steaming broth for the next day's meal, I moved in a stupor of exhaustion.

Dono had been right: Doing such each evening, on top of the day's heavy labor, would've soon broken me.

See, cooking a meal meant not only butchering an animal each eve, but fetching water from the stable pump, sifting sufficient featon grit and sesal nuts from the silo located behind the third courtyard, and, once back at the hovel courtyard, coaxing the embers beneath the cauldron to new life. Once the ingredients were all simmering in the cauldron, the thick mess required constant stirring to prevent the bottom from burning and the top from remaining unheated.

I cursed myself many times for having taken on the project, albeit only for the one night. Hunger would have been preferable, surely. And I'd *not* elevated my status in the slightest by my show of defiance; it had only underscored how aberrant a creature I was and given Dono the opportunity to emphasize the danger my presence posed to the lives of all present.

To what lengths would Dono go, I wondered, to rid the stables of me? And how would Temple deal with the dragonmaster, and, by extension, me?

Ringus followed my every move as I prepared the next day's meal. He was a slender servitor with lips so pale and glossy, they looked like ribbons of pomegranate-seasoned oil. He had a gentle manner, somewhat nervous, and eyes so wide they looked perpetually awed. I soon discovered that he had an unconscious habit of stroking things, as if ladle and table needed reassurance.

I stirred the cauldron while Ringus fitfully dozed, leaning against the butchering table and jerking awake every now and then to check my progress. I dozed off twice, too, only to awaken abruptly when my hand that held the ladle slid into the gruel.

At middle-night, with dew heavy and chill about us, I spoke. "It's cooked enough, yes?"

Ringus hauled himself upright. He took the ladle from me and stabbed the gruel a few times. With a shrug, he grabbed one of the chipped and unwashed bowls stacked haphazardly upon the butchering table and filled it with the slop. He held it out to me.

"Eat."

I did so, his sleep-heavy eyes watching my every move. I thought it ridiculous, though. If I wanted to poison the lot of them, what was to stop me from tainting the slop while they all slept? Perhaps the same thought occurred to Ringus, for he sighed and helped himself to some gruel before I was even halfway done.

My exhaustion increased a thousandfold with the warm food in my stomach. Ringus placed his empty bowl on the table and nodded at me. Together, we hefted the cauldron's heavy wooden lid over it.

I was done, free to go.

It was then that she came to me.

I didn't recognize her at first, understand, so deep was my fatigue. I saw only the benign form she took. A pigeon.

The pigeon flapped across the courtyard, pearly gray in the moonlight. It landed an arm's span from Ringus and me, cocked its head, and began approaching, walking in a jerky bob, its beady eyes as red and waxy as incarnadine berries.

Closer it came, unafraid. Unnatural.

"What . . . ?" Ringus said, and a blue mist oozed up from the ground beneath the pigeon, viscous and sulfurous.

Both Ringus and I backed up. Our rumps jarred the butchering table behind us. Without turning or looking away from the pigeon, I fumbled on the table for the machete I'd used to slaughter the renimgar.

"Kwano the One Snake, the First Father, the progenitor and spirit of all kwano everywhere, I bid you begone," Ringus gasped. He was uttering the Gyin-gyin, the Dragon Temple chant every child, every father, every mother and Holy Warden knows. "I evoke the powers of Ranon ki Cinai, governed by the exalted Emperor Mak Fa-sren."

The pigeon began swelling. The blue mist rose into the air in a column and began swirling about the bird in a tight spiral. My fingers closed over the machete.

"I evoke the authority of the Omnipotent Dragon," Ringus breathlessly intoned, eyes bulging, "the One Dragon, the progenitor and spirit of all dragons everywhere."

The pigeon swelled to the size of a melon. Its feathers stood out like quills; its eyes sank deep into its flesh. Its beak gaped as wide as the mouth of a fish out of water.

"Shut up," I hissed at Ringus. "You're making it worse."

"I evoke the power of Re, holy bull of Clutch Re—"

The obscenely bloated pigeon emitted a strangled squawk and exploded. Shreds of flesh splattered against our shins. Feathers rained down upon us, charred and smoking. The blue, sulfurous mist coalesced and turned into the flickering form of . . . my mother.

"Re help us," Ringus squeaked.

Her long ebony hair fanned out behind her like wings, and the green and brown pigmentation of her Djimbi skin glowed, the green as bright as fireflies, the brown as ruddy as a lit kiln's bricks. The bitoo she wore fell in blue luminescent pleats to her feet, shivering as if alive. My heart swelled and pounded painfully in my chest.

She reached a trembling hand out to me, an uncertain smile on her face. "Zarq?"

I dropped the machete and ran into her embrace.

I buried my face against her bosom and wept. She was warm and soft and real, and her arms about me were forgiving and loving both.

Oh, Mother, you who used me so cruelly in your madness, who'd led me to mutilation at the convent and then abandoned me through death, why did I crave your love so?

She lifted my hair from my nape, pressed her lips against my skin.

"Forgive me, forgive me," she murmured, and her tears ran sweet and warm down my back. "My baby girl, forgive me."

"Mother," I wept. I held her tight against me, the curve of her spine welcome and familiar beneath my hands.

"Hush now, child," she murmured. "You know I love you."

But I didn't know such, not after the Sa Gikiro of my ninth year, when my sheltered world in the pottery clan had shattered.

"Mother," I said, inhaling the soft warmth of her neck, below her left ear, her glossy black hair draped over me like a benediction.

"Listen to me, Zarq." Her voice became a little sterner, the strong, gentle tone so familiar from my infancy. She held me at arm's length, studied me as tears sparkled like stars upon her cheeks. "My beloved. Listen."

"Mama—"

"Listen."

I bit my lip, held my breath. Silently, I prayed that she wouldn't break this magic spell of love and sanctuary by uttering the last name I wanted to hear right now.

"Waivia needs you, Zarq."

I closed my eyes and felt my insides wither, felt the sanctuary and certainty of her affection draining as swift as a gutter torrent away from me.

"You need to find her, Zarq. Leave this place. Forget this apprenticeship madness of yours and find her."

"Mother."

"She's all alone."

"Mother."

"She needs me." Her voice turned gravelly; her hold upon my elbows became a grip. I dared not open my eyes, wanted to turn back time to moments before, when she'd wept and whispered love against my neck. I wanted to lock myself forever there in her embrace.

"They hurt her, Zarq. She was only a baby and they hurt her." No more was it the voice of my mother, but a gritty rumble of earth and rock. "I thought that my kindnesses to their own children would protect her, but I was wrong. I chose wrongly. I should have fought them. Despised them. They were no clan of mine, those pottery women. They hurt my Waivia."

"Mother."

"Leave here, Zarq." She abruptly released me. "Find her."

The smell of sulfur burned my nostrils. The light behind my closed eyelids turned a luminescent blue. The stench of carrion began souring the air.

I opened my eyes. No longer did my mother stand before me in the shape I loved, but in the shape of my mother's haunt, large and nacreous, a six-foot-tall buzzard with scaly legs the slick reds and whites of viscera, strips of rotted flesh impaled on hooked talons. Luminescent blue feathers bristled upon a breast inflated with growing anger. Red eyes above a beak lined with tiny shards of teeth glared at me.

"Find her."

"She's dead," I whispered.

"She's not!" the haunt cried, and somewhere a mouse shrilled as an owl snapped its spine. "She lives."

I backed away from the haunt, weeping. "She was sold as kiyu almost ten years ago. Sex slaves don't live long. She's dead, Mother. Dead."

"Find her!"

"No."

The haunt shrieked rage, and its eyes sank into its head and rattled like pebbles down its throat, so that I stared at dark caverns instead of eyes. Maggots writhed within those pits, and they dripped over feathered cheeks and wriggle-fell down a feathered breast to gray talons.

"Go away!" I cried, tears streaming down my face, wanting her to stay, but stay in the form she'd once been, long ago, the mother who had sung lullabies to me, laughed like the clear trilling of a bunting bird, tenderly picked splinters from my palms and kissed away all tears. "I won't look for her, Mother, not now, not ever! Let me live my life—"

"You waste your life here!" the haunt shrieked.

"No. I can change things, I know I can. Just listen to me; just *believe* me: I can make it so no daughter is ever sold from her mother as kiyu again. Please, let me try."

"I don't care about other daughters! I care only about Waivia!"

"Waivia is dead!" I shrieked. "She's dead, understand? Now, go; leave me alone. Go!"

The haunt shook its feathered head at me, clacking its beak. With a hiss, it launched into the sky and flapped upward, into the night, luminescing like a lost star.

I shuddered, soaked in chill sweat, and wept tears of anger and frustration.

Beside me, I heard a gasp. I turned.

Ringus stood there panting, eyes glazed with fear. He was pressed against the edge of the butchering table, fingers gripping the thick wood for dear life.

"Eidon," he breathed, ineffectually trying to call the veteran to his aid. "Help me, Eidon."

"Tell no one about this," I said, my voice choked with threat.

He nodded, eyes locked on mine.

"Now, get out of here," I said. "Find your Eidon and throw yourself into his arms. Get."

Ringus turned and fled toward the hovel, stumbling as if his knees no longer worked. He fumbled with the gharial hides draped over the hovel's entrance and nigh on tore them down in his desperation to get inside.

I watched him go, the fingernails of each of my clenched hands digging flesh from my palms. I watched him go, knowing that he'd tell Eidon of what he'd witnessed tonight. But really, I didn't care.

I'd remain a dragonmaster's apprentice and become a dragonmaster myself one day, no matter what obstacles were hurled at me. Just to spite the haunt and prove that I *could* do it, I'd stay. I'd show Mother that I was every bit as clever and worthy as her precious Waivia, and then some.

I would.

# FIVE

*"Get up, deviant."*

Dono stood before me, where I lay on my hammock in my stall. *Splash!* He upturned a bucket of cold water over my face.

Spluttering and gasping, I bolted upright.

The servitors and inductees gathered at the threshold of my stall snickered. Dono turned and walked out, his audience hastily parting to let him pass.

I had not the energy to leap after him. Every part of me was stiffer than old rawhide. I glowered at my unwanted audience and swiped water from my eyes.

"What are you looking at, hey-o?"

They muttered and returned to their hovel, where others were just starting to stumble from its depths and stagger across the courtyard to the latrines. My latrine, roofless, looked decapitated.

I remembered my mother's visit. Shivering and sodden, I buried my face in my hands.

There was so much to fight, within and without me, and it would always be that way. Every moment of the life I'd chosen as a dragonmaster's apprentice would be a fight, a fight for respect amongst my peers, a fight to survive the dragons while serving, a fight to survive Arena, when that time came. I needed to daily battle the iron will of my mother's haunt, and would also need to fight against the conventions of society, the formidable laws of

Temple, and the hatred of those rishi whose lives I strove to change for the better, even while defying the conventions they held so dear.

And where, in all that fighting, lay my goal of revenge, of ousting Waikar Re Kratt from his own Clutch, of ruining his life? I had not the spirit for any of it.

I was so desperate for sleep, my eyes felt like clots of clay-sodden straw, my bones like glass pipettes, my muscles like heavy, rotten melons.

What had I been thinking, to undertake such an impossible journey? I had been naive. My situation was outrageous. Perhaps I *should* just give it all up, follow my mother's bidding, seek a sister long lost and most likely dead.

Oh, Re. I needed venom to stave the haunt off. I needed venom to fight, to continue.

No sooner did I think it than the tang of the dragons' poison was suddenly sharp in my nostrils. Startled, I pulled my hands away from my face, then reared back from the dragonmaster, who was standing right next to my hammock. His palms cupped a filled gourd.

He didn't say anything. Didn't have to. That effervescent, citric tang said it all. As if it were a fragile glass bauble, he proffered the gourd.

I shook my head. Pain from yesterday's labor ran down my neck and across my shoulders like hot oil.

He proffered the gourd again.

My heart beat a little faster.

"No," I whispered, meeting the dragonmaster's blood-rivered eyes.

"No," I whispered again as he stood there still, but no conviction was in my voice, none at all. Indeed, a rush of saliva was filling my mouth.

"No," I said a third time, my voice husky. In answer, the dragon-master lifted the gourd to my lips.

I drank.

With venom singing through my veins, I cobbled together a roof for my latrine before the sun was even full into the sky.

Temporarily freed from the bondage of my mother's will by venom's shield, and my aches and uncertainty eradicated by the same poison, I stood back and regarded my building with pride. It would serve its function admirably, regardless of its extreme lean to the left and the fact that a crawl-hole at shin level stood in lieu of a door. All the humble structure required to validate it was the monthly purification rite of a daronpu.

A glimmer of green and purple up under the roof's overhang caught my attention. I shielded the sun from my eyes with one hand and squinted.

I was looking at a dartanfen.

Such spiders were considered a sign of luck, understand, a sign of favor from the Pure Dragon, for they bore the same colors as a bull. I grinned absurdly at the spider as it spun fine silk in the shade of the slanted roof I'd built.

"You'll not learn how to serve Re, standing there like a fool," a voice growled behind me. I turned and met the gaze of the dragonmaster. His bald head gleamed in the sun's glare, and for a moment, the venom in my blood made his pate look like a moss-splotched chestnut.

"Think you that I've angered Temple just to have you gawk at insects in my stables? That's not why I've spent the last days arguing with the Ranreeb over ancient scrolls and debating with Temple fools!" He jerked a calloused thumb to the east. "Get you to the ve-balu course with the other apprentices, or I'll whip you for your sloth."

I flared my nostrils. Alas, venom brings out the worst of my temper. Always.

"Temple can't refute my legitimate claim to serve Re," I argued. "The Scroll of the Right-Headed Crane clearly states that anyone who has been rendered clean by a holy knife and has been chosen by a Temple-sanctioned dragonmaster may serve a bull."

"I don't need reminding what the scroll says, girl. And what is stated in the scrolls and what actually occurs in Malacar are frequently two different things!"

"Temple can't deny me this position. It *can't*."

The dragonmaster's face turned puce as he struggled to retain his anger. I remembered, then, how precariously balanced he was upon the knife-edge of insanity, after years of venom exposure.

"But I'm sure that your clever arguments will have swayed even the dullest Temple minds in my favor," I hastily added, to assuage him.

His teeth chattered briefly, as an excited cat's do before it pounces upon a bird, and then he shuddered and his shoulders convulsed once, violently.

"We'll see if I have or not," he rasped. "Doesn't matter now, anyway." He smiled maniacally. "There was an uprising last night. Several Hamlets of Forsaken joined forces and launched an attack on Clutch Maht. The Ranreeb flew out this morning to deal with the rebels."

"So I'm safe."

"Safe, gaah! Unless you train hard and survive this year's Arena, you'll not be safe. Re will gut you with one swipe."

"You're not sending me into Arena until I'm ready!" I cried, alarmed.

"Don't tell me what I can and can't do! There are rules, Temple governs Arena. . . ." He sputtered angrily, then pointed wildly to the east, as if he could fling me away with the gesture. "Get to the vebalu course and start training. Now!"

I bit my tongue and turned from him to pack the tools back into the crate.

As I crouched to open the lid, a hot ember snapped against my back, burning through the cape I wore into the flesh of my left shoulder. I yelped, leapt to my feet, and spun around in one movement. Venom-tainted, my vision spun several heartbeats after my eyes did, and I swayed like one drunk.

The dragonmaster stood with a short braided whip dangling from one hand.

"Yes, Komikon!" he shouted.

I licked dry lips. "Yes, Komikon."

"Don't forget it again!"

"Yes, Komikon."

"And never turn your back toward anyone, understand? Ever."

"Yes, Komikon," I replied. But he was already walking away.

I walked east, in the direction the dragonmaster had pointed, into the adjacent stable courtyard. I say walk, but it felt as if I drifted, my venom-oiled muscles moved that easily. As I passed stalls of frisky dragons, some growled at me, while others merely stared intently at me with their still, slitted eyes. The diamond-shaped membranes at the ends of their short, twiggy tails slapped against stone at my passage. *Slap-slap, slap-slap.*

It took me several moments to realize that the sound synchronized with my heartbeat, that the sound of muscle and blood caged behind the bars of my ribs was in precise rhythm with the dragon muscle and blood caged behind the stable's gated stalls.

*Slap-slap.*

The synchronicity unnerved me, even while under the spell of venom. I didn't want to be one with the dragon in *that* manner, didn't want to experience the dragons' captivity deep within my breast.

I hurried on, averting my gaze from the dragons.

The vebalu course was located behind the grain silo in the third courtyard of the stables, the same silo I'd hidden behind during my first day in the stable domain. The grunts and cries of young men hard at work acted as my compass. No sooner did I appear at the dusty outdoor gymnasium than Egg lumbered over to me.

"Sit there!" he bellowed above the activity, pointing to a group of inductees squatting on their haunches. "And watch!"

I knew at once by Egg's manner that Ringus hadn't told him of the haunt's visit last night. As I joined the inductees, I scanned the gymnasium for Eidon. There he was, locked in a wrestling match with Dono while other veterans wrestled in pairs around them. Eidon hadn't seen me. Yet.

Overhead, the sun blazed like it had a vendetta against all things green and living. The ground of the gymnasium was as dry and red as a brick, and the peculiar equipment within the gymnasium was so thickly furred with rufous dust that in the heat it seemed to glow like live coals.

So this was where I'd learn vebalu, the exercises that developed a dragonmaster apprentice's physical agility, coordination, mental faculties, reaction time, and skills with Arena goading tools.

I'd expected something more refined.

I spotted Ringus. The slender servitor was leading a group of his peers through a furious drill of calisthenics. He had his back to me, hadn't seen me enter. I wondered what had ensued after he'd fled from me last night.

Abruptly, Ringus stopped exercising and gave a long whistle. The servitors began hurling themselves over, under, and along the assorted gymnasium equipment at his signal.

First, they leapt onto and raced across a waist-high narrow bar, then leapt off the bar with a somersault. Upon landing, they snatched up one or more of the many goading tools scattered about the ground, and, while dodging around and whacking a series of tall, straw-wrapped pylons, they antagonized and hindered one another with their tools.

The action during this obstacle race grew quite fierce, shields, lances, capes, and bludgeons all swirled and stabbed with malevolent vim. Grunts and the occasional cry of pain peppered the air.

Upon completing eight circuits of the sparring obstacle course, the servitors then sprinted back to the balance bar, dropped their weapons about its base, and hurled themselves at a domed structure.

Twelve feet high and constructed of steam-bent bamboo, the hide-covered dome clearly represented the back of a dragon. The aim was to vault directly onto the bamboo dragon's back, using its nearest hind leg as a springboard to flip oneself up onto the dorsum, whereupon one tossed oneself off the other side with a half twist, to land facing the opposite flank of the beast.

At that point, Ringus dodged in and out under the dragon's scrotal sac, an impertinent bulge I thought surely more prominent than that of a real bull, though I couldn't be sure, as the only male dragons I'd seen had been the senile kuneus of Convent Tieron; the testes and penile forks of *those* beasts had been as withered as their infirm wings.

Each time Ringus darted toward the bull's testes, he spread his arms wide, embraced as much of the scrotal sac as he could, and rubbed his torso and hips against the bulge as if trying to scribe circles upon the thing.

I flushed furiously.

This was the ignoble part of an apprentice's duties, the part children giggled over and women sniggered about, and the moment in Arena when men lustily roared their approval and their lewd taunts. This was where we apprentices used our hands and bodies to bring the bull to full penile arousal. This was when we became Temple's dragonwhores.

Understand, a bull only achieves erection during shinchiwouk, display and combat with another bull dragon. But due to the scarcity of bulls, no Clutch lord wanted to risk his prized bull in such a conflict. Thus Abbasin Shinchiwouk, oft called Arena, was created. This, then, is what I knew of Arena at the time:

Situated on the outskirts of Fwendar ki Bol, Village of the Eggs, Arena was both a place and an event. Each year, for eight days, the bull dragons of every Clutch in Malacar underwent shinchiwouk in an enormous Temple stadium. Many wagers were laid concerning how long it would take the dragonmaster apprentices of each Clutch to arouse their bull, how many apprentices would die in the process, and how many female dragons each bull would mount once aroused. The bloody, ribald spectacle was attended by the elite from both Malacar and the Archipelago. The lower stands of Arena, nearest the action, were always filled to capacity by rishi, Xxelteker sailors, and lower-class merchants. The status, wealth, and political standing of each Clutch was determined annually at Arena. Half a dragonmaster's apprentices never left its bloody grounds.

During shinchiwouk in the wild, much butting of domed head against flank and scrotum takes place between bulls, with the intent, of course, of driving away one's competitor. The few extant accounts of shinchiwouk sightings in the jungle all state that the weaker bull withdraws before real damage occurs. All that physical stimulation of the testes, combined with the excitement of battle and the odor exuded by the female dragons witnessing the conflict, causes a bull to achieve erection. Remove even one of those elements from shinchiwouk—butting of the scrotal sac, battle lust, or the scent of gathered female dragons—and a bull is unable to mate.

For shinchiwouk to be successfully re-created in Arena, then, a dragonmaster apprentice must incite battle lust in a bull while stimulating the bull's testes. The young female dragons witnessing the mock battle behind a series of huge iron gates exude the necessary pheromones.

Flushing from the roots of my hair to my toes, I looked away from Ringus as he continued his vigorous, full-body manipulation of the bamboo dragon's scrotum.

There were more stations on the vebalu course; I just couldn't see them clearly, my view obstructed by target pillars, bamboo dragon, and whirling bodies. But this much was obvious: Vebalu training would be intense and exhaustive.

After leaping several times over the bamboo bull, Ringus came to stand before us inductees. His skin gleamed with perspiration and his lean chest heaved deeply and easily; he looked bright-eyed and exuberant. He was good at vebalu, very good. No doubt he'd be granted veteran status soon.

His eyes fell upon me.

He stopped still. Paled. Shot a look toward the wrestlers, where Eidon trained. Ringus's larynx jogged up and down a few times, then he turned stiffly back to face us, avoiding my eyes, his exuberance gone. Clearly, he *had* told Eidon of what had occurred last night.

Anger flooded me, swift and thin, and then was gone. In its wake, I realized I'd expected as much. I'd now have to find a way to use Ringus's fear of me to my advantage.

"On your feet," Ringus cried at us inductees. "Do as I do and don't fall behind, or Egg'll beat you."

Standing scowling to one side like a gandi, a herder, Egg thwacked a leather baton into one meaty palm. We all flinched. A sloppy grin broke through Egg's frown and a chortle of delight escaped him before he could pull his somber mask back into place.

"Like this, keep up, follow me," Ringus shouted, and he began leaping high into the air to briefly grab his heels before landing again.

Venom-charged, I felt as agile as a jungle cat, my muscles like coiled springs. I kept my eyes on Ringus and matched his every move. Then I began trying to speed up the pace, press him into a competition, and sure enough, aware of me from the periphery of his gaze, he accelerated his pace to keep even with mine.

I accelerated my pace further, leaping so fast my toes only grazed the ground with each landing. Ringus matched me leap for leap.

Soon the inductees on either side of me were falling, gasping, wheezing, our ranks in chaos. Egg charged from inductee to inductee, bellowing and thwacking his baton with abandon, a harried look on his swarthy face.

"Stand up! What's wrong with you? Jump, jump, all together!" He threw his baton to one side with an aggrieved roar, grasped a young boy about the waist, and hoisted him over and over into the air.

"In time with Ringus!" he bellowed. "Jump. Jump. Jump!"

I kept pace effortlessly with Ringus, whose eyes were now locked upon mine. We were in an open contest, one that he was clearly determined to win. Soon all the inductees collapsed in a chest-heaving heap about us. Egg quit badgering them to watch us in amazement, his jaw slack.

My lungs began to burn, as if the air were turning into thick, hot blood in my throat. My vision began to swim. But I would not give up. Not yet.

Ringus, too, was struggling. Although he had the advantage of years of training, I had the advantage of the dragonmaster's venom draft soaring through my limbs. Both of us were failing badly, though, jumping no longer swiftly or gracefully, but as if stones were tied to our ankles.

After a clawful more lung-burning leaps, I decided I'd pushed Ringus far enough. That he'd been willing at all to engage in a contest of wills after witnessing my unnatural rapport with a haunt the night previous garnered my respect for him. If I wanted to restore his sense of worth before me and earn *his* respect—and possibly his alliance—I needed to gracefully lose this challenge I'd lured him into.

So, with a shuddering wheeze that wasn't at all feigned, I collapsed upon the ground. After a few more leaps, just to prove his win fair, Ringus likewise stopped.

While he and I heaved for air like hooked fish, Egg pulled his wits together.

"That's enough warmin' up, hey-o," he muttered, thoroughly disgruntled. " 'S not normal."

He gestured at the inductees and took his unease out on them. "Sit up, sit up, get yourselves ready for the next part! You're going to learn your weapons now, an' I want you all to pay close attention."

While the veterans began target practice with bullwhips, the servitors gathered in one corner of the gymnasium to practice drills with capes, bludgeons, hooked nets, and staffs capped by great, bulbous knobs. Poliars, Egg called these, as he explained the different goading tools to us.

"But you'll be usin' only capes an' bludgeons today," he said, nudging one of the leather-covered clubs piled atop a filthy mound of terracotta-colored capes at his feet. "Remember, you're trainin' for Arena, hey-o. If you want to survive, you'll move fast an' hit hard. The idea is to get your opponent down, so's he'll be bait for Re while the dragonmaster and whatever servitor or veteran is in Arena with you can work the bull."

Work the bull. A euphemism for whoring the beast, for arousing Re.

"When you hit someone, you wanna hit him *real* hard, so he goes down screamin' and writhin'. That sort of thing gets Re's attention fast. When Re goes into Arena, he ain't been fed for a couple of days, hey; he's hungry an' mean, and he's frustrated as anything 'cause he can smell the onahmes in the holding pen, but he can't get at 'em.

"Don't run when the bull comes at you," Egg continued, swatting at a fly that buzzed about his oily locks. "Movement is what Re goes for, movement an' noise. You have to learn to stand still when he charges, wait till he's close, *then* move, when he's built up so much speed he can't maneuver fast. You get behind him, then, an' work him good."

From the mound of frayed hempen cloth at his feet, he picked up a cape. It was exactly the same rufous color as the ground, so much so that it looked woven from dirt.

"Every apprentice wears one of these in Arena. Never let a stronger apprentice grab your cape; if that happens, you're locked in hand-to-hand combat, an' as an inductee, you'll go down. A cape can garrote you, smother you, an' blind you. But,"—and here he squashed the persistent fly with an audible splat between his meaty paws—"it can also save your life."

I was uncomfortably aware of how dry my mouth was turning during his lecture, how sweaty were my palms. On either side of me, my fellow inductees shifted about, restless with *their* increasing anxiety.

"All of you know what a pundar is, right?" Egg asked us, scowling.

Nods all around. Pundars were lizards with remarkable camou-flage abilities. Their skin could turn from the green of a leaf to the red of the earth in seconds flat, and they could hold their breaths and remain as still and stiff as a clod of earth far longer than a child could.

"One of the skills an apprentice learns is the art of pundar," Egg said, and even though such an announcement would have caused hilarity elsewhere, we all remained sober and listened intently. "If you've been hurt bad in Arena an' Re is chargin' at you, your only hope of survivin' is pundar. You drape your cape over yourself, drop to the ground, keep your mouth shut, an' don't move."

Shivers rippled over me at the thought of cowering beneath a worn cape while a bull dragon the size of a large hut came charging toward me.

"Remember, Re goes for sound an' movement. I ain't sayin' his eyesight is poor, hey-o. But if you've just clobbered a fellow inductee, an' he's howlin' and writhin' on the ground, Re's gonna go for him, not go snootin' about the ground tryin' to figure out where you've disappeared to. Every veteran in this stable has survived Arena an' aroused the bull at least once by using pundar, after strikin' down a fellow apprentice as bait for Re."

I cleared my throat. All eyes turned on me.

"What happens to the person that's fallen? What exactly do you mean by 'bait'?"

Egg snorted derisively. "Whaddya think happens? Anyone who falls gets ripped apart by Re, and while he's feedin', the survivors work him good. What's there not to understand about that?"

I couldn't answer.

"If you *do* get your opponent down an' survive Re's charge an' manage to work him, you'll be promoted to servitor when you return here. Your chances of survivin' next year's Arena are better then, 'cause you'll spend more time vebalu training instead of mucking stalls, an' you'll form alliances with veterans who'll watch your back in Arena. And most important of all"—here he wagged a thick finger at us—"as a servitor, your name might not even end up on the Ashgon's Bill, which means you won't be required to enter Arena at all."

The wide eyes of every inductee were riveted on Egg. Each boy's jaw was set with the conviction that he would survive Arena and move on to become a servitor.

I couldn't look at the boys, so filled were they with childish determination.

Understand, the majority of the inductees were eight to ten years old—most of them a good nine years younger than I—their knees overlarge on their twiggy legs, their bellies as round and smooth as cooked eggs. Their chests were slight, their ribs visible, their arms thin. They were children, to me, and I knew with both frustration and sadness that the dragonmaster had chosen the majority of them solely as temporary stall muckers, their ultimate purpose to incite bloodlust in our bull dragon with their lives a year hence in Arena. Fodder, he had called them, before going to round them up on Sa Gikiro a few days ago. "Now, get on your feet, all of you," Egg ordered, "an' pair up."

In a mad scramble, all the inductees claimed one another as opponents. A dark-skinned, scrawny boy with an unruly cowlick sprouting like a parrot's plume from his crown was left without a partner. Shoulders hunched, he had no choice but to stand opposite me.

He was ten years old if he was a day. He should have been learning his clan's guild trade, and in his spare time, making peepholes in mating shacks in hopes of glimpsing naked women. His was an age for foolish play and wrestling with siblings in the dust, for eating much and sleeping heavily. Yet here he stood, learning the brutal art of fighting to the death.

"Grab a cape, snap it on, an' start on the balance beam!" Egg bellowed at us. "C'mon, get movin'! An' remember, you're *trainin'*; don't use full force and really break someone's kneecaps, else you'll be whipped for it."

I grabbed one of the filthy camouflage capes and, after fumbling a bit with the heavy, rusted chain, clasped the cape about my neck. I could easily see how an opponent could garrote me, with that coarse chain about my throat.

With my reluctant opponent standing a generous arm's length away from me, I queued up to start the sparring course.

All those years balancing atop mill wheel and convent roof

while at Tieron, fixing cogs and replacing roof tiles, stood me in good stead on the beam, despite the trembling in my fatigued legs. My technique for swirling my cape in my young opponent's face and obscuring his view was also more than competent, and my reflexes for darting out of reach of his bludgeon were superb, learned after years of darting away from tail lashes and head butts from the retired bulls I'd served as an onai.

But my bludgeon hung limp in my hand.

Egg lumbered over to me, scowling, as I and my young opponent danced about the straw-stuffed pylons on the obstacle course.

"Wassa matter with you?" Egg bellowed in my ear. "Use your bludgeon!"

I gritted my teeth and gave the straw pylon nearest me a mighty whack, which unfortunately left me open to attack from my opponent. He promptly thwacked his bludgeon across my lower back. I cried out from the blow but was not felled, only bruised.

"Turn round an' hit him back!" Egg screamed.

Panting, sweat running down my dust-coated face in rivulets, I faced Egg. "No."

"Eh?"

I took a shuddering breath. "No. I won't do it."

We were blocking the obstacle course; the inductees sparring behind us were forced to come to a stop.

Egg gawked at me. "Whaddya mean, you won't do it?"

"I won't fell someone as bait for Re," I gasped, heart pounding not just from the exercise but from defying Egg's order.

"What do you think your purpose in Arena is, hey?"

I swallowed. "To serve Re."

"You think you can do that, with every inductee that's out in Arena alongside you tryin' to bring you down?"

"I . . . I intend on trying." I sounded as confused and uncertain as I felt.

Dumbfounded, Egg's great jaw moved up and down several times before he sputtered, "You're completely cracked."

"There's no law that says an inductee *has* to sacrifice another to save himself in Arena, is there?" I asked.

"Common sense says so!"

I frowned, shook my head. "I didn't join the apprenticeship to commit murder."

Egg let out a string of curses, then spun on the inductees pooled behind us.

"Don't stand about starin'!" he shouted. "Get trainin', get movin', go!"

Word of my refusal to attack another inductee spread quickly amongst the apprentices after that, and with every new circuit through the vebalu course, I was challenged by a different opponent. Each young boy attacked me with bold glee. As the sun poured wrathful heat over us, my quick reflexes began to slow, and some of the inductees' hits landed hard against kneecap or ankle and felled me.

But I persevered.

Though more than once, my bludgeon twitched in my hand as anger exploded in me, prompted by pain, and I almost gave in to brutal retaliation.

Gradually, a crowd began to form about the obstacle course. The servitors and veterans had heard of my refusal to attack. Pausing from their training during the worst of the day's heat, they gathered to watch me parry and dodge.

The venom was all but gone from me by then, understand, and only my high threshold for hard labor after years at the convent was keeping me upright and moving. Jeers and hoots began peppering the air.

"Set a servitor against her!" someone called out. "See how long she keeps her vow then!"

"No, set a veteran against her!"

Laughter.

Then someone did step between me and my current opponent, and I came to a swaying stop and blinked through sweat-salted eyes at who it was.

Dono.

Relief flooded through me. He was ending this ridiculous show, was coming to my rescue.

"I'll spar with her," he said quietly, his eyes never leaving mine. "Hand me your bludgeon, boy."

My young opponent swiftly obeyed and joined the sidelines.

Dono slowly began circling me, and I, instinctively, mirrored his every move. Then I stopped.

"Wait," I said, my voice rasping from my parched throat. "I don't want to spar you."

"You'll spar me or be beaten."

"Fine," I said softly. "But first I need a drink."

Taunts and slurs from the crowd.

Dono considered, then magnanimously held up a hand for silence. "All right. You need a drink, go."

I staggered off in a side-walking manner toward the dust-filmed cistern located in the far corner of the outdoor gym. I'd learned my lesson from the dragonmaster: Turn your back on someone, and you're likely to get struck. Dono had agreed to allow me to seek water with the confident expectation that I *would* turn my back on him, and that he could then humiliate me by felling me with his first blow. He stood tensed as I moved away, his bludgeon twitching in readiness for felling me.

Of course, I gave him no such satisfaction.

While the gathered apprentices began laying wagers on how long I'd last against Dono, I plunged my head into the cistern's algae-slick waters to invigorate myself. The water was miserably lukewarm.

I didn't want to spar with Dono.

Not at all.

I craved his friendship, his support, even his indifference, anything but this hostility. Did he not remember how as children we'd raced crickets at dusk? How we'd napped side by side in the heat of midday during the Fire Season? We'd once shared a concoction of dead hornets, in the childish belief that drinking the mashed insects would furnish us with stingers. I'd had my first sip of maska wine at age seven, when Dono had had the audacity to steal some from his blood-uncle's domicile and share it with Waivia and me.

He remembered none of that, apparently. He cared not that I was clan, was his milk-sister. All that mattered to him was that he should remain a cinai komikonpu, a dragonmaster's apprentice proper, a veteran, and that my deviant presence in the stable domain be removed before it caused Temple to denounce the dragonmaster, end his reign, and oust all his apprentices.

I cupped water in my palms and did what I'd come to the cistern to do: I drank.

Have you ever experienced the queer rebound sensation that occurs, the morning after imbibing too much fermented drink, when, upon drinking water on a stomach empty of all food, the alcohol in your blood is temporarily reignited? If so, you can perhaps see the cunning behind my request for water: I had had nothing to eat all day save the dragonmaster's venom draft, and, as had occurred more than once during my venom-dependent days in Convent Tieron, the moment I drank the water from the cistern, the venom in my blood was slightly reignited.

But only slightly.

I returned to face Dono. To a chorus of catcalls and gibes against me, Dono and I began circling one another.

When he attacked, I didn't see it coming. He moved and was instantly upon me, and I was stumbling backward under a flurry of blows. *Thwack, thwack, thwack!* About my head, about my arms, about my waist. I couldn't see, and I lifted my arms automatically to protect my head. He delivered a short, blunt blow across my stomach, winding me, then grabbed my cape and pulled it tight about my neck. I gagged and clawed at my neck.

He released me and nimbly leapt back, out of range.

Stunned, I tried to gather my wits, catch my breath. He came at me again.

Backward I stumbled, almost tripping in my desperation to avoid his blows. The purpose of his onslaught was clearly to humiliate and overwhelm, not injure me, for no blow was damaging, merely dizzying. My ears rang; I couldn't focus. I couldn't catch my breath or gather my wits enough to effectively dodge his rainfall of strikes.

I tried weaving. I tried ducking. I tried parrying his blows. But I avoided or stopped about only one in eight.

He grabbed my cape again, briefly strangled me, then let go and leapt back.

I gaped at him, wheezing, sweat running off me in grimy rivulets. The apprentices jeered and laughed.

"You can't do it, Zarq," Dono said, and I was somewhat pleased to realize that he was breathing hard. "Go home."

That hurt far greater than any blow.

I *had* no home. My clan had exiled me. Convent Tieron had been purged by Temple Auditors, and all my holy sisters had been executed, save for one named Kiz-dan, who'd fled the convent with me; even she and her child had, to my never-ending sorrow, eventually deserted me.

The closest thing to a home that I had now was the dragonmaster's stables.

I swallowed, shook my woozy head. "I'm not leaving, Dono."

He attacked again.

I fell.

I lay in the dust, dazed, staring at sun-seared sky. Dono loomed over me.

"Give in and leave."

I licked my lips. "No."

"Yield, Zarq, or I'll hurt you."

I closed my eyes, summoned my strength, and staggered to my feet. I braced myself for his next attack.

When it came, it was swift and angry, and I landed facedown in the dust with the back of my knees smarting from his felling blow.

Reeling, I slowly clambered upright again. The hoots and cat-calls about me began petering to a stop. Dono swam drunkenly before me.

"If you won't yield, you'll have to hit me," he panted. "I'm leaving myself open, Zarq."

"No."

"You've got to hit me, or you'll go down."

"I won't strike," I said.

"Then you'll go down." He swooped in and felled me before I even had time to blink.

Grit was in my eyes; grit crunched like sand between my teeth. My calves throbbed hot and painfully, taut with swelling bruises. The crowd slewed first one way, then another, as I tried to stand. My vision oscillated and clouded.

"Stay down, Zarq," Dono panted. "You don't have what it takes to be an apprentice."

I ignored him and dragged myself upright. I swayed, staggered, and almost fell. Blood from a cut on my cheek dripped into the dust.

Silence in the gymnasium.

The silence stretched long and hot.

Dono finally spat on the ground. "I'm wasting my time. You won't survive Arena, Zarq. Doesn't matter how hard you train, doesn't matter if the dragonmaster keeps Temple away from you. If you can't play the game by the rules, you won't make it."

He approached me and placed a hand on my forehead.

It would have been so easy to strike him then. So easy to smash my bludgeon across his face. But I did not. I would not strike an apprentice down, would not turn my back on honor in my quest to obtain that which I desired. I would not become like my mother's haunt.

With barely any effort, Dono pushed me over into the dust.

# SIX

Dusk.

The hovel courtyard.

And there lay my latrine, the walls separated, the roof fallen, as if a giant fist had bowled it over. I stared at it in disbelief as twilight drew a star-shot cape over Re valley.

"Who did this?" I asked hoarsely. I turned about and faced the shadowy forms of the apprentices, who, like me, had just entered the hovel courtyard. My disbelief flooded into fury.

"Who did this?" I cried again, and from the adjacent stables, a dragon bugled, challenged by the anger in my cry. The other dragons shifted in their stalls and rasped talons against stone. "By the power of holy Re, I demand that you declare yourself!"

From the east, a sputtering white star blazed across the sky. A spume of unearthly green scintillated in its wake. It shot high over the adjacent courtyard and scribed a perfect arc above the sandstone archway leading into the stables beyond.

Through that archway, amongst the stragglers just returning from vebalu training, walked Dono.

"You!" I stabbed a finger at him. The shooting star exploded into a coruscating nimbus of white and green. The unearthly light showered over Dono and turned him the mottled colors of a corpse.

Dono had destroyed my latrine, I was sure of it. He'd lost a little self-respect that afternoon, lowering himself to repeatedly attack someone who had refused to fight back. So he'd rashly taken out his pique by dismantling the coarse structure that I'd so carefully crafted the day before.

A section of the dark detached itself from one corner of the stables and drifted wraithlike toward Dono. It materialized into a form we all simultaneously recognized: the dragonmaster.

"Did you do this?" the dragonmaster hissed at Dono, and even though I stood some distance away from them both, I heard the dragonmaster clearly, his voice whispering through the courtyard like an invidious wind.

Dono lifted his chin a little. "Yes, Komikon."

I recalled that brash tone from my childhood, from when Dono had first audaciously demanded inclusion in the dragonmaster's apprenticeship.

"You will be whipped for it." The dragonmaster faced us all. "Whomsoever opposes my choice of any apprentice here will be whipped. Do you hear? Twenty lashes, meted out with a venom-free whip! No one opposes my will, regardless of whom I've chosen to enter our ranks. Ever!"

He turned back to Dono. "Now, strip."

Dono did so, narrow chin held steady. With his loincloth on the ground, he looked somehow larger than life in the moonlight, his nakedness before us all a powerful statement of his humanity. The Komikon ordered Dono to brace himself against a wall. Dono did so, muscles tense. The Komikon uncoiled his dragon whip from his waist. Dono took a deep, slow breath and visibly forced himself to relax, to unclench tight muscles. So the whip wouldn't cut so deeply, understand.

I jumped at the first crack of the whip, tensed for the second, bit my lip at the third.

After ten lashes, my fury at Dono was gone. Teeth clenched, I listened to the whistle of whip through air, the tight snap of leather against skin, and saw, with eyes unable to look away, the red, raised circles already peppering Dono's back. Those welts would, with one more forceful strike, split like the peels of rotted plums.

Dono fell at fifteen lashes, staggered upright again, panting, his sweaty palms leaving visible marks upon the sandstone wall. The moonlight made the blood running down his back and buttocks look like rivulets of dark wine.

He fell again at eighteen, and again at twenty. He didn't rise then.

We all stood motionless as the dragonmaster toyed with his corded bullwhip, which lay stretched long upon the dusty ground. He flicked it, gently; the whip undulated in a slow wave, barely rising from the earth. The muscles in his whip arm were roped with protruding veins, and a smile played upon his face, like that of a mother well pleased with her child.

"Eidon," he said, and Dono's red-haired adversary strode to the Komikon's side. "I'll be gone on the morrow again. You'll act as wai-komikonpu in my absence."

"Yes, Komikon."

"Any who shirk their duties are to be publicly lashed each dusk, by your hand, on the lane. Eight lashes, meted out with a venom-free whip. And any who oppose my will regarding my choice of the girl receives three times that number. Understand?"

"As Re wills, Komikon," Eidon replied. "As Re wills."

After the dragonmaster left, the apprentices shuffled toward the hovel and lounged about the ground, untying their leather sacs of destiny wheels and dice from their waists with studied ease. But their poise was contrived as they petitioned Re to favor their dice; the broken skeleton of my latrine was a presence as disturbing as a relentless noise, and Dono's bloodied form, kneeling still before the sandstone wall, loomed as large as a sepulchral tower behind our backs.

I staggered over to my broken latrine's roof, which lay upon the ground like the half shell of an enormous nut, and sank wearily upon it.

Ringus blew the embers to life beneath the cauldron, then gave orders to this inductee and that to begin preparing the next day's meal. Servitors bowed before the veterans they had chosen to serve during the day and chanted komikonpu walan kolriks, the dragon-master apprentice prayers for guardianship, on their behalf. The chants were threnodic. They suited my mood.

I watched as the servitors sat around the outskirts of the veterans, who began their complex contests of darali abin famoo. I knew virtually nothing about that game of prognostication, though I'd known, as a child, that the pottery clan men had indulged in darali abin famoo during men's celebrations, when maska ran freely and inebriation ran high. The veteran apprentices, however, played with great intensity and somberness, and the servitors sitting about them watched each veteran's spin of destiny wheel, each fall of dice, and every forecast those combinations made with equal fervor. No party amusement was this, but a game with serious intent.

Groans, curses, taunts, grins, and even the occasional scuffle broke out amongst the servitors as alliances swiftly formed and re-formed according to the destiny wheel forecasts. I needed no such forecast for myself: I knew I had no allies.

Yet.

For as Eidon spun his wheel and tossed his dice, I saw both him and Ringus glance more than once from their game of prognostication to me.

I didn't stand aside to let any queue before me that eve, and no one attempted to make me forfeit my turn, either. I ate what was allotted me by Egg, which looked to be more than on the previous evening, and then I retired to my hammock. I fell asleep instantly.

I bolted into a sitting position sometime later, heart pounding. Someone had entered my stall, breathing like an angry dragon.

Darkness all around me, the dense darkness of deep night, lit thinly by weak moonlight. Dono stood hunched and crooked at my side, his features shrouded in shadow. His hands gripped a weapon.

He raised the weapon. I reared back with a cry.

"You've got a latrine to rebuild," he said, his words thick with pain.

I stared at him, mind spinning, and realized that the weapon he held was a shovel.

"Komikon's orders," Dono growled, and he lowered the shovel and leaned on it for support.

I licked my lips. "I'll rebuild it tomorrow."

"Tonight. Komikon's orders. Me and you, together."

I flared my nostrils. "It's dark, Dono—"

"Why?" he said, and he abruptly lurched closer, using the shovel as a crutch. "Why're you doing this, Zarq? What in the name of Re motivates you?"

I paused, then answered slowly, carefully. "Kratt killed my father. Temple took my brother away just after his birth. Kratt crushed her face beneath his boots."

"Whose face?"

"Mother's."

A pause. Then: "People die. All the time."

"Our clan sold Waivia as kiyu, Dono."

That penetrated his facade of indifference. Emotion worked over his face, then he turned aside and spat.

"You think being an apprentice is a safer life?" he growled.

"I can change things."

"What things?"

"The way things are. Temple laws."

He stared. "You're talking revolution."

"Yes."

"You're cracked. You're a *woman*, Zarq, a woman. You can't start a revolution. Look at you. You can't even bring yourself to strike down a fellow apprentice. You don't have what it takes to be an apprentice. Shit, you don't even have the strength to rebuild a latrine."

Anger came then, from somewhere hot and unwanted deep within me, from the hole gouged in my spirit from all I and my family had suffered and lost, a hole I'd filled with the promise of vengeance, a promise I now had turned my back on with the outrageous hope of achieving something greater.

"Give me the shovel and I'll build that latrine," I said, and I snatched the tool from his hand and jumped from my hammock, causing him to step back as my chest struck his.

"Watch me, Dono," I said, and I pushed by him, hoisting the shovel up, and strode to the dragon stall adjacent to mine.

The dragon within was sleeping, standing with snout brushing the ground. At my footsteps, she awoke, slitted pupils dilating, nostrils flaring, head rising. I stood outside her stall's gate with my hips butted against the stout iron.

"Hey-o, dragon," I murmured. "I'd have you know me."

The forked tip of her tongue quivered from her gums. Slowly, I set aside my shovel. Slowly, I unknotted my cape.

From the corner of my eye, I saw Dono lurch out of my stall. He stopped at my stall's threshold, stunned, as I untied the remaining knot in my cape.

"What're you doing?!"

"Obtaining the strength to build a latrine," I snapped, and I let my garment fall to the ground, snatched up my shovel, and jabbed it lancelike at the destrier.

She rose up on her hindquarters, and the domed slope of her crown butted against the ceiling as talons the color of newly minted steel shredded the air. Her tongue shot out, thick with venom, straight for me.

Dono tackled me just as she lashed out. Her tongue glanced off my neck with brutal strength as Dono threw me sideways, and I landed hard on the ground, Dono atop me.

He launched himself away from the dragon's reach, knees and feet scrabbling over me; then I, too, scrambled on hands and knees away from the destrier's stall.

Talons slashed air and scaled muscle slammed against stone. The bitter reek of agitated dragon fogged the air like smoke from burning oil.

I collapsed across Dono's calves. The violence of the dragon's strike and the strength in her tongue shocked me. Numbness blazed up my throat, and my neck instantly began swelling with great bruises.

"Idiot," Dono gasped, and he shoved me off his legs and swiftly rose to his knees. With one broad palm he swiped the welt of venom from my neck. "They're trained to go for the face; they're destriers."

I couldn't breathe. The swelling bruises were acting like a garrote. Wide-eyed, I clawed at my throat.

"Hold still!" Dono barked, and he whipped off his loincloth and scrubbed furiously at my neck. "Don't die on me, hear? The Komikon'll kill me. Don't die on me, Zarq."

His words became a roar. My vision tunnelled into darkness.

I regained consciousness. Warm lips pulled away from mine. The taste of someone else's breath lingered in my mouth like broth-scented steam.

A face floated above mine, floating, fading, a strange demon moon.

"Don't move. Y'agitate yourself and your throat'll close over again."

Dono.

I closed my eyes, concentrated on keeping my breathing slow and even. Each breath was hard-won, felt as if I'd drawn it through the confines of a burlap bag held over my head and tied tight around my throat with wire. It would have been easy to panic, to succumb to the terror threatening to overwhelm me.

But a growl in my ear stayed the urge. "Breathe, Zarq. So help me."

I focused on inhaling and exhaling in measured, even breaths. My lips felt foreign and partially detached, my cheeks as if cold starch water were hardening upon them. My ears hummed as though a swarm of insects clouded my head, and as the venom that had touched my skin sank into my bloodstream, I was filled with a familiar illusion of puissance, which had been my goal in provoking the dragon, understand. Though I'd not expected such strength, such violence, in her lashing, and I'd not expected her to go for my face.

The earth beneath my back breathed with me, gently swelling with each inhalation and deflating with each sigh. The destriers in their stalls likewise began to breathe in harmony with me, and even the apprentices asleep in their hovel inhaled in accordance to my demand. Indeed, every man and woman, child and beast, within Clutch Re breathed in rhythm with me, blithely unaware in their sleep that I controlled their very air. Or so I believed, in my inebriation.

I felt that even Dono's breathing synchronized with mine. I glowed in the triumph of mastering his lungs.

He broke the harmony. "What d'you do that for? No, don't answer. Keep quiet."

I cracked an eye open, saw him sitting alongside me, one knee up, arm draped over it. He was looking down at me, running a hand through his locks. Sweat slicked his body silver in the moonlight, and stars like flecks of fine glazed porcelain glittered upon the dark table of night above him.

I had a grunu-engros, then, a dragon-spirit moment. You know of what I speak, yes? That illusory feeling of having already experienced a similar situation, a situation that is a portent of your life yet to come, that muddled, powerful feeling of familiarity and omen.

And I remembered, suddenly, when I'd last seen the sky so

illuminated by starlight. It had been the eve following the Sa Gikiro of my ninth year, the night Mother broke Temple Statute for what was to be the first of many times, when she hid glazes and pottery tools in the jungle. On that night, like this, the sky couldn't be described as black, for it was so bright with luminescence that it looked as if white liquid porcelain had been gently swirled through it.

I shivered.

"How come you know venom so well, Zarq?" Dono said, bringing me back to the present. "Onais aren't allowed to touch the venom of the kuneus they serve. But you must've, hey-o, to have built up the kind of tolerance you've got. You should be dead from the amount of venom you just received, so close to your face." He looked away from me, across the empty courtyard.

After a moment, he spoke again. I realized, then, by the lilting tone of his voice and the unnaturally still focus of his gaze that he, too, was intoxicated by venom. Of course. With his bare palm he'd first scraped the dragon's poison from my throat.

"They always go for the face, Zarq. It's instinct. Hatchlings right out of the egg do it. I've seen them. They always aim for the mouth."

He shifted a little, still gazing into the dark. "Y'know how many inductees I've seen die that way? Dozens, most of them boys too young to understand what was happening. They convulse on the ground, blood streaming out of their eyes and noses, blisters erupting on their faces so fast it looks like something is crawling around underneath their skin."

A breeze pushed a strand of hair into his eyes and he brushed it aside, staring into his past. "You think you've seen people suffer, Zarq? You've seen nothing so far, not compared to what I've seen."

He fell silent. We breathed in synchrony.

I closed my eyes against the brilliance of the stars and my mind against the images evoked by Dono's words, and concentrated on breathing slowly, carefully. I envisioned the swollen welt across my neck unknotting, the way the muscles in a man's shoulders loosen beneath the oiled fingers of a woman. I pictured my breath flowing like a ribbon of sweet, dark honey down my throat, smooth and unhindered, imagined the warm glow of it in my lungs. Around that pooling honey buzzed a horde of bees, their wings fluttering fast and furious, the hum of them vibrating my entire torso.

The hum became a rhythm that rocked me slightly, as if I were in a cradle.

No, the hum was more guttural than that, more urgent, and the rocking was something less soothing, something focused against one of my hips, not affecting my whole body. I opened my eyes.

Dono still sat alongside me, one knee up. But no reflective look resided upon his face now, and he no longer stared into the dark. He was looking at me. Not me, the person, but me, the body. He saw only breasts and belly, vulva and thighs, body parts exclusive of a whole.

He was stroking himself hard and fast as his eyes roved over me. His lips were parted, and intense concentration that could at any moment turn into profound frustration had set his features.

He stiffened, suddenly. His head jerked back and his eyes snapped shut. A groan sounded from his belly like a thorn was being drawn from deep in his flesh.

He began stroking himself anew, each move slow, teased out, full of savor, and a series of small grunts escaped him. He shuddered, glut easing the intensity from his face.

Warmth and want bloomed in my own groin. I lifted a hand as cool and heavy as marble to touch myself. Dono's eyes snapped open.

"Don't," he said huskily.

I let my hand fall back. By lifting it, I'd disturbed that warm honey flowing down my throat. It began forming a viscous clot, threatening to choke me.

Dono cursed. "Breathe easy, Zarq. And don't move, hear? I mean it: Don't move."

I lay there motionless, his eyes upon mine. Self-loathing filled his face and he looked away from me. The air about him smelled different now, a bitter salt smell redolent of ocean weeds. The odor of his seed, that, spilled upon sanctified ground. An offering to Re: Temple Statute did not forbid such, for a man.

I closed my eyes again and concentrated on breathing. After a while, when my breath flowed easier, Dono spoke.

"The Komikon told me to wake you, hey-o. To help you rebuild the latrine. He gave me a potion to give you first." A pause; I kept my eyes closed. "You keep your mouth shut and tomorrow morning I'll let you drink the draft he bid me give you tonight. Understand? Or I'll drink it myself. Re knows I'll need it."

I gave a tiny nod. I understood.

It was not my provocation of the destrier Dono wanted hidden from others, which was an impossibility, what with the turgid bruising across my neck, but his own reactions that he wanted kept secret. That he'd given in to lust in my presence was something he wanted no one to know.

He shifted and looked about the glowering courtyard. "You've got no idea what you're taking on, Zarq. You can't defy Temple Statute like this. You can't defy the Emperor."

He rose stiffly to his feet and looked down at me.

"I'll carry you to your hammock when it's safe enough to move you, and I'll rebuild your damn latrine myself. Hear? I'm not getting whipped again because of your stupidity."

But if you'd given me the draft as the dragonmaster bid you, I wouldn't have acted so rashly, I thought. I couldn't say so aloud, though, not with my throat so swollen. Instead, I merely gave another infinitesimal nod.

"If you're clever, you'll just disappear," Dono grunted. "Tomorrow.

Or the day after. But I don't believe you're that clever, are you, Zarq?"

He picked up his venom-soiled loincloth and disappeared into the far corner of the courtyard to wash it free of the dragon's poison. Unlike me, his tolerance of venom was low, for he'd not had unwatched, free access to the substance as I had had as an onai. No, I imagined that the dragonmaster kept a very close eye upon his apprentices, that they not partake of the dragon's fire of their own accord and thus not only flout Temple Statute but descend into the dizzy world of addiction as well.

I stared at the stars, feeling their white twinkle like cold water droplets upon my belly. From the corner where Dono had disappeared came the grating squeak of rusted iron, followed by the gush and splash of water pumped forth. I shivered.

Dono returned moments later, his damp, wrung-out loincloth knotted back around his hips, Kratt's cape in his hand. He draped the cape over top of me and started pacing. He studied the stars, studied the stables. Time slid on, unhurried. Equally indolent, the moon and stars drifted languidly through the sky. He paced some more.

Finally, his patience wore thin. He crouched on his haunches beside me, face drawn from exhaustion despite the venom in his veins.

"I'm going to lift you now," he said. "I've still got that damn latrine to build. Just relax and keep breathing. Hear?"

I nodded.

His hands slid beneath my back and rump, his calloused palms strong and warm against my buttocks. The muscles in his arms flexed as he tugged and hefted me against his chest. I felt the unleashed strength that lay coiled within him, like the muscles in the haunches of a wild dog poised to fight.

This man lifting me was no longer the orphan who had nursed alongside me as a babe. He was something else entirely, and the heat of him, his musk of sweat and semen, made my pulse race.

He pulled me close. My cheek lay against his muscled chest. I could feel his heart beating. My forehead rested against one of his nipples. I stayed the urge to lift my mouth to it.

He inhaled and tensed, and I felt the wild dog within him coil tight, ready to leap into action, teeth bared. Then a grunt reverberated from beneath his ribs as he rose with me in his arms. He started back to my stall.

With each step that he took, the effort of carrying me quivered up his body from his thighs. A muscle in his lean jaw twitched as he concentrated on his destination. I wondered what he felt, carrying a naked woman in his arms. Even one such as I. I could not resist; I couldn't. It was the venom that made me do it, venom and the giddy pluck it always inspired in me: I parted my lips, lifted my head a little, and closed my mouth around his closest nipple.

He froze. I didn't release him. No. Instead, I sucked. A gentle pull, as if I were nursing.

His larynx punched up and down.

"I'll drop you," he said hoarsely.

I continued suckling, slowly, evenly, in rhythm with my frail breathing.

"Zarq." His eyes closed; he was pleading with me. I slowly let his nipple slide from between my lips.

Then I bit it.

Not hard, understand. But not a nibble, either. I drew no blood, but I did cause pain. Pain, to a veteran apprentice, is oft mingled with pleasure. It's the way of venom.

He sucked in a breath, sharplike, and his hands on my back and beneath my knees tightened. I sucked anew, harder now, insistent, in full control.

"Zarq," he hoarsely gasped, only the word was a cry, a sigh, a request, an ache, a contradiction. He wanted me to stop, yet he wanted me to continue.

I stopped and blew gently on his nipple, firm now as a green flower bud.

Slowly, his eyes opened again. His breathing was ragged and uneven, as if he were the one with bruised and swollen flesh obstructing his throat. He swallowed and refused to look down at me. Trembling, he resumed carrying me to my stall.

I think, perhaps, he longed for more, for as he lay me in my hammock, his arms and hands slid out from me slowly. Our eyes locked, his inches from mine. Our body heat merged. My breathing quickened. That was enough to send his lust scurrying away.

"No," he said thickly. "It'd kill you, like this."

He withdrew from me and stood up. Once the contact was broken, his will was no longer mine. Not completely. He looked away and his nostrils flared like the nares of a dragon in distress.

"Leave the stables, Zarq. Or Temple'll kill you. And if they don't, you'll die in Arena. You know it."

# SEVEN

Did I still fear my lust for venom, still fear that I might descend, completely, into addiction? Oh, yes. If I'd had an alternate means of obtaining the strength necessary to get up the following morning and fulfill my responsibilities as an apprentice, I would have chosen it. But in my condition, with my neck so tight with bruising it felt as if sinewy hands were wrapped about my throat and relentlessly squeezing, I needed the medicinal properties of venom.

So as much as I had resisted the dragonmaster's drafts only days before, I now sought the same.

I joined the apprentices for the morn's repast, the massive bruising across my neck tender and pulsing. I ignored Egg's gawping mouth and ogle-eyed look as he stood behind the cauldron, ladle hanging loosely from one paw. I reached forward, placed a hand over his, and scooped gruel into my bowl. He barely noticed my touch, just continued to stare.

"I'm waiting for bull wings to bless Clutch Re," I said. The ritual greeting came out hoarsely, as if I'd just gargled raw, minced chilies.

Egg gathered himself. "May your waiting end, may bull wings hatch."

I moved away with my bowl of gruel and stood at the edge of the unwashed pack of boys. Nudges and stares followed me.

I slid two fingers into the gruel and scooped some into my mouth. I let it rest there, a clot of broth-swollen grain. With difficulty, I swallowed it.

Overhead, the dawn's light tainted the pearly sky pink. Dew glistened upon sandstone wall and tiled stable roof, turning as red as fresh blood the rufous dust that coated everything. The citric tang of venom lay so heavy in the chill morning air, it was as though the dragons' poison, not the sky's clean dew, slicked roof and ground.

Slowly and steadily, I finished eating my gruel. Morning noises rose and fell about me: The clunk of ladle in cauldron, the slurp and burp of food being ingested; hacks and nose clearings, ritual greetings exchanged. A hungry dragon lowed. A tail thwacked stone in impatience. Snouts snuffled audibly through empty mangers in search of stray nuts.

Soon Egg would herd the inductees to whichever section of the stables demanded our labor. I needed my venom draft.

I scanned the yard for Dono, saw him returning from a visit to the latrines in a stiff, lurching shuffle, still using the shovel as a crutch. The latrine he'd rebuilt during the night, aided by venom-induced energy, was a ramshackle affair, sloppily cobbled together and unlikely to withstand the first monsoon. But it was finished, roof perched askew on top.

I detached from the milling boys and intercepted Dono.

He came to a stop and swayed briefly. A muscle in his jaw twitched.

"Give me the draft," I murmured. "Give it to me now and I'll share a little with you."

He paused. Swallowed.

"What'll it do to me?" he asked hoarsely.

He'd not swallowed diluted venom before. Yes, as a veteran apprentice he'd been exposed to venom via the Komikon's poison-saturated whips, and yes, he'd accidentally received venom-slick tongue lashes from the destriers, but no apprentice would have ingested venom before. Of course not. Against Temple Statute, that.

"You've tolerance enough; it won't harm you," I murmured. "The impact of venom is a clawfold more intense when you swallow it. Your pain will disappear for the day. Well into the night, too."

The poison had certainly given him the strength to rebuild my latrine last night, for under normal circumstances, he would have been prone on his belly, groaning from the whip welts upon his back.

He tottered briefly upon his crutch. He needed venom as much as I did. "Fine. Come back here after Egg leads you all out."

He turned and lurched away from me. I averted my eyes from his back.

Shortly after, Egg led us inductees through a side door in the second courtyard. It opened onto yet another courtyard, a small one with but a few stalls, each filled with dragons convalescing from wounds, intestinal trouble, or some such malady. A low wooden building ran two-thirds of the way round this courtyard. The building's worn wooden verandah squeaked underfoot as the inductees followed Egg along it. Unexpectedly, the lot of them moved slowly, matching my careful pace.

Egg chewed a callus on one palm as he shifted his weight from foot to foot beside me. "Eidon didn't say nothin' about you not workin' today, so you have to work, y'hear? It ain't often we work in the Tack Hall, so count yourself lucky he gave us such an easy job today."

He ducked through a creaky door into a dark interior. I and the rest of the inductees followed him.

The smell of brass. Beeswax. Stiff new leather. Oiled wood and dry hemp cloth.

As my eyes gradually adjusted to the gloom, shapes resolved themselves, peculiar shapes perched upon braced racks jutting from the walls. Clawfuls of them, there were, all in orderly lines. Moth-eaten blankets were neatly stacked waist high beneath them.

"This is the Tack Hall, hey," Egg said, his voice condensed by beam and wall. "This is where all the gear is kept, reins an' saddles an' parade stuff. Not the battle gear. That's kept in the Cafar. Eidon wants us to clean and repair all this. Understand?"

Egg lumbered over to one wall and hoisted a bulky object down from one of the many racks. A saddle, that's what it was. Great leather riding saddles straddled the racks protruding from the walls, saddles with handgrips and foot stirrups jutting from them, fore and aft. As Egg lumbered back to us, huffing under the weight of the enormous saddle he carried cradled over his arms, he nodded at a chest-high wooden table, the top of which was peaked like a roof.

"Don't just stand there! Pair up an' carry a saddle to this bench." A pause as he demonstrated with his own saddle, heaving it atop the long table so it sat astraddle the peak, stirrups dangling on either side. "Watch what I do an' do it yourselves!"

In the ensuing noise and scramble, I slipped out the door and returned to the hovel courtyard.

Dono was waiting at the threshold of my stall, as though he were reluctant to enter without me present.

"Where is it?" I wheezed, looking for the venom gourd.

His eyes darted over me, then darted away, as keen and quick as the beak of a bird that impales its prey upon thorns.

"How do you know it won't make things worse for you?" he asked.

"Venom?" I was stunned at the very idea. That caught a piercing glance from him and I could see him realizing that, yes, I *had* drunk it before, a great deal.

"It could close your throat over," he rasped. "You don't know that it won't. I bet you've never been hit on the neck before, not like that."

"I've drunk it enough to know how it affects me, Dono. It won't hurt me. It was the force of the tongue lashing that hurt me, not the venom itself."

"It was the combination of the two."

"My tolerance of the stuff is higher than that of any apprentice here."

Dono's dark eyes studied me from beneath a veil of hair. "Temple'll kill you for sure. You *are* a deviant."

"No."

"Egg says you called yourself a Dirwalan Babu. Those are Djimbi words, Zarq. Djimbi is the language of deviants."

I frowned, nonplussed. Then I realized what he meant. No term existed for *daughter* in the Emperor's tongue, and so to describe myself as the Skykeeper's Daughter to Egg, I'd used the old Malacarite term *babu*. The dragonmaster had likewise called me such.

"It's not Djimbi; it's ancient Malacarite."

"How would you know?"

"I learned the old language as an onai, while learning the hiero-glyphic arts."

"It sounds like Djimbi to me."

"Just give me the draft, Dono."

"The Djimbi are deviants. Temple executes all those who aid a deviant."

"The Komikon is piebald," I countered. "Djimbi blood flows in his veins. Is *he* a deviant?"

"He shouldn't be giving the draft to you. It's against Temple Statute to consume dragon flesh."

"Venom isn't flesh."

"It's wrong."

"So you're going to defy the Komikon's wishes? Refuse me the draft?"

We stared at each other, both of us tense and unflinching. Finally, Dono shrugged. "You'll give me half, understand? Half, and say nothing to the Komikon."

"Half," I agreed, though it angered me to do so. I'd planned on giving him only a few sips, not half of my potion.

With a nod, Dono limped out of the stall. He returned moments later, lips compressed with the pain of walking. Without speaking a word between us, we moved into the shadows at the very back of my stall.

He held the gourd cupped in his palms. We stood close, facing each other. Our breathing synchronized. His eyes blazed amber, like a dragon's.

"It'll lift you high," I whispered. "It has a fiercer thrust when ingested, and a longer burn."

He nodded. Outside, the buttery light of dawn was turning into the heat of morn. Beyond the stable domain came the muted sounds of rishi at work.

Dono lifted the gourd to his lips.

I couldn't help it; I reached out and placed my hands over his. To control how much he drank, understand, so there would be enough left for me. He didn't shake off my touch.

His lips parted and he tipped the gourd. His larynx bobbed up and down. I heard the liquid slide down his throat. After several swallows, and with the slightest hesitation, he lowered the gourd.

I watched him, waiting for the venom to flare into life within him. I saw the exact moment, too: His eyes widened briefly, then turned bright and brittle, as if sugar glaze had been poured over them and was instantly setting.

He shuddered and closed his eyes. I knew what furious fire raged through his sinus cavities, blazed in his belly, and devoured the pain of his whip welts. I knew what puissance and ecstasy swelled him beyond mere mortality. I knew what lust burned hard and undeniable in his blood.

His erection touched my thigh.

I swiftly downed the remnants of the draft and waited for the effects. They would be nowhere near as instant or intense as what Dono was experiencing during his virgin swallow of dragon's poison. But I would take what I could get.

I stroked his penis while I waited, emboldened by his inability to control his body, empowered by his weakness, his need, his nearness. I craved some sort of affection from him, any sort.

You don't know what your lust is for, I felt like whispering against his ear. You don't realize such lust is intended for a woman, to encourage her to lie with a dragon, that she might hear the dragon's thoughts.

The theory had only just occurred to me, upon the fiery wings of venom, surmised from what I'd witnessed and experienced at Convent Tieron. It at once made absolute sense.

I continued stroking him, his phallus as smooth and hard as burnished clay in my hand. Want started to pulse within me, too, muted by how paltry the dose of venom had been compared to my tolerance of the poison.

Dono climaxed with a cry, an arched back, a fierce look of elation on his face.

I leaned forward, then, and whispered in his ear, "You don't want me to leave, Dono. You want me here with you, in the Komikon's stables. Tell me you want me to stay."

His eyes cracked open and his lips parted slowly.

"I want . . ." he croaked. And then he bit his lip and looked away, trembling.


There was a time, nearly a century ago, when a woman could not walk the dusty, narrow alleys of Clutch Re unaccompanied by a man.

She was required to wear a bitoo, an inviolable cloth garment manufactured by a Temple-sanctioned guild clan, at all times. Outside of clan walls she was forbidden to speak or to touch a man, be it her son or aging father or the man accompanying her outside of her ku compound. She was forbidden to gesture in the direction of a temple or a dragon, and forbidden to shed any dirty waters upon the ground as she walked. Quilted handkerchiefs called difees were used just for the purpose of sopping perspiration during an out-of-

clan-compound journey; the more damp a woman's difee upon return, the greater her sweat-sopping vigilance and therefore her
piety. With much insincere groaning about laundering, women
would compare their difees after journeying outside their clan
walls.

Men were embarrassed, impatient, and uneasy when circumstance forced them to accompany a gaggle of women outside clan
walls, but such journeys were routinely necessary. Women were
needed to cart goods to one of the Clutch markets so that the men
could trade the wares for Temple chits or other staples. Women
were required to fetch water from the nearest Deep Well during
the height of Fire Season. Who else could do such chores? In my
youth, my father's mother, who lived to the extraordinary old age
of fifty-two, would recount tales from those times to us girl children each eve, as reproach and reminder for how easy our childhood was compared to hers. Her tales were inevitably gruesome.
The heavy pleats around her rheumy eyes would glisten with remembered grief, and her words would haunt our dreams. Although
she died before I reached six, her stories remained with me always.

One story she'd been particularly fond of was that of her eldest
navel auntie.

It was at the height of an unusually stubborn Fire Season, when
muay plants lay limp in clan gardens, wilted leaves curling with
brown. Under the sun's relentless onslaught, the timbers of the
women's barracks creaked like the old bones of a dying beast, and
the clan water towers grew thick with stagnant scum and the
bloated corpses of thirst-maddened vermin that had fallen into the
great vats and drowned.

Trips to the local Deep Well took place frequently, and on one
blistering-hot day, my grandmother, then seven, was allocated the
chore of fetching water along with her mother, her eldest navel
auntie, and two other strong young girls. They waited in the tor-
pid, interminable queue at the Deep Well from dawn until almost

high noon. Roasting beneath their bitoos, their skin as feverish wet as the glazed skin of a fire-roasted boar, they lost the ability to think, to move, to breathe almost. They took turns between waiting in the line under that unforgiving sun and seeking refuge in the shade of the nearby temple, but the latter did little to relieve the smothering heat of bitoo and sun.

Finally, their turn at the well. Finally, the dank, metallic water splashing into their enormous urns.

On their return to their clan compound, unwieldy urns filled with precious water balanced upon their heads, my greatmother's auntie stumbled on a bit of brick fallen from one of the ancient walls that divide clan from clan, guild from guild. Her ankle twisted. She cried out. One hand shot out to steady her balance as a natural reflex. She inadvertently grabbed the arm of her adolescent nephew, assigned the job of viagandri, girl herd, for the day.

A heat-embittered daronpu with a cheek swollen from a rotting tooth witnessed such.

My greatmother's navel auntie was arrested on the spot for the dual crime of speaking in public and trying to seduce a man while upon Temple grounds.

Justice was meted out two days later, after enough stones had been gathered by daronpu acolytes and stacked neatly in strategic spots in the market square. Greatmother's navel auntie, encased alive in a grudrun, the heavy, hempen shroud that encloses a dead woman's body during transportation to the gharial basins, was herded out of the temple prison shortly after dawn. Beneath the grudrun, she'd been firmly gagged and tightly bound with rope from shoulder to knee. She walked rigidly, blindly.

She was placed upright in a hole in the ground, picked up as though she were a fence post and shoved into place. The hole was thigh deep. Two daronpu acolytes shoveled dirt back into the hole, burying her in place. Their spades moved carelessly in anticipatory haste.

My greatmother, then only seven, was required to watch because she'd witnessed her aunt's transgression and therefore needed pimala-fuwa, the instructional cleansing of watching justice meted out.

She was required to throw the first stones.

As an old woman, she still remembered the sound those stones made as they struck her aunt's body. Small, resonant sounds, like rotten plums dropping upon the ground from an untended tree. She remembered her aunt's silence and the way her aunt's body shivered with each stonefall. She remembered the seething crush of the crowd, the roar of hysteria emitted from obscenely open mouths. She remembered the spittle gathering like curdled milk in the corners of her cousin's mouth as he screamed at his aunt in fury and shame, because of what she'd brought on him and herself with her careless footstep, her thoughtless cry, her forbidden touch.

Things had changed somewhat on Clutch Re since then.

Although a woman was still required to wear a bitoo when beyond the walls of her clan compound, she could journey forth unaccompanied by a man. Although forbidden to address or touch a daronpu, she might talk amongst other women while in public. Not that such conversation was encouraged, understand. It was merely overlooked, conveniently unheard by any man within earshot.

Another change that had seeped into acceptance on Clutch Re by the time I was a dragonmaster's apprentice was that women not only transported clan goods to marketplace for trading; they also carried out the marketplace transactions through inoffensive gestures and brief, modest dialogue. Indeed, it was uncommon to see a man squatted before a mat of wares anymore, and was, in fact, deemed unseemly for a man to be engaged in such subordinate work.

Those changes that had slowly come about since my greatmother's youth could be attributed to the ever-increasing discord and disorder plaguing the Emperor's instrument of power in Malacar: Temple. The Temple of the Dragon. In the Emperor's tongue, Ranon ki Cinai.

The Temple of the Dragon was but a theocratic dictatorship, first imposed upon our nation of Malacar nearly two centuries ago by the foreign autocrat Emperor Wai Fa-sren. Like all inhabitants of the Archipelago, the Emperor believed that dragons were divine. He was, however, a practical man unwilling to destroy the economy of the nation he'd vanquished. He therefore decreed that, although the eating of dragon flesh was forbidden, the consumption of unfertilized eggs laid in Temple-sanctioned Clutches within Malacar would be permitted. He also decreed that dragons could continue to be used as transportation and beasts of burden, but only by those people deemed worthy of such a sacred honor.

Only those people with Archipelagic ancestry, unquestionable loyalty to Temple, and considerable wealth and resource were ever deemed worthy enough.

One hundred and seventy years later, Emperor Wai Fa-sren's fourth successor, Emperor Mak Fa-sren, still ruled Malacar from his Archipelagic throne, and he still did so through Temple.

Hivelike Temple vaults, each pitted with floor-to-ceiling hexagonal cells, each cell containing an ancient holy scroll, contained all there was to know about dragons and how Emperor Fa's subjects had to live in regards to them.

But Temple was now rotting from the inside out.

While the Emperor's Malacar-stationed militia leaders vied for power with his Temple Superiors, the landed gentry acting as overseers upon the Emperor's Temple-controlled Clutches grumbled about self-governance. Wealthy Malacarite natives in the city muttered louder and more frequently about autonomy, while Clutch rishi and the city populace, aware of the in-house corruption and political squabbles plaguing Temple, chaffed under Temple's yoke more and more openly.

The deepest thorn embedded in the Emperor's flesh at the time of my apprenticeship was the sudden increase of Hamlets of Forsaken springing up throughout Malacar. Such nonpartisan agricultural communes, under the protection of no Temple-sanctioned warrior or dragon estate lord, were an unacceptable outrage, a bold, treacherous disregard of Temple Statute and allegiance to the Emperor.

But none of that was my concern as I returned to the Tack Hall where Egg and my fellow inductees polished silver and leather alike. Indeed, it wasn't until nearly two years later that I even learned of the depth of Temple's woes. What did concern me at the time, in that relentlessly obsessive way only venom can provoke, was the fact that I was still clothed, ridiculously, in Kratt's cape, and that should a daronpu visit the stable domain, he could order me stoned on the spot for such indecency.

By the time I stepped onto the Tack Hall's creaking wooden verandah, I'd determined to fashion myself a man's short tunic from a couple of the blankets I'd seen stacked against the walls inside. I *could* have made a tunic from Kratt's cape, I suppose, but I had no desire to wear that man's cloth against my skin any longer if I could prevent it.

Egg and the inductees were hard at work, the smell of beeswax and polished leather thick in the air. Despite my ardent wish to slip in unnoticed, my arrival was instantly noted by all.

"Where've you been?" Egg squealed. "We have work to do!"

Venom hummed in my veins like hornets with raised stingers. I brushed by Egg, went straight to the nearest stack of blankets, and hefted it into my arms.

"These are riddled with holes," I said in as accusing a tone as I could muster.

"What're you doin'?" Egg cried.

"Mending these. They're in a disgraceful state. What are they used for, hey-o?"

"Dryin' the dragons, after exercisin' in the Wet."

"Right. Needles?"

Egg gave a strangled moan, then lurched down the length of the Tack Hall, elbows knocking saddles perched upon wall racks, disturbing the rows of neatly hung reins so that they rustled and hissed like snakes in his wake. At the end of the hall, he rattled through the drawers of a tall, broad cabinet.

He returned with an aggrieved expression, a spool of what looked to be more coarse string than thread, and a bodkin the size and thickness of a woman's stout hairpin.

"It's a needle for workin' leather," he said defensively. Then, petulantly, "Eidon said nothin' to me about mendin' those old blankets."

I shrugged, took spool and enormous needle from him with muttered thanks, and turned for the door.

Egg's squeal stopped me in my tracks. "Where're you goin' *now?*"

"Outside. I can't see enough in here to sew." Before he could grant or withhold permission, I walked out of the Tack Hall, my fellow inductees gaping at me.

My insolence toward Egg was unacceptable. No woman should display such behavior toward a man, especially one outside of her clan. But not only did I not quite view Egg as a man, I thought of the stable domain as my new clan, and therefore experienced only the slightest qualms about my audacity, quickly quashed by venom-induced insolence.

Perhaps I possessed more of my mother's traits than I had hitherto thought; after Waivia had been sold as a sex slave, my mother had shown no compunction whatsoever in such similar displays toward men.

I sat down on the worn verandah and immediately set to fashioning myself a tunic. As long as the garment covered me from neck to knee, I felt it would suffice.

I was never clever with a needle and thread, so my work was

clumsy. More than once I stabbed a palm or finger with the bodkin. The flare of pain each time ignited the venom in my veins anew, sending my senses spinning so that my eyesight blurred, my ears were filled with a spiraling whine, and the verandah briefly swooped from my bottom, leaving me suspended in vertigo.

The chaos ended each time within heartbeats, leaving me swelled with a glowing puissance.

The garment, when I was done, hung off me askew but concealed far more of my skin than Kratt's cape had. Pleased, I fumbled beneath my new tunic, undid Kratt's cape, and stepped out of it. So I wouldn't be accused of lying to Egg, I then darned and patched the remaining blankets and folded them neatly back into a stack.

Just as I was about to enter the Tack Hall again with needle and mended blankets, a muted cheer rose up from somewhere in the stables. I looked in the direction of the noise and saw, some ways off, two destriers rising into the sky.

With pellucid, tawny wings beating down the air, and scales the color of wet rust and ivy glimmering in the sunlight, the two beasts riveted me to the spot. The power inherent in those muscle-corded shoulders as wings flexed and stretched filled me with an empathetic tension and exhilaration.

Turning my back on the sight, I entered the Tack Hall and joined my fellow inductees.

There is a joy to be found in polishing fine, sturdy leather, as if by rubbing wax into the grain, one is breathing life into the object, soul back into the empty hide. I worked steadily throughout the early hours of morn alongside my fellow inductees, polishing leather until my fingers were glossy and soft with beeswax, and as the sun shone madly at itself, unable to touch us in the shadowed Hall, a feeling of camaraderie settled upon us all.

Like all women, I knew the art of braiding, and by late morn it had fallen upon me to teach the inductees how to do such, for the parade saddles were heavily garnished with tassels, braiding, and fist-sized flower knots made of looped leather tethers, many of which needed repair. Although Egg knew how to mend them, his brawny fingers worked clumsily, and his attempts to help the inductees learn the skill often ended messily.

At first, the hands I corrected skittered out from under mine and the shoulders I looked over crouched low, to avoid my touch. But as the morning progressed, such recoiling decreased, and although I was never directly addressed during the occasional bouts of chatter and banter that crept into our midst before Egg squelched it with a bellow, I wasn't excluded from conversation by turned backs, either.

And then came a moment when one of the inductees mentioned that he'd heard a rumor that several Hamlets of Forsaken had joined forces and attacked Clutch Cuhan.

"Can't be true," said one sable-eyed boy of about nine. "The Forsaken don't have dragons, so what're they gonna use as weapons? Pitchforks?"

Scorn from a clawful of his peers:

"Don't be yolk-brained; they have scimitars and dirks and things."

"Axes, too, and crossbows alight with fire."

"I've heard they even use Djimbi blow darts dipped in poison."

The sable-eyed boy shook his head and said with great conviction, "Doesn't matter, hey. No one attacks a Clutch. Ever."

"Not true," I murmured, tying tight a tassel I'd reshaped upon a saddle. "The Komikon himself mentioned such an uprising to me."

Silence, and every eye in the place looked at me. A few mouths opened, wanting to ask questions, but then closed again, the would-be speakers uncertain of whether they should acknowledge me or not. Egg solved their dilemma.

"When did he say that?" he demanded.

"Yesterday morning. After flicking his whip at me for turning my back on him," I added with artful rue.

Fleeting empathy crossed a clawful of faces.

"An' is it true, then?" Egg asked, a touch of belligerence in his tone. "Clutch Cuhan's been attacked?"

"Clutch Maht, he said."

Egg grunted. "That makes more sense. Maht ain't as big as Cuhan."

"But why?" asked Sable-eyes. "It's stupid. The Emperor'll just crush them."

"You don't know that for sure," I said.

"It's most likely," said another boy. "The odds of the Forsaken taking over Maht have to be one in a thousand."

"But is that a reason for not trying?" I asked. "Don't we some-times have to try, despite the odds?"

"Not against those kind of odds."

"Well, I dunno," Egg said slowly, a deep frown furrowing his great forehead. "*We* face pretty big odds each time we go into Arena, hey."

"That's different," Sable-eyes stubbornly insisted. "We ain't Forsaken."

"No," Egg growled. "That ain't what I meant. All I was sayin' was, we face big odds too."

"Especially us," one boy muttered glumly. "The inductees."

"Exactly," Egg said, pleased someone had understood him.

"That's what our apprenticeship is all about," I added quietly. "Trying against the odds to survive Arena, to attain servitor, then veteran, then one day dragonmaster status. Not a one of us would be here if we didn't harbor the hope we could attain such."

A moment of silence as young minds digested that. Expressions changed subtly.

"Maybe it's that way for the Forsaken," I continued. "They fight because they believe, because they *have* to believe. Despite the odds."

"Like us," Egg grunted. "Yeah. Like us."

My debate with the sable-eyed boy preyed on my mind for the rest of the morn with as much venom-induced insistence as had my previous fear that the cape I'd been wearing would earn me a stoning by a visiting Holy Warden. See, even though I'd convinced Sable-eyes that the Forsaken's rebellion *may* have met with success, he'd convinced me that of course it would have ended as an utter failure. The thing that worried me concerning such a failure was the expedient return of the Ranreeb to the Jungle Crown and Daron Re to our Clutch. Once back, their thoughts would naturally return to me, and, their bloodlust whetted by the rebellion of the Forsaken, they'd press for my immediate execution.

Or so I became convinced.

So feverish grew this belief, and so numerous and logical the reasons supporting it, that by noon I'd persuaded myself with venom's typical frantic conviction that neither the dragonmaster's fervent pleas on my behalf, nor Kratt's intervention, could save me. One thing and one thing alone would prevent the executioner's axe from decapitating me: proof positive that one such as I could serve as a dragonmaster's apprentice.

And that, I knew, meant a journey to the Zone of the Dead to procure the Scroll of the Right-Headed Crane.

Understand, I'd only but once glimpsed the crumbling scroll upon which was written, in exquisite, ancient hieroglyphs, the stanza that stated that a circumcised woman, chosen by a Temple-endorsed dragonmaster, could serve a Clutch bull. That scroll had been in Geesamus Ir Cinai Ornisak, Clutch Re's dragon-sanctioned Zone of the Dead, in a decrepit temple mismanaged by Daronpu Gen, an eccentric giant of a Holy Warden.

As the heat of noon began to penetrate the Tack Hall, I grew increasingly restless, convinced I needed to obtain that unique and ancient scroll lest Temple, in its determination to be rid of me, discover it and destroy the only extant copy of a two-hundred-year-old decree that unequivocally stated who could serve a bull.

I'd like to believe that this rationale was sound, regardless of it springing from a font of venom. To this day, I insist on believing such.

As I knotted and braided leather thongs, as I sewed and stitched horny saddle leather together, I reasoned that if I slipped out of the Tack Hall soon, I could run the distance to the Dead Zone, locate and steal the scroll, and return before nightfall. Perchance I would not be missed. If I were . . . Well. I would fabricate some story or another, say I was working or training elsewhere in the stables. And if I were not believed, I would, quite simply, be whipped as punishment.

While the prospect of a whipping appealed not in the least to me, far greater was my fear that should I leave my fate in the hands of the dragonmaster—a man conspicuously struggling to retain a hold on his sanity—I would be dead before the full moon.

No. I needed to secure the Scroll of the Right-Headed Crane, even at the cost of a flogging.

My chance to slip out of the Tack Hall came suddenly and unexpectedly: While awkwardly returning a saddle to its wall rack, two inductees jarred said wall rack loose. The weight of the saddle pulled it away from the wall with a soft, papery sound, and after the briefest of pauses, a swarm of bees poured into the hall, buzzing furiously from a hive located, apparently, in the wall itself, directly behind the torn-out rack.

Chaos as we all stampeded for the single door. Chaos as nineteen frenzied inductees capered about outside, flailing limbs and swatting themselves, shrieking. I ran just like my peers. Only, I didn't stop running.

Under the cover of the noise and confusion, I once again slipped out of the Tack Hall courtyard unnoticed.

How foolish I had been to have thought I could walk to Temple Ornisak in the Zone of the Dead, find what I sought, and return to the stable domain by nightfall.

Late noon found me staggering down the dust-thick tiers of the Dead Zone's decrepit temple. I was focused to the exclusion of all else on reaching the antechamber where Daronpu Gen stored his scrolls. Though the venom I'd drunk with Dono had worn off, the swelling around my neck from my throat injury had receded just enough to permit me to swallow without choking, to breathe without feeling as if at any moment I might suffocate, and to walk without each footfall causing an agony of reverberations through my bruises. I'd slowly slaked my thirst at the Dead Zone's Deep Well not long ago—the sodden front of my crude tunic attested to that—and I was somewhat revived. Several times during my journey, the heat and my injury had forced me to rest by the shade of a sunbaked wall. Not just once had I wondered whether I would reach my destination before nightfall.

I had.

I was unprepared for the emotion that flooded over me when I entered the Dead Zone, though. I stopped, throat tight with sudden tears, as I looked upon the charred acres crowded with the huge sepulchral towers of Clutch Re's bayen dead.

Thrice I'd sought sanctuary in the Zone of the Dead, and each time it had been granted. The first time had been with my mother, when I was but nine: We'd lived as hidden, working tenants in a disintegrating sepulchral tower whose caretakers were brothers, brothers who'd loved each other much more than brothers should. The second time I'd sought sanctuary within the Dead Zone, I'd been fleeing a Temple purge in Convent Tieron many mountains and jungle-clotted miles away from Clutch Re. That time, I'd not been alone, though my mother had been many years dead; I'd traveled with Kiz-dan and her babe.

The third time I'd sought sanctuary in the eerie silence of the Dead Zone, I'd been wounded by a Cafar guard's sword. I'd received the wound when, in a fit of venom inebriation, I'd attacked a bayen woman, mistaking her for Kratt. The subsequent retaliation from the aristocrats of Clutch Re led to the razing of the Zone of the Dead. Dozens had died in the flames, and Kiz-dan and her babe had disappeared.

As I stood there, swooning in the heat, I felt anew the guilt of my past actions and the wrenching loss of Kiz-dan and her child. I'd loved them both fiercely, had vowed to the holy sisters in Convent Tieron that I would protect them always.

And here I was, in the Dead Zone once more. Not seeking Kiz-dan and child, though part of my heart wanted that, but seeking a scroll that could save my life.

Why is it that so often that which we want to do lies so far from that which we are actually doing?

Temple Ornisak was empty, of course. The dilapidated building with its dust-thick tiers descending to a sunken floor had rarely been attended, even before the razing. Since the fires, the inhabitants of the Dead Zone were too concerned with rebuilding their lives to be pious.

The temple's ground floor was smooth and cool beneath my bare feet as I staggered over to the burrowlike hole in the far wall, where the first few rows of tiers bluntly ended to accommodate the antechamber's entrance. With one hand braced against the stone wall, I descended three small, hardpan steps into the dense dark of the unlit antechamber.

I stood there a moment, inhaling the familiar ashy air as my eyes adjusted to the dark. A shudder swept over me, from chill or memory or anticipation I could not say. Probably all three.

Nothing had changed since I'd last been there. Of course not.

Though so much had occurred to me since I'd slept upon one of the two grimy hammocks slung from the antechamber's low stone ceiling, less than a clawful of days had actually passed since I'd left.

Nothing had changed. Nothing, that is, except that the scroll I sought was not in its place.

Understand, there were scrolls everywhere. Underfoot. Piled atop the heavy potbellied oven that squatted in the chamber's center, awaiting use during the Wet to prevent the scrolls from spoiling with damp. Scrolls littered the hammocks and crowded the antechamber's sole desk, vying for space with inkstone, quill, fresh parchment, and unlit candle. A weevil-ridden cabinet that almost touched the antechamber's low ceiling was stuffed to spilling with scrolls corked within bamboo casings. Atop the cabinet, a clackron mask leered at me, the protruding red tongue a taunt.

The holy mask, which was vaguely fashioned in the shape of a dragon's muzzle, was the kind routinely worn by Holy Wardens while they recited stanzas in their temples; the mask's large, flared mouth amplified the daronpu's voice so that all could hear his holy words. But this clackron mask, though similar to all others I'd seen while attending various Temple ceremonies in my youth, set my pulse skittering like a hunted cockroach. Not because of how it looked, understand, but because of what it did *not* look like.

I shall be clear: The scroll that I sought was not in the place where I'd last seen it, was not resting upon the protruding tongue of the clackron mask that sat atop the weevil-ridden cabinet.

Indeed, *no* scrolls were piled atop the cabinet, which was odd in itself, as every other surface of the antechamber was littered with them, loose or encased in bamboo.

Hands trembling, I lit a candle from the desk and stiffly approached the cabinet. I stood on my toes, lifted the clackron mask, and shook it. Insects fell out and skittered away. I thumped the mask back into place.

Slowly, I surveyed the room, not daring to move too fast, lest by moving quickly I'd unleash the panic building like a thunderhead within me.

Reining in my panic, I turned back to the cabinet and began methodically checking each scroll and casing that was stuffed into the cabinet's compartments.

None of the scrolls, encased or not, bore the hieratic I sought: the Scroll of the Right-Headed Crane.

Heart pounding, I finished examining the last scroll in the cabinet. I turned in disbelief and growing horror to survey the mess of scrolls littered about the antechamber.

It would take me days to search through all of it. Days.

The candle burned down to its midriff. My eyes felt engorged with thistle. My head threatened to fall like a rock from my shoulders.

It was evening. I could tell so by my exhaustion and the warm, humid smells wafting in from outside. Daronpu Gen and his acolyte, Oteul, would be returning any moment.

Stiff and cramped and dull witted, I rose to my feet and snuffed the candle. I staggered out of the antechamber into the circular, tiered ground floor of the decrepit temple. At once, I was surrounded by the sounds and smells of the jungle at twilight, for the jungle surrounded the Zone of the Dead like the arms of an unwanted lover. The earthy scent of fungus, decaying wood, and decomposing bract and vine was as thick and warm about me as if I were embedded in compost. The sap-tart scent of new growth lay like a foundation beneath it all, and another smell lay like a blanket over everything: the dry, smoky smell of charred wood, of old fires. *That* odor belonged not to the jungle, yet it would linger long in the Zone of the Dead, day and night, year after year. The smell had been present ever since the razing.

From where I stood on the ground floor of Temple Ornisak, looking up its bleak tiers, I could see bats flittering about the maroon-shot twilight sky, could hear their chirrs of triumph as they caught insects with their tiny clawed feet and stuffed the bugs into their little mouths while in flight.

I would wait for Daronpu Gen to return, I wearily decided. I would beg him to give me the scroll. Surely he would, surely. He'd be executed for treason and blasphemy if any of his Temple colleagues ever learned how in the past he'd hidden and disguised me. If need be, I'd threaten him with such.

I crossed the ground floor of the neglected temple, skirted the crumbling stone altar at its center, and sat upon the bottommost tier in the women's section, to await the Holy Warden's arrival.

Oteul, his acolyte, arrived first.

Understand, Oteul had never liked me. He had regarded me charily throughout the months that I'd worked disguised as an acolyte alongside him and Daronpu Gen, finding homes for the children orphaned in the Dead Zone's razing, healing bones and welts, extinguishing fires that flared up from the smoldering wreckage strewn about the zone.

Oteul's aversion toward me stemmed not just from my gender and the sacrilege of my disguise, but because he'd witnessed how the fatal wound I'd suffered from a Cafar guard had healed impossibly overnight. The day after my arrival at Temple Ornisak, he'd stared in consternation at the otherworldly scar as it cast a faint, luminescent blue upon his cheeks. From that moment onward, he'd regarded me with mistrust.

I, in turn, had regarded him warily.

Given that he'd seen my wound prior to its miraculous healing— a wound so obviously made by a Cafar guard's sword—and given Daronpu Gen's eagerness to disguise me from the eyes of Temple interrogators, I was certain Oteul suspected that *I* had been the one who'd attacked a bayen lady (mistaking her for Kratt), and that *I* was therefore responsible for the retaliatory razing of the Zone of the Dead.

Correct assumptions, both.

Yet however much I'd suspected him of suspecting me, he'd not turned me over to his superiors during Temple's interrogation of the Dead Zone's living inhabitants. With his silence, Oteul had therefore become an accomplice to my crime.

A brooding, unwilling accomplice.

Thus my first instinct upon seeing him descend Temple Ornisak's tiers, tunic besmirched with soot and hem entangled with twigs, was to distrust him, to remain hidden in shadow. But he noticed me immediately despite the gloom, despite my stillness and silence.

It wasn't until he was several feet away from me, long-fingered hands outspread as if to appeal to yet another beggar to leave him be for one night, that he could see my features. He stopped still in his tracks.

"You." Said in a voice taut with loathing.

I rose to my feet. "I'm waiting for Daronpu Gen."

"You'll have long to wait, then."

"Why?"

"He's gone. Disappeared."

"What! When?"

"Several days ago."

"Why?"

"*Why?*" He was incredulous. "We were there, at the lane. We saw what you did. He'd harbored you, healed you, and you repaid his kindness by defying Temple so openly? By daring to join the dragonmaster's apprenticeship? By shedding your *clothes* in public . . . ?" He looked away, swallowed hard, and looked back at me with great effort. "The daronpu acted bizarrely after that."

But he always acted bizarrely, I thought to myself dizzily.

"He was agitated, restless, unhinged. He feared you'd be traced back to us, at Temple Ornisak."

"And he's gone," I said stupidly.

"To save his own life."

"Where?" I asked hoarsely.

A derisive snort. "I wouldn't tell you if I knew."

A cold draft slid across my nape like the steel of an Auditor's blade.

Daronpu Gen, gone. The Scroll of the Right-Headed Crane, gone. My execution therefore a certainty.

I turned about, not seeing my surroundings, unconscious of my movements.

"He saved my life, once," Oteul said, voice low behind me. "I would never harm him over you. But hear this: I know what you did. I know why the people of this zone suffered the losses they suffered. You were the cause, hey-o. If not for how it would implicate Gen, I'd inform Temple about you."

His tone turned as dark and bitter as the thin black juice of an unripe walnut. "He should have turned you in instead of hiding you. His kindness is his weakness.

"But Temple will execute you soon enough," Oteul continued, voice now fat with certainty. "The day fast approaches when Clutch Re will be cleansed of your evil. I pray for that day. I pray for your death."

I fled the temple.

# EIGHT

Wheezing and devoid of all rationality, I staggered toward the little side door in the apprentices' hovel well past middle-night, the same door from which I'd left the stable domain at noon. In the starlit chill, my hand looked sallow and slight as I reached to shove the door open.

A boulder outside the door lumbered upright.

"Not that way," croaked a voice thick with anger and sleep. For a wild moment, I thought it was Oteul. I stared dumbly at the person that had risen from the ground, and only after long moments did I recognize him as Dono.

"This way," he said, and though the face belonged to Dono, the bitter tone belonged to Oteul.

Dono turned and started walking alongside the stable domain's sandstone wall, his shoulders hunched, his stride impatient. He stopped when he realized I wasn't following.

"You can't go through there," he hissed. "You'll wake everyone. *This* way. Komikon's waiting for you."

The Komikon was waiting for me.

How much fear must a person experience before the heart collapses with dread? For certain, fear addles the mind. Leastways, it addled mine, for I could not shake the impression that the lithe young man before me, clad only in a worn breechclout, was not Dono, but the robed acolyte who'd stood before me at Temple Ornisak. A young man who wished me dead.

Dono strode to my side, grabbed one of my arms. Pulled. "I'll break your arm if I have to, Zarq. Now *come*."

I struggled; he neatly pinned my arm behind my back. The flash of pain cleared my head somewhat and I realized it was not Oteul leading me to certain death, but Dono acting upon the Komikon's orders.

"Walk," he snarled, shoving me in the back, propelling me forward.

So I walked. Dono, warm and tensile with strength at my back, cursed me roundly as we followed the sandstone wall. It was clear from the way he moved, despite the welts and ruin of his flayed back, that venom still thrummed in his veins from the draught we'd shared that morning.

"What'd you come back for, hey-o?" he growled at me. "He's going to whip the piss out of you; you realize that, don't you?"

I trembled from exhaustion and chill. My thighs and calves were inflamed beyond endurance from my mad run from the Zone of the Dead. Dono walked too fast for me.

"Slower," I gasped. "Please."

A snort that conveyed disgust and incredulity both. He didn't slow down in the slightest.

"I couldn't find it," I said through chattering teeth. "It wasn't there; he's taken it; it's gone."

"What?"

"The scroll. I'll have to find another one; Re save me, they'll execute me . . ." I turned boneless, vision reeling. Stars fell about my head like strewn shards of glass.

My senses cleared as pain shot sharp through the arm Dono held pinned between my shoulder blades.

"Here," he said, coming to an abrupt stop. He reached forward with a free hand and rapped on a wooden sally port inlaid in the sandstone wall. *Knock, knock, knock!*

Dono's three brisk raps sounded puny in the deep of night. On the other side of the sally port came the splintery rasp of a wooden bar being lifted.

The small door creaked open. Dono shoved me through it. The dragonmaster stood on the other side, his bandy simian form silhouetted against one of the ubiquitous courtyards of the stable domain.

The dragonmaster reached forward, snatched the front of my tunic, and roughly pulled me through the sally port. Dono followed, shutting the creaking door and barring it behind me.

The dragonmaster was practically quilled with rage. His entire body quivered from it. He thrust his face into mine.

"Where went you today?" he breathed.

I swallowed. "I worked this morning in the Tack Hall—"

"I didn't ask what you did," he snarled, and I recoiled as his spittle landed like hot steam on my face. "I asked where you went."

I hesitated.

Immediately he grabbed one of my hands, spread my fingers, and before I could comprehend what was coming, he rammed something small and sharp underneath one of my nails.

I screamed. His free hand jammed sideways in my mouth to mute my cry. I writhed, struggled, tried to bite; his grip on my violated hand was as tensile as steel and the fist in my mouth was too big to exert much pressure on with my teeth, and what little I could exert mattered not a whit to him.

He jammed me against the sally port and pinned me there with his considerable strength.

"You go nowhere without my permission," he hissed into my face. "You do nothing, *nothing*, without my authorization. You understand that? Do you?"

The pain was deafening; I could scarce comprehend his words.

"Do you understand?" he hissed.

I nodded, tears streaming down my face.

"Did I not tell you that I've been dealing with Temple in regards to you?"

Again I nodded.

He withdrew his fist from my mouth and reached beneath his loincloth. A flash of metal: I cried out. He slapped me and lifted my fiery hand to his chest, brought the metal instrument toward my already swollen finger, and yanked.

Blood spurted in a thin line against his skin. My blood.

He stepped away from me, grinning, holding like a trophy a bloody bamboo splinter pinched in his slim pliers. Clutching my hand to my chest, I melted to the ground and folded over my lap.

After a while, I realized that the dragonmaster was crouched on his haunches before me, asking a question. Impatience and ire were stark in his voice.

"Where went you today?" he said.

"Temple Ornisak," I responded quickly. "In the Zone of the Dead."

"That was stupid." His voice was as tart as an unripe lime. "You say, 'Yes, Komikon. I was stupid.' "

"Yes, Komikon. I was stupid."

"Hold out your hand."

My head flew up to meet his eyes. I clutched my hand closer to my chest. "Please, no, I won't go again. I was only trying to find the scroll that would stay my execution; I thought—"

He rapped my forehead hard with his knuckles. "You weren't thinking. You have nothing to think *with*. You are a rishi via, the witless girl child of some lowly Clutch serf. Repeat that."

Breathless and too fearful to be humiliated, I obeyed.

"Without my instruction and training, you are unable to think for yourself. Understand?"

I nodded.

"*I* will do your thinking for you from now on, until you're ready to enter Arena. If such a scroll is needed to prove you can serve me, *I* will procure it. Is that clear?"

I nodded again.

"Yes, Master!" he roared in my face.

"Yes, Master!" I gasped.

"Now hold out your hand so I can bind it. Wounded apprentices don't agree with me." A grimy cloth lay over one of his knees.

He was insane.

He bandaged the finger, wrapping it so tight that the digit instantly felt as cold as stone despite the consuming agony steadily pulsing from beneath the nail.

"Now," he said, dropping my hand and lifting my chin so that I looked into his eyes. "You will return to your hammock and sleep the night away. You'll tell no one where you went today, but you *will* fashion a credible reply for them if they ask. And you will never again leave my domain without my permission. Understood?"

"Yes, Komikon," I whispered.

"Good." Wiping away the spittle that had gathered in the corners of his mouth, he rose to his feet and gestured to Dono.

"Take her back."

And Dono obeyed, helping me to my feet with a surprising, and much needed, amount of gentleness.

The next morning, I explained my previous day's absence to Egg by way of the bees that had swarmed us. I told him, with a face sunburned and swollen from my mad journey to the Dead Zone, with my damaged hand swathed in bandages, that I had been stung repeatedly by bees, and that I'd suffered some sort of fit, whereafter I'd blacked out beneath the verandah of the Tack Hall.

"Didn't you think to look there for me?" I said to him, in a tone replete with wonder that he could have been so obtuse. "I could have died there!"

He grumbled an apology, and my absence wasn't remarked upon again.

That day, after feeding and watering the dragons, we inductees labored long and hard mixing mortar and repairing the walls of whichever stalls had been too oft gouged by talon or battered by dragon bulk. Masonry is exhausting work that requires the use of two hands; by dusk, the hand that the dragonmaster had violated was swollen and hot, and I clutched it to my chest and walked lopsided, for it felt like the pain was radiating down that entire side of my body.

Near to tears with pain and fatigue, I collapsed outside the apprentices' hovel while Ringus stirred the communal cauldron of gruel.

"Hey," a voice grunted above me, sometime later. "You have to eat, else you'll be no good to me tomorrow."

Egg stood over me, a scowl on his oily face, a bowl of gruel in his hands.

"I ain't gettin' whipped just 'cause you let yourself get stung by bees," he said petulantly. He crouched and thumped the bowl down beside me. "Eat."

I ate.

Despite my exhaustion and pain, I found that once I started eating, my appetite was huge. I scraped my bowl clean and looked toward the cauldron. It was empty, obviously, for no one stood queued before it. With a weary sigh, I gingerly moved my swollen hand into a more comfortable position on my lap and looked over the apprentices sprawled about the hovel.

As with all other previous nights, they were engaged most seriously in games of darali abin famoo. Eidon and Ringus glanced my way several times; on the fourth glance, Eidon barked something to Ringus, who took a deep breath and nervously approached me.

"This is for you," he said, stopping a goodly distance from me. He tossed a dusty twig at my feet. "For your hand. Chew it slowly."

A maska root.

I murmured my thanks and picked it up. Ringus returned expediently to Eidon's side.

With a thumbnail, I scraped most of the skin off the root, then warily began chewing one end of it. It had the bitter, milky taste of maska wine, highly unpleasant to my palate, for I'd rarely imbibed in the fermented drink. After several minutes of dragonish chewing, a great lassitude dulled my mind and, by extension, the pain in my hand, so I continued to suffer the chalky, bitter taste in my mouth. Maska imparted nothing of the bright, light analgesic properties of venom, though; this was a heavy, cloddish substitute, with no accompaniment of giddy puissance. I couldn't for the life of me understand why men so readily drank the stuff.

After some time, I felt as sleepy and dumb as a sloth, and I watched those around me with heavy lids. Eidon and Ringus continued to glance at me throughout their game of dice, and several times the apprentices gathered about them inhaled sharply and looked my way as well.

My curiosity was piqued. With leaden limbs, I hauled myself upright and shuffled toward them.

I stopped close enough to Eidon's game of prognostication so as to watch but not intrude. He looked up. The servitors and inductees who were clustered about him likewise looked at me, many with amazement shining in their eyes, some with flushed cheeks.

After several long moments, Eidon nodded at the two dice he'd just cast.

"You played this before?" He had a rich voice, deep and low.

"No," I said, my own voice maska-slurred.

"D'you understand it?"

"No."

"Watch, then. Ringus'll explain it."

And Ringus did. In a soft murmur that I had to strain to hear, he explained how the fall of the destiny wheel, which was not a wheel at all but a spindle with an octahedron atop it, announced whether the prognostication was good, evil, indifferent, or divided, depending upon which direction of the compass the spindle pointed to upon falling. Each face of the octahedron bore a different crude picture, the interpretation of which varied, depending upon the compass direction the spindle pointed to and the numbers of the accompanying tossed dice.

"What are the images on the spindle?" I asked, for Eidon's destiny wheel was so worn, the carvings on the octahedron were all but obliterated.

"Earth, air, water, fire," murmured Ringus. "Dragon, grain, stars, snake."

He explained the dice next.

Each digit on the dice not only had numerical value but represented the hierarchy within our society: One, the lowest number, was feminine, while six was masculine. Number two was rishi; three, bayen. Four represented a warrior, and five, ludu fa-pim, or landed gentry of dragon-blessed pure blood.

"Look. There you are again," Ringus said as the spindle Eidon had just spun landed in the dust. The spindle was pointing in the Season of Fire direction, the octahedron facing east, the spindle pointing west. The face on the octahedron was that of a dragon, the number on one of the dice two, for rishi, and on the other, one, for feminine.

"It's a good prognostication, according to the destiny wheel's direction, which counters the low numbers on the dice," Ringus explained. He looked at me with cautious expectation. "That's the eighth time tonight Eidon's spun those exact combinations. Last night, too. You know the odds of that happening?"

It was a rhetorical question.

I looked about the other veterans and servitors. They had paused in their games. They were watching. All of them.

"Everyone knows he's spinning this," I murmured to Ringus.

"Yes. It's . . . never happened before. This kind of combination, over and over. Eight times."

Eight. A portent number, that. Eight for the number of talons on a dragon's forelegs. Eight for the number of battles the Pure

Dragon had won against the One Snake. Eight for the number of Skykeepers that guarded the Celestial Realm.

A breeze suddenly stirred dust about the seated apprentices, an alarmingly chill wind that smelled slightly of carrion. A blue phosphorescence glittered over us all in its wake, then dissipated into the dark.

Beside me, Ringus shivered.

"Eidon wants you to sit with us tomorrow eve," he whispered, voice hoarse, eyes nervous. "And every eve thereafter. For as long as the wheel dictates, you sit with us."

I nodded.

By whatever peculiar gravities that guided the fall of the destiny wheel, I now had an ally.

The days bleached into weeks under the relentless Fire Season sun, and my life in the dragonmaster's stables settled into a routine of hard labor, intense training, and wary camaraderie with my fellow apprentices. While labor and stable politics filled my days, my nights were governed by visits from my mother's haunt. I would dream then.

Of Waivia.

The dreams were always harrowing, fraught with sexual degradation and torture, or replete with all the cruelties Waivia had suffered, as a child, from the Djimbi-despising members of the pottery clan. I woke from the former sweating and gasping in horror, and from the latter subsumed in guilt that Waivia had suffered such a miserable childhood while mine had been the blithe, carefree one of a child without piebald skin.

These dreams weren't the only way my mother's haunt plagued me during that Fire Season in the dragonmaster's domain; she followed me, in her mundane disguise of a buzzard.

Most days I could ignore her, the same way one ignores a nagging, muffled headache, but on those days when my fellow inductees sought to test again my vow never to strike an apprentice down, and on those days that I remembered, painfully, how I had once had the opportunity to kill Kratt and had let it slip away, and on those days when no breeze blew and the sun blazed and the air felt as thick and hot as smoke, I found myself glancing too frequently at the tongues of the dragons I served, found myself inhaling the citric fragrance of their venom with great longing.

But as I said, most days I could ignore the haunt's presence.

Readily done, when there was so much work in the stables.

Each day, my hours were filled from dawn to dusk with grooming, mucking stalls, repairing tack, replacing roof tiles, or rehinging stall gates. Poultices had to be ground to treat wing sores and claw pad ulcers. Purges had to be distilled and forced down the throats of sick dragons by means of leather tubes, to treat intestinal parasites. Fodder had to be fetched from the grain silos, mangers scrubbed clean of all food residue, and faggots for the cooking pit made from manure and straw. The renimgars—our sole meat source in the stables—had to be fed and watered, and their hutches regularly cleaned. We inductees squeezed in our vebalu training between our stable chores, and truly, I could see why attaining servitor status and earning a decrease in tasks was so desirable. With all the work we inductees performed, we learned little of Arena fighting skills. With each passing day, our chances of learning enough to survive against Re decreased as Arena drew relentlessly closer.

But despite the constant, low-grade presence of the haunt, the nagging realization that I'd given up on killing Kratt, and the intense, ever-increasing anxiety concerning Arena, I did find pleasure in my work. As soon as Egg and Eidon discovered how adept I was at grooming dragons, I was told to work alongside the servitors doing that job, instead of mucking stalls with the inductees. All those years at Tieron, sweeping snake poles beneath the partially detached scales of the kuneus in search of kwano snakes, made me an expert in grooming. More than once, an impromptu race between myself and another servitor would interrupt the monotonous work, and amidst the wagering and shouts of spectators, I'd again and again prove my grooming mastery.

And, because I refused to strike an apprentice during vebalu, I concentrated all my efforts on learning how to dodge and parry and swirl my cape in an opponent's face. I even developed a new technique, one that no one had used before, and while at first my clumsy attempts were jeered at, my eventual proficiency garnered much grudging admiration. My technique was this: I'd whip off my cape during vebalu, swirl it fast into a ropelike whip, and snap it, chain end out, at my opponent's testicles. I'd had to revise my opinion slightly about striking an apprentice during vebalu, see, given the brutal reality of my situation; I'd decided that although I would never fell someone with a strike, I *would* strike to repel their attack against me.

Each evening in the privacy of my stall, I therefore practiced my maneuver over and over, so that I could perform it smoothly and swiftly *and* slip my cape back over my head while my opponent was dancing away from me, testicles smarting from where I'd stung him with the whip flick of cape chain.

Even though I never whipped hard enough to fell, I was sorely tempted many a time to do otherwise.

The dragons, too, were occasionally a source of pleasure for me, because each had her own personality and quirky character. While one dragon would submit to grooming with grunts of contentment, eyes closed, another would roguishly seek to toss me off her back, or snatch my snake pole in her mouth. There was the odd dragon that was feisty and foul tempered, but I'd had much experience in the convent with such a humor, for Ka, one of the retired bulls, had had an aggressive, touchy spirit. I soon gained a reputation of being able to handle such temperamental beasts, and while I welcomed the respect it garnered me, I didn't relish being stuck grooming most of the unpredictable destriers.

I was lashed, on occasion, by venom-drenched tongues, when a displeased dragon vented her anger upon me. The infrequent attacks left me with blistering welts, venom-induced puissance, and giddy hallucinations. My high tolerance for the dragons' poison also earned me some respect from my fellow apprentices, though that admiration was tinged with much trepidation, for a new inductee such as myself should show nowhere near as much familiarity with venom as I did, regardless of my history as an onai.

Where was the dragonmaster, in all this? Often in the exercising fields, a place I'd yet to see, instructing the veterans how to saddle and fly a dragon, or aiding them in the giddy, terrifying task of exercising Re, our holy bull. Sometimes I saw the Komikon in the vebalu gymnasium, correcting a servitor's hold on a bullwhip or improving a veteran's bull-whoring style. Occasionally he could be found in Isolation, the stables near the Tack Hall, where we housed ill and wounded destriers. The dragonmaster's rough affection for the dragons gradually became apparent to me, and his skill with the beasts was manifest in the way no dragon, no matter her temperament, ever misbehaved with him.

On two occasions, he joined us at dusk outside the apprentices' hovel and regaled us in his hoarse voice with stories of past Arena battles. We listened raptly, though tensely, for the Komikon was as temperamental as our most unpredictable destrier, and we never knew when his delight in storytelling would switch to disgust at our reactions, or lack thereof.

He also whipped those of us who shirked our duties.

He cared little if an inductee was ill from exhaustion, and he was impatient with strained muscles, torn ligaments, or broken bones. We had no infirmary in the stables where we could go when injured, only the Isolation court for injured dragons. If ever any of us fell ill, we'd splint our own broken bones or medicate ourselves using dragon-meant supplies from Isolation.

On two separate occasions during this time, an inductee disappeared overnight from the dragonmaster's domain. Each disappearance was met with communal silence and unease, as if we were all involved in a conspiracy to pretend such a thing hadn't occurred, as if none of us, at any given time, had entertained fleeing the dragonmaster's domain.

Throughout those days, Dono gave me as wide a berth as he could. Those who believed as he did—that I was a threat to their livelihoods—challenged me in small ways, frequently, to wear me down. I'd be given a snake pole that was bent, its guillotine dull and useless, or the axle of the fodder barrow allotted me would need repairing before I could use it. I'd be tripped, jabbed, or whacked with a pitchfork handle numerous times each day. Such relentless, subtle hostility was, thankfully, balanced by Eidon's guarded favor; no bruises did I suffer when Eidon was close by.

Despite this constant, low-grade opposition from some of the apprentices, there *was* a sense of temporary reprieve in the stables in regards to how Temple would deal with me, for the uprising that had taken the Ranreeb away to Clutch Maht had been surprisingly successful. The Forsaken who'd invaded that Clutch had gone straight to the destrier stables, and rumor had it that a clawful of Lupini Maht's best fighting dragons had been stolen by the rebels and couldn't be located. Temple was too involved in ferreting out the rebel leaders who now hid in mountain, Clutch, and city alike to dwell much on the presence of a deviant woman in Dragonmaster Re's stables.

Then one day, in Temple's bid to purge Malacar of all insurgents, the Daron of Clutch Re remembered me.

Acting upon the orders of the Ranreeb, he spoke harsh words to Waikar Re Kratt concerning my ongoing presence in Roshu-Lupini Re's stables. The Ashgon, the sacred Temple advisor to the Emperor and Malacar's titular head of Temple, was sorely displeased with Dragonmaster Re for sanctioning my enlistment in his apprenticeship, regardless of what the as-yet-unfound Scroll of the Right-Headed Crane said. And Kratt, in a thoroughly foul temper, came direct to the stables to see me that evening.

I sat astraddle a destrier, grinning, having just won a grooming contest against one of Dono's allies. The handsome, full-lipped veteran who'd challenged me just before we quit work for the evening had thought he'd stood a reasonable chance of winning, for only the day previous, I'd been beaten yet again during vebalu training, for my refusal to strike a fellow apprentice down. My back, arms, and calves bore the bludgeon bruises to show it. Despite the aching stiffness and pulsing tenderness of my bruises, I'd still won the contest. Standing to one side of the crowd of apprentices that had gathered to watch, Dono looked comically exasperated at my win.

I thought, too, that perhaps I saw reluctant admiration in his eyes.

I was just sliding off the destrier I'd groomed, my bruised and aching back turned to the crowd, when of a sudden everyone fell silent. The hairs on my nape tingled. With a feeling of presentiment, I turned around.

Waikar Re Kratt stood at the threshold of the stall, eyes shadowed by lack of sleep and brimming with deep purpose.

"You turn my stables into an exhibition ground, girl?" he said quietly, his voice replete with threat.

"No, Bayen Hacros," I murmured, eyes cast down. Bayen Hacros: First-Class Citizen Lord Dominant. It is custom for a rishi to address the highest-ranking lord present as Bayen Hacros, and because Waikar Re Kratt's father was not yet dead, Temple had not yet granted Kratt the title Lupini Re, Lord of Clutch Re.

Though most addressed him as such regardless.

My somewhat impertinent use of the title Bayen Hacros flamed his brooding fury. I'd been stupid, cocky with my recent win; I realized it the moment the words left my mouth. I should have addressed him as Lupini Re.

"You there," Kratt said, and I glanced up to see him gesture at Dono. "Restrain the girl for me."

Dono came toward me, eyebrows knit with uncertainty. He grabbed my left wrist.

"So that's how one of the Komikon's men restrains a woman, hey," Kratt murmured. "As if holding the hand of a child. How disappointing."

A muscle in Dono's cheek bulged. He swiftly stepped behind me and forced my wrist up between my shoulder blades. I gasped and rose up on my toes.

"An improvement," Kratt said. He approached, moving with languid ease, his blue eyes overbright in the gathering dusk. The crowd of apprentices moved back a short ways, instinctively creating space between themselves and Kratt's smouldering anger.

Kratt stood before me. Not daring to meet his gaze, I stared at his chest, covered in a white silk shirt artfully unlaced at the front to reveal his lean muscles. He smelled so strongly of ambergris, the pungent perfume coated my teeth with bitter fumes.

I waited. Kratt didn't move. My arm, pinned by Dono, began to throb.

Kratt's chest rose and fell before me. Smoothly. Hypnotically. His stillness was a threat, his proximity menacing. My anxiety increased with each passing heartbeat.

When he backhanded me across the cheek, my head rocked back and bounced off Dono's chest. He slapped me again, and again, then stepped away.

Reeling, eyes watering, I tasted blood in my mouth. My bleary vision focused on Kratt.

"Now, rishi whelp, I want you to free yourself," he murmured, tilting his head slightly to one side.

Panting, I could only stare at him, uncomprehending.

"Free yourself," Kratt repeated, his voice lower, insistent. I pulled against Dono's grasp. Unclear as to his role, Dono relinquished his hold.

*"Do not release her, boy."*

Dono jerked my hand into place again.

"Release yourself, girl," Kratt ordered, and he slowly began circling Dono and me. I could smell Dono's fear, sharp and sour, and the overfast rhythm of our breathing grew synchronized. "Show me some of your power and release yourself."

I pulled with an arm that felt as heavy and useless as a roll of sodden cloth, and was answered by stabbing pain across my neck, down my shoulder, and through my biceps.

"Release yourself." A whisper from Kratt's dark shape near my elbow.

Dono stepped away from me slightly, still holding me—Kratt must have guided him to do so with a commanding finger upon his torso—and then *thwack!* Kratt struck me with a quirt upon the fresh bruises of my back.

I cried out, and he hit me again, and I felt myself falling, heard Dono's grunt as he instinctively reached with his free hand to catch me around the waist, and for a moment there was blackness.

But the blackness did not last.

Kratt's face before me. Again.

"Summon your bird, rishi whelp. Summon your Skykeeper to save you, hmmm?"

"I can't," I gasped, panting. "It won't come; it won't obey me."

"That's not what you told me before. Did you lie? I deal harshly with liars, rishi whelp."

"No!"

"Then summon her," he demanded. "Prove to me that you are what the dragonmaster says. Prove to me that you are this Dirwalan Babu."

"But I can't; she won't come; she only appears when my life is threatened," I babbled, fear running rampant throughout me.

"Only when your life is threatened, hey-o?" Kratt said.

A slow, humorless smile spread over his face.

Oh, Re.

I gaped at him, aghast at what I'd said, at what power I'd just given him.

Because, of course, I knew what was coming next.

"Bring her out into the courtyard, boy," Kratt murmured to Dono. "I think I'll require more space."

The past oft repeats itself, hey-o.

This is how my father died, when I was but nine years old: Four bayen lordlings dragged him from his pottery studio into our clan courtyard, and with the leather laces from his own sandals, they bound his hands and ankles. They led a yearling over to him, man height and twice as long, wings a-tremble and scales contracted, its claws fully intact: one of the warrior lord's own dragons.

Using bullwhips, they drove the yearling into a frenzy; it attacked my father. Between drawing one breath and another, he was disembowelled.

Dono had seen none of that, had already begun serving his apprenticeship to the dragonmaster. So as he bound me upright against a barrow in the center of the stable's courtyard, my gibbering story meant nothing to him.

No, not nothing. Confusion flitted across his features and his hands fumbled badly.

Waikar Re Kratt stood some distance away from us, pacing slowly to and fro, examining the long whip he'd uncoiled from his belt as the first evening bats began swooping over the stables. The rest of the apprentices stood clustered some distance away. At a subtle signal from Eidon, I saw Ringus slip away, unnoticed by Kratt, and disappear at a run through the adjacent stable yard.

Dono finished lashing my ankles together and rose from his knees. His narrow, never restful eyes darted over my face.

"Waivia," he said, voice guttural.

I stared at him, uncomprehending.

"Did she see it?" he said.

Waivia, my sister. He wanted to know if she'd been present when my father had been killed, if she'd witnessed the horror; he *had* been listening to my babble as he'd lashed me to the barrow.

"No," I said, the truth coming thick as old gruel from my tongue.

He nodded and dropped his eyes. He took a deep breath and mumbled, "You should've left when you had the chance, Zarq. I'm sorry."

He quickly turned away and went over to Kratt.

Words were exchanged. Kratt pointed to one of the destriers in her stall. He knew the dragons in his stables, certainly; he'd chosen the most temperamental of them all.

Dono hesitated, then turned and barked at two of his allies to give him aid. The trio approached the feisty dragon.

Kratt snapped his whip at my belly. It ripped a hole right through my coarse tunic and snapped like fire against my skin. I gasped.

"Now, summon your bird, rishi whelp," Kratt ordered, and *snap!* the tip of his whip cracked a hand's breadth away from my mouth. "Summon your bird or be killed."

The destrier Dono and his helpers led from the stall fought the muzzle hooks inserted in her flared nares. She was a beautiful creature, her crop dewlaps hanging from her throat like milky opals. Even in the gloom of dusk, her quivering wings—hastily bolted by Dono while in her stall so she couldn't burst into flight—looked like amber, rich and tawny and almost pellucid. The finger claws at the end of her wings twitched like jointed ebony needles, and the talons on her forelegs were as curved and wicked as scimitars. She shied at the sight of me strapped against the barrow, and the muscles in her hindquarters bulged beneath scales green and glossy brown.

She was a magnificent beast, powerful and high-strung. Her talons would easily cut me in half. My vision swooned and my heart thundered like a thousand beaten kettle drums.

Kratt circled behind me and began flicking his whip at the dragon. She reared back, shied left, shied right, snorted and tossed her head. *Flick, flick!* The whip snapped against her muzzled snout. Infuriated, she bugled in her throat, charged forward several feet, and reared up. Her great, wicked talons slashed the air several feet before me.

I inflated my lungs and screamed. I screamed as if expelling my soul. Out of my wits from fear, I screamed and screamed.

Silence from the darkling skies. The slash of talons direct before me, the next blow sure to slit me open from throat to groin.

Then: a scream from the skies. Gravelly, earth-trembling, blood-curdling.

"Mother!" I shrieked, and the Skykeeper appeared overhead.

She didn't descend from the heights as she had done at the Lashing Lane, when the crowd had intended to stone me to death. No. She merely circled above us, her vast form casting a chill as cold as ice. Even at that height, her wings filled the air with the stench of carrion.

The smell of death: the smell of my mother.

Those unearthly shrieks: the sound of her love.

The dragon before me bucked and yawed against her restraining muzzle, rage turned to fright. Dono and his helpers could no longer control her. The restraining hook notched into one of her nares ripped loose with a spray of blood, and she whirled and bolted out of the courtyard, dragging, for a short distance, one of the two apprentices holding the reins to her muzzle.

Waikar Re Kratt moved from behind me and came into my view. With an inscrutable glance at me, he gestured at Dono to untie me.

I slumped against my bindings and wept.

When next I looked up, the Skykeeper was gone. The first star twinkled at me in her stead.

By the time Dono finished unlashing me from the barrow, the dragonmaster had appeared. Ringus slipped from the dragonmaster's side and unobtrusively joined the gathered apprentices before Kratt noticed him.

The Komikon marched up to Kratt, chin braid swinging like an angry cat's tail.

"Lupini Re!" he barked. "What's the meaning of this?"

Kratt began languidly coiling his whip, running one palm over it, checking if any grit was embedded in the tightly woven braiding. He looked completely at ease, as if he'd just supped at banquet, not provoked the appearance of a deadly, supernatural creature.

He didn't answer the dragonmaster.

Flushing, the dragonmaster whirled around to face his apprentices.

"Get yourselves to the hovel, the lot of you! Have you nothing better to do than gawk at your future lord? Go, eat, sleep!" He turned back and stabbed a finger at me. "You stay."

A superfluous demand; I couldn't have moved if I'd wanted to. My legs were trembling violently and I was dizzy, breathing too fast. I shivered, feeling terribly, terribly cold, and the desire to curl up on the ground and close my eyes was intense.

"Now, Lupini Re," the dragonmaster said, his lower jaw thrust out pugnaciously, his eyes rolling as he struggled to retain a measure of control over his emotions. "Please tell me what in the name of Re just occurred here."

Kratt finished coiling his whip, hooked it back onto his belt, and with a lazy smile, regarded the dragonmaster.

"I had need of proving that your deviant is indeed what you declared she was. Temple is anxious these days, Komikon, and that anxiety spills over into the Daron of my father's Clutch. He pressures me to execute the girl as a rebel."

"She's not Forsaken," the dragonmaster said, glaring at me. "She's no insurgent."

Forsaken?

For a moment, I had the absurd notion that the dragonmaster knew I'd been abandoned as a child by my mother, that being forsaken had somehow branded me. Then I realized he was referring to the Hamlets of Forsaken, the agricultural communes that were springing up throughout Malacar without Temple's consent—communes that functioned extremely well without Holy Wardens, egg stables, overlords, or Temple Statute.

Communes reputed to be inhabited by insurgents plotting to overthrow the Emperor.

"Insurgent or not, she challenges Temple," Kratt said. "And Temple looks very unkindly upon any challenges as of late."

"You must ensure that the Daron leaves her be," the dragonmaster growled, and his shoulders convulsed once, violently.

"You will not direct me on what I should and should not do, old man. I believe I've warned you before."

The dragonmaster flushed. He rocked to and fro on his feet, muscles in his cheeks twitching in agitation.

"Forgive me," he eventually rasped, though he sounded anything but contrite. "I'm alarmed that you doubted her identity in the first place."

"Are you, now? I find that peculiar. You see, I've done much reading over the last few months, and I can find no mention of your precious prophecy anywhere."

"The Djimbi don't record their prophecies!" the dragonmaster cried. "They sing, they tell stories, they . . . they . . ." He tugged his chin braid as he spluttered. "You've twice witnessed the appearance of the Skykeeper; what further proof do you need that the girl is what I tell you?"

"The Daron is emphatic that she possesses an evil spirit. He says"—and here Kratt's lips twisted with wry amusement, though his eyes went hard and bitter—"that the creature she summoned on Mombe Taro was but a demon."

"And now that you've seen it again, what do you think?" the dragonmaster demanded.

Kratt studied me almost indifferently. "The renderings of Sky-keepers that I've seen upon velum and parchment look remarkably like the creature she just summoned. Her creature does indeed appear to be a Guardian of the Celestial Realm."

"It is; it is! And think you what power you have, with a Skykeeper answering to this girl's summons!" The dragonmaster clutched Kratt's arm in his fervor. "Think what you might achieve with such a creature by your side!"

Kratt looked back at him and disdainfully shook off the dragonmaster's touch. "I require the Scroll of the Right-Headed Crane, Komikon. The Ranreeb insists upon seeing it himself. Now."

"It is safe, with someone I trust."

"That does me little good."

"The Ranreeb will destroy it."

"He'll destroy this deviant if he doesn't see the scroll for himself. Now is the time to bring forth your proof. I insist."

The dragonmaster gnashed his teeth.

"Fine. I will . . . have it brought forth."

Kratt nodded in lazy satisfaction. "And does she understand dragonspeak yet?"

The dragonmaster scowled and hunched his shoulders. He mumbled something. Neither Kratt nor I heard it. I found myself leaning forward, breath held, heart pounding.

"Speak up, old man," Kratt barked.

"I said: She's not yet undergone the rite in my stables." A defensive, slightly defiant note crept into the dragonmaster's tone. "I've been loath to subject her to it yet."

Kratt narrowed his eyes. "Is she or is she not the Dirwalan Babu?"

"She is!"

"Then why your reluctance?"

The dragonmaster's nostrils flared and again his eyes rolled. "I would first practice upon a few more inductees."

"I'm not known for my patience, Komikon. You told me your dragon was trained."

"She is."

"Then delay no more. Is that clear? I want the dragons' secret before the Daron guesses my true purpose behind keeping the deviant in my stables. I want to see bull wings hatch."

One of his hands touched the whip coiled at his belt. "I'm under much pressure from Temple concerning her right now. Don't force me to exert equal pressure upon you, old man. Get the Scroll of the Right-Headed Crane to me, and get her to lay with the dragon. Tonight."

# NINE

After Kratt left the stable domain, the dragonmaster summoned Dono from where he stood amongst the other apprentices, feigning interest in palm calluses and splinters. The dragonmaster spoke to him in a tense whisper, shot a harried look at me, then stalked out of the courtyard and disappeared into the night.

Dono didn't once look at me while we ate.

Though truth to tell, I barely touched my gruel, which was cold because Ringus hadn't the time or inclination to reheat it thoroughly, so addled was he—as were we all—from what had just occurred. Cold or hot, I had not appetite for the gruel, for I was badly shaken from Kratt's deliberate provocation of the Skykeeper, and my thoughts were too cluttered to be concerned with such mundane matters as eating.

For Kratt had talked about the rite, see.

I was astonished that he knew of the secret rite where a woman and a dragon joined, and that he knew, too, that such an intimacy imparted the dragon's unintelligible memories to the woman; dragonspeak, Kratt had called it. I'd spent half my life in a convent where such a rite had been routinely and clandestinely performed by a small group of holy women, and I'd learned of the act only late in my adolescence.

Certainly, rumors abounded throughout Malacar about perversions committed by the jungle Djimbi, but a wide assortment of atrocities were lavishly ascribed the Mottled Bellies, regardless of accuracy, and most were readily dismissed. So where had Kratt learned about the validity of the bestial rite?

From the dragonmaster, I guessed.

Somehow, Komikon Re knew about it.

*I want the dragons' secret before the Daron guesses my true purpose behind keeping the deviant in my stables. I want to see bull wings hatch.*

That's what Kratt had said.

Which insinuated, shockingly, that those of high status in Temple might know of the rite, too.

I clutched my head between my hands, my thoughts whirling.

What did it all mean, Temple and dragonspeak?

It came to me then, and I actually bolted upright with the epiphany.

*I want to see bull wings hatch.*

Kratt would only defy Temple if he had something great to gain by it. What greater thing than the answer to the mystery as to why eggs laid by domestic dragons never produced bulls?

What unprecedented power and wealth would fall into Kratt's hands if he learned the answer to that riddle, if he could one day hatch bull dragons in captivity!

The very fabric of Malacarite society revolved around the scarcity of bulls, understand. The social and economic clout Kratt would have, should he have a stable filled with bulls, would be unparalleled. He could rent out stud services cheaper than every Clutch in Malacar. He could breed his bulls to his Clutch brooder dragons whenever he wanted, increasing his herd exponentially, without waiting to attend the Temple-controlled Arena. Indeed, he could even have his own Arena, one with fewer regulations, fewer tariffs than Temple's.

He could build his own empire. Waikar Re Kratt, child of a blue-eyed Xxelteker ebani, would *become* Temple.

But first he needed the answer to the dragons' secret, and he plainly thought that I, as the Dirwalan Babu, would understand the beasts' ancestral memories and learn the secret if I lay before one of his destriers.

A pair of feet appeared before me. I looked up, mind reeling, scarcely able to comprehend my situation. Dono stood before me.

"Get up, hey-o," he said, not unkindly. "You're to follow me."

I licked my dry lips and my heart raced. I didn't move.

"Where are you taking her?" Eidon asked in his rich, low voice.

"Dragonmaster's orders," Dono barked. In other words: Mind your own business.

After a moment's hesitation, Eidon nodded once, brusquely, and turned back to his game of darali abin famoo. He would show me guarded favor, yes. But he'd not raise a finger to protect me against the Komikon's will.

Dono extended a hand to help me upright. I stared at it. Here, finally, was the support from him that I'd so longed for. With a trembling hand, I reached out. His fingers closed warm and strong about mine. He wouldn't meet my gaze, though, as I rose to my feet.

"This way," he grunted, and he started across the courtyard. Taking an unsteady breath, I followed him.

We walked in silence. Not side by side, but with me several paces behind Dono. I shivered as I walked and trembled, and at first my thoughts raced wildly, dashing from Temple to Kratt, dragon tongue to enigmatic dragonsong. The maelstrom of emotion accompanying each half-formed thought overwhelmed me, and my thoughts grew more erratic and incoherent still. Eventually my mind shut down into a sort of catatonic state, and I walked as if in a trance.

Through the stable yards we walked, beyond the grain silos, into a quadrant of the dragonmaster's domain that I'd not yet entered. A great stone byre with a steeply peaked and tiled roof and massive upswept eaves loomed ahead. Our footsteps sounded muted as we approached it. The pungent musk-and-leather smell of a bull dragon, laced heavily with the citric tang of venom, dominated the air.

Huge ceramic Skykeepers encircled the entire building, each shadowed visage more contorted and fierce than the last, each outspread wing touching that of its neighbor. As we passed the sentinels, clay eyes bored into our backs.

It felt as if I were being watched by a thousand of my mother's haunts.

A breeze skulked about us. Above our heads came an eerie rainfall of rattling. I stopped and looked up. Hundreds of miniature skeletons dangled from the byre's eaves.

Dono paused, then turned to me.

"Chimes," he murmured, and his voice seemed intrusive in the sinister silence that followed the rattling from above. "Made from the foot bones of eight hundred dragons."

"Why?" I croaked.

"The Gyin-gyin is carved onto each bone," Dono explained. "Each time they clatter, it represents eight hundred recitals of the Temple chant."

The Gyin-gyin: the chant that evoked the triumvirate power of the Temple of the Dragon, the One Dragon in the Celestial Realm, and our Clutch bull. No evil could penetrate such protection.

Then why did I feel that the place was so dark?

Dono bent, picked something up from the ground. He hefted its weight a few times in his palm, then thrust it out to me.

"Take this," he said gruffly.

I did. A coarse, dusty rock fell solid into my outstretched hand.

"Hit me over the back of the head with it," Dono said. "Then run."

I stared at him.

"Do it, Zarq. Hard enough to knock me out. Make it look real."

I looked down at the rock in my hand.

Looked back up at him.

"The Komikon'll whip you," I whispered.

His larynx worked in his throat. "I know."

"Dono—"

"Just do it."

He turned his back on me.

I stared at the round part of his skull I should hit. Stared again at the rock in my hand. I dropped the rock at my feet.

Dono flinched at the dull thud, paused a moment, then turned.

Disbelief, then anger, flooded his face.

"I won't do it," I said. "I won't strike another down."

"Don't be yolk brained, Zarq! Do you have any idea where I'm taking you, what the dragonmaster's going to make you do?"

"Yes," I said. "Yes, I do."

He digested that a moment and the muscles in his neck bulged. "You *are* a deviant. Aren't you?"

"It's not the way you think it is."

"Those two inductees that disappeared from the hovel last month were brought here, Zarq. I'm the one who dragged their bodies out when the dragonmaster was finished with them."

"How many others, over the years?"

He looked away, could barely answer. "Too many."

"What other apprentice knows?"

"Just me." He looked back at me and swallowed hard. He bent, picked up the rock. "I'll knock myself out, then. Just run."

I reached out and placed a cold hand over his warm one.

"I'll survive it, Dono. Take me to him."

We turned the corner of Re's byre, and beyond the great stable stood yet another sandstone archway. The dragonmaster stood beneath it, his bandy form silhouetted against a vast oval field of dust and scrub and great tree stumps. At our approach, the dragonmaster turned and began crossing the ravaged field.

Dono followed. He walked slouched, as if against a gale, and refused to look at me.

Trembling under the black sea of glittering starlight, I followed the dragonmaster and Dono across the blighted oval field, around the tree stumps, which, I could now see, weren't tree stumps at all but stout stone pillars rising up from the ground, each topped by thick downward-pointing hooks. The ground itself had been rutted and scored by hundreds of dragon talons. A long, low building crowned by a silver-plated dome stood on the far side of the field. We were walking directly toward it.

My heartbeat skittered and a dreadful anticipation pimpled the skin on my arms.

We reached the domed building. A wide, walled stone ramp ran the length of it, leading down to a gated tunnel that appeared to run directly beneath the building. In silence, the dragonmaster started down the ramp.

How dark that tunnel at the ramp's base. How chill the air wafting from its maw. I came to a stop.

The dragonmaster reached the bottom of the ramp and paused before the gated tunnel. He bent over something, moved his arms; rusted steel screeched as he winched open the tunnel's iron barricade.

Shoulders hunched, Dono stared at the oval field. In the starlight, I saw a muscle in his jaw flicker. "This is where I wait," he growled. "You go in there alone, with him."

I shuddered, shuddered again. Wrapped my arms about myself to stave off a little of the damp chill emanating from the tunnel.

Slowly, I started down the ramp.

The walls on either side of me were as high as my chin; I felt blinkered, felt as if I were being funneled into blindness.

It was coarsely pebbled, that ramp, constructed from a stone-hard, seamless material, and it was as slick underfoot as if it had been recently dredged from a swamp. The slickness increased to an algae-thick film the closer I drew to the maw of the tunnel. Mosquitoes whined about my head.

I entered the tunnel.

One step. Two steps. Two clawful steps forward and then my feet touched water. I stopped. Cautiously, I shuffled forward a bit farther. Yes, water. The tunnel descended into water. What in the name of Re was this place?

I would *not* descend blind into unknown waters. No. Clenching my jaw to still the clacking of my teeth, I looked back toward the entrance. Revealed by the incline behind me and the starlight seeping into the tunnel was that which I'd not seen before: a raised, narrow pathway that ran alongside the walled ramp I stood on. A raised pathway that was so narrow it would only just accommodate a fully grown man.

With much scraping of knees and elbows, I clambered out of the walled ramp and landed, panting, on the adjacent pathway.

Narrow the pathway was, indeed. One of my elbows grazed the tunnel wall as I continued my descent into the bowels of the domed building, my opposite hand trailing lightly over the slick surface of the ramp wall to guide me. Mosquitoes buzzed thicker about my head the deeper I descended.

A glow ahead. Faint. Unmistakable. Had it been there all along?

The pathway abruptly opened up. I stopped and tried to take in what I was seeing.

A vast, perfectly circular pool lay before me, oily black in the dark and streaked amber in places by the light cast from a lantern the dragonmaster now held, where he stood on the rim of the pool. Above the pool stretched a dome.

I cleared my throat. The noise rattled around the dome like a hail of rocks cascading down a cliff.

"What is this place?" I asked.

The lantern the dragonmaster held guttered, as if my sibilance had threatened it.

"Use your wits," he growled. "*You* tell *me* what this place is."

My wits? I had none, I was confusion and uncertainty personified.

"Use your wits, girl!" the dragonmaster bellowed, and his words boomed round the dome high above our heads. "Think you that I'll be at your side in Arena, giving guidance, explaining the obvious? Train yourself to overcome your fear and think through your terror, or else you'll not last beyond the year!"

I bit my lower lip.

I looked about me, at the oily pool, at the wide, walled ramp that led down into it, at the small, raised pathway alongside the ramp. At the dome high above. None of it made sense to me; it was all scattered puzzle pieces.

"Look at the details!" roared the dragonmaster, my silence infuriating him, my fear intolerable.

Details. Details. What details?

Then: scales, floating on the water. Dragon scales, palm sized and gray with the beginnings of rot.

I looked back at the wide ramp that led into the pool. It was the width of a dragon. I looked anew at the walls enclosing the ramp down the length of the dark tunnel: Those walls were shoulder height to a dragon, would easily prevent a dragon from lunging about. I looked with dawning comprehension at the narrow, raised pathway that ran alongside the ramp: That was a path where a veteran might walk while leading a dragon by means of a muzzle pole down the adjacent watery ramp.

"The dragons," I said hoarsely. "You swim them here."

"And why in the name of Re would we do such a thing?" the dragonmaster growled.

I thought furiously, pictured a dragon in the water, forelegs churning water as powerful hindquarters likewise kicked to keep the beast afloat, the wings pinioned against flanks by means of bolts.

And then I had it.

"Their forelegs. If they damage their forelegs during training, you exercise them in this pool. To keep them active while they're healing."

"And that happens, hey-o," the dragonmaster conceded. "Dragons're aerial beasts, not meant to spend so much time walking about the ground. In the wild, they use their forelegs for grabbing prey in flight, for climbing about the jungle's crown, for defending their territory by slashing opponents in aerial combat. They don't walk on the ground as much as we force 'em to, and never forget that. Dragons are predominantly aerial beasts."

Lantern light turned the dragonmaster's face into a skeleton's skull, dark hollows where mouth and eyes should be.

"An apprentice damages a destrier's forelegs by riding him too hard on the ground, I drive bamboo splinters under the apprentice's nails. Understand? I pound 'em in deep and leave 'em to fester and abscess, and I don't remove 'em from the apprentice till the destrier is healed. Remember that, rishi whelp."

I shuddered and instinctively clutched my wounded hand to my chest.

He turned and walked toward a side door located in the circular wall surrounding the pool.

"This way."

We descended down a short, dark passage. As the side door swung shut behind me, the dank smell of the exercise pool was immediately cut off and replaced by the smell of old wood and manure and the dusty scent of bedding chaff. The salty odor of dragon scale and the leathery reek of dragon hide, laced with the tang of venom, overlay everything.

Cobwebs clouded the low beams overhead. Vermin skittered in the dark. My breath sounded loud and quick. I heard the muted snort of a dragon.

The short passageway leveled, abruptly turned. A row of stalls, all empty save the last one, stood directly before me. In the last stall, an old destrier stood, her wings folded along either flank.

The dragonmaster stopped at the first empty stall. He set his lantern on the ground, turned to face me, and waited for me to stand before him. I did so stiffly.

He leaned into my face.

"Now. You will do something for me. You will do it without question or complaint, and you'll do it the moment I ask it. Understand?"

I swallowed, knew full well what he was going to ask me to do. Knew, too, that I was eager to do it.

"Yes, Komikon," I murmured, cheeks flaming, eyes downcast.

His face glowed with pleasure and he threw back his head and cackled. The veins in his neck stood out like rivers of tar.

"Disrobe."

Heat began flaring in my groin. My skin pimpled with expectation. My nipples hardened.

I lifted my tunic over my head and dropped it to the floor. I stood naked before the dragonmaster, eyes closed.

"She's old, this dragon," he murmured. "Been long in my service, mine and mine alone. She's practiced on many a reluctant apprentice that I've drugged and gagged and tormented into submitting to her tongue, apprentices who're no longer alive to tell the tale. But you don't need such persuasion, do you, Skykeeper's Daughter? Because you've done this sort of thing before."

His fingers closed on my chin. "Open your eyes," he whispered, and I did so.

"Ah, yes. You can't hide them from one who knows. I saw it the day we met at Mombe Taro: You've got dragon eyes."

His own eyes glittered brightly, and his shoulders twitched. "You're hungry for it, aren't you?" he breathed. "You want the venom."

"No," I whispered, but he only grinned madly at the lie.

"You know what I expect from you, after you lie with the old destrier, hey?"

I refused to answer. His fingers tightened on my chin.

"You'll tell me what you heard, Skykeeper's Daughter. You'll reveal the dragons' mystery to me. Understand?" He leaned closer, closer, and I closed my eyes as his lips touched my ear.

"And with that secret, you'll grant me the power to set the Djimbi free," he hissed into my ear, and I shuddered as if he'd driven another splinter under my nail.

The Djimbi Sha. The Mottled Bellies. They are Malacar's true natives, their lineage unsullied by Xxelteker or Archipelagic blood.

There are tales of the Djimbi Sha. Obscene tales, told behind the closed doors of mating closets during men's parties, lewd stories whispered by children when adults aren't within earshot. Tales of the sage-and-tan-skinned Djimbi and the undomesticated dragons of Malacar's jungles.

Because of these tales, all races have felt at liberty throughout Malacar's history to kidnap, enslave, and rape Djimbi women and children. Djimbi men have been slaughtered, or gelded and enslaved. With their profane chants and blasphemous beliefs, with their glottal language and uncivilized lifestyles in the jungle, with bestiality so interwoven within their culture, the Djimbi have been oppressed and reviled with a dedication that has been unflagging.

Of course, I knew the Komikon of Clutch Re had Djimbi blood in his veins. *All* knew of it, even those who had not attended the

annual Mombe Taro parade and glimpsed the dragonmaster's piebald pigmentation beneath the multitude of scars he wore like a
tunic. Aside from the color of his skin, the Komikon's infamous
freakish behavior and his renowned skill with dragons all marked
him as a Djimbi's get.

Half a century before my birth, one such as he would never have
been allowed to retain his testicles, let alone attain the status of
dragonmaster. Instead, such a dragon-skilled Djimbi man would
have been gelded in his youth and pressed into service as a stable-
man, his Archipelagic lord receiving the accolades due a dragonmaster in his stead.

Convention is a river that oft changes its course, hey-o.

Here stood the dragonmaster over me, the mottled pigmentation of his skin somehow highlighted by lantern light, and here lay
I, obeying his will and offering my sex to a tethered female dragon.
Yes. I was about to enact one of the very tales I'd snickered over as
a child.

Perhaps it was fitting, that, for I was not free of Djimbi taint. My
mother had been born to a full-blooded Djimbi woman who had
been captured for slavery and raped in the process by an Archipelagic warrior. Mother had lived on Clutch Xxamer-Zu with her full-
blooded Djimbi mother, had loved a half-blood Djimbi youth on
that dragon estate, and had illegally borne his child. Unions between piebalds were strictly forbidden by Temple so as to dilute
the Djimbi blood; my mother was therefore traded to Clutch Re as
punishment for her act, traded along with her piebald babe, my sister, Waivia.

Or half-sister, if one insists on pedantry.

Although I'd been sired by a Clutch Re man with not a drop
of Djimbi ancestry in his veins, I *did* have Djimbi blood in me
from my mother, though oddly, the pigmentation of my skin
showed it not.

It didn't seem to matter. The Djimbi lust for dragons was strong within me.

"Lift your knees," the dragonmaster growled. "Spread your thighs."

I shivered on the cold ground and smelled the venom of the dragon as she strained against her creaking leather tethers to get at me.

"Spread your legs," the dragonmaster repeated impatiently, and I readily obeyed. I parted my knees and let them fall to either side of me, my mouth dry with want.

I'd done this once before, in Convent Tieron.

But at Tieron, intoxicating Djimbi chants had strummed magic through me. The image of hands stroking nipples erect, of human mouths teasing belly and thigh, had shimmered like golden pollen in my mind's eye. No such intoxicant existed for me now. In lieu of beguiling Djimbi chants singing passion through my heart, a greed to hear the dragon's divine memories and experience venom's fire governed my actions.

And that was more than enough to make me slippery with want.

The dragonmaster straightened with a grunt from where he'd been crouched between my legs. The grunt held no lechery in it. For him, this was not a sexual act. He had but one aim: to procure the dragons' secrets. The impending act was but a means to that end.

That he expected me to understand the dragonish thoughts I received during the intimate exchange, and that he intended to use the secrets gained to empower the Djimbi, astounded me.

He moved toward the destrier and murmured something incomprehensible. She snorted and clawed the ground with her talons. Steel clicked as he unclasped her tethers.

She pounced at me in that sloped lunge peculiar to all dragons, and I gasped, half sat, and pushed myself away from her as

far and fast as I could, but my shoulders butted against the passageway wall. The dragonmaster roared, but I couldn't hear his
words over the pounding of my heart and the breaths heaving
from my chest and the snort of the old destrier as she shoved my
clenched thighs apart, one tawny, slitted eye staring direct into
mine.

The cleft tip of her tongue slid out and flicked over my sex, the
venom-black forks of her tongue trembling like slim fronds in a
wind.

"No," I whispered.

The forked tip of her tongue dove within me.

A furious, muscled burn, hot, slick, and expansive. The venom's
warmth radiated throughout me, melted my muscles and anointed
my skin, and the taste of licorice and limes bloomed in my mouth.
My head inflated, turned diaphanous.

I dissolved into the hard ground beneath me.

And then I heard her. I heard her thoughts.

I heard the thoughts of her mother, of her greatmother, of the
bulls that had sired them both. I heard snatches of the memories of
all dragons in her lineage, was joined to that continuous, indu-
bitable string of song-thought, was privy to the touching emotions
and impenetrable sagacity of the divine beasts.

But I could not understand what they were saying.

Frustration spread throughout my body like rot through a
spoiled plum.

"No!" I hissed, wanting to understand, to delve further into that
compelling mystery, to comprehend the musical whispers weaving
through my mind like strands of silk and spun gold.

But the destrier withdrew from me.

She stood above me a moment, head cocked to one side, her
opalescent dewlaps glittering with an orange sheen in the lantern
light. The eye that locked upon me—so melancholy, so wise—

glowed bloodred and chestnut. She was beautiful and unattainable. She was, truly, divine.

With a snort, she back-shuffled into her stall.

"What heard you?"

The dragonmaster crouched at my head and gripped one of my shoulders.

"What heard you?" he repeated, and I tried to focus on his face, but my vision swooped and oscillated as though my eyes were swallows in flight.

The amount of venom I'd received was too intense.

Understand, when I'd but once offered myself to a dragon in Tieron, it had been to a kuneus, an infirm bull whose venom had been dilute from age and malnourishment both. Although the destrier that had just invaded me looked near senility herself, she was far from malnourished. The venom imparted by her tongue had therefore been the strongest I'd yet experienced, and despite my tolerance for the poison, built up over years of ingesting drafts of the stuff, I was reeling from the dosage I'd just received.

In fact, I was nigh on incapacitated.

My legs, my arms, my very head did not belong to me. My face was numb, my chest a block of granite. I could not focus, had difficulty comprehending the dragonmaster's words. My surroundings heaved about me, cobwebbed timbers, stone stalls, dirt floor, all undulating as if they were seaborne.

I passed out.

When I revived, something was pressed against my lips. I thought a rat was atop me; I tried to swat it off and found that my arms were disobedient entities.

"Drink," the dragonmaster ordered, his voice disembodied in the darkness that surrounded us, for no guttering lantern light bathed wall and stall now. Perhaps the Komikon had doused the light, or perhaps it had burned all its fuel. Or perhaps he'd carried me someplace else, someplace deep within the bowels of the cold earth.

"Drink," he said again, and I realized that thirst raged within me, and so I drank.

Cool, clean water flowed down my throat and ran over my lips. A dragon snorted some short ways in front of me.

Ah. We were still in the stable beneath the pool, in the domed building of the training grounds.

Venom smoldered within me, flickering here and there in mind, belly, and limb like so many embers, provoking smugness and potency like showers of fire-thrown sparks.

I finished drinking and relaxed in the dragonmaster's embrace.

"What did you hear?" the dragonmaster said in my ear, voice hoarse with fatigue.

"The dragon," I mumbled, lips thick. "I heard her. Not just her, but the bull that sired her. Not just the bull, but the brooder that laid the egg he hatched from. Her greatmother, her greatfather. All her ancestors."

"And what did they say?" the dragonmaster said in a voice so clotted with anticipation he was all but unintelligible. His arms about me were steely. No embrace, that, but confinement. What had I heard? Divine mystery. Indecipherable words. No, not words: Muddled music, enigmatic melody. Compelling whispers composed in an outlandish tongue. What I'd heard had been emotion subtilized, sentiment turned into sensation, ancient memory conveyed by divine passion.

The emotions those memories had stirred within me were fading. The harder I tried to cling to and define them, the quicker they faded. A profound sadness filled me.

"I don't know," I whispered, the hoarseness of my voice matching that of the dragonmaster's, only mine laden with grief and not greed. "I couldn't understand the music."

"Music?" the dragonmaster roared, and my heart stuttered. "Are your wits addled?"

"They speak in music, not words," I cried. "And emotion. And I couldn't understand it, and then she pulled away from me, and then it was gone!"

Stunned by my outburst, the dragonmaster said nothing. But after some time had passed, he released me. He stood.

"Then we'll repeat the experience," he growled. "We'll repeat the experience until you learn this music and unravel the words within. Understand?"

I didn't reply. No response was necessary.

We both knew I would comply.

# TEN

*~e~*

"Make sure she keeps breathing," the Komikon growled as he passed my prone form into Dono's arms. "You know venom's tricks."

Dono didn't respond. Or perhaps he did. Perhaps I just didn't hear his response as I swooped in and out of venom's silken void.

Dono carried me from the training grounds back to my hammock.

I felt like I was floating, suspended somewhere between ground and sky. The stars danced above my face like glass baubles whirled by an invisible juggler. Venom trickled down my thighs, filling the night air with the lusty odor of womanly brine and the citric tang of dragon.

"Keep breathing," Dono growled at me as he slid me onto my hammock an indeterminable time later, and I saw his voice as a cockroach skittering over a dusty rock.

"Why breathe?" I asked thickly.

A good question, that, or so I thought at the time: *Why* should I keep breathing? Understand, my lungs felt as if they might erupt into molten pools of lava within my chest, then swiftly solidify into porous rock, and this was not at all a terrifying or disagreeable sensation. In fact, I felt certain that if I could only stop breathing long enough, I might comprehend the dragons' music. Not that I wanted to die. No. I just wanted to hear dragonsong.

"Keep breathing," Dono growled again, a heartbeat later, a lifetime later, the passage of time incomprehensible to me. But I obeyed. I breathed. Whether from obedience or the body's natural need for air only, I continued breathing.

So passed the night. Dono stood over me the entire time, and as my desire to stop breathing decreased, it was replaced instead with lust. I reached for Dono; he pushed away my hands and tried to ignore my indecent whispers.

But toward dawn, his resolve broke and he coupled with me. Somehow, we ended on the stable floor.

Fresh chaff had recently been forked into my stall, shin deep and smelling sharp and sweet, like bark stripped from a freshly felled sapling. The light stuff cushioned my back, gave my hips extra thrust. Clinging tight to me, biting my neck, Dono climaxed in my womb while featon chaff drifted down on our heads, much the way kaolin dust had graced us in our infancy, when we'd crawled about my mother's feet as she'd worked at her potter's wheel.

Because my vulva was slicked with venom, Dono was soon transported on new wings of lust, venom induced, and he flipped me onto my belly and took me again, from behind. As he did so, he whispered my sister's name like an incantation, evoking her presence so that no longer were only the two of us on the stable floor, but a third joined us, ethereal yet as tangible as an insatiable need.

"Waivia," he groaned. "Waivia."

That was my first time with a man, and I found Dono's performance somewhat lacking compared to that of a dragon. No dragonsong did our couplings provoke in me, nor any whispers of profound, ancient thoughts. After a while, I begged Dono to desist.

He did.

And as I wept, he held me and began to talk of our childhood and himself. And Waivia.

"She was mine, you know. If it wasn't for you, I wouldn't be here today and she'd be alive." He stroked my back absently as he talked. "When you stole my whip, you stole her away from me, Zarq."

With clarity and certainty, I suddenly realized that he despised me—and himself—for his past audacity in demanding inclusion in the dragonmaster's apprenticeship, which had led to the anger of Temple, the ruination of our clan, and the subsequent sale of Waivia to mitigate a little of that poverty.

I sat up slowly and wiped away my tears.

"It wasn't my fault, what occurred," I said quietly. "Nor yours. Temple didn't observe the Sa Gikiro rite, didn't give our clan the restitution they should have for losing you to the dragonmaster."

I hesitated, then placed a hand upon Dono's closest knee. "It's Temple's fault Waivia was lost to us. Neither you nor I are to blame. We were only children."

The moment I said those words, something dark and heavy lifted away from us both. I saw it lift. Dono sensed it and shuddered. The great black shape rose into the air, grew wings. It flapped ponderously across the courtyard, rising higher into the sky. As it rose, stars shone through its darkness like flecks of quartz at the bottom of a silty river. The wind from the dark shape's wings feathered Dono's hair and caressed my cheeks. It smelled like a river bottom, of things long rotted, of muck long out of sunlight. A dense, fertile odor, redolent of birth and death.

We watched it go, Dono and I, though I think he saw it not, only sensed its leaving. But although his anger toward me and his own self-condemnation may have departed, I knew he still yearned for his first love. Waivia.

The dragonmaster gave me many weeks to process the experience of being with his destrier and recover from venom's giddy sting. At first, my training suffered from the intimate encounter with the old destrier and I shook badly for days. I stumbled often and my balance in the vebalu course was poor. Sunlight hurt my eyes; I was grateful for the approach of the Wet Season and the increasing number of clouds that smothered the sky.

Though my fellow apprentices didn't know the reason behind my ineptitude, they surmised that I'd suffered from something the dragonmaster had subjected me to and, thankfully, all but a few of them treated me as if I were a fragile egg they had no wish to break. The few apprentices who attempted to treat me elsewise were beaten by Eidon.

As Dono wrestled with his own complex emotions, his treatment of me still vacillated between solicitude and anger. The passion we had shared together that night on my stall floor had not only renewed our childhood bond, but created something else, that feeling one experiences after having shared that vital, vulnerable part of oneself with a lover. And, too, after coupling with me while under the influence of venom, Dono had, in his mind, inextricably linked the memory of his first love to me. To some extent, I had become Waivia to him.

He often found an excuse to place a hand upon my back, waist, or shoulder while instructing me on how to repair that which I already knew how to repair. When he could, he worked alongside me, grooming dragons, mending stone walls, scrubbing mangers. More than once when he brushed by me in close quarters, I felt the press of his erection against my rump.

But, also, he could not forget that I'd chosen to perform bestiality rather than flee the stable domain, and this chafed him sorely. So while one day he might spar easily with me in vebalu and give me advice on how to better my reflexes, the next he would bludgeon me ruthlessly.

Throughout, the dragonmaster watched me closely and questioned me each evening, hoping I'd had an epiphany during the day regarding what I'd heard while joined with his destrier. I could tell him nothing more than what I'd told him in his hidden stable: The dragons' ancestral memories were a divine, enigmatic song that I could hear but not comprehend. His frustration with my unvarying response increased. I knew I'd soon be asked to lie again before his destrier.

I looked forward to that night.

\*     \*     \*

"Harder!" Egg roared in my ear. It was my third time through the vebalu circuit that day, and I was parched, tired, and vexed by Egg's boarish voice. And I hated that part of vebalu: scrotum rubbing. Eyes closed, I lightly rubbed my spreadeagled body upon the hide-covered bamboo sac.

"Harder, harder!" Egg roared in my ear. "You have to make the thing move, hey! And don't spend so long under there; you think Re's gonna to be standin' still while you're doin' that? You have to get in an' out, in an' out, else you'll get trampled!"

With gritted teeth, I increased both the pressure I was exerting on the thing and the speed at which I moved. The whole structure rocked against my torso.

"Better!" Egg bellowed. "Now, move on!"

I lurched back to the balance bar for yet another circuit of the vebalu course.

Ringus stepped in front of me, his cheeks flushed, his eyes bright.

"You've got a visitor," he said in a breathless rush. "Rutkar Re Ghepp."

I gaped at him, then followed the direction of his thumb with my gaze.

My heart stopped, ran backward several beats, then rushed forward again. He spoke the truth: Rutkar Re Ghepp stood at the entrance of the gymnasium's courtyard, clothed in a rich emerald waist shirt and slitted, fawn pantaloons. He was flanked by Cafar guards and chancellors.

Rutkar Re Ghepp: Third Son of Roshu-Lupini Re, warrior-lord of our Clutch, and the would-be inheritor of Clutch Re if not for Waikar Re Kratt. Born from the loins of the Roshu-Lupini's First Claimed Woman, Ghepp had appeared in the world long after the Roshu-Lupini had given up hope that any of his roidan yins, his claimed women, would ever produce a living son.

All infants conceived by the Roshu-Lupini had died during childbirth, understand, regardless of which roidan yin bore the child. The Roshu-Lupini had tried to solve this tragedy by claiming more and more women, but after his fourteenth roidan yin produced yet another stillborn boy, he turned his back upon all his claimed women and took his pleasures only with the best ebanis. Then, unexpectedly, his favorite ebani—a blue-eyed Xxelteker woman exquisitely trained in the arts of pleasuring men—conceived a child by him. Although any child an ebani accidentally bears with her claimer is legitimate, such a child is traditionally regarded as far lower in status than the children begotten from the claimer's household roidan yins. The Roshu-Lupini made an exception to the cultural norm and declared that should the babe not only survive birth but be born a boy, he would regard the child as his legitimate heir.

Waikar Re Kratt was born several months later.

Overjoyed by his success, the Roshu-Lupini again took himself to the mating closets with his roidan yins, and a second son was born to him nine months later, a child who, tragically, died of snakebite at age two. Undaunted, the Roshu-Lupini continued to vigorously service his women, and seven years after Waikar Re Kratt's birth, Rutkar Re Ghepp was born from the womb of the Roshu-Lupini's First Claimed Woman.

And here Ghepp stood, in the dusty coarseness of the vebalu yard, demanding audience with me.

"You stink," Ringus said, jerking my attention away from the bayen lordling. He pointed a slender finger toward a cistern in the far corner. "I'd wash first."

"Yes," I mumbled, addle headed. "Yes."

Ringus pursed his slim, sweet lips, then came to a decision. "I'll fetch the dragonmaster. In case you need him."

"Thank you," I said, heart pounding, and turned and walked quickly to the cistern.

What could Ghepp possibly want with me?

Ghepp was rumored to be a thoughtful, predictable man, somewhat staid in habit. Like many Clutch Re rishi, I thought he'd make a far better Clutch lord than Kratt, whose sadism and impatience had already caused misery and death for many in our Clutch.

Seeing Ghepp standing there, in the vebalu courtyard, suddenly made me aware of my vengeance vow to ruin his brother. In the daily swarm of activity as an inductee and the ever-increasing anxiety over the approaching day of Arena, I'd completely forgotten my ulterior motive for joining the dragonmaster's apprenticeship.

Being abruptly reminded of something so profound as that mad ambition filled me with unease. It had been pleasant to not be preoccupied with ruin and social revolution for awhile, to just enjoy each day's successes and battle each day's failures and feel like I belonged and had clan and home once more.

Hastily, I splashed water over myself, then shook off the excess water much as a cur does. Taking a deep breath, I started toward Ghepp, dodging the servitors who grappled each other along the far side of the gymnasium.

I could feel their eyes following me as they wrestled.

Dressed in his ivy and fawn silks, Rutkar Re Ghepp was a startling figure in the vebalu yard's drab surroundings. He stood flanked by two men garbed in the heavily embroidered blue and red gowns of Cafar chancellors, and on either side of the chancellors stood Cafar guards, resplendent in short skirts and plastrons of steel-studded black leather.

I came to a stop before Ghepp, and, as custom dictates for a woman, stared at his boots. They were made of a soft leather I'd never seen before, a suede from some jungle-caught creature perhaps, or an Archipelagic or Northern beast that I would never lay eyes upon. I could smell the opulence of the chancellors, a perfume-and-pomade scent that was so intrusive that it was a bitter taste upon the tongue. One of the chancellors breathed heavily through his nose, as if he suffered a blockage. A fire ant ran over my bare foot.

"What is your purpose here, in the stables of my father's Clutch?" Ghepp murmured.

I raised my head, couldn't help it, and met the steady gaze of his canted chestnut eyes. His dark hair was slightly tousled above his slender brows, and his full lips, centered below high cheekbones the color of fine aged ivory, were slightly parted. His was a beautiful face, one many a woman spun romantic fantasies about, and many a man, too.

"I want to be an apprentice, Bayen Hacros," I replied.

"Women don't apprentice. Women don't serve dragons."

"Onais serve dragons. I've been circumcised by a holy knife in the manner of those women."

"I've heard my brother use that argument against the Ranreeb and our Daron."

Of course he had. I dropped my eyes. "Yes, Bayen Hacros. Forgive me."

His soft suede boots shifted. "So you wish to be an apprentice. You wish to serve Roshu-Lupini Re's dragons."

"Yes, Bayen Hacros."

"To one day become dragonmaster of this Clutch?"

Blood roared in my ears.

"Do you see yourself one day as dragonmaster of Re's estate?" Ghepp asked again.

My head lifted higher than it should have. "I mean to survive Arena and survive it repeatedly, and I mean to bring glory to Re in the process. Yes, Bayen Hacros. I *will* become dragonmaster."

He cocked his head to one side. "A great ambition, for a rishi via."

"I am no ordinary rishi via."

Though he didn't look skyward, I saw what flashed through his mind: the Skykeeper.

"No," he murmured, "you are not."

Several heartbeats passed. We stood so close, I could see a minuscule cut on his jawline, where a servant had carelessly nicked him while scraping away stubble that very morn. I stared at that tiny cut in skin so smooth it reminded me of the taut muscles beneath the pale yellow pelt of a wangiki deer.

"And why become dragonmaster?" he finally said. "What need has a Clutch and a bull of a female dragonmaster?"

I studied him from under the fringe of my dark hair. I decided to risk it, then, encouraged by his calm mein, his gentle beauty, his captivating, canted eyes that glowed like polished chestnuts streaked with gold.

"A dragonmaster has power, Bayen Hacros. The status of a Clutch is determined by the dragonmaster's performance each year in Arena." My voice dropped, went hoarse. "I would use that power to elevate those I feel are deserving of advancement, and depose those whose cruel natures I feel only threaten the prosperity of a Clutch's populace. My womanhood grants me the vision and scope that another apprentice, who is driven only by glory and fame, lacks."

His beautiful eyes never wavered from mine. "You assume much, rishi via."

"I have a Skykeeper at my command, and I make those assumptions with the confidence of having that creature as my ally."

He studied me some more, then looked away and stroked an earlobe, from which protruded a rigid teak earring, spiral carved in the shape of a dragon's tail. To either side of him, his chancellors remained impassive, though they watched me closely. The Cafar guards who stood sentinel a short distance away watched none of us, but kept a vigilant eye upon their surroundings. They were pretending to be deaf.

"One of our great tale spinners has said that nobility without virtue is but a fine setting without a gem," Ghepp finally murmured, as if to himself. He looked at me again. "You would agree, it seems."

"I do."

"My brother risks much by succoring you in my father's stables. Clearly he has not heard your views."

I licked my dry lips, tried to speak past the unsteady pounding of my heart. "I've not expressed my views to anyone until this moment."

"You take a risk expressing them now."

"The person who risks nothing and does nothing *is* nothing."

"You are rishi. You know nothing of politics. You know nothing of duplicity and scheming. You have no subtlety."

"I'm rishi; I know of hardship and loss. Strength alone knows conflict."

A smile played briefly upon his lips at our exchange. "Temple looks to execute you, oh-clever-and-courageous deviant."

I took a shuddering breath. "If I fail, then my failure will be but a challenge to others. But I won't fail. I have perseverance, the Scroll of the Right-Headed Crane, and the Skykeeper on my side."

We held each other's gazes for a long moment. Then he nodded, once.

"This has been a most interesting conversation. I'll be watching closely what becomes of you." He tapped his lower lip thoughtfully with one finger. "Very closely."

He turned and gestured to his retinue, and they swept from the gymnasium just as the dragonmaster stormed into it, Ringus by his side.

As the dragonmaster stopped at the doorway to let Ghepp pass, he bowed. The bow was perfunctory; Ghepp barely acknowledged it. The two men disliked each other, clearly.

After Ghepp's departure, the dragonmaster strode to my side, scowling and tugging his chin braid in agitation.

"What did he want?" he demanded.

I frowned, shrugged, and answered truthfully, "I don't know. Komikon."

"What did he ask you?"

"Why a woman would want to be an apprentice."

He gnashed his teeth. "And your response?"

The dragonmaster's bristling anxiety gave me pause. I prevaricated somewhat. "I told him the Skykeeper guided my actions."

The dragonmaster grunted and his shoulders twitched. He looked toward where Ghepp had exited. "You realize it's in his best interests that Temple execute you, yes?"

My blood ran cold.

"How so?" I asked, as coolly as I could.

"Temple won't grant governorship of Clutch Re to Waikar Re Kratt if they can find lawful grounds for executing you, despite the Scroll of the Right-Headed Crane," the dragonmaster snapped. "They'll appropriate the inheritance of this Clutch to Ghepp instead, on the grounds that Kratt succored a deviant and permitted her into his stables. Make no mistake; that man there"—and he stabbed a calloused finger in the direction Ghepp had left in—"is no friend of ours."

Of course. I hadn't thought of that. With a sinking heart, I realized that Ghepp had been right: I *was* naïve; I knew nothing of subtlety and politics.

It now remained to be seen what would become of my impulsive conversation with Kratt's scheming brother.


"You're to come with me, hey," Dono muttered, standing before me.

It was dusk and we were all sprawled outside the apprentices's hovel, stomachs full of gruel and limbs heavy with fatigue. I was sitting with Eidon's crowd of favorites, mulling over Ghepp's visit and my rash disclosure to him. Dono had entered our ranks without care; he and Eidon had an unspoken truce between them in regards to me, since Dono treated me well most days and since the dragonmaster had favored him as my escort for my last mysterious appointment to see him.

"You're to come with me," Dono repeated, and he added, for emphasis, "Komikon's orders."

The Komikon was summoning me.

To the old destrier, I instinctively knew.

As I looked up at Dono, my pulse quickened and a flush rose to my cheeks. Shivering as if cold, I nodded, rose to my feet, and followed Dono unsteadily across the twilight-shadowed courtyard.

Our feet kicked up red dust; it clung to our sweat-beaded shanks like droplets of blood. I glanced at Dono as we walked. Even in the gloom of dusk, I could see that color had flushed his own stubbled cheeks. His jaw was set as if in argument.

When we reached the silo courtyard, he abruptly stopped and faced me. I almost stumbled into him, so sudden was his stop.

"Zarq," he said, and the flush on his cheeks heightened. "I can give you what you want. Every night. During the day, too, if your passion runs that strong."

I didn't know how to respond, so far from the truth was his ingenuous offer. He *couldn't* give me what I wanted. He wasn't a dragon.

I glanced down at his groin. He had the beginnings of an erection at the mere thought that I possessed an insatiable sexual hunger he must try his best to assuage.

As I grappled for a reply, he licked his lips and shot a look about the silo courtyard we stood in. It was empty save for stalls of heavy-lidded dragons grooming or watching us with disinterest.

"Look. I've made my decision," he continued, his voice dropping lower. "I, danku Re Dono, hereby give up my apprenticeship and claim you, danku Re Darquel's Zarq, as my roidan yin."

I gaped; he ploughed on.

"You've good enough hips; you'll bear me fine children. We'll live in Liru, the capital city. No one will find us there. I've already mapped a route to the coast."

Flabbergasted, I could do nothing but stare at him. He misread my silence.

"Don't be afraid, Zarq. I'll protect you. I vow it as your claimer."

"I . . . I don't know what to say," I stammered. "This is so unex-pected."

He agreed with a brusque nod. "I could claim a much finer woman, that's true. But rest assured that I mean to uphold my vow as claimer. I *will* provide for you and the children you bear me, regardless of how many women I might claim in the future alongside you."

I spluttered. He reached out and stroked my arm. His erection was prominent now.

"You look like her, sometimes," he said huskily, and I realized his eyes were glazing over with memory.

"I'm not Waivia, Dono," I said, as gently and firmly as I could.

His hand stilled on my arm. I took a quavering breath and cov-ered his hand with one of my own.

"I'm profoundly honored you would choose me as your roidan yin, and I'm overwhelmed that you would give up the apprentice-ship for me. Truly, I am."

His eyes cleared. A frown crept over his face. "I don't understand what you're saying."

Oh, Re, this was not going to be easy.

"Dono, I'm staying here. In the apprenticeship. I'm not going to leave."

He let go of my arm and stepped back a pace, so that my hand fell away from him. Color seeped into his cheeks. Not the glow of passion from before, but an angry, white-speckled flush.

"You're refusing to be my roidan yin?" he asked in disbelief.

"I'm grateful for your offer—"

"It wasn't an offer." His voice was climbing. "I claimed you. A woman can't refute such!"

"I'm a dragonmaster's apprentice."

His turn to gape at me, speechless.

"You want to go there, don't you?" he finally said, hands clench-ing into fists at his side. "You want to do the Komikon's bidding."

"I . . ." My rebuttal died on my lips. We both knew how badly I wanted to obey the Komikon in this matter.

"Dragonwhore," he spat.

"You don't understand."

"I understand, all right. You prefer the dragon to me. You're a deviant."

"No."

"You only use me to glut your lust for the dragon. When I touch you, you close your eyes and think of a dragon's scales and claws."

"And you? What do you think of when you lay with me, hey-o? Not of me, Dono. You don't think of me. You close your eyes and imagine you're with my sister."

"She's human."

"A dragon is divine," I countered.

"You're depraved."

"You're desperate."

"I'm offering to give up my apprenticeship!" he roared. "I'm willing to risk my life for you, save you from execution!"

Dono's fury blazed over me and I experienced a moment of vertigo. When my vision returned, I was staring at his outraged face.

I shook my head slowly.

"I'm sorry," I whispered. "I'm a dragonmaster's apprentice. This is my home. This is my . . . destiny."

Then I staggered away from him, in the direction of the dome-covered building and the old destrier that awaited me.

# ELEVEN

The Komikon himself carried me back to my stall and lay me in my hammock that night. Not because he'd guessed at the rift between Dono and me, but because he'd hoped that, while still freshly drunk on venom, divine inspiration would strike me and I'd decipher the dragons' song.

No such thing happened.

Once in my hammock, I fell into a stupor that submerged me swiftly in a fevered sleep. I woke once to find the dragonmaster standing impatiently over me, awaiting my revelation, and the second time, Dono, who watched me with visible resentment, clearly there only at the Komikon's insistence.

The third time I awoke, it was to find an Auditor looming over me.

Hands chalked the pallor of bone were reaching for me. I stared at them, scarce comprehending, then screamed and bolted upright.

Dono stood on the other side of my hammock, his face an obsidian shadow. Behind him stood a cluster of daronpuis, their porphyry and turquoise robes gleaming like dew-slicked orchids in the spluttering light of the torches they held.

"You are charged with committing impurity with a beast," boomed the Auditor. "You are hereby sentenced to life imprisonment."

Fear reignited the excessive amount of venom I'd received at dusk from the Komikon's destrier; I flung myself at the Auditor and fought like an ocelot, all teeth and claws and writhing body.

"Dono," I screeched, "get the dragonmaster!"

The Auditor possessed unnatural strength. He pinned me down, bound my hands, hobbled my ankles, and threw me sacklike over his back. Surrounded by the circle of daronpuis, Dono still silent amongst them, I was carried into the courtyard.

Three winged dragons pranced and shuddered in the courtyard's center, their unbolted wings fanning up great clouds of dust. To the right of them, a goodly distance away, stood Eidon, arguing with a Temple acolyte. Behind him, Egg bellowed for the dragonmaster, who was nowhere to be seen. Ringus sprinted for the sandstone archway. Temple wardens jabbed lances at the rest of the apprentices, ordering them to stand still, while a Temple acolyte raced after Ringus.

I turned my head, cheek rasping over the Auditor's incense-perfumed robe. Dono still stood on the threshold of my stall, his eyes looking as if they were forged from pewter.

He'd told Temple.

Furious because I'd spurned his offer to flee with him to the coast, insulted that I favored a dragon's tongue over his phallus, outraged because I preferred to risk death by staying in the dragonmaster's stables rather than become his roidan yin elsewhere, Dono had informed Temple of my interactions with the Komikon's destrier. And Temple had come for me.

Despair flooded me, and grief and loss. Dono's betrayal was like losing my childhood all over again. I was outcast. I was forsaken.

The Auditor threw me atop one of the winged dragons and four Temple acolytes leapt forward to hold me there.

"No!" I howled, tears streaming down my cheeks, and the agitated dragon shivered and pranced beneath me. "Dono, you don't know what you're doing!"

Or maybe he did.

Like most Malacarites, I'd heard rumors about Temple's prisons for women. I'd heard how the women were little more than kiyu, sex slaves for the Retainers who guarded the prison doors and windows. I'd heard how the Retainers were but criminals themselves, serving their sentences in a jail located adjacent to each of the prisons for women. Every imprisoned man who showed piety and displayed recalcitrance for his crime was awarded with Retainership duty at a women's prison.

The hard light in Dono's eyes suggested that he knew very well what he was doing, that he knew precisely what my fate would be from that moment on.

Sobbing, I writhed, bucked, and bit. The Temple acolytes caught my flailing fists and legs, and they lashed my hands and ankles to the dragon's saddle while the Auditor climbed up behind me. The Auditor leaned atop me, his weight pressing me hard into the saddle as he assumed the half-lying position of a dragon rider.

"No!" I shrieked, and then the ground lurched away from me so violently, I briefly thought my head had been separated from my body by the Auditor's blade.

I was in flight.

Massive wings beat the air on either side of us, fighting the sky down, thrusting us upward. Dragon muscle lurched and heaved beneath me. I pitched forward, then sideways, and felt as if I might be tossed off at any moment. All was noise and heaving motion.

I scrabbled for a handhold along the dragon's neck, grasped knobbed hide instead, and clung tightly to that. I relented to the Auditor's weight, so that I was pressed flat against the dragon's dorsal ridge. But with each lurch of the dragon's wings, the Auditor's body likewise lurched. What if he fell and pulled me down with him?

"I'm falling!" I yelled, but the wind devoured my words. I held my breath and pressed my cheek against the dragon lunging beneath me.

Something violent occurred within me, as if an unseen fist

buried behind my liver and diaphragm punched outward, toward my navel. At once cold rippled over the skin of my abdomen and a sulfurous taste coated my tongue.

Mother. Her haunt. I was leaving Clutch Re and, in doing so, was entrapping the haunt within my psyche.

I struggled to sit up. "No, we have to go back; stop, stop!"

The Auditor thumped my nape with the heel of one hand. "Stay still, else we both fall to our deaths!"

The haunt roiled within me. Clenching my teeth against the invasive struggle, I clung tight to the dragon and closed my eyes while the dragon's great membranous wings battled the air.

An eternity later, the violent wing thrusts stopped. My eyes snapped open and I tensed for the fall.

Nothing to see to either side of me but cold, damp darkness that sucked the blood from my marrow. I raised my cheek a little. Beyond the dragon's outstretched wing to my left, I saw only darkness below. To the right, more darkness.

No. A thin, silvery ribbon that for a moment I could not comprehend. I then realized it was a river.

"Lie still," the Auditor barked, and he shoved my cheek hard against the dorsum of the dragon to make me lay flat again. Then: an explosion on either side of us as wings battled air once more. I clung tight to the dragon's hide as we lurched up and down.

After flapping a few times, the wings fell still and stretched out in another glide. Wind rushed past.

The horrific flight went on and on, until I was drenched from chill mist and I shuddered from cold, until I lost all sensation in my hands and lower legs. The Auditor occasionally shifted, yarding back this way or that on the reins he held, his arms stretched along the dragon's neck.

The dragon began huffing.

I stiffened; her strength was flagging.

A short time later, the Auditor barked at the dragon, shifted the position of his legs, and flexed his arms. The pitch of the dragon abruptly changed, pointed sharply earthward. We were landing.

I clung to knobbed hide, hardly daring to breathe from tension, and kept my eyes shut tight. Our descent was so steep, I was glad of the weight of the prone Auditor pressing me against the dragon's back, for I felt sure I'd slide right off and dangle by the ropes binding me to the saddle if not for his bulk.

Down we flew. I espied a flickering light below: A fire atop a cliff.

The dragon abruptly changed direction and flew toward the light. Her wings exploded into action again. I'd had no idea flight was so violent, such a battle. All was motion and sound and muscled chaos about me, and suddenly I was smelling jungle, the damp, earthy smell of rotting bracken, the astringent smells of sap, leaf, bud, and bract. The air grew warmer as we neared the firelit cliff.

The dragon's wings beat in short and furious movements and she changed position, her neck and breast rising upward, pointing skyward, her hindquarters pointing down in an almost vertical position.

"Hold strong; we're landing!" the Auditor bellowed in my ear.

There was a violent lurch beneath us, a coiled sort of impact as we landed.

I stared about me, shaking as if I had palsy.

Some distance from us stood a ring of torch-bearing men. One of them came forward and handed the Auditor his torch. He wore no Temple garb but only a frayed hempen tunic that reached just below his knees. Both his face and midriff looked pudgy and soft. In a stupor, I watched him untie my ankles from the saddle, watched my wrists likewise unbound.

"Dismount," he ordered in a voice oddly sweet.

A eunuch. The man was a eunuch.

I was exhausted to the point where I felt sapped of all fight. I obeyed. I dismounted.

My knees buckled upon my feet contacting the ground. I didn't fall, though, but merely slumped against the dragon's heaving flanks. The eunuch clucked and pulled me upright. His pulpy hand about my biceps held me firmly but did not crush, did not bruise.

He propelled me forward, into the circle of torchlight.

Thick eyebrows, hooked noses. Stern mouths set in dense, groomed beards. Hair meticulously oiled and plaited in the many looping braids befitting a Temple warden of high stature.

And one face recognizable to me, an impassive face set above a multitude of turgid chins, upon a broad-shouldered, corpulent body: the Ranreeb, the Holy Overseer of the collective of Clutches to which Clutch Re belonged. I recognized him from the Mombe Taro parades of my youth; Mother had always pointed him out to me.

"That's her," the Ranreeb rumbled, his voice dredging from the pit of his vast belly, his inset eyes steady upon me. "Bring her closer."

The eunuch tugged on my arm and brought me to stand directly in front of the Ranreeb, so that the Holy Overseer's torch bathed my cheeks with warmth and ochre light.

Over the terraced hills of his chins, the Ranreeb looked impassively down at me as I looked up at him. The smell of incense cloying to him was so powerful that I could taste the scent as if I were sucking on a cone of oily tree gum.

He studied my face. I should have dropped my eyes but did not.

"The apprentice-informant spoke truth," the Ranreeb rumbled, and my chest vibrated as if the sound of his voice were rocks tumbling atop my breast. "Look to the eyes. She knows dragons."

The circle of men drew closer about me, their torches a constellation of crackling light. The eunuch obliged those gathered by firmly grasping my chin and tipping my head this way and that for all to examine me.

"Dragon eyes," one of the gathered daronpuis muttered. His tone carried both disgust and satisfaction.

"Dragon eyes," the others one by one confirmed, silk gowns rustling.

Dragon eyes.

Suddenly I was back at Tieron Nask Cinai, the sanctuary for retired bulls where I'd served since the age of nine. And the Convent Elder, whom I'd named Yellow Face for the color of her jaundiced skin, was standing before me, bidding me farewell as I fled the upcoming visit by Temple Auditors.

"Mind, now," Yellow Face had said, fussing with a bladder of venom she was about to give me. "It marks you. Your eyes, understand. Anyone who knows anything about dragons will see how much you've used, and anyone who knows of the rite will guess how intimately you've received it."

Dragon eyes. She'd had them, Yellow Face. Bloodshot eyes with unnaturally small pupils. Eyes that were stationary as they looked upon you. Eyes that blinked slowly, rarely. Like a dragon's do.

I closed my eyes so that those about me could look no further.

Pointless, really. They knew.

Dono had told them: I lay with dragons.

After a grueling march along a rutted, overgrown trail, I was taken into a stone labyrinth of unlit corridors. No one walked those mossy corridors but me and my retinue. No sound but the swish of robe, the phlegmy wheeze of Holy Warden, and the soft crackle of torchlight in those stooped passageways.

The eunuch leading me stopped, fumbled with a set of rusted keys at his waist, and opened a wooden door.

Hands grabbed me from behind and shoved me forward. Immediately I was assaulted by a musty stench, like that of a long-abandoned latrine. I spun about and caught a last glance of the Ranreeb surrounded by a torch-lit circle of daronpuis, before the door was slammed closed upon me.

Shock paralyzed me for several moments. My enclosure was dark, the only light a meager strip shining beneath the doorway. Beneath my feet, the wooden floor was soft and wet with rot. Small stones poked through. My head grazed the ceiling, which was also constructed of rotten wood. I threw myself at the door and attacked it. It relented not in the least to my pounding fists, my gouging nails.

I screamed like one gone mad.

Sometime later—long after I'd fallen asleep slumped against the door, and woken and shuffled to a corner of my prison cell to urinate—the door in front of me rasped as if it were being opened.

It was not.

A rectangle of light appeared in the closed door, at chin height. A leather bladder was shoved through an opening. Something else was shoved in after it, a white block that landed with a squelch atop the bladder.

I smelled the unmistakable scent of paak, baked egg whites, and saliva sprang painfully into my mouth. That's what the damp white block was, see: paak. I staggered forward and snatched up the food.

The paak was cold and outrageously salted, and I devoured it eagerly. With trembling hands, I then unscrewed the lid of the bladder and drank.

"Hand back the bladder when you're done," a voice barked on the other side of the door.

"Let me out," I gasped. "Please."

"Hand back the bladder."

I knew instinctively that once I handed it back, the portal in the door would slide shut and I'd be enclosed in darkness once more.

"I'm not finished drinking," I lied. My jailer responded with only a grunt.

By the flickering torchlight coming through the portal, I slowly examined my wooden cell.

It looked to be a perfect cube, six feet long, wide, and high. No cot existed for sleeping on, no pot to urinate in. Other than the rotting floor and walls, the dark, and the spiders that crawled about the place, I was alone.

Then I noticed how the walls appeared to shift in the torchlight. Something writhed over them.

Wait. No. Writing: The walls were covered in coarsely rendered glyphs that flickered in the torchlight.

Trembling, I read the verse nearest to me:

> Twenty-two years have I, and the name Bayen Lutche Rit's Limia. But, too, I have an unnatural interest in ancient Malacarite literature.
>
> Or so I was told by the Auditor who waylaid me in Wai Bayen Temple square.
>
> He also informed my smirking claimer that I displayed wanton tendencies, that I would be imprisoned for life. My claimer held a scroll, and though it was rolled, I recognized the broken seal as my own. He'd intercepted my last letter to X. I pray X learns of my fate and flees.

Directly beneath those lines, carved into the wood by another hand:

> Two years into her imprisonment, Bayen Lutche Rit's Limia expired in the Retainers' bunks. I now voice her name and free her spirit from these walls.

Heart thudding, I moved on to the next verse carved on the wall.

I am twenty-seven years old, and my name is Bayen Ka Ryn's Tak. While speaking from the lectern in Ondali Wapar Liru Third Lecture Hall, I was arrested and charged with teaching subversive literature. I have no intention of remaining imprisoned for long. Any who read this must have courage and believe they can endure and escape.

But again, beneath the lines, glyphs that slanted in a different direction from the original writer's finished the woman's history.

Six years into her imprisonment, Bayen Ka Ryn's Tak died in the medic's den during her third medic-induced miscarriage. I now voice her name and free her spirit from these walls.

A shiver raised the fine hairs on my nape. Almost every surface of my cell was carved with epitaphs.

That meant two things. One: All who had been imprisoned here had been able to write. They had, astoundingly, been educated women from elite bayen families. Yet they, too, had had lives controlled by the whims of Temple and powerful, displeased men.

The second thing I realized was that all who had entered these walls had expired within them.

"Hand back the bladder," the voice on the other side of my cell door growled, and I startled.

"Hand back the bladder," the voice again demanded.

"Don't shut the window," I begged.

"Hand it back, or else I won't bring you food and drink again."

I shoved the bladder through the slot of light but didn't withdraw my fingers. "Keep it open, please. I can't see in here."

A bamboo switch slashed my fingers. I cried out, snapped my hand back inside. At once the portal slid closed again.

"No!" I yelled, and I banged the door with my fists. "Open it, I can't breathe, I can't see, don't leave me here!"

No answer.

Time blurred. The slot opened, food and water were pushed through, I drank and ate, and then the slot closed again, entombing me in stench and darkness. My teeth rattled in my head from chill, my legs trembled incessantly. My feet and ankles swelled and pulsed like pulpy bruises.

Dono's betrayal sat on my shoulders and shattered my heart anew each time I woke from fitful, nervous sleep.

My mother's haunt made its presence known; it was trapped within my body. Each time I slept I felt its presence pulsing within me. I saw it in my sleep, embedded in my belly in the shape of a yamdalar cinaigour, the mucus-coated cocoon an old brooder dragon secretes about herself in preparation for death. I could see claws trying to rip open the cocoon, that the haunt might fully invade me, might take over my body as its own. Only the residual venom left in my body held the haunt trapped in that cocoon. I knew it was only a matter of time before the weak enclosure would disintegrate, and then each time I slept, the haunt would occupy my frame and entrap me in limbo, and upon waking, I'd have to fight my way back into my body and subdue the presence occupying my flesh by giving voice to the haunt's desire: Waivia.

Understand, such had happened to me before.

And, as the haunt gathered strength, I knew, too, that it would next begin to invade my waking hours. It would start to control me as a puppeteer controls a puppet.

I feared sleep, for it offered no escape, only provided a different source of misery and fear. So I kept myself awake, chanted the stories carved into the walls, even the few stories I'd found that had not been completed.

After some time, it became utterly necessary to include my name upon those walls, that my fate not go entirely unremarked, that my demise not be completely insignificant. I chose a stone from the filthy floor, ran my fingers over the wooden walls about me, and found an unmarked section.

It was not easy to carve hieratics upon those walls, despite the softness of the wood. But I persevered, triumphing with each cursive symbol I inscribed, feeling I'd won something great, something worthy, by my meager mastery. Yet picking up the stone each time I woke from a restless, chill sleep was supremely difficult. Rousing myself from despair, forcing myself to take action, however slight that action was, became a monumental task. Sometimes I could not bring myself to do it and instead spent my time rocking on the floor, my head between my knees.

Courage is the price that life exacts for granting peace. Anyone who does not know this, knows not the livid loneliness of fear. And when I could find the courage to pick up that stone, I found, for a little while, a strange sort of peace.

This, then, is what I inscribed on those foul walls:

> **Some call me danku Re Darquel's Zarq, but others call me Zarq-the-deviant. Both are correct, for at seventeen, I _am_ a deviant. I am rishi, yet I can read and write. I am woman, yet I have served bull dragons. I am a deviant because I once dared believe I might one day attain the status of dragonmaster.**

Writing this gave me purpose, kept me half sane. It felt as if I were burying Dono's betrayal by stretching out a hand to the women who had known this cell prior to me, and I dreamed of them and knew them as dear friends. I was not alone, not with their names constantly rolling off my lips. Not with my history inscribed alongside theirs.

At some point during that dark eternity, it dawned on me that my litany was similar in a small way to the dragons' music, to the ancestral ladder that connected each dragon with the dead, the living, and even the unborn. The act of scraping glyphs into damp wood joined my heart and breath and spirit to the women who had died in that place, and, by extension, it joined me to all women and men, for all of us would one day die, whether in cell or hammock, in childbirth or by mishap. Death was an undeniable unifier.

Then the door in front of me one day opened, shockingly, and I fell face-first into life again.

# TWELVE

A plump eunuch bathed me in tepid waters, in a blue-tiled room stained with ochre watermarks. I flinched from his touch, from the lantern light that glimmered overbright upon the cracked and chipped tiles. I was suspicious of the wooden tub he dipped water from, was overwhelmed by the feeling of tepid water poured over my head. I gasped, I spluttered, I trembled and hid my face behind my hands as I stood there naked, accepting his ministrations.

He used a grainy bar of soap on me. It smelled like crushed vines and stung my pressure sores, which he scrubbed vigorously.

Clucking, murmuring, occasionally patting my belly or back or shoulder as if each were a separate creature requiring soothing, he washed me thoroughly, and then, while I shivered and wept in anxiety, for I knew not what this washing meant and was terrified of it, he scrubbed my hair clean, running his fingers through the snarled mess until it lay in neat, wet ribbons to just below my chin.

He dried me with a linen sheet that at one time must have been very fine indeed, judging by the embroidery stitched along the edges, but was now stained and worn thin in multiple places.

When I was dry and my scalp throbbed hotly from his attentions, he dressed me in a bitoo, and I was astonished and unsettled anew by how fine the light, pale green linen was, by how softly it pooled about my ankles and how precisely it covered my arms.

He pulled the bitoo's cowl up over my damp head and stood back. He beamed as if he'd created, not washed, me.

The eunuch looked about twenty years old, though because he was a eunuch, his age was difficult to guess. His cheeks were as full as a baby's. His worn hemp tunic, wet from where he'd washed me, clung to his chest. Breasts bigger than mine and each jutting sideways a little, in perfect symmetry with his large, splayed feet, rested on his paunch. His hairless shins and thighs looked as soft as chamois, and his toenails had been painted orange with henna, as is the custom of all eunuchs.

As he beamed, dimples appeared on either side of his full lips.

"Better, hmmm?"

I felt like running from him, had a mad urge to find my prison cell and bar myself in it, for there I knew what to expect from each day, and a certain comfort may be derived from knowing such.

"I'll introduce you to the rest of the viagand. Come."

Viagand: herd of girls.

He took my left hand and gently but firmly tugged me forward.

He was to do that a great deal, over the months that followed. Carefully take my one of my hands in one of his own and lead me about, whether it be to the Retainer's bunks to be raped, the bathhouse to be washed, the latrines, the viagand chambers, the brooder stalls, the recovery berths, or the medic's den. Always his grasp was gentle.

But firm. Undeniable. Absolute. Or so I let myself believe.

I get ahead of myself.

That first day, he led me through a labyrinth of stone corridors, upstairs and down, the verdigris-slicked walls lit here and there by a guttering sconce or greenish sunlight that trickled through long, narrow casements high up in the stone walls. We saw no one, heard no human sounds. Once, as we passed beneath the grassy light streaming through a casement through which liana vines had grown, I heard the squawk of a parrot, followed by the hooting of a troop of howler monkeys. Instantly I knew: Jungle surrounded this dank stone fortress. Jungle and nothing else.

And then we did see people, two of them. Men, standing sentry outside a door at the end of a dead corridor. Dour, stinking men with long snarled hair. They were dressed in a shabby mockery of a Cafar guard's uniform, though they were unarmed. Their steel-studded leather skirts and plastrons were cracked with neglect, their sandals in equal disrepair.

My heart rattled against my chest as the eunuch led me toward the two, down that corridor, which ended only at the door they guarded.

The eunuch kowtowed to the two men.

"Retainers," he murmured, either addressing the two or informing me of their titles, I knew not which. Nor did I care; the Retainers looked at me with such knowing lechery and smirking confidence that I instantly feared them.

The eunuch pushed open the wooden door and pulled me through, past the Retainers.

"The viagand chambers," he said, beaming. "Your home." He shut the door behind us.

My eyes roved over the chamber before me, skittering from one dark niche to the next. My "home" was a dark, vaulted stone room, lit only by the greenish sunlight that slid through the few narrow casements in the stone walls. Fraying draperies hung upon the stone walls in dusty folds. Once-fine rugs in faded greens and purples covered the stone floors, some overlapping others, most worn through in the center and unraveling at the ends. Pillows and musical instruments, floor tables and divans, art easels and inkwells, lay scattered about, intermingled with the occasional hand puppet or forsaken destiny wheel.

Everything looked shabby, as though decades of dust had been ingrained into every surface. The smell of women impregnated the damp air, a soft, briny odor that was familiar from my childhood in the pottery women's barracks but was altered radically by the stone walls behind the mildewing draperies, and the fusty pools of darkness that lay beyond the rays of light seeping through the narrow casements.

Altered, too, by the unmistakable scent of venom pervading the entire place.

Saliva rushed into my mouth, a painful, puckering burst, and my heart stuttered and danced.

"Greatmother," the eunuch called. He released my hand, clasped his belly. "Greatmother!"

From various dark corners—caves hollowed out here, niches ferreted away there, crannies that notched the circumference of the vaulted room we stood in—came slow, swishing sounds, as if the dead were rising from eternal slumber and shambling toward us.

My heart rattled against my chest and I half turned back to the door we'd just come through. I remembered the two guards, the Retainers so confident in their lechery. Swallowing hard, I turned away from the door and faced whatever was about to befall me.

"Come, come." The eunuch clucked indulgently at the approaching sounds.

I saw them then, drifting toward us, as slim and pale as if they'd been shaped from moonlight.

Women.

"Here she is: One Hundredth Girl. Introduce yourselves to Najivia, girls."

I stiffened, bit my tongue to hold back a scream.

The women shuffling toward me were unnatural, their skin almost as white as a Northerner's but as waxy as an orchid's petal. Their shoulders hung off them as if made of melting wax, and their hands hung slackly at their sides, as if too heavy to lift. Their hair hung long and thinly to their elbows, and their scalps were clearly visible beneath their hair roots. To a woman, their eyes were ringed in oozing red skin and looked too big, as if plucked from some larger creature and embedded like fat rotting plums in the glossy dough of their faces.

Not that their faces were plump, understand. No. They were lean. But nary a wrinkle, nary a crease, marred their cheeks, so that their faces reminded me exactly of the dough used to make holy cakes: round, smooth, damp, covered in a thin coat of lard.

It was their eyes, though, that made horror ripple along my spine. Overlarge eyes ringed by irritated, weeping skin. Dragon eyes.

Dragon eyes like I'd never seen before, like I'd never thought possible.

The whites of each woman's eyes were so thickly webbed with broken blood vessels, her irises appeared to be suspended in pools of blood. And the irises, well. *They* were marbled with shards of white. Not a clean white, like that of an egret's down, but the blue white of starlight on a cold, clear evening. The blue white that remains imprinted upon your eyesight for several heartbeats after a celestial feather has exploded like a spark upon your skin.

And they were as immovable as rocks set in mortar, those eyes.

"Hello," said one of the women, coming to a stop before me. The air she exhaled was heavily perfumed with the scent of venom. Her front teeth were missing. Gray streaked her long black hair. "You're Naji."

"She is, Greatmother," the eunuch said. "Fresh from the Prelude."

"I see." Her eyes dropped into mine like rocks sinking through silt. "I'm Makwaivia, Forty-one Girl. But call me Greatmother."

The women lethargically formed a semicircle before me. The smell of venom pervasive throughout the place increased as they drew close. There were five women, all dressed in pale bitoos, and they all looked identical.

"I'm Sutkabdevia," murmured one of the women. Sixty-seven Girl.

"Kabdekazonvia." Seventy-two Girl.

"Misutvia." Eighty-six Girl.

"Prinrutvia." Ninety-three Girl. "But please, call me Prinrut, as the others do. It's shorter."

I stared at them in horror.

The eunuch clucked beside me. "Can you remember what your name is?"

He talked nonsense.

"Najivia," he said gently. "One Hundred Girl. Remember that, hey-o?" He turned back to the gathered women. "You'll orient her, won't you, girls? I've got noon feast to prepare. Wait until you see the delights in store for you today!" He licked his lips and rubbed his soft hands together in anticipation.

One of those hands landed heavily on my shoulder. "You listen to Greatmother and the girls closely, hey-o? Greatmother's been here a long time; she knows what's best for you. Don't you, Great-mother?"

Moving his hips like a cur with dysplasia, he departed through the solitary door.

One of the women standing before me sighed. "Let's sit. It's tire-some standing."

A murmur of agreement. The women drifted to the various cush-ions and divans scattered about the room and melted atop them, boneless.

"Come, child," the gray-haired woman called Greatmother said, pointing to a worn carpet across from the tattered cushion she sat upon. "You haven't had the pleasure of sitting upon a cushion for a long time."

Stiffly, I approached her and tried to sit. I found myself unable to, without a wall to slide down as support. I was astonished by my body's inability to perform what should have been a natural motion.

"Give her aid," Greatmother instructed, gesturing at the two women seated closest to where I stood.

With sighs of exhaustion, the two women helped me lay upon a wine red carpet, their touch gentle, their words soft. A kiss brushed my brow. The scent of venom was momentarily as strong as if breathed from the throat of an uncut dragon.

"Your flexibility and strength will return to you soon enough, Naji," Greatmother said. "Eat well, stretch your limbs, rest."

Five bloodshot pairs of overlarge, unblinking eyes stared at me.

"Listen closely to me and you won't return to Prelude, not unless you wish to. Understand?"

She required an answer of me.

"Yes," I breathed, wanting only to close my eyes and hide.

"Twelve of us currently live in the viagand. You are the thirteenth." Greatmother's motionless eyes grew roots into mine. "Some of us are not present. They're either in the stables or a recovery berth. You'll meet them if they all return. I'll warrant *your* chances are good for surviving the stables; your eyes speak of prior experience with venom."

"I—"

"You'll not talk about the life you had before here; you won't so much as tell us your old name. If you do, your transgression will be reported to the Retainers and you'll be punished accordingly. Each one of us here will do that, understand, inform on each other. It keeps us pure. And it garners respect from the Retainers and thereby increases one's longevity. You'll learn to do such, too, in varying degrees."

Her tone was that used by an elder sister instructing a younger on how to cook paak for the first time.

"But we must know your age," said another woman, someone who, in different circumstances, might have looked not that much older than me.

"Patience, Misutvia, I was coming to that," Greatmother chided, though her tone was almost flat. She stared at me, waiting.

"Seventeen," I said hoarsely. "I'm seventeen."

A brief silence as everyone absorbed this seemingly relevant information. Then Greatmother continued.

"As the eunuch informed you, I've been here the longest. You'd be wise not to think of me as your friend. I won't ever think of you in that manner. Understand?"

I gave a small nod, head rasping along the worn carpet beneath me.

"Your survival here depends upon three things. The first of these: your ability to please an authoritative Retainer, that he prefer your attentions and prevent other Retainers from receiving your services. The second: your ability to survive the touch of venom. The third: your ability to interpret what you hear in the stables, and your willingness to divulge such in a useful manner in the recovery berths. This, of the three, is the most crucial."

I didn't understand.

"You haven't explained her purpose here, Greatmother." Again from the younger woman called Misutvia. "You haven't explained that this is no ordinary prison for women."

Greatmother tilted her head to one side as if listening for a worm turning beneath the stone floor. "Did I forget?"

Murmurs in disaffected tones all about us.

"Yes, you did, Greatmother."

"You forgot."

"Yes."

Consternation flickered over Greatmother's glossy face, though no emotion was revealed in her blood-bathed eyes, in her white-flecked irises. "That's not a good sign. Not at all. I should be punished accordingly."

A concurring murmur here and there.

"Well. Let me continue where I should have begun. Your purpose here, Naji: to lay, on a rotational basis, before one of the four venom-intact dragons housed in the brooder stalls. There you will permit the dragon to insert her tongue into your womb, whereupon you will become privy to her divine thoughts. After the dragon withdraws from you, you will be carried by Retainers to a recovery berth, whereupon you will in great detail divulge to the waiting daronpuis everything that you learned during the divine exchange. If you claim that you did not understand what you heard, the daronpuis will employ various methods to encourage you to refrain from hoarding the information to yourself. Understand?"

I stared at her in mounting horror. I looked at the other women draped here and there about me, their red-rimmed, expressionless eyes glittering in their dough-glossy faces.

"But the dragons' thoughts are incomprehensible!" I gasped.

"You've undergone the divine experience before. That explains your eyes, hey-o."

"I can't understand what the dragons are saying, I can't!"

"You must. Your life depends upon it."

"Interpret the images you see, connect them with the emotions they provoke," Misutvia said, interrupting Greatmother for the third time.

"Do not color the way she might translate the dragons' thoughts by informing her of your own methods of interpretation, Misutvia," Greatmother said, a subtle urgency behind her flat tone. "That's a transgression. I claim the responsibility to report it. You'll be punished accordingly."

Misutvia dropped her eyes to her hands and I saw then that her hair was not as thin and oily as that of the other women about her.

"You're correct, of course," Misutvia murmured. "And I claim the responsibility of reporting your forgetfulness, Greatmother, which you moments ago defined as a transgression."

"No one else has claimed the responsibility to do so before you, so certainly the right is yours. I should have claimed the responsibility myself. Clearly, my mental faculties are weakening. I will discuss this with the eunuchs and my Retainer. Perhaps my execution is warranted."

A moment of silence about us while I stared in disbelief at Greatmother. She'd spoken in a sensible, unhurried manner, as reasonably as if discussing the merits of a bitoo she might purchase.

"You strive admirably toward purity, Greatmother," Misutvia finally murmured, without looking up from her hands.

"Yes. I do," Greatmother said.

At that moment, the door behind us sighed open. The women languidly turned, as did I from where I lay on the floor, to watch the eunuch reappear bearing a platter of food. Behind him walked another man bearing a platter, also clearly a eunuch. He walked in a peculiar, mincing manner, as if thorns stabbed the soles of his feet. A third eunuch followed, a mere boy, bearing two buckets slung over either end of a pole, balanced across his shoulders and the back of his neck. He kicked the door closed behind him and set his burden down with a groan.

"Noon feast, girls," sang the plump eunuch, the one who had bathed me. "Pastries and nerwon, and I want you all to eat more than you did at breakfast, hey-o."

The women about me sighed or closed their eyes wearily.

I, on the other hand, was gripped with an immediate, shuddering hunger, and if my body had been able to obey my wild need, I would have leapt pantherlike upon the eunuch and mauled the contents of his platter. As it was, I watched with a territorial intensity as he set the platter upon a worn rug not far from me. I didn't want anyone touching the food upon that tray. I wanted it all to myself.

Cubes of nerwon—breaded and fried egg yolk glazed with hot fat and bittersweet crushed plums—steamed in a chipped crock. In another bowl alongside it, white strips of paak lay like islands in a sea of yolk yellow sauce delicately laced with minced muay leaves. A third bowl gave off a vinegarish scent. Neat stacks of quanis formed a steaming pyramid within a large bowl, the vinegar-soaked muay leaves rolled around a traditional stuffing of crushed coranuts, diced dried oranges, and slivers of fiery chilies. Tarnished spoons lay haphazardly about the three large bowls, as if tossed upon the platter as an afterthought.

The eunuch who walked as if upon thorns placed his platter alongside the first: pastries the hues of a splendid sunset—wine red, tangerine, old-gold yellow—sat artfully arranged in a sunburst display, all oozing amber honey.

I whimpered.

"Yes, we'll feed you first, Naji," the plump eunuch clucked indulgently. "Watch how well she eats, girls, hey-o? Think how much it pleases the Retainers when a woman has a little flesh upon her hips. Think of how popular Naji will be."

He shuffled toward me. The yolk sauce slopped over the sides of its bowl.

"A little of the jalen for you; no nerwon or quanis. Too rich. Tomorrow maybe, yes?" He picked up the crock of paak slices floating in the yolk and minced muay sauce. Jalen, he'd called the dish. I'd never tasted such rich food, not even during my youth in the pottery clan, for the dishes required ingredients and preparation time rishi could ill afford. With one of the spoons from the tray, the eunuch began feeding me.

He did it in an odd way, carefully placing each spoonful in my mouth and, after I'd swallowed, sucking the spoon clean. I was revolted but too hungry to care.

Before my hunger was anywhere near appeased, the eunuch licked the spoon one last time, sighed, and beamed at the women draped about us.

"Didn't she do well? She'd eat more if I let her, wouldn't you?" He clucked. "Tomorrow. Small amounts only today, hey-o. Now, who's next? Greatmother?"

Incredibly, he then fed Greatmother in the exact same manner, with the same spoon, sucking it clean each time after she swallowed. He also coaxed her to nibble part of a quani, to swallow two cubes of nerwon. When she closed her eyes in protest and weakly waved away further offerings, the eunuch clucked and moved on to another woman.

The mincing eunuch likewise began feeding those about me, wheedling and cooing as if he were feeding fussy toddlers and not grown women. The boy at the door squatted on his haunches and dozed.

A few of the women wept, helplessly, as the eunuchs badgered and coaxed them to eat.

"You're skin and bones; no wonder the Retainers use you roughly," the plump eunuch snapped. "They hanker for some softness, some flesh! Eat, eat, you'll live longer; they'll hurt you less. Eat!"

I closed my eyes to the tyranny, wished I could close my ears, too.

At last the eunuchs stopped, then woke the boy dozing near the door, and the three finished the remainder of the noon feast themselves. They ate melodramatically, loudly sucking the dripping juices from their fingers, rolling their eyes as they popped cakes into their sticky mouths and licked grease from their chins. I watched it, fascinated and detached both, as if I were living a strange dream from which I'd soon awake. The women about me watched with their huge, unblinking eyes, their faces expressionless.

Torpidity began descending upon me, bringing the threat of deep, long sleep.

"Hey-o, girls, on your feet. Come, come," the plump eunuch sang, clapping his hands briskly. The mincing eunuch tiptoed to the door. The young boy now held a whisk and dustpan in his hands; as the women listlessly rose and shuffled toward the door, the boy darted about the rugs and cushions, carelessly sweeping up crumbs.

The plump eunuch lifted me to my feet brusquely, almost impatiently.

"You can sleep later, Naji. Walk now. I know you can walk."

But my legs didn't want to obey. *I* didn't want to obey. Nor, really, did I wish to sleep, for then Mother's haunt would pulse strong within me, its angry necrotic presence, which had been growing stronger as of late, bulging and sweating in my body, trying to burst from its cocoon within me and infest me with its will, control my mind and limbs, and eradicate all I truly was.

The eunuch took my wrist and pulled me forward. I stumbled and almost fell. Clucking irritably, he gestured for the boy to leave his crumb-sweeping and instead act as a crutch for me. The boy darted forward and slid one of my arms over his narrow little shoulders with practiced ease. His toenails were painted henna orange too.

The mincing eunuch opened the door and gestured the women forward. Before each woman shuffled out, he dipped a ladle into one of the two buckets of water the young boy had carried in. Each woman drank greedily and requested more. The mincing eunuch either granted or denied their requests, according to the dictates of the plump eunuch.

"You ate well today, Greatmother; drink your fill. Good girl. No, no, Prinrut, no more for you. You ate very poorly; I'm very disappointed in you. And you, Kabdekazon, only half a ladle of water for you. You'll be dead in a clawful of days, I'll warrant."

When it came time for me to shuffle out the door, the mincing eunuch held the ladle to my lips, too. The water tasted like it had been filtered through moss, slightly muddy, but I drank gratefully anyway. I didn't ask for more, for I didn't crave water the way the venom-saturated women did, and the eunuch didn't offer it.

Again the Retainers at the door watched me with greedy anticipation. The plump eunuch perfunctorily kowtowed to them and pushed to the head of the line of women.

We followed him along one moisture-slick corridor to a set of stone stairs, climbed them, turned left down another corridor, then right down another. I longed to collapse. The boy holding me pinched me to keep me awake and moving.

We arrived at two stone latrines, stinking and perched at the end of a corridor like two crumbling thrones. No doors on those latrines. We were required to void bladder and bowel in full view of all.

Then back to the viagand chambers, whereupon the boy led me to one of the many small stone burrows notched in the circumference of the vaulted central chamber. Only shadow and darkness granted the burrow privacy; no doors or curtains existed across its entrance. Not that the entrance needed much in the way of concealment beyond shadow, for it reached only my knees, it was that low, and I had to kneel to crawl into the dank place. You'd have thought I would have balked, after so many weeks in Prelude. You'd have thought I would have been deathly afraid to squeeze myself into a dark, unknown place so cramped that my head brushed the slick stone as I crawled within. But I did nothing of the sort. I was too exhausted, too overwhelmed, to summon the energy and wit required for defiance. Thus I began submitting to the will of my jailers.

Inside the burrow: darkness, mildewed cushions, and the scent of venom so strong it seemed as if I knelt not in a stone den but in the venom sacs of an intact dragon. I lay down upon those mildewed cushions and curled into an infant's position.

"Drink this," the eunuch murmured. His bulk was crouched in the entrance to my burrow, silhouetted by the greenish jungle light trickling through the central chamber's casements. "Take it, Naji; drink. To ease your aches, to help you sleep. Drink."

He thrust a gourd at me. A citric tang wafted from it. Venom.

With trembling hands, I reached for the draft.

The venom blazed down my throat, and my eyes stung and itched as if rubbed with coarse salt, then streamed tears. My nostrils burned as if coated with chili paste. Lusty heat radiated through my groin.

Bliss.

"Thank you," I gasped, overwhelmed with gratitude toward he who held me prisoner. "Thank you."

The eunuch chuckled benignly and took the empty gourd from me. I closed my eyes and sank back onto the damp cushions. They felt as soft as down. I was floating on them. The burrow was constricting no longer. It cradled me gently, like a mother's arms. Cradled me and rocked. I sighed, contented.

Then, for the first time since being arrested in the dragonmaster's stables, I slept. Truly slept. Unhindered by my mother's haunt.

# THIRTEEN

The next clawful of days fell into a routine of draft-induced sleep punctuated by the plump eunuch's summons to eat. I couldn't recall the last time I'd slept so much. Not since I was a child in the pottery clan compound, certainly. I luxuriated in venom-induced sleep at night, wallowed in it during the day, felt glutted yet greedy for more. Oh, haunt-free bliss! Oh, black escape!

I spoke with no one during those days, and no one spoke with me, either. Each day passed like the one previous: We were spoon-fed by the eunuchs and rewarded accordingly with water rations; we were led to the latrines, then returned to the viagand chambers. We slept.

Sometimes as I slept, I roused slightly, heard the merry whistling of the boy eunuch as he dusted or swept or scraped lichen from the walls. Now and then I heard apathetic voices in brief conversation. To sharpen a venom-dulled mind so that it could better interpret the dragons' memories, the plump eunuch occasionally badgered a woman into splashing paint onto a canvas in a parody of creating art, or harassed her into a game of darali abin famoo with the destiny wheel. But mostly, all I heard was a wilted, damp silence that clogged the ears like sodden chaff. We all lay in our little caves sleeping, see. Immersed in escape.

Sometimes, other noises penetrated my slumber.

Recognizable sounds, they were, which, upon waking, I realized must be the coo of wild doves, the whisk of feathers across stone, the wet slap of frond against frond.

Those sounds came to me in the form of dreams, woven with the golden threads of memory: I dreamed of the mating shack in my birth clan. I dreamed of its paper-wall cubicles, of the gasps and groans and wet, gentle slaps I'd heard as a child when sleeping in a cubicle across from my parents, during those sultry nights they joined each other there.

In the beginning, the sounds were comforting. They evoked the security and warmth of a childhood long lost.

But as the days and nights stretched on, the sounds began provoking adult emotions within me, magnified a hundredfold by the venom in my veins. My sleep was no longer restful then. I'd dream of Dono pawing at my breasts, kneeling while I stood, tonguing me so that I arched and clawed his hair with insatiable want.

And I took to examining the women about me, each time we gathered for feeding.

Did they feel the same as I did, whenever they curled in their burrows? Were they gripped with the ache, the loneliness, the need that only venom and dragon union could alleviate? I couldn't tell, from looking at them. The women gazed at ground or wall, studiously avoided conversation, touch, and each other's eyes.

I wondered which of the two women who had helped me lie down before Greatmother for instruction, upon my arrival in the viagand, had brushed her lips across my forehead. I wished I had paid more attention to who was whom, but alas, they'd all looked alike to me.

Not now.

They did not look the same, not at all. Yes, they moved more or less in the same lifeless shuffle, and yes, their eyes bore the mark of the dragons' poison. But as the days dripped into each other, I realized that each damp face differed from the other, and that those who had been in the viagand longest looked palest, moved slowest, had suffered the most drastic hair loss, burned with the fiercest thirst, and displayed the least interest in food.

Greatmother looked eldest, by mere dint of her missing teeth and the gray so heavily streaking her long, thin hair. Yet a core of purest steel seemed to hold her erect, and I realized that determination to survive her imprisonment as long as she might, coupled with her absolute belief in the justice of her situation, made her the most formidable person I'd ever met.

Sutkabde and Kabdekazonvia, Sixty-seven and Seventy-two Girls, looked like figures made of melting tallow, and their eyes, surrounded by swollen, serum-weeping flesh, were harrowing. But whereas Kabdekazonvia seemed unable to eat more than a morsel here, a nibble there, Sutkabde would allow the plump eunuch to spoon exactly as much food into her mouth as Greatmother had eaten. Often, she'd gag in the process. Once, she retched up all she'd swallowed. Prinrut swiftly and quietly announced such waste a transgression.

Prinrut, the newest arrival save for me, looked and acted almost normal. I say almost, for she suffered a tendency to fall into short spells of fear-induced catatonia; fear, after resignation, hung as thick as the scent of venom in the chamber's air. Prinrut's shoulder-length hair had a tendency to curl about her face in a disarray that softened her pallor and hid the reddened skin around her eyes. Her meek voice gave the impression that before her imprisonment, she may have been a comely, plump, docile sort. I wondered what crime she'd been accused of, that she'd ended up in such a prison.

Misutvia, Eighty-six Girl—also relatively new, going by the numerical order of her name—was also least marked by her time in the viagand. Occasionally color would flood her high cheekbones, most usually while pouncing on any transgression Greatmother inadvertently performed. I oft felt that Misutvia ceaselessly watched the rest of us beneath her jet-black bangs, cut so severely and attractively in a straight line across her forehead. Her posture while reclining upon a divan during feeding was always provocative, almost defiant: one arm draped above her head, breasts out-thrust,

one leg dangling over the divan, shapely calf exposed. In this respect, she reminded me of my sister Waivia, though with her
frighteningly bloodshot eyes, deathly pallor, and languid walk,
there could be no mistaking the one for the other.

As quick as Misutvia was to pounce on any transgression Greatmother performed, I noticed that she never claimed the responsibility of reporting the transgressions performed by other women.
Ever.

With each passing day, my regard for Misutvia increased. In her
treatment of all save Greatmother, she was ethical and sane. Occasionally, I noticed her realizing that a transgression against someone had gone unclaimed; I'd watch her struggle with the conflict of
wanting to claim that transgression for herself, yet time and time
again, she would choose not to.

Those transgressions, hey-o. They ranged from the outrageous
to the unfathomable, and I flinched each time a woman claimed
one against another.

"Greatmother, I noticed you didn't have a bowel movement
today. You're failing the dragons and the daronpuis by allowing
yourself to fall into ill health. This, surely, is a transgression. I claim
the right to report it."

"Misutvia, you slept uneasily during the night; you kept others
awake. This endangers their health. I claim the right to report this
transgression."

"Prinrut, you suffered a catatonic spell during feeding this noon.
You missed a meal."

"Kabdekazonvia, you ate even less today than you did yesterday."

"Sutkabde, you haven't engaged in creative expression for a
clawful of days. Such mental laxity is remiss; it encourages sloth
and physical deterioration."

Hearing those transgressions was an instruction for me. I ensured that I moved my bowels once each day, regardless of how
much straining it required. I scraped dry, clotted paint onto a

canvas to avoid the transgression of mental laxity. I ate heartily, even though my appetite decreased with each venom draft the plump eunuch gave me. I took to stretching my limbs in the presence of others, prior to each noon feast, so that I couldn't be accused of not recovering from Prelude fast enough to please the daronpuis.

As I said, at all other times I curled into my stone burrow and escaped from life through sleep.

That was the safest way of dealing with the monstrosity of my situation: ignoring the reality of it as much as I could, much the same way, I suppose, that Prinrut did each time she plunged into catatonia.

But I couldn't completely avoid the whole issue of transgression reporting, for each evening, after being force-fed dinner, any woman who had claimed a transgression against another during the day would stand before the plump eunuch. He would solemnly mark the transgression in a ledger with a quill, dipping it meticulously in an inferior inkwell whose gray glaze had crazed during firing in the kiln. He'd mark down both the name of the transgressor and that of the woman who had reported the transgression.

I surmised that it was a tally system of sorts, whereby informing on others decreased whatever demerits had been logged against one on prior days, or earned one a merit to be used in the future, should there be no demerits scribed next to one's name. I didn't ask when or how the recorded transgressions would be turned into punishments, and, by staying in my little cave at all times except meals and my brief forays to scrape paint upon a canvas, I avoided the company of others who might inform me of such.

I knew, though. I knew how important those tallied transgressions were.

I knew by the way each woman reacted when caught committing a violation, guessed that the eventual punishment would be no mere knuckle caning. Each time a violation was claimed against a woman, the transgressor would freeze. Stare fixedly at the air. Remain so for long moments while a frantic pulse beat visibly in neck or temple. Each such trance would end with noiseless tears or a paroxysm of shudders.

Their fear created my own.

I took great care to remain well fed, silent, and mostly unseen.

Then, deep into a humid, honeysuckle-sweet night when the first monsoon of the Wet thundered outside, I committed my first transgression, and I committed it with a hungry passion that astonished me.

I was asleep, and then I was not, staring at the slick cave ceiling mere inches above me, uncertain whether it was star-flecked night I gazed into or quartz-flecked rock. Maybe it was both. It felt that way, at the time, the enclosure of rock as immutable as endless sky, the flecks of quartz as hypnotic and scintillating as starlight.

Something had woken me, a feeling, a presentiment. A presence that whispered something forbidden and unknown into my ear. My name? Not that, no, even though I'd been prohibited from speaking it to any. Yet the feeling pulsing over me, emanating from the little mouth of my stone burrow, was as familiar as my name, as forbidden as such.

I turned my head. A figure crouched at the entrance to my burrow, a hand's breadth away.

I held my breath and realized, belatedly, that I'd been practicing solitary intimacy in my sleep again: my thighs were spread, the fingers of one of my hands satiny with my brine.

I realized, too, that the figure had been crouched there for some time. Watching me. Her own thighs were spread, one of her hands tucked into the dampness of her cleft.

We held our breaths, she and I.

Oh, yes, it was a she. Not one of the eunuchs, no. The figure before me had hip, had breast. The moonlight seeping through the casements in the central chamber lit her curves, clothed in the linen of her bitoo.

I knew not what to do. The woman crouched on her haunches at the threshold of my burrow seemed likewise paralyzed, and in her fear, I recognized her, despite her features being shrouded entirely in dark. Prinrut.

I felt safe, then, for her withdrawn, docile demeanor made her the least frightening woman in the viagand. I withdrew my hand from between my thighs and offered it to her. I was instantly befuddled, not having expected myself to do such, taken aback by my own action. My hand wavered, but she withdrew her hand from between her legs and clasped mine before I could retract it.

Her fingers were warm, wet. They interlocked with mine. I found my grip tightening. She responded likewise. My body quickened. The heat in my groin swelled, pulsed, and I began to breathe too quickly.

I tugged her forward at the exact moment she came toward me.

I pushed my back against the burrow's wall, that she might squeeze in beside me, and I wondered, trembling, at what I was about to do, wondered whether it was not too late to avoid it, wondered whether I wanted to avoid it, wondered whether I'd gone mad. Wondered, too, at the intensity and immediacy of my reaction to her smell, her wet fingers entwined in my own.

Her breath sounded loud in my little burrow. Her form and warmth filled the cave. She lay down beside me, on her side, the both of us squeezed together, facing each other. One of her knees lay between my thighs. One of her arms draped over my ribs. Because there was no room, no room at all, I placed an arm over her. My hand perched uncertainly atop her hip, like a nervous bird that could at any moment burst into flight.

Never before had I been with a woman in such a situation. I was surprised and delighted by the curve of her.

Her breath, so venom laden, breathed warmth against my face. She moved closer. I swelled with want. Then her lips pressed against mine, and oh! the hunger in me.

Her breasts against mine felt so different from the firmness of a man's chest, felt so welcome and warm and giving, and at once I was filled with a need to feel those breasts against mine without the cloth of our bitoos dividing us. I tugged at her bitoo, she at mine. Elbows grazed stone, mouths panted; it was impossible to remove our bitoos in such a space. I thought I heard something rip. Her neck tasted salty and was soft, so soft, beneath my lips.

Oh, Re, I wanted her breast in my mouth, wanted her nipple on my tongue.

And then her fingers were in me, and I gasped, arched. Melted. Her arm moved, fast. My need built greater. I needed the dragon, needed its tongue, wanted its song.

I think I climaxed, but it was so incomplete, the need that rolled after it so fierce, that I pushed my hips against her in greed. I realized that her own want was huge, and in craving divine merger, I sought her moist depths in hopes I might alleviate a little of the immense need in the both of us.

How new and warm and welcome the wet of her. How intoxicating the push of her muscle, the soft curve of her breast and hip and belly.

We invaded each other, over and over, until I felt swollen and raw and could scarce breathe from exhaustion. Soaked through with sweat, we lay in each other's arms.

Finally, our breaths slowed.

She moved, then, and placed her lips against my ear.

"Someone will have heard us," she whispered, so quietly that I had to guess at half her words. "Even above the sound of the monsoon outside. Please, may I report our transgression tomorrow morn? Before anyone else does? Will you give me that gift?"

I went cold. Was stunned.

"Someone *will* have heard us," she repeated, and by the catch in her throat, I knew she wept.

She was afraid. Afraid of the inevitable report of transgression. Afraid of the mark the plump eunuch would make in his ledger against her name.

She was asking me to allow her to announce our intimacy to all on the morrow, that in declaring such, she could earn a merit, thus detracting a demerit or so that would be marked against the both of us. She was also calling our beautiful, passionate embrace a transgression, which I knew in my soul it was not.

Befuddled, I shrugged.

Agreed.

I didn't realize until later that I could've claimed the right to announce our transgression myself, and thus reduce somewhat the punishment that was to shortly come my way.

I'd not make that mistake again.

Shortly after weeping her thanks against my neck, Prinrut crawled out of my burrow and melted into the dark, to her own cave.

"Naji slept restlessly last night," she announced the next morning, before even half of us had crawled from our respective burrows. She avoided my eyes. "I claim the responsibility of reporting her transgression."

"You, too, slept restlessly, made noise that interrupted the much-needed sleep of others," Greatmother said, her white-flecked irises swimming in orbs of blood. "I claim the responsibility of reporting that transgression."

It became clear to me then.

Those dove coos, those feather whispers I'd heard in dreams I'd attributed to childhood memories, had been the kisses and gasps of viagand women joined in need within their burrows. I realized, belatedly, that the phrase both Prinrut and Greatmother had used, *you slept restlessly*, was code for the intimacy we'd shared. It was an intimacy that Greatmother would not name for what it was, for it was an act she, too, performed on some nights, out of insatiable need and loneliness.

I wondered what ludicrous phrases represented other acts committed in the viagand chambers.

And though I resented Prinrut claiming the transgression against me, and though I burned with fury that she would even call the passion we'd shared a transgression, I forced myself to let go of that anger and, if not forgive her, then move on. I decided that I had to let go of my ire, see. Because I wanted affection with Prinrut far more than I wanted to hold a grudge against her.

I craved affection. Acceptance. A sense of family and belonging.

Prinrut visited me each night thereafter. She would answer none of the questions I asked of her, though, would turn away from me as I pressed my love-swollen lips against her ear and breathed my questions softly so that none could hear. After several nights, I stopped asking, for her continued silence aggravated me and saddened her, and I did not want to lose her companionship. No. If not for our intimacy and the venom draft the eunuch gave me each eve, I would have given in to a madness of despair.

After our first time together, I was smarter: I refused to concede Prinrut the right to claim a transgression against me. We agreed in hushed voices that we would announce our own actions each morn, using the accepted code. After the first few announcements, I easily deceived myself into believing those marks against my name in the eunuch's ledger meant little.

I don't know how long I would have mindlessly gone on in such a manner, obediently quaffing down drafts and engaging in pleasure with Prinrut, if one dusk the plump eunuch had not refused me my venom.

I stared at him, on the threshold of panic. We'd just returned from the latrines after being force-fed an evening meal. Instead of waddling to my stone burrow alongside me, to hand me a venom draft, he clapped his hands together and made an announcement.

"The rest of the viagand returns from the recovery berths two days hence. Make sure you're all well rested for their return."

Rigidity amongst those around me. Prinrut gasped. Her eyes glazed over and her limbs locked picket stiff. At once her face wore that slack, vacant look of catatonia.

The eunuch clucked with annoyance. "Greatmother, see to it that she revives before morn, hmmm?"

Greatmother murmured acquiesence. The eunuch turned to leave.

I stepped forward, one hand outstretched. "My venom draft?"

Again he clucked irritably. "Naji, don't be noisome."

"Will you bring it later?"

He frowned. "You're walking, eating, quite hale now. You've recovered from Prelude nicely. You'll not require the drafts further."

"But—"

"One mark against you, for insolence!" he cried, and he drew forth the ledger he'd held tucked under one flaccid biceps and furiously leafed through it.

"I claim the responsibility of reporting her transgression," Kabdekazonvia said.

"You," the eunuch snarled. "I'll not waste my ink giving you the benefit of Naji's effrontery. You've eaten nothing for three days now. Nothing! Stupid girl; stupid, stubborn girl."

Kabdekazonvia stared groundward, her sloped shoulders appearing to melt off her.

The eunuch scratched the ledger angrily with his quill, slapped the book together, and tucked it back under an armpit.

"Good evening, girls," he said primly, and he jerked the sole door in the chambers open. I caught a glimpse of the Retainers beyond; the eyes of one man met mine and he licked his lips lewdly.

The eunuch closed the door after himself and I shuddered.

"Naji, Misutvia," Greatmother said wearily, "carry Prinrut to her sleeping quarters."

We did so, draping one each of Prinrut's arms about our necks and drag-pulling her forward. I avoided looking at her vacuous stare, closed my mind to how the cool rigidity of her arm about my neck reminded me of the death-lock of a corpse.

With force, Misutvia and I managed to fold Prinrut inside her cave. I crouched at the entrance of the burrow, paralyzed by her glazed eyes and vacant face. I felt impotent and useless.

"Prinrut, wake up," I murmured, and I shook her nearest arm. It was like shaking a felled tree. I dreaded a night without both her and my venom, didn't know how I would survive the dark with only the reality of my imprisonment to keep me company. "Wake up, Prinrut!"

"You've become attached to her," Misutvia said, from where she was crouched beside me. "It'll be hard on you, when she goes."

My heart tripped against my ribs. I studied Misutvia's cool eyes, shadowed beneath her severe ebony bangs.

"Goes?"

"She won't enter the barracks again, Naji. She's decided to die rather than submit once more. Isn't that clear?"

Greatmother appeared behind us, a rigid, toothless, blood-eyed wraith.

"You engage in idle gossip, Misutvia, and poison Naji's mind with your gross speculations. I claim the right to report your transgression on the morrow."

Misutvia shuddered, then pulsated with silent anger.

"Of course, Greatmother," she finally whispered, downcast eyes blazing. "That is your choice."

I didn't sleep that night, not at all. I stole to Prinrut's burrow a clawful of times and pleaded with her to come back to me, to wake up.

Toward dawn, she did. She gasped once, like a fish out of water, eyes protruding, lips gaping wide, then clutched my wrist tightly.

She stared into my eyes, dread as sharp as knives in her look. Panting, she formed her lips as if to speak. She stopped herself, bit her lip, closed her eyes. Squeezed my hand tighter, gripped by a dread she would not share with me.

"Sleep now," I murmured, crawling in beside her, melding my form to fit hers. She felt as cold as rain-slicked bone. "I'm here, we're together; sleep."

I cradled her as if she were my child, and I rocked the two of us until the scream of a jungle bird beyond our prison's stone walls woke everyone in the viagand. Pinch lipped and sallow, all of us, save for Kabdekazonvia, crawled from our stone caves. Morning.

"You slept poorly last night, Najivia," Greatmother began, turning her blooded eyes upon me the moment I straightened from my knees. "I claim the right—"

"I slept soundly," I snapped. "I only woke to do your duty, to wake Prinrut as the eunuch bid you do. You shirked your duty, and *that's* a transgression. I claim the right to report it."

Silence from the viagand women, all standing as stiff as dead songbirds impaled upon roasting skewers. They turned their unblinking dragon eyes upon me.

Misutvia spoke. "She's quite correct, Greatmother. You slept when you should not have. Naji has made a legitimate claim."

"You have no need to inform me of such," Greatmother whispered, and her words were a stale, frail wind. "I strive to be pure."

"Yes, Greatmother," Misutvia said, malice dripping from her lips. "You do. It is your choice."

# FOURTEEN

Kabdekazonvia didn't crawl out from her burrow at all that morning. Just before the eunuchs showed up, Greatmother bid Prinrut and I bring Kabdekazonvia forth. I crouched before her burrow; a putrid, honeyed stench wafted from within.

I quickly stood up and pulled Prinrut away.

"No," I said, head buzzing. "Don't."

Prinrut looked away from me, toward one of the narrow casements high in the central chamber's stone walls. Outside, rain thundered down. The air was heavy with damp. "So. She's free."

"She's dead," I snapped, unnerved. "There's a difference."

"Is there?" Prinrut looked back at me, the red skin about her eyes dewy. I wanted to hold her, love her, protect her. I wanted to slap her, shake her, rail against her apathy. But I did none of it. Instead I informed Greatmother that Kabdekazonvia was no more.

Upon learning of Kabdekazonvia's demise, the plump eunuch fell into a formidable rage, hurling expletives and cushions at the rest of us, howling, beating his chest, and running circles about the central chamber like one gone mad. He fell upon Sutkabde, the poorest eater of us all now that Kabdekazonvia was dead, and rammed pastry after pastry down her throat until she turned blue about the lips and passed out. He dragged her unconscious body to the water buckets by the door and plunged her head in to rouse her. With a gurgle, she came to and vomited all he'd forced her to eat. He dragged her back to the pastry platter and with unrelenting determination, forced a clawful more pastries down her throat.

The rest of us melted into air by remaining motionless with fear. Prinrut plunged into catatonia again.

That night, I could not revive Prinrut, no matter how frequently I visited her, no matter how I pleaded with and shook her, no matter how I cursed and cried. Dawn came. Prinrut remained lock limbed and vacant eyed in her burrow. The eunuchs arrived.

"To Prelude with her," the plump one said, flapping his hands as if shooing out a cur. The boy eunuch dropped to his knees and skittered into her cave to drag her out. He reminded me of a carrion beetle.

I staggered forward to protest. Misutvia caught my arm and shook her head imperceptibly.

"Let her go, Naji." Her lips barely moved, her voice was hardly audible. "It's what she wants."

"But—"

"Let her go."

I could not watch as the mincing eunuch and the boy hauled Prinrut from the viagand. Turning my back against the whispering rasp of her bare feet dragging across stone, I stared at a wall.

I never saw her again.

I awoke at noon from a restless, chill nap during which I'd dreamed constantly of the cocoon-encased haunt writhing in the pit of my belly. Noise had woken me, a sound of activity. I crawled from my burrow, stiffly stood, and shuffled out of the shadows just as six unfamiliar women staggered into the viagand chambers, reeking of venom.

They stood there several moments, wobbling, dazed. As if from an unseen signal, they staggered off in separate directions, seeking caves they'd clearly inhabited before. One woman approached me, blood-punched eyes locked upon my burrow. I stepped aside and watched her crawl into it.

I inhaled the rich citric trail of venom scent she left behind. Greatmother approached me.

"We'll be taken to the bathhouse after noon feast," she said tone-lessly.

I turned cold. Bathhouse? Should I dare ask why we'd be taken there? I should not, I should not.

"Why?" I asked, tensing in anticipation of her declaring my question impudent and therefore a transgression.

But instead, Greatmother said, "To be washed."

I left it at that, knowing that something terrible would happen shortly. Something from which I could escape only through death.

At noon feast, we were joined by the six women who had returned to the viagand. At the plump eunuch's summons, they crawled from their caves, some dragging themselves out by their elbows, looking like belly-slithering salamanders exposed upon the brackish bottom of a drained pond. At Greatmother's behest, we helped the six totter to the feeding cushions. The woman whose arm I held was the color of glair and her skin felt gelatinous. The smell of venom gushed from her as if she were an aquifer of dragon poison.

All of the six refused even the smallest morsel of food. I expected apoplexy from the plump eunuch, but he merely clucked indulgently.

"Good girls, you've worked hard; a reprieve today, then. But tomorrow, hey-o! I want those cheeks filled, those bellies plump. Yes?"

"Yes," they breathed, staring from unblinking eyes that were surrounded by oozing creases of red skin.

The three eunuchs theatrically finished off the remainder of the meal. Afterward, they led Greatmother, me, Misutvia, and Sutkabde to the bathhouse.

At the plump eunuch's orders, we stripped and stood with legs spraddled and arms outstretched. The mincing eunuch and the young boy washed us. Commanded to not touch ourselves while they scrubbed our skin with boar-bristle brushes, we stood immobile, save for our collective shivering.

They had a system, the mincing eunuch and the boy. The mincing eunuch washed from the waist up, while the boy slid along the blue-tiled floor on his knees, scrubbing vigorously at our ankles, poking between the folds of our vulvas, scraping little rolls of old skin and dirt from our thighs.

When the process was finished, we weren't permitted to dry ourselves. This the plump eunuch did, praising or vilifying our bodies at great length.

I did not fight it. Fear and the resignation of those around me sapped me of any inclination toward defiance. Indeed, the thought never once occurred to me to refuse, to rebel. Instead, I made an effort to please, to do exactly as told. Obedience would shield me, would convert the eunuchs from jailers to friends. Or so I wanted to believe.

From the bathhouse, we were led to the Retainers' bunks. It was there that I discovered that the demerits marked against me stood for how many Retainers I was commanded to pleasure. My mother's haunt writhed in its venom-wrought cocoon within me, talons desperately scoring the psychic aegis in an effort to billow into my body and attack those who defiled me.

"There, there, Naji," the plump eunuch crooned as he led my shattered body down night-darkened corridors an eternity later. "See how well the Retainers like you? When you learn their ways a little better, as Greatmother has, your skills will help you bleed less."

The medic's den was a cobwebbed and dank grotto. An apothecary's chest and a three-legged table covered with steel instruments stood across from a bamboo cot. The eunuch led me to the cot. He then departed, taking his lantern with him, and I lay there shivering until at last a man swept in, gowns reeking of tobacco smoke.

His many coiled braids gleamed in his lantern's light as he stood above me, lips compressed above his neat, sharp beard.

"Could you not have washed first?" he asked in disbelief. He thumped his lantern down on the table and sutured closed my wounds.

I dreamed that night while alone and venom-deprived in the medic's den. I dreamed of Kiz-dan and her babe. Kiz-dan, understand, was the holy sister I'd taken with me when I'd fled Convent Tieron, but after we reached Clutch Re, my dependence upon venom almost killed Kiz-dan's babe. One day I'd returned to the home we'd made for ourselves in the Zone of the Dead to find her and her child gone.

Perhaps I dreamed of her as my violated body shivered uncontrollably in the medic's dank grotto because, by my brutal treatment in the Retainers' bunks, I'd had the deceptive security and sense of community in the viagand chambers wrested violently away from me. I had had, once again in my life, lost a sense of home to violence, however illusory and peculiar that feeling of home had been.

In my dream, Kiz-dan stood upon a rickety rope-and-wood bridge, suspended far above a deep chasm, and she held little Yimyam in her arms. He was playing with her chin, trying to open her mouth and toy with her teeth. He babbled merrily. I stood on the chasm's bank, twining grass stalks into twists. I didn't know why I did so. I was compelled. Stacks and stacks of the twists surrounded me, teeming with vermin.

Kiz-dan lifted a hand to wave at me. Little Yimyam followed her hail and gurgled with delight at the sight of me. The bridge snapped.

The sound was like the crack of a whip, magnified a hundredfold, and Kiz-dan cried out and lunged toward me, one hand clutching Yimyam to her chest, the other outstretched in my direction. Her hand was close; her fingertips brushed my leg.

But I did not reach to grab her.

No.

I turned and walled myself deeper within the vermin-infested stacks of grass twists, while mother and child plunged wailing to their deaths.

I woke sweating and sobbing, and it took me a long time afterward to fall back into sleep.

I was left alone in the impenetrable dark of the medic's grotto for an indeterminable time. I slept, I woke, I hungered, my wounds wept. Then the plump eunuch appeared, lantern swinging. Misutvia limped in after him, her sallow cheeks caved in with pain. She held one arm to her chest.

"Sit on the floor," the eunuch said curtly. "The medic will come shortly, hey."

He took the lantern with him and thumped the door shut, congealing us to the dark. After a pause, I heard Misutvia slide down a wall to the floor.

My teeth clacked together from a shudder.

"We'll be taken to the stables on the morrow. The venom will help," Misutvia said. Her voice was hoarse, as if strong hands had recently wrapped about her throat.

"The Retainers look after the dragons here, mucking their stalls, feeding them, grooming them. They're criminals all, serving a life sentence in Temple's employ. They're also superficial guards, though even they don't take that duty seriously; we're surrounded by jungle, hidden and unknown to all but the Ranreeb and the few deranged daronpuis that are stationed here on a rotational basis. Understand me, Naji?"

She spoke quickly, and I realized that she was not only distracting both herself and me from what we'd been subjected to, but also using this rare opportunity to impart information without the presence of others impeding her tongue.

"How many Retainers are there?" I asked, teeth chattering.

"Seven."

There had seemed many more of them than that. Many more.

"And daronpuis?" I asked.

"Five residing here each season. Zealots, all."

"Will the daronpuis . . . ?" I choked on my question. She understood it nonetheless.

"No, they won't touch you in that manner. But they will hurt you if your interpretations of what you hear during your union with a dragon don't please them. They have methods."

"How do I please them?"

"You've lain with a dragon before?"

I hesitated; we were forbidden to talk of our previous lives.

"You know I don't claim transgressions against any but Greatmother," Misutvia said impatiently. "Answer the question. We've little time before the medic shows up."

"Yes. I have," I breathed. "I've known a dragon."

"So you've heard the so-called canticles."

Canticles. An excellent word for what I'd heard: a dragonchanted text, a melodic composition of dragon scripture and historical lore.

"I've heard snatches of them, yes."

"Focus on the emotion those hallucinations provoke, splice them with your own experiences in life, and create an interpretation from that. Think of what Temple wants, what it needs: power. Feed them names that suggest how they might increase that."

"I know nothing of politics. I'm a Clutch Re rishi."

A pause. I could hear her wondering how and why a lowly invisible serf had ever ended up here, in this secret jail for women, where the imprisoned were forced, at the behest of the Ranreeb, to be intimate with dragons.

"I see. Well. It will go harder for you. The rest of us are bayen; we know Ranon ki Cinai politics, know people of influence and power. We've gleaned, in our lives outside these walls, a little of the alliances and conspiracies woven throughout the fabric of Malacar and the Archipelago. We use that knowledge in our interpretations."

Alliances. Conspiracies. People of influence and power. I knew none of that.

Wait. Kratt and his dragonmaster.

In remembering them, I remembered what motivated them: They sought the answer to the mystery of why no eggs laid by domesticated dragons ever hatched a bull. Surely Temple sought the same. Of course they did. Did Misutvia guess at such? What *did* she think her purpose here was?

I asked.

"Purpose," she said bitterly. "To glut the Ranreeb's sick fantasies. To provide him with venom-inspired babble that might strengthen Temple. To suffer and die as a prisoner, for wanting more freedoms than a woman should want."

She did not believe the rite to be sacred. Nor had she guessed at the Ranreeb's true goal.

"If you are able, Naji, endure this life as long as you can," Misutvia said, her voice quickening. "I'm from the Caranku Bri of Lireh. Surely you've heard of our clan? It's the wealthiest merchant guild in Malacar, and I *know* my mother must have sent news of my disappearance to my brother by now. I'm certain he's returning early from his expedition north, even as we speak. He'll find me yet, Naji. I have to endure until that time."

Her excitement was infectious, but I couldn't share her view so facilely.

"How will he possibly find us?" I asked. "This prison and what goes on here will be a secret known only to a select few."

"Malaban, my brother, is well connected. He owns lands and factories, and his fleet of ships is one of the finest on the coast. Surely you've heard of Malaban Bri of Lireh?"

"I'm rishi," I reminded her. "Does he own dragons?"

"Temple has never granted him the right to own a Clutch, but he's been granted license to own a clawful of dragons. He has fifteen at the moment, five of which retain their wings."

The man was as powerful as she said, then. Perhaps she was right; perhaps her brother *could* find us here. But I was still somewhat doubtful. After all, she'd been imprisoned, despite her status.

So I asked her how that had occurred, how one of her status had ended up imprisoned in the Ranreeb's unknown jail.

"Do you think that just because we are bayen women, our lives are ones of luxury and ease?" Misutvia replied. "Some of us are here because we wanted too much. Too much knowledge, too much equality, too much freedom. We weren't docile and domestic enough for whoever it was that eventually applied sufficient pressure on Temple to have us imprisoned. Others of us are here because we just didn't please. As women, we are disposable and replaceable, remember."

"Even bayen women."

"Bayen, rishi, it makes little difference." Her tone grew brusque. "The medic will be here soon, and there's one other thing we have to discuss: Prinrut. After we're returned to the viagand chambers from the dragons, one of us must return to Prelude, to record Prinrut's history on the walls. You read the histories while you were there, yes?"

"Yes."

"No one knows of them but the viagand. The Retainers, the eunuchs, the daronpuis, they've never entered Prelude, even to clean it. I've heard tell they send a cur in, to eat the filth from the floor. The histories on the walls are one of the secrets Greatmother, in her unfathomable piety, has always kept."

"How long has she been here?"

"I'm talking about Prinrut," Misutvia said sharply. "Listen. One of us has to return to Prelude: You should request such. This is the way it's done. You stop eating, act despondent around the eunuchs, and state that you require the cleansing of seclusion to purify your mind from the insidious thoughts plaguing you. In Prelude, you search the walls and find the incomplete histories. Identify Prinrut's story by her age. She was twenty-two years old. Remember that: twenty-two."

"I can't return to Prelude," I said in horror.

"You have no wish to do this for her? To learn who she was?"

"I can't return," I stammered.

"It'll be for a short time only."

"And if I don't go?"

"Her history goes unrecorded and her name never joins those on the walls. You'll never learn who she truly was, and her spirit will remain trapped here, as Prinrut, until you voice her free name and release her."

"You do it. You go."

"Think about it."

"I can't."

"Oh, and Kabdekazonvia, inscribe her demise upon the walls, too. She was twenty-six years old."

Lantern light and footsteps outside the door.

We both stilled, and the medic entered.

My blood rushed loud in my ears and I felt certain that he would know Misutvia and I had been talking, just by the guilty pounding of my heart. But after a cursory examination of my wounds, he merely turned to Misutvia and set her arm.

We didn't have a chance to talk further, Misutvia and I, for as soon as the medic had set the broken bones, the plump eunuch came and fetched us both. I could scarce walk, so the eunuch pulled me along, my wrist held firmly in one of his paws. He murmured words he meant as encouragement.

"Just a little way to walk, Naji; not far and we'll be at the stables. Not long now, not far. One more set of stairs and you'll be there."

It was day. Verdigris light filtered through the vine-choked casements we passed, and diurnal lizards skittered lightning quick along the stone walls. Outside, rain thundered down; the Wet had started in earnest. Rivulets of rainwater streamed in a ceaseless flow down the insides of the casements, splashing upon the invasive vines divaricating along the corridors, forming brackish pools on the corridor floor.

Obviously this shabby stone fortress had been built in slipshod haste, solely that the Ranreeb might learn the secret to breeding bulls in captivity. I felt an empathy for the stone edifice. Situated where it should not be, invaded and disfigured by aggressive, indifferent life, it was no different from my body. I didn't hate the stone walls about me. No. I understood, only too well, that the enemy lay within the hearts of my jailers.

What I didn't understand yet was that my enemy, too, lay within me. Within the complacency my fear had wrought.

If banished loneliness were to have a smell, if the promise of ecstasy were to be a scent, it would be that of venom.

As the citric tang of the dragons' poison grew thick on the air, I knew we were near the stables. I stumbled, gasped, felt unbidden tears trickle down my cheeks. Despite my shattered physical and mental state, or perhaps because of it, I longed for the dragons' embrace with a shuddering intensity. Without knowing from where the words sprang, I began muttering.

> *Embrace with thy obsidian-jeweled mouth,*
> *a creature made of blood coagulated.*
> *Embrace! and the honey light of wings ignited*
> *will teach that which they give not unto men.*

The eunuch abruptly stopped. Annoyed by the pause, I looked from him to Misutvia. The eunuch wore a look of utter astonishment. Misutvia was an ocelot crouched in shadow, all dilated eyes, wariness, disciplined muscles poised to spring.

"What spoke you?" she whispered.

"The dragons are calling," I answered, and I pulled the eunuch forward, toward the light.

The stables were steeped in venom, flagstone and flaxen chaff tacky with toxic mildew. Light blazed from sconces upon the venom-sweated walls, banishing shadow. Four stalls, four dragons. Four snouts huffed below eyes slant and amber and unblinking. Five daronpuis chanted stanzas while dashing oiled whisks over the heads of two women knelt in supplication. The daronpuis each chanted different stanzas, their murmured voices rolling and merging into one another like waves stirred from opposite shores of a lake.

> *I make thee mine own peer,*
> *reckless of what must come when thy luck must turn*
> *in the turning of time.*
> *My shame!*

The words hissed from my mouth, as splendid and shocking as imported perfumes and pearls, ebony and coconuts, as threatening as the heaving seas upon which ships carried such varied treasure. The daronpuis shambled to an incredulous halt. The dragons' eyes bored into me.

The dragons were bony with neglect, citrine scars where their wings had been amputated at birth running like accusing fingers along their flanks. Their dorsal ridges, briskets, and eye sockets protruded. Scales the dull green of desert cacti and the brown of dried blood hung as loose as rotting teeth upon wrinkled hides. The putrid stench of pressure sores on claw pads riddled the venom-rich air.

Words unreeled from my throat like kite silk lifted by wind.

*I saw what I hoped never to see alive,*
*the cur that fouled me pampered and well fed,*
*the black snakes in plumes, the good yearning for death.*

From where they knelt, beads of consecration oil dripping off their long, thin hair, Greatmother and Sutkabde stared at me, their pallid faces turning like orchids toward light.

"What blasphemy is this?" one of the daronpuis hissed. "Eunuch, control your charge! Is she mad? Make her kneel; how dare she foul the air with her voice."

The eunuch shoved me forward, angry in his fright, and forced me to kneel alongside Greatmother and Sutkabde. Misutvia joined us, eyes hooded beneath her lowered lids.

"The effrontery!" another daronpu growled. "Is she like this always?"

I shuddered where I knelt, fearful, remembering the Retainers' bunks, the ledger wherein the eunuch scribed marks against our names. What madness had gripped me to speak so?

"Holy guardians of Ranon ki Cinai," the eunuch murmured, kowtowing to the daronpuis from where he stood behind my back. "She has never acted this way before."

"It's the venom," one daronpu said, voice rich with certainty and not just a little smug with his own knowledge. "I've seen others react this way, from time to time. The Canon of Medicine recommends the juice of celery and honey, mixed with galangale and taken with the juice of a mouse ear, to remedy such venom fever. Failing that, tongue amputation, with white pepper applied thrice daily to the stump."

Grunts from the gathered daronpuis.

"I'll prepare the concoction at once, holy guardians," the eunuch murmured. "I doubt she'll require tongue amputation, though if necessary, I will not hesitate to do such. But you won't give further trouble, will you, Naji?"

His corpulent form leaned over my shoulder and he pinched me, hard, in the small of my back.

"Forgive my impudence," I mumbled, kowtowing.

More grunts from the daronpuis.

The eunuch departed. After several moments, the daronpuis resumed their circumambulation, fat-swollen cheeks pulping out holy stanzas. *Splatter-splat* went their whisks above my head, and their consecration oil stung the knuckle cuts on my cheeks. But I blinked away the pain and concentrated upon the immediate future, upon my expectation of venom's burn.

As if sensing my impending descent into the toxin's realm, the haunt trapped within me roiled like a maggot exposed to sunlight. My belly rippled beneath my bitoo much as a woman's does when she is with child.

Shuddering, I awaited submersion, immersion, a merging with the divine.

# FIFTEEN

Time passed, in the viagand.

I experienced the madness and euphoria of dragonsong, was violated in the Retainers' bunks, and "slept restlessly" with Misutvia, though our familiarities with each other were never as tender as what I'd experienced with Prinrut.

I babbled in the recovery chambers while greed-cruel daronpuis hung on my every word. I spoke of nests and good dragon fodder, bull hatchlings and well-groomed scales, intimating in my delirium that by improving the health of brooder dragons on all Clutches, a bull might hatch from an egg laid in captivity.

The daronpuis avidly recorded my words and I realized I'd struck gold. The imprisoned women, bayen all, knew nothing of the debilitating effects of hunger, knew nothing of the needs of a dragon. Dream fevered, they all spouted politics, intimating in their interpretations of the dragons' song how Temple might fortify its pillars and rid itself of destructive weeds.

I, on the other hand, spoke not of Temple or political stratagem, but of the dragons themselves. Of rich yolks produced only through the best fodder, of clean nests that a brooder might sit a clutch of eggs in comfort. I spoke of what I knew: how starvation and ill health reduced fertility.

For awhile, the novelty of my interpretations earned me much favoritism, so that my obligatory visit to the Retainers' bunks prior to each visit to the stables was perfunctory, a brief sojourn where I was subjected to the crude ways of only one Retainer, he who by brawn and brain was deemed highest in the criminals' rank.

During this time of favoritism, when my health was still somewhat with me and the promise of merging with the divine shone star bright before me, I found the strength of spirit to request a return to Prelude. During my brief, dark stay in that stinking sarcophagus, I released the spirits of Prinrut and Kabdekazonvia from imprisonment.

Prinrut, I learned, had come from Clutch Ka. Her name: Yimplar's Limia. She'd been accused by her claimer of thrice provoking miscarriages of boy infants, and had been arrested for those heinous crimes. What little I knew of Prinrut, I was sure she'd not had the nature for such acts. She would have wanted a babe, certainly. The miscarriages had been natural and tragic. Her claimer had been impatient and influential enough to rid himself of her using Temple, and had probably assumed she would be made an onai, a holy woman serving in a Temple sanctuary for dying bulls. Or maybe he hadn't cared what her future would be. Maybe he'd forgotten her the moment Temple had arrested her and his next claimed woman lay beneath him.

Kabdekazonvia had been arrested for recurrent insubordination toward her claimer, her kin, and Temple daronpuis. I could not reconcile the image of a defiant woman with that of sallow, gaunt Kabdekazonvia. Her apathy had been so complete. How could anyone who had once been so bold succumb to such lifeless submission?

I never thought to look at myself when I asked such a question.

When I'd completed Prinrut's and Kabdazonvia's histories, meticulously carving the words into the damp wood with a stone, I whispered their names. I thought I felt Prinrut's spirit enfold me briefly, tenderly, before dissipating beneath the crack under Prelude's door. I imagined Prinrut taking flight as a trembling mist through stone corridors, to spiral out a vine-choked casement in a helix column.

A Skykeeper appeared then, I was certain: It coalesced from the green jungle air, scooped the misty helix of Prinrut into its beak, and carried her to the One Dragon, safe in the Celestial Realm, where her life force was fed into its maw. Her essence combined with the Dragon's and, fortified through recombination, the Dragon continued its eternal battle against evil.

Prinrut was free and whole.

Upon murmuring Kabdekazonvia's name, I thought lights exploded about Prelude, white-orange sparks thrown from a temporal fire. Sharp and turbulent, the sparks zinged chaotically off Prelude's walls, eventually discovering the crack under the door. Crackling and hissing like compressed bonfires, they disappeared from my sight.

This is what I thought I saw, and though I've never seen such since, I'm convinced that it was no hallucination evoked by the foamy residue of venom in my blood. No. I'm convinced that what I saw was the numinous release and regeneration of the essence of the women I'd known.

Understand, we didn't lie with the dragons often. Such would have killed any woman, regardless of her tolerance for the dragons' poison. Only thrice did I lie with the dragons during those long months in the viagand. Three times only. Yet how memorable they were.

What did I learn, during those pleated, undulating, wildly contracting and expanding days in the brooder stalls and the recovery berths? What did I hear?

Song that glorified and cleansed, melody that redeemed and transcended. Whispers melancholic and grief laden. I heard earth, heard water, saw fogged images of blood and radiance. I smelled loss and constraint, tasted barbarity and amputation. Rapture was a sound, had texture, knew grief.

Images sometimes flitted through the songs, fractured and

blurred, seething, fuming, fermenting. Words belched from my mouth, disgorged by the tumult rampaging through me. Convulsive and savage, scorching and bestial, the images I saw and the eruption of words clashed and howled in orgiastic storm.

I felt my cloaca stretch as thin as fine paper as I laid an egg.

I flew from tree crown to tree crown, seeking my hatchling while the scent of humans burned like sulfur in my nostrils.

My hind legs trembled as, flanks heaving with exertion, I fought the young upstart that would mount my brooders.

But the images were not like this, not as I've presented them. They were frayed jigsaw pieces, worn at edge by time, and my intoxicated mind pieced them together as a confused whole, a collage that made little sense without the song and empathy that structured them. It was only during the dream-dizzy days and nights I slept in my burrow back in the viagand chambers that my mind assembled the pieces into coherent images, and in such assembling, many jigsaw pieces were lost, and pieces from the puzzle of my own life inserted instead for a logical picture to result.

Certain images *did* recur from each visit to the stables, though. Over and over, I experienced shinchiwouk as a bull. Over and over I felt territorial rage against my opponent, fought young bulls and old ones that I might prevail and mount the brooders gathered to watch. Long after I'd been returned to the viagand chambers, my limbs would twitch in a flashback of lunging, striking, turning, protecting flank and wing and throat. Over and over I triumphed, or was subdued and retreated.

And over and over, I felt the harrowing grief of losing a hatchling to python, vulture, or man. Over and over, I felt the agony of knife amputating wing from flank, felt hobbles about my forelegs, felt the burden of yoke across my shoulders.

But never once did I receive even an inkling as to why an egg laid in a Clutch was never an involucre for a bull dragon.

Never once.

\*     \*     \*

My time of grace, if any stage of imprisonment can be deemed one of grace, was not long-lived.

After awhile, the uniqueness of my interpretations of the dragons' music wore off and the daronpuis tired of my talk about fodder and brooder health. That, coupled with my increasingly irrational rambling while in the grips of venom's embrace, only frustrated the daronpuis. Other strikes against me: my rapidly declining appetite; my disinterest in even pretending to create art, that I avoid sloth and animate my mind; the frequency of my "restless sleeps" in the viagand chambers, claimed against me by Greatmother and others as transgressions; my pallor and pustulant eyes; the frequency with which I wept for want of venom while in the presence of the eunuchs.

When Najiwaivia, One Hundred First Girl, arrived in the viagand chambers one afternoon, and shortly after, Najikazonvia and Najirutvia, I knew my time of favoritism was over. Those three would provide fresh interpretations of the canticles. My waning advantage was gone. Even in my debilitated, hazy state, I realized that my next obligatory visit to the Retainers' bunks would go very hard indeed, and those unfathomable steel instruments in the recovery chambers would be employed by the daronpuis upon my person, that I might interpret the dragons' song better.

I knew, then, that I'd become like Kabdekazonvia. I yielded to the knowledge as I yielded to everything else my jailers subjected me to.

I don't know who said it first—Najiwaivia, if memory serves—but it roused us all from our individual stupors.

"Please forgive my insolence, Greatmother, but haven't the eunuchs usually come by now?"

My lids rasped against my eyes like sacking as I blinked. Slowly, my gaze focused on Greatmother, who sat across from me on a cushion.

We had gathered, by rote, upon the cushions and divans in the central chamber for the morning feeding and were sitting there staring unblinkingly inward. I'd had a poor night, as I oft did after a clawful of days had passed since my last union with a dragon and the venom in my blood was as cold and brittle as rime. My mother's haunt had maggot-roiled within the cocoon in my psyche all night, clawing wildly at the membrane that enclosed it. Even in daylight as I sat with the rest of the viagand on the feeding cushions, waiting for the eunuchs to show up, I could feel the abhorrent squirming.

"She's right," another one of the new women murmured. "Haven't the eunuchs usually come by now, Greatmother?"

Greatmother cocked her head to one side and stared hard at the jungle hues slipping through a casement.

"It would seem they are tardy today," she eventually said in her measured, toneless voice. "I'm sure they have good reason."

"How long do we sit here?"

"Until they come."

"But we've been sitting for some time already. It's past noon. I have need to relieve myself, Greatmother. Forgive me."

We *all* looked at the light streaming through the casements, then, looked at the angle in which it fell as weak, wavering fingers upon floor and wall. I felt the merest nudge of surprise at noticing it was true: We'd sat there since dawn, and noon had come and gone. I also dully realized that I needed to visit the latrines.

Greatmother licked her chapped lips. "We must wait further."

Silence. Beside me, Misutvia drew air into her lungs as though with great effort. "This hasn't happened before, not since I've been here."

We all looked at Greatmother, waiting for her to defend the eunuchs' behavior or explain it by way of stating that such a thing had occurred before in her many years of imprisonment.

She did neither; merely stared unblinking straight ahead of her, wan face expressionless.

"Please." One of the newest women spoke, her voice a strained whisper. "I must relieve myself."

The urgency in her voice made my own need urgent. Others shifted about me, aware of their own states. We all sat there, unmoving, until one of the new women cried out in dismay. She clambered to her feet, ran to a painting easel, snatched at a crock of dried paint, placed it on the floor, hefted her bitoo, and straddled it.

I almost wet myself at the sound.

At once, we were all struggling to stand. A moment of chaos followed. Greatmother and Sutkabde were too debilitated to move quick enough, and they soiled themselves. The rest of us jostled for the few remaining paint pots and filled them to capacity.

In the ensuing silence, we stared at each other in horror.

"We shall be stoned," one of the newest said, trembling.

"That would be preferable to what will happen instead," Sutkabde replied.

"You instill debilitating fear in the viagand with your remark," Greatmother chided. "That is a transgression. I claim the right to report it."

"And I claim the right to report that you soiled floor and bitoo both," Misutvia swiftly said.

A pause. Then chaos ensued as we all breathlessly claimed the right to report everyone's transgression of urinating in paint pots. Our world was so fearful and narrow, understand, that it not only made sense at the time, but seemed an integral part of survival.

Transgressions claimed, heads thumping from tension and thirst, we drifted back to the cushions and divans and sat. We waited. We dozed. We woke raging with thirst in darkness. No day-shine drifted through the casements, only the night's chill. In the blackness, fear blossomed.

"What is this? Have we been abandoned to die?" a disembodied voice whispered in the dark.

The silent quickening of our hearts.

"Who spoke?" Greatmother said. "Such fearmongering is a transgression. Identify yourself."

A wondrous silence as no one responded. A thrill pimpled my skin and I momentarily felt brave.

"We could ask the Retainers guarding the door for water," I suggested. "It's unlocked. Someone could crack it open a little."

No one would dare such temerity.

"We will wait," Greatmother pronounced, her hoarse voice part of the dark. "It is a test of our purity, of our obedience. We will wait."

"So this *has* occurred before," a clipped voice stated. Misutvia.

A pause before Greatmother replied. "No."

"We have no reason to think this is a test, then," Misutvia argued. "We've never been tested before. I've never heard tell of such testing, either."

"You admit to idle gossip. Gossip is a transgression. I claim—"

"I admit to no such thing," Misutvia said with an anger as wondrous as the defiant silence that had met Greatmother's command, a short while ago, that the unidentified speaker distinguish herself. "It is the one who imparts the gossip who transgresses, not the one who overhears."

A cumbersome silence from Greatmother as she strove to find the resources to respond.

"If not for the receiving ears, there is no gossip, only mutters into air," Greatmother finally said. "Thus, you have transgressed."

"And by extension of your argument, you also have transgressed, Greatmother," Misutvia countered. "For if ears overhearing the words of another are guilty of transgression, then so too are eyes that witness such. And you, Greatmother, as our uncontested and recognized elder, said not a word to prevent our earlier transgression of voiding bladder into paint pot. I therefore hold you responsible for all our ills, and claim the right to report this great transgression."

A profound silence as the lot of us slowly realized what nest of snakes Misutvia had just overturned.

Who was responsible for a transgression, the witness who could have prevented it or the transgressor? Both? But to what degree? What then if the transgressor knew not that she was violating some esoteric law, but the witness did?

My sluggish mind wrestled with the questions. Irritated, I spoke without thought, licking lips shrivelled for want of water.

"It won't matter who transgresses and who witnesses what if there's no one to report to."

I tensed at my own nerve, waited for a bodiless voice in the dark to pronounce my statement as fearmongering and therefore a transgression. From the direction where Greatmother sat like a ghostly wraith, I heard her gather breath and strength to declare such.

Misutvia spoke before Greatmother could utter her first word.

"We'll return to our burrows to sleep. Pointless to sit here further." Misutvia's voice was firm. "In the morning, if no one appears, we'll do as Naji suggested. We'll ask the two Retainers outside the door for water."

"We'll need it," I croaked hoarsely, and thirst moved all the women into murmuring fervent agreement. With venom in our veins, thirst was a constant, unwanted companion. We all craved water, ceaselessly. Going without it for this one day had given us pounding heads and a restless, irritable mien. "We won't last long without water."

"No," Misutvia agreed. "We won't last long."

With the unexplained, unexpected change in our routine, the entombing darkness of night suddenly seemed thicker, chiller, fraught with crouched menace. I made my way to Misutvia's burrow and crawled in with her.

Her bony frame and gelid skin offered little by way of comfort, but it was not physical succor I sought; it was solace of spirit.

"The other viagand women," I whispered into her ear. "The ones currently in the dragon stalls and recovery berths. I wonder if they're also being tested in such a manner."

"Don't be sensational," Misutvia snapped.

I shuddered against her and held my tongue, and I realized, by her very irritation, that she too was greatly unnerved by this sudden turn of events.

Sleep came grudgingly that night to both of us, and when it eked my way, I dreamed ceaselessly of the haunt clawing its way free within me. Just before dawn, I could no longer bear the vision and the accompanying sensations. I left Misutvia's burrow and returned to mine, passing in the vapid light the gray shadows of others slinking back to their dens. We averted our eyes from each other in a tacit complicity of pretending we never saw each other. A short while later, we crawled from our burrows.

My thirst was paramount. I could scarce swallow. My eyes felt gummy. We waited, swaying, for someone to claim the first transgression against another, for the violation of sleeping restlessly. My spittle was too scarce to waste; I would not speak lest someone claimed first against me.

We all remained silent, muted by thirst. Greatmother stood in a stupor, seemingly unaware of us, of our predicament. Exhausted, I broke the spell by staggering over to the feeding cushions. The others shuffled after me.

Long moments passed as sunlight oozed through the narrow casements in the stone walls, obfuscated by entangled vines, thick tree trunks, curtains of moss, and ceilings of leaf and frond. No rain fell outside, but fog dew dripped incessantly upon bract and leaf.

I could stand it no longer. I rose, went to the cool, dew-beaded stone walls, and licked. The dust-gritted pearls of condensation at once disappeared upon the swollen surface of my tongue. Lizard-like, I continued lapping the walls. It wasn't long before others copied me.

With our thirst not so much satiated as masked by the dampness now in our mouths, we returned to our divans. Greatmother, I no-ticed, had not permitted herself the dew on the stone walls. She sat rigidly staring at nothing, eyes slightly wider than usual. Her lips were parted, the gap of her missing front teeth visible to all.

We waited, and with each passing heartbeat, the tension and our thirst climbed higher. At last, one of the new women spoke. She addressed Misutvia.

"Who will do it, then? Ask for water?"

We all looked at the door. On the other side stood two Retain-ers, burly criminals permitted to assault us at scheduled dates as re-muneration for their service to fortress, Temple, and dragon.

"Naji will do it," Misutvia said.

"Why me?" I cried.

"Someone must, else we expire from thirst."

"I went to Prelude. You do this."

She shook her head. One of the new women whimpered.

"And what if the Retainers' answer is rape?" Greatmother said, and her voice husked from her parched throat like sand rasping over a reed mat. "Or simply an order to get back inside and remain silent? Then what has Naji gained for her audacity? Nothing but shame and punishment. No, we stay. We wait. It is our duty."

Sutkabde neither nodded nor disagreed. She merely stared at Greatmother. One of the new women began weeping.

Misutvia met my eyes. "I'd rather know I'm to die, and suffer in gaining the knowledge, than have death creep gradually over me."

"Isn't that what happens here regardless?" gasped the weeping woman. "Death by slow degrees."

Misutvia colored and pursed her lips.

"Our duty here," Greatmother rasped, "is to serve Temple. We know not in our ignorance the great workings of holy minds, of holy ways. We will sit here and wait for the eunuchs' return."

"We're prisoners, not acolytes," Misutvia growled. "I have no duty to Temple. I don't willingly serve it. I'm enslaved."

"You have lain with the dragons," Greatmother breathed. "You are privy to divinity. You are blessed by being permitted such a hallowed touch, by performing such a sacred service."

"I'm a prisoner!" Misutvia barked.

"You deny that you've experienced divinity?" Greatmother asked.

"Of course I do. We suffer nothing but hallucinations provoked by the venom. There's nothing divine about whoring to a dragon."

"A hallucination does not preclude the divine, but is merely the form the divine dialogue takes," Greatmother rasped. "As recipients of such, as the dragons' chosen servants, our duty is to submit and obey."

"To rape? Humiliation? Death?"

"We earn with our suffering the reward of lying with the dragons. The blood we spill cleanses us, washes away our impurities."

"You're mad, to believe such."

"If I did not believe such, Misutvia, how could I daily submit to all I'm subjected to?" Greatmother said, chin lifted, blood-bathed eyes unblinking. "Who is mad, you who submit for no reason, or I who submit out of faith?"

Misutvia stared, words eluding her, and I suddenly saw myself for what I'd become.

"Greatmother's right," I said slowly. "If we don't want to be here, why do we remain? That door"—I pointed a bony, pale finger—"is unlocked. It's guarded by unarmed men. There are seven of us to their two. At night, when their snores rattle the door, what's ever stopped us from overcoming them?"

"With what?" one of the new women asked. "Look how feeble we are."

"We use those." Misutvia nodded at the art easels. "We break them apart, use the wood as bludgeons and stakes."

I frowned. "The Retainers would hear us smashing the easels. They'd come in and stop us before we were armed."

"We wrap the easels in carpet before breaking them apart, place pillows over the door to muffle the sound." Misutvia's color was high.

I licked my lips. "How do we break them?"

"With our feet. The easels are old, the joints rickety. I've checked."

"You've thought of this before," I said, and Misutvia nodded slowly. "Then why . . . ?"

But no sooner did I start asking the question than I stopped. I knew why she'd never suggested it before: Revolt required collective effort, required teamwork and collusion. Until now, we'd been too set in our submissive ways, too focused on gathering transgressions against each other. We'd been unified by our sudden abandonment by the eunuchs. The old order was broken.

The other reason why Misutvia had never before suggested revolt was because to escape was to turn away from the dragons' numinous embrace. Even if she scoffed at the divinity of the rite, she was not immune to venom's addictive power and pleasures. Where else but here would these women ever have the opportunity to offer themselves to a dragon's tongue?

Greatmother echoed my thought by speaking it aloud. "Once you leave this fortress, you leave forever the dragons' grace. Never again will you be lifted to the great world of light that lies behind our paltry destinies. Never again will you be embraced by celestial glory, merged with bliss. You forgo ecstasy for starvation in the jungle, celestial union for the tear of feral teeth through heart and brain."

"No," I countered, heart beating as if I'd recently quaffed venom. "Some onais do this thing, too. They've trained the infirm bulls in their care to perform this rite. We could survive the jungle. I've survived it before. We could join a convent somewhere. We'd have access to dragons then."

Misutvia and the three new women gaped at me.

Greatmother shook her head. "You're forbidden to speak of your former life, Naji. In doing so, you turn the devout away from their duties here, beguile them with your tongue."

I swallowed, defiance brewing a spume of turmoil in my gut. "My name isn't Naji. It's Zarq."

Silence followed, as great as a sail that a gust has just blown full and taut.

"Zarq," Misutvia said slowly. "Named after Zarq Car Mano. A woman named after a rebel, then."

I lifted my chin. "Yes."

"Extraordinary."

"Evil," Greatmother breathed. "Do not listen to the beguiling tongue of evil."

"You no longer plan to ask the Retainers for water and direction," Sutkabde breathed. "You plot murder and escape."

Misutvia and I refused to glance at her.

"Shall we make ourselves bludgeons and stakes, then?" I asked.

"Yes," Misutvia said, and she smiled for the first time and last time behind those walls. "Let's arm ourselves."

# SIXTEEN

Not only did we break apart the art easels, but I taught the three new women how to break a nose by slamming the heel of a palm against the bridge, a skill I'd learned as a nine-year-old while living in a traveling merchant's train. They were the strongest of us, those three new women, and the most energetic. They were therefore the most likely to subdue the Retainers and survive. They listened closely, eyes bright.

"If you're close enough, use your forehead, like so," I said, and I clasped Misutvia's temples and, without making contact, demonstrated how to shatter bone and cartilage and stun a victim by slamming forehead against nose. "Remember the testicles: A man's strength is sapped by a blow to the area. But move fast and decisively, yes?"

Swaying from the effort of so much speech and dizzy from lack of water and ill health, I leaned against a wall to steady myself. We all rested for some time, high-strung yet motionless, eyes flitting to and from the door, guarded on the opposite side by the Retainers. At last, Misutvia spoke.

"We know what to do. We'll act now, then."

"Now," I whispered, heart hammering insanely inside of me, my fingers as charged as lightning.

"Now," the three new women breathed.

"Kwano the One Snake, the First Father, the progenitor and spirit of all kwano everywhere, I bid you begone," Greatmother intoned, sanguine eyes riveted upon me. She was uttering the Gyin-gyin, which I'd last heard back in the dragonmaster's stables on Clutch Re, when Ringus had feverishly murmured the incantation against my mother's haunt. "I evoke the powers of Ranon ki Cinai, governed by the exalted Emperor Mak Fa-sren—"

Sutkabde wrapped her arms about herself and began rocking, much as a child about to witness the murder of her father might.

Holding our primitive spears with jagged ends thrust forward, we approached the door. Misutvia laid a hand upon the wooden handle.

"We know what to do. Do it fast; don't hesitate," she mouthed.

"We can do this," I said. Nods all about me.

"On the count of eight, I open the door." She began counting, and for a moment, the room swooped, I tasted death, and my mother's haunt was an oyster-cold clot in my mouth, lodged at the back of my tongue, trying to thrust its way to freedom.

"Eight," Misutvia said, and she flung the door open and we spilled forth, wraithlike and murderous.

Our charge was short-lived.

We spun right, left, turning this way and that in confusion, so intent on clubbing and stabbing that we almost fell upon each other with each dizzy turn. We stopped, chests heaving, and looked about in confusion. Cold bumps shivered over my skin.

"There's no one here," I gasped.

The gloomy corridor was unlit save for the grassy light crawling through the narrow, ivy-choked casement high up at the corridor's end.

"There's no one here," I repeated, and the reality soared through us on hope-feathered wings. As one, we dashed to the end of the corridor, though by the time Misutvia and I reached it, we were stumbling and wheezing and scarce able to stand upright.

We all stopped and stared in disbelief.

Where the corridor turned right, into what had been another

corridor only days before, stood a stone wall. One of the new women reached out with a trembling hand and touched it, checking that it was real.

"We've been sealed in," she whispered. Horror rippled over us and turned my scalp prickly. "There's no way out."

We returned to the chambers and shut the door. It felt safer, somehow, to have that door shut.

Misutvia walked straight toward Greatmother, who sat motionless, still droning the Gyin-gyin.

"Close your lips, old woman," she snapped. "No murder has been done. We've been sealed in by stone."

Greatmother stopped breathing for long moments. Then her chest swelled mightily and she exhaled her words on a rattled breath. "The One Dragon has subverted your evil plans. Now we shall await whatever befalls us next."

Sutkabde stared at the floor, face expressionless.

Gloom crept through the casements in the chambers and the air grew cool and damp with the promise of rain. A gust slapped broad hosta leaves one against the other, sounding like meat fillets smacked upon a butchering table. I collapsed on a divan, heart and thoughts racing.

I remembered, now, how uneasy the plump eunuch had seemed when last he'd visited us, and how cold, paltry, and ill prepared that evening's feast had been. His shins had been scraped, too, as if he'd recently fallen . . . or as if he'd had to clamber over a partially constructed wall to reach us. The water boy had glanced repeatedly over his shoulder, toward the door, the entire time he ladled water into our mouths.

Of course. He'd been afraid he'd be sealed in with us.

Why had we women not been concerned by those subtle yet portentous changes? Especially the greatest change: The mincing eunuch had not led us to the latrines that night, but instead produced two chamber pots and ordered us to use them. Why had we not questioned his hasty explanation that the latrines were undergoing repair and could not be used until morn?

Passivity can be smothering. Passivity can be as lethal as an adder's poison.

The eunuchs had known, at least three days ago, what was to be our fate. They'd brought us a cursory last meal even as the Retainers were erecting a stone wall to seal us in. Had Greatmother guessed then that something had been amiss? Or had she truly believed, in her unwavering faith, that the latrines were being repaired? And as for the rest of us, how could we not even have heard the activity at the corridor's end, beyond the chamber's door?

Little it mattered now.

Outside, a sudden rain squall drummed against frond and leaf alike. My throat clenched at the watery profusion and my swollen tongue cleaved to the roof of my mouth as if it were a block of chalk.

"We need water," I croaked. My eyes fell upon the paint crocks overspilling with urine. "Misutvia. If we pushed three divans over to that wall, and if we stacked them, might we not climb up to the casement and catch water in those crocks?"

"And drink it?" squealed one of the new women. "We've soiled those crocks, we can't drink from them! And we most certainly can't consume water unpurified by Temple."

"Rainwater is clean enough," I said shortly. "Rishi drink it all the time without Temple's interference."

"I am not rishi," the woman declared, outraged.

"That's right, you're a prisoner. A difference, there."

She pointed a trembling finger at me. "You're a serf, aren't you? A filthy second-rate cur."

"I'm no different than you."

"You aren't worth the spit in my mouth!"

"For what little spit you've got right now, I'll warrant you're right again," I muttered, dragging myself upright. "I'm worth more."

"How dare you!"

"Fighting amongst ourselves will achieve nothing," Misutvia snapped. "Zarq is right. We need to trap rain. Those that help will drink, regardless of their status outside these walls. Understand?"

No one replied one way or the other. After a moment, Misutvia ordered two of the new women to help move a divan beneath the casement.

My suggestion didn't work, though. The casement was too narrow to thrust a crock through. Instead, we pulled a drapery from a wall, shook dust from it, rolled it into a rope, and fed it outside. When it was heavy with water, we hauled it back in and wrung the water out. It was laborious work and fetched little to drink. Sutkabde sucked the cloth each time after we'd rung it out, but didn't offer to help, and therefore was given nothing to drink. Greatmother sat resolutely with her back turned to us.

Evening fell.

Exhausted and at the cusp of lapsing once more into passive despondency, we abandoned our efforts. Outside, rain blew in gusts against the surrounding foliage. Less than two spoonfuls of water we'd each drunk, yet just beyond our reach water fell in delirious profusion. I shuffled to my burrow and curled inside, stoppering my ears to block out the mocking sound.

At once I became aware of the haunt trapped within the cocoon in my belly.

The membranous walls surrounding it were as thin as a newborn's skin. I'd been many days without venom, and the haunt had grown strong within me. If all had gone as normal in the viagand chambers that day, the eunuch would have led Misutvia, Greatmother, Sutkabde, the new women, and me to the stables. Sensing the abrupt change in the unscheduled lack of venom, the haunt roiled within my psyche the harder.

It would overcome me soon, and incarcerate me within the walls of my own flesh. I would be imprisoned twice at once, then: by stone, and by the invidious spirit of a deranged haunt.

I crawled out of my burrow, too fearful to be alone.

Misutvia hadn't retired to her burrow for the night. She sat against the wall beneath the casement, beside the stacked divans, a rug draped over her shoulders. Without a word, I collapsed beside her.

Outside, rain slapped the jungle. Wind blew in gusts.

"It doesn't make sense," Misutvia said, stirring me from stupor. "Why enclose us if they wish us dead? Why not decapitate us, or abandon us to the whims of the Retainers?"

I shrugged. I was too exhausted to think. I closed my eyes, but all I saw was stone. Stone walls above me, beside me, surrounding me, keeping me from water and light and life.

My eyes snapped open.

"They're hiding us," I said, and I sat upright with the truth of it. "They'll have done the same to the brooder stables, walled them off."

"What do you mean, hiding us?" Misutvia said bitterly. "From whom? No one knows of this place; the entire fortress is hidden in jungle."

"Someone's here. Someone who shouldn't be. Someone who can't be murdered to ensure silence. They've walled us in to hide us, to hide the purpose of this place."

"As if the very seclusion and impenetrability of this place doesn't suggest its true function."

Her scorn made me feel defensive toward my conjecture. "Not necessarily, no. Daronpuis and Temple officials are always secluding themselves behind walls—"

"Not in the heart of the jungle. Holy Wardens like their comforts, Zarq. Such an austere place like this would hardly be a retreat of choice for any but the most zealous of—" She abruptly broke off, and then I felt her quicken, as if lightning rippled over her skin.

"A mobasanin," she gasped. "They've walled us in to make this place look like a mobasanin."

"A what?"

"A retreat for zealous daronpuis seeking purification through seclusion. They're reputed to be austere places, isolated always in dense jungle."

"That's it, then," I said. "That's what they've done. But who's found this place, that they need to conceal its real purpose?"

Silence, the both of us thinking furiously.

"My brother," Misutvia tremulously breathed. "Malaban has come for me."

She turned, clutched my wrist with a bony hand.

"I told you he would, Zarq. He's found me!"

Her excitement was infectious, but I was afraid to believe such was possible, was afraid to be duped by blind hope.

"How?" I asked.

"I told you before! He's well connected, owns lands and factories, a fleet of ships. Are you sure you haven't heard of the Caranku Bri of Lireh? Our guild clan is mighty, our family influential. Malaban is here, I'm sure of it!"

I dared allow the conviction in her voice to instill a modicum of belief in me. "We must summon him, then. Make noise, hang draperies out the casements. The daronpuis will have kept your brother in their living quarters under some pretext or another while the Retainers walled us in."

"He may have toured the fortress already," Misutvia said, nervous energy spilling from her in an almost visible flood of prismatic color. "He may be convinced this *is* a mobasanin. Quick, we must make noise and summon him!"

My turn to grab her. "He won't hear us, not with this squall outside. Conserve your energy for morning."

"And risk him leaving here without me?!"

"Nonsense. Think rationally. How did he arrive?"

She shuddered and pulled herself together with difficulty. "The only way possible is upon dragonback."

"And you said he owns winged dragons?" I remembered that much from our conversation in the medic's den. It was a fact hard to forget.

"Five escoas, yes."

I nodded slowly and hope as hard as a full moon's light shone within me.

"If he's here still, he won't be flying out until daybreak," I said, thinking aloud, heart beating fast. "Why fly at night, during a squall, if there's no need?"

"Oh, Zarq. We *can* survive this; we will."

I realized, then, that neither of us had truly believed we'd escape the fortress or survive the surrounding jungle. We'd been willing to chance death for attempting both, but we'd not truly believed we'd succeed at either.

Until now.

"So we wait," she said, twisting her fingers together in agitation. "The moment the squall dies, we climb the divans and scream out that casement."

"We'll call his name," I said. "More likely he'll hear. One hears one's name, no matter how muted the cry."

She studied me, head cocked to one side. "You're clever, for a rishi."

If she meant ill by it, I didn't hear it in her voice. She placed one hand over her belly, the center of a woman's being, and offered her other hand to me. I took it and placed it over my womb, as if we were two strangers meeting for the first time and exchanging our trust.

"I am Caranku Bri of Lireh's Yenvia," she said. "My brother and friends know me as Jotan Bri. Please call me such."

"Jotan? You're known as Teacher?"

"I was an academician at Ondali Wapar Liru. I was apprehended after organizing a demonstration in protest of the arrest and disappearance of a colleague."

"I don't know what this Ondali Wapar Liru is."

"You've never heard of the Wapar?" she said in disbelief. Then she remembered. "Oh. Forgive me. You're rishi."

She gave me a moment to recover from the shame of my ignorance.

"Ondali Wapar Liru is the Academia Well of our nation's capital," she murmured. "It's a place of great learning. Sciences, arts, foreign religions, and great philosophies, they're all discussed and taught there."

"To whom?" I asked, for it was my turn for disbelief.

"To any who pay to learn such."

"Of course I've never heard of it, then. It's not a place for rishi."

"I wouldn't say that," she said defensively. "Certain patrons support the impoverished who possess a true desire to learn."

"Do these patrons travel to Clutches, gather interested rishi from the kus laboring within?"

"No," she admitted slowly. "But surely if a rishi has that much drive and interest, to attend the Wapar, he'll find a way to reach a patron."

"Surely a prisoner who has the drive and interest to escape her dungeon will find a way to flee," I murmured in response.

She drew in a breath.

"Poverty and circumstance can be as immutable as a stone prison, Jotan Bri," I said. I touched her knee to mitigate a little of the harshness of my words. "But please, tell me more of this place, this Well of Knowledge. Women attend?"

She shifted, clutched her rug about her shoulders as it started to slip. "There are more now. There's been a contentious battle over the issue of whether women should attend, let alone teach. The women of influential merchants, as well as those of the Emperor's militia stationed in Liru, have much sway when in mass. Together we've won against Temple in this regard: We can attend the Wapar. And, recently, teach."

"Yet women teachers are arrested on charges of committing vice with other women," I said. "Many of the names in Prelude list that as the reason behind their arrest."

"I was protesting such a thing when *I* was apprehended."

I studied her pale face, bit my tongue to hold back a question, then found myself asking it regardless. "Didn't you realize *you'd* be arrested?"

She stared into darkness and remained silent for so long that I thought I'd offended her terribly and that she wouldn't answer me.

"I'd not expected this, Zarq," she finally murmured. "Not this."

Another question pushed at me. "Would you do it again, if you could reverse time? Would you protest despite knowing where you'd end up?"

Her head swung round and her eyes looked as bloody and granular in the gloom as pulped meat. "If no one protests an injustice, it becomes ordinary and acceptable. In time, a greater injustice creeps in on its heels. Society is shaped by dissent, Zarq, justice birthed by complaint."

It was then that I remembered my vow to become a dragonmaster and use my influence to oust Kratt and bring a measure of equality to the rishi of Clutch Re. That ambition was so great, my current situation so far removed from it, that I was dazzled by the disparity and by my former naïveté.

I shook my head and spoke to myself more than her. "I don't know if I want the strife and instability that comes with dissent. I don't think I'm capable of being a martyr for my beliefs anymore."

"I'm no martyr," Misutvia hotly replied. "Don't compare me with Greatmother."

I started at the vehemence of her response. "I wasn't thinking of Greatmother. Nor you."

She hung her head and inhaled jaggedly several times.

"I hate that woman," she whispered at last. "I've dreamt of strangling her many times, of staving in her lunatic skull with a rock."

"Lunatic?" I murmured. "Or pious? Is she a madwoman or a martyr?"

"Her faith is merely an excuse for her passivity. She is no heroine."

"Are you sure of that?" I looked at my glycerin hands, my protruding bones looking as delicate as those of a fish. "You've heard the dragons. Do you really believe they aren't divine? Perhaps Greatmother is right. Perhaps that's why you hate her so. Her faith is formidable. Yours is nonexistent."

"Close your lips, Naji," Misutvia said, reverting to my prison name in her anger. "I need sleep now. We both need sleep. Let's not waste our energy discussing a delusional old woman who's on the brink of death."

Although I slept, I did not rest. My stuttering, relentless dreams grew hale in the night's void, pulsed systole and diastole, mutated, propagated. I was surrounded by cocoons that were stacked and compressed above and around me. I moaned in my sleep, opened my eyes and saw the maturing dark as traitorous, saw pillow and divan as proxy for oscillating star-spume forms that crouched and coupled with malevolent vim. The haunt within me roiled, assonant with my breath rhythm.

A claw shredded the cocoon asunder and punched forth into my being.

I gurgled and scrabbled at Misutvia, slumped in oblivion beside me. Another claw ripped its way free of the cocoon in my psyche, and my mother's haunt erupted from the involucre, splattering my soul with septic fury. My shattered, darkened mind howled as the assimilation began, as my mother's haunt oozed through my tissues, obsessing and possessing.

I convulsed on the floor.

"Venom," I cried.

A pillar of melting wax dripped over me: Briefly, I knew it to be Misutvia.

Then I saw no more, my sight stolen by bilious, otherworldly eyes. My body was hollowed out as I was infected; I felt myself draining out of finger and arm, rushing waterfall down neck into chest cavity. All of me was draining into one place, a polyp embedded within my own womb. I was compressed. I was darkness folded in on itself.

From that cramped prison, I felt the body that held me move. Fury, spasm, hectic fever. Violence and great effort. Wreck and ruin, purpose in disorder.

The haunt couldn't hold me within the polyp, not with its berserk energy so focused on destruction. I writhed, felt the polyp about me turn as viscous as fruit pulp. I struggled harder. The pulp turned as thin as serum and evaporated in the heat of my determination. Triumphant, I surged back into my body. Depleted from her rampage, my mother's haunt splintered into thousands of minute shards and scattered to the far corners of my frame.

Sight. Sound. Sensation.

My chest was heaving, air scoring down my throat and lungs as if sucked from a hot kiln. My legs could not support me, and I crumpled against a wall. Splayed out before me, I saw that my shins were blood chipped, fragments of mortar and rock embedded in my calves. Slowly, I looked up.

Dust floated upon dark air, a thick, gritty texture that filmed my eyes. About me lay a jumble of stone.

I was slumped in the corridor outside the viagand chambers. Misutvia stood at the chambers' door, gripping it for support. Clustered about her stood the new women, gaping fearfully at me.

I looked down at my hands. They glowed with strange blue light. My fingertips throbbed in the peculiar way they had done once before, when, in Convent Tieron, the haunt had possessed me and fire had blasted from my hands. Only now no fire had raged from my hands, but some dark force that had shattered a rock wall.

For the wall that had enclosed us lay strewn about the corridor in ruin, and two Retainers, dressed as acolytes, lay dead amongst the rubble.

The viagand women left me there and withdrew to the chambers, shutting the door against me. Outside the fortress, the monsoon raged on. Teeth chattering, stupefied and exhausted, I stayed sprawled on the stone-strewn floor, my bones turning as cold and stiff as the corpses twisted beneath the debris.

Eventually, as middle-night drew near, the wooden door to the viagand chambers cracked open. Misutvia approached me slowly, looking like a glaucous spindle in the dark. As she picked her way over stone, her pale bitoo snagged on spars of mortar.

She came to a stop several feet from me and waited, silent and wary.

"The rain," I rasped, nodding at the dark stretch of corridor ahead of me, beyond the rubble. "Puddles."

A pause, then she understood. She picked her way over the moraine and the dead Retainers and staggered into the corridor beyond. Through the ivy-choked casements notched in the corridor's walls, water dripped from leaf and trickled along vine, creating a murky pool of water on the ground, as dark as a slick of tar. She folded to her knees and dipped her head to the ground. She sucked her fill, then drenched a corner of her sleeve in the puddle and returned to me.

Holding her sodden sleeve above my mouth, she carefully squeezed the water onto my tongue.

"More," I gasped.

"I'll get a crock," she whispered, and returned from the viagand chambers with an emptied paint pot a short time after. The three new women followed her out. In their haste to skirt me and reach the water, they fell over the rubble a clawful of times.

Misutvia crouched again before me and I drank from the crock she held to my lips.

"More," I gasped.

"I'll find another puddle, in another corridor."

"No. You might run across a Retainer."

"Or Malaban," she said.

"We need a plan."

She nodded. "We'll talk, back in the chambers. Can you stand? Can I touch you?"

"Yes. It sleeps, recovering power."

"The demon within you."

To explain was too much effort. "Yes."

"Why haven't you used its power before now? Why did you even allow yourself to be arrested and brought here, if such a demon obeys your command?"

"It doesn't obey me, not at all." I gave the slightest shake of my head. "When I'm on the soil of my birth Clutch, the creature you call a demon can't invade me like this and use its powers through my body. It can only try to exert its will upon me, by plaguing my every waking and sleeping moment with visions and whispers. Venom shields me from the haunt's presence."

"And when you're off your birth Clutch?" Misutvia prompted.

I sighed. "The haunt becomes trapped within me. I don't know how or why, but that's the way of it. When I'm away from my birth Clutch, the haunt rides within me, holding the reins, blinkering my eyes. It uses me like a puppet, when and how it wants, and I become a prisoner within my own flesh. It's like being buried alive."

I closed my eyes, exhausted. "That's when I need venom the most, see. When I'm off my birth Clutch and the haunt rides within me. Venom envelopes the haunt, creates a membrane about it that it can't penetrate. And because I've been without venom for some time now, it burst free from its shell and overpowered me tonight."

"I see," Misutvia murmured, though it was clear she did not. All she knew was what the evidence of her own eyes could tell her: Forks of blue power could blast from my hands, and I was capable of hewing down walls and killing men with it. "I've heard rumor of such invasions occurring amongst the Djimbi."

I licked my lips and opened my eyes. "I'm not demon possessed, Jotan. This is celestial strength."

"A celestial demon? Ah." She didn't believe me; she thought me an instrument of the One Serpent.

But she didn't care.

As long as she wouldn't be harmed in the process, she'd use me to escape. I could feel the truth of it emanating from her.

"I'll help you stand," she murmured.

Back in the viagand chambers, the both of us sank upon floor cushions, exhausted by our efforts. Sutkabde and Greatmother sat there, too, ashy mounds in the dark. The three new women cautiously joined us.

"You have removed the obstruction," Greatmother rasped. "You have killed two Retainers. Defying the will of the Retainers and the daronpuis is a transgression, as is murder. I claim the right to report both."

An abrupt, humorless snort from Misutvia. Greatmother obviously hadn't witnessed, nor been told about, how I destroyed the wall, or else she'd have more to concern her than just claiming the right to report disobedience and murder.

I ignored her and drew in a quavering breath. "Do we know the layout of this fortress?"

"I've memorized every passage I've walked," Misutvia answered.

"Sketch it."

Moments later, I was studying the glistening streaks she'd made with paint upon the pearly surface of one of her torn-off sleeves. I pointed.

"The daronpuis' quarters are over here, yes? Two corridors lead to it, if your memory serves correctly: here and here. Both will be guarded by Retainers dressed as acolytes. The entrance to the fortress will most likely be in this area, too."

"If Malaban is here, he'll lead us to the entrance."

"We have to reach your brother and escape without the Retainers' notice. The daronpuis stationed here will have us all murdered, your brother included, before they allow the truth of this place to escape. They don't care how influential your family is, Jotan. They won't let you out alive, knowing what you do of dragons."

"They wouldn't murder Malaban Bri merely for fear that I'd speak of what I've been subjected to," she said. "To murder my brother would earn the wrath of many powerful families in the merchant guild, not just the Bri."

So it was true; she did not believe the dragons divine. She really thought this fortress, the bestiality we were subjected to, were all just to enhance Temple's political power by obtaining venom-induced counsel concerning alliances, conspiracies, and stratagems. She had no inkling what Temple really sought.

But I knew differently.

The dragons *were* divine, and the daronpuis stationed here wouldn't let a viagand woman go just to avoid confrontation with an affluent merchant guild. Temple wouldn't take the risk that Clutch lords might learn of the rite from an escaped viagand woman, didn't want them knowing what happened when a woman lay with a dragon. Because some lord, on some Clutch, at some point, would see the true potential behind that telepathic exchange.

As Kratt had done.

Only unlike Kratt, those Clutch lords would know that because Misutvia was merely an ordinary woman, *any* woman could lie before a venomous dragon and hear its song, not just the Skykeeper's Daughter of a little-known prophecy. And with the many venomous dragons each Clutch lord possessed, and with the thousands of rishi women Clutch warrior-lords could force into dragon union, chances were Temple would be the last to solve the riddle of the bulls.

Temple wanted a monopoly on that answer, to make the Emperor's power vast and unassailable. Malaban Bri of Lireh was but a gnat Temple would swipe aside.

"Let's not be hasty," I said to Misutvia. "Let's think this through."

Greatmother stirred. "There is nothing to think through. Our duty is clear. We're to stay here, as the daronpuis so clearly desired."

Misutvia made a strangled noise in her throat. In the brackish night-gloom eking through the chamber's casements, her hands convulsed.

Greatmother smacked dry gums. "I should never have sat here while you plotted murder against the two Retainers you believed to be guarding our door. I failed in my duty then. I will not do so now."

I stared at the ashy mound that was Greatmother. "What do you mean?"

"I must go. Report your actions."

"You wouldn't."

"You deranged old crone," Misutvia hissed.

I leaned forward. "Greatmother. As soon as you approach the Retainers, as soon as they realize you've breached their seal, they will strike you down. They won't risk this Malaban Bri learning of your presence, even though you're doing them a service by informing on us."

Silence, ripe with the conflict fomenting in Greatmother's conscience. I sat tensely, wondering how strong her faith was.

"If death is to be my lot for alerting the daronpuis that you've breached their wall," she finally husked, "then so be it. But they must be warned of your corruption. It is my duty."

"I'll kill you!" Misutvia shrieked at Greatmother, and she threw herself on her. "Deranged whore, I'll rip you limb from limb!"

A shredding noise, flailing arms. A gravelly, choking wheeze from Greatmother. A thud, awful in its melon-thick resonance.

Greatmother lay upon her back, clutching her throat to catch her breath from Misutvia's attack. Misutvia lay motionless atop her. Sutkabde knelt at Greatmother's head, paint crock in hand; she had slammed it against Misutvia's skull to save Greatmother.

"If I'm to die," Sutkabde said hoarsely, "it will be at the mouth of a dragon. I won't be killed over your futile attempt at escape, rishi via. I believe in the divine. I serve the dragons."

# SEVENTEEN

**W**hile Sutkabde helped Greatmother to her feet, I frantically checked Misutvia, seeking blood, broken bone, a pulse, life.

"Sutkabde, don't do this," I said, even while my fingers found a gross swelling beneath Misutvia's thin hair. "You don't want to remain imprisoned. You can't believe it's holy and right."

"What Temple does here is an abomination," she said, steadying the wheezing, teetering form of Greatmother. "But I know this much: I won't live without the dragons and their venom."

"But the Nask Cinai, the sanctuaries for infirm bulls! As an onai you can lie with dragons in such a place and receive their venom."

"Temple would search such places for me."

"Sutkabde, you go down those corridors with Greatmother, and they'll kill you. What venom will you experience then?"

"I mean to survive this debacle, rishi via," she said. "I'm not leaving the corridor beyond these chambers. I'll help Greatmother over the ruins, that's all. Greatmother is determined to do her duty, aren't you, Greatmother? She doesn't need me by her side the entire way."

"I strive," Greatmother breathed, her voice withered and thin, "to be holy."

"You strive admirably, Greatmother," Sutkabde said. "You strive admirably."

I watched in dismay as she led the wobbling old woman to the chamber door.

"Now what?" cried one of the new women the moment Sutkabde and Greatmother disappeared.

I thought furiously, stroking Misutvia's cheeks to rouse her. Her pulse staggered under my fingertips.

"Greatmother can barely walk," I said, thinking aloud. "It'll take her some time to reach the daronpuis' quarters. Bring me the map Misutvia drew."

The pearly, torn-off sleeve fluttered before my face as one of the women draped it shroudlike over Misutvia.

"Look," I said, stabbing at the diagram. "This corridor is shorter than the other one, and it leads directly to the daronpuis' quarters. Greatmother will take the short route, surely. At the rate she moves, we can reach the daronpuis' quarters just after she does. When the Retainers guarding the corridors see her—and there will be Retainers, make no mistake—they'll leave their posts to deal with her as quickly as possible, before Malaban Bri is roused. They'll immediately rush here to contain us, perhaps divide to check that the seal they constructed over the stable entrance stands intact."

I looked up at the black shadows of the three women standing before me, my heart a crazed thing. "This might work to our advantage. If we're quick and quiet, we may be able to escape yet."

"What choice do we have?" asked one.

"I won't do it," another gasped. "I'm going to stay here, stay in my burrow. To leave is to defy them at their weakest moment. I won't do it. They'll kill you, but they won't kill me for staying here, where I should."

Hesitation in the other two.

"All that remains here for you is rape and torture," I pressed, knowing by their newness that their taste for venom and their desire for dragonsong was not yet fevered. "No one survives here long. This chance for escape will never come again. Don't you want to feel rain on your face once more, sun on your back? Embrace loved ones?"

I threw a frantic look at the door; Sutkabde would have helped Greatmother over the rubble, would be returning any moment.

"A bludgeon, quick," I gasped, holding out a hand and rising. A swirl of shadow and cloth as a woman moved. Coarse wood slapped against my outstretched palm.

The door to the viagand chambers creaked open.

I flew toward it, tripping over cushions. I staggered, almost fell, floundered on. Sutkabde came through the door.

Astonishment crossed her wan face, making human her blood-soaked, pustulant eyes for the first time since I'd known her. I slammed my bludgeon broadside across her belly. She folded over with a shuddering sigh and collapsed onto the floor.

Chest heaving, I gestured to two of the new women. "She won't stop us now. Lift Misutvia between the both of you and come. We've little time."

I was gripped in a delirium of panic.

Flee, flee, flee!

Across the rubble of the ruined wall, ankles cut by spars of mortar, soles bruised on rock. Splashing through puddles, hems dragging like sodden tails along slick earthen floor. Unnerving dark, alarming uncertainty of what lay ahead. Pelting rain deafening us each time we passed a casement, our hearts thundering louder in our chests. Misutvia a dead weight dragged between the two women who followed me.

The corridor branched.

Left or right? Which way was shortest, which way had Greatmother gone? I couldn't remember in my panic, had not thought to bring Misutvia's cloth map with me.

Left, I decided, and I lurched down it, the women who followed me wheezing under their burden.

Slower now, slower. Surely we'd run across a Retainer soon.

The corridor branched again.

I came to a standstill, stupefied. There shouldn't have been another fork, not according to Misutvia's map! But alas, none of us had ever walked that part of the fortress: She'd not known. We were lost in the night-shrouded maze of stone, would never find an exit before we were discovered.

Slap of feet approaching at a sprint.

I gestured wildly to the women. We ducked into the branching corridor and cowered against one wall, exposed save for the sable cloak of night.

Heavy breaths, approaching feet, and a Retainer dressed in an acolyte's tunic and scapular shot from the adjacent corridor and sprinted down the corridor we'd just traveled. Several heartbeats later, a second, third, and fourth Retainer dashed after him, bearing spears.

Greatmother had reached the daronpuis' quarters already. They knew we'd breached their seal.

"Quick, down the corridor they came from," I said, and we started to move, and then we heard heavy breaths and rapid footsteps approaching: A fifth Retainer, running last in the pack sent to check the viagand.

"Back, back," I hissed frantically, and we staggered back into the shadows of the branching corridor, dragging Misutvia with us.

We froze. The sound of running feet drew near. A Retainer dressed as an acolyte, in pursuit of his cohorts, shot into the corridor leading back to the chambers. His back passed a hair-raising body length from us as he ran. I could smell his filthy sweat.

Misutvia groaned.

The Retainer lurched to a stop.

"Quick, attack!" I cried, and I flung myself toward him even as he was turning and raising his spear. I heard the soft thud of Misutvia's body dropped to the floor as the two panicked women obeyed me, and I bent, head down and chin tucked to chest, and barreled into the Retainer's soft belly like a battering ram. He staggered back a pace with a gasp and his spear clattered to the ground. Then all was a blur as we flew at him, frenzied and silent, gouging, hitting, biting, kicking. He faltered under our onslaught. My teeth found the soft cartilage of one of his ears and I bit. I drove a fist again and again into the soft flesh above his left kidney, and one of the women clawed at his face, shredding skin with nails as if it were cold lard.

He buckled over his testicles and fell to his knees. Hysterical, we kicked him into unconsciousness with our bare feet.

Quaking at our own brutality, shaking with battle lust, panic, and a macabre triumph, we stood over the body. Misutvia groaned again and retched. We looked at each other.

"Pick her up," I wheezed.

"No," one of the women panted. "We leave her."

"I'll help carry her, then." I nodded curtly to the woman who hadn't spoken. "You help me."

"We leave her," the first repeated, but I was already walking back to the albescent puddle of cloth on the floor of the branching corridor.

I bent and draped one of Misutvia's clammy arms over my neck. My legs felt boneless and weak. Still bent, I looked up, waiting for the other woman to join me. She hesitated.

"I won't leave her behind," I said angrily.

"We part ways, then," the dissenter said, and she tugged her undecided companion's arm, pulling her down the corridor without me.

"I don't know," the second woman began, and then she was picked off her feet by a spear and thrown backward several paces, to the ground. The dissenter cried out, turned, and broke into a run. A swift whistle: Her body jerked and she was thrown against a wall. She slid down it, fingers clawing stone. The oiled shaft of a spear protruded from her back.

I dropped Misutvia, turned, and ran.

Shouts from behind me. I staggered into the dark, my spine crawling with dread, awaiting the bite of a spear in my back.

"Down there, that way," a voice cried behind me, and I knew I'd been spotted. My viridescent bitoo was like a beacon in the dark, and I understood then that all the viagand women had been purposely clothed in pale gowns, that we would always stand out in the fortress's gloom.

Hopelessness engulfed me. I could not outwit them, could not outrun them, would not escape. Yet even so, I stumbled down the corridor.

Dim light ahead, cast from a flickering sconce situated in a junction where the corridor forked yet again. Two silhouettes appeared in that pool of light, one bandy-legged, one cloaked in a cape. I was trapped, front and behind. I stumbled. Fell.

"Mother!" I hoarsely cried, willing the haunt to appear and endow me with inhuman strength, even at the cost of being imprisoned forever within my own flesh.

Opalescence danced before my eyes, stippling the dark with blanched blue. Shattered into a thousand grains throughout me, the haunt incandesced, tried to coalesce. It felt as if hot drops of wax were trying to join together in my veins, yet cold water solidified them as isolated beads. The haunt was depleted, hadn't had sufficient time to renew its strength.

"Mother, save me!"

"That's her," one of the sconce-lit silhouettes cried, and they broke into a run toward me. I looked wildly to the opposite end of the corridor: A Retainer dressed as an acolyte emerged from the darkness. He stopped and raised his arms, elbows akimbo.

I would be impaled on his spear.

"Mother!" I cried again, and metal streaked through the air like a blade of lightning, a dagger thrown by one of the two sconce-lit silhouettes. The dagger glanced off the Retainer's left shoulder just as he loosed his spear; the spear sailed drunkenly through the air and hissed onto the ground a hand's breadth from my body.

The scent of perfumed oils rushed by me as the caped figure launched itself at the Retainer and engaged in combat.

The second of the sconce-lit silhouettes reached me. A familiar face leered at me beneath a bald and scarred pate. I reeled, incredulous.

"You've led us a merry chase, rishi whelp," the dragonmaster cackled.

I looked wildly at the wrestling shadows: Sconce light glinted upon golden locks. Kratt.

"No," I said, baffled. "No."

Sinewy fingers bit into one of my arms and hauled me upright. "We'll be leaving now, hey-o," the dragonmaster said.

"But Malaban Bri. Where's Malaban?"

A thud: The Retainer fell to the ground. Kratt bent over him and a minnow of steel flashed in his hand. With a grunt, Kratt straightened, wiped his bloody dagger upon his cape, and approached us.

"To our dragons," he grunted, barely casting a glance my way.

"Wait," I gasped. "We can't leave Misutvia."

"Shut your lips, rishi get," Kratt snarled, and I thought he'd strike me.

"She's sister to Malaban," I cried. "From Caranku Bri of Lireh."

Kratt paused. A muscle in his jaw clenched like a fist. "We have the Dirwalan Babu," the dragonmaster hissed, calling me Sky-keeper's Daughter in ancient Malacarite as he held up my arm as proof. "We leave *now*."

Kratt ignored him and pierced me with battle-bright eyes. "You're sure the woman hails from Caranku Bri?"

"She was imprisoned with me," I answered breathlessly. "We talked. She's at the end of this corridor, unconscious."

"We waste time!" the dragonmaster growled, eyes rolling.

"I'd have the Caranku Bri of Lireh beholden to me, Komikon," Kratt said, sheathing his dagger.

With a swirl of cape, he raced down the corridor. The dragon-master twitched and gnashed his teeth until Kratt reappeared, Misutvia draped over his shoulders like a gharial carcass.

"We leave this place," Kratt said shortly.

We reached the sconce-lit fork at the end of the corridor just as three daronpuis lumbered into view, robes and coiled braids askew from hasty dressing. Their collective bulk formed a wall in front of us. Beards trimmed into sharp arrowheads glittered with oil in the light of the torches they held.

"You should not have come, Waikar Re Kratt," a daronpu with an aquiline nose growled.

"This is no mobasanin," Kratt said, his voice as smooth and muscled as a python's body. "This is a den of deviance, hidden from the eyes of all but a few. Now, step aside."

"You'll have to remain here a while longer, I'm afraid."

"Will I, now?" Kratt said softly. "I doubt that very much. Unless I return to Clutch Re by tomorrow eve, the outriders who accompanied me here are instructed to inform not just my brother of the location and suspected purpose of this stronghold, but the Lupini of Clutch Cuhan and the Roshu of Ka as well. All will learn of the Ranreeb's secret then, holy man, and Emperor Fa will be ill pleased."

Eyes narrowed.

"I propose instead that you stand aside," Kratt murmured. "Alert the Ranreeb to what's occurred here. He'll deal with me as he sees fit. I've no intention of sharing what I know with other Clutch lords once I've returned to Cafar Re. Better Temple competes with just one man to learn the dragons' secret, than with all the Clutch lords in Malacar."

"No one would believe you," sneered a daronpu, though he twitched as he said it.

"Shall we lay a wager on that, hmm?" Kratt murmured. "Now, step aside. You've no skill in combat, I'm sure."

Nostrils flared. Hate was an acrid taste in the air.

A daronpu flicked a hand and ordered his colleagues to stand aside.

The journey back to Clutch Re lasted several days and a lifetime, knotted together like a ball of twisting, nested snakes. Starved and dehydrated, I swam in a sparkling fever, drowning, surfacing, sinking once more. I knew the exact moment we reached Clutch Re, though, for the thousands of incandescing grains of the haunt, scattered throughout me, burst from my skin in a visible cloud, and my psyche rushed into the gaps left behind from the haunt's departure.

My body was mine, truly mine.

My anima stretched into my form with aching ease, too-long cramped by the haunt's invasion. A bluish buzzard coalesced from the cloud, some distance to the right of the dragon I rode. The buzzard glided on an updraft, carbuncled neck outstretched.

The haunt.

When next I awoke, I lay on a bed of dusty featon chaff, surrounded by lantern-lit stone.

I bolted upright with a cry. It had all been a dream; I was in the viagand chambers still!

A dragon snorted.

Heart pounding, I tried to place where I was. I struggled to my feet, using the stone wall beside me as support.

I was not in the viagand chambers, no. I was in an underground stable comprised of three small stalls, all of which were empty, save for the last, and in that stood an old destrier. She watched me with melancholic, sage eyes. Her wings trembled, folded tight over her dorsal ridge.

"Where am I?" I asked the old destrier, my tongue swollen from want of water.

Her cant eyes blinked slowly, slitted pupils not moving from mine. The diamond-shaped membrane at the end of her twiggy tail slapped against stone. *Slap-slap. Slap-slap.* The sound of blood and flesh imprisoned in stone. My heart beat in synchrony, blood and flesh imprisoned in rib.

I knew where I was, then.

In the gloomy stables beneath the domed pool of Cinai Komikon Re's domain.

Home.

The dragonmaster woke me sometime later, and gave me broth to drink, paak to eat, a blanket to wrap myself in, and an enamel pot to use when the need took me. I pushed the paak aside, turned my nose up at the broth, and slept again, dreaming of dragonsong.

Again the dragonmaster woke me. Again the broth, the paak, the insistence that I eat and grow strong. I pushed the food away, teeth clacking together from cold. Chill slimed my skin.

The smell of the old dragon housed beside me was a maddening tease. It enticed, seduced, whispered of divine grace and union. The licorice-and-lime scent of venom was a memory of wholeness, of isolation transformed into unity and joy.

"Venom?" I asked the dragonmaster, though I'd not meant to; the words tripped from my self-willed tongue.

The dragonmaster stared at me, displeased. "You look to have enough of it in your blood, girl. I won't give you more."

A great weariness overwhelmed me at his words. I turned away from him and curled onto my side in the bedding chaff.

"You have to eat, hey-o," the dragonmaster growled. "Your sole purpose from this moment on is to recover, to train, to survive Arena! Are you listening?"

I was listening, but his words evoked nothing but weariness in me. I saw no reason to recover, to train, to survive, if I were to be deprived of venom the rest of my life. A harsh admittance, that, and one I'm not proud of, but it is the truth nonetheless: I had escaped the viagand chambers only to imprison myself in the desire to further my decline into addiction.

I was, once more in my short life, utterly dependent upon the dragons' poison.

Perhaps you would not blame me, if you could but once experience venom's numinous embrace, coupled by the stupendous passion of dragonsong. To hear such power and through the hearing *become* the power is a lure I'm certain no mortal could refuse. And how much more powerful a lure for one such as I, who had stood so close to understanding the dragons' divine music!

For yes, I had been on the cusp of understanding the memories in the viagand chambers. I was convinced of it. I'd been able to recognize certain refrains, had oft guessed which images would appear with what strains. The polyphony was not all wild sound uncivilized by time and otherworld tune; order lay within the dulcet mosaic, and I alone—I felt sure of it—stood at the brink of understanding the enigmatic score.

I had climbed the ladder closer to the Realm. Given enough time, I *would* reach the uppermost rung of that ladder. But to reach said rung, I required more venom. More and more and more of it.

Over the next clawful of days, the dragonmaster grew to loathe me for my dependency and lust. Each time he visited me in his underground stable, he railed at me to eat, stand up, begin training for Arena, but as each day passed, I sank further and further into stupor and asked only for venom.

On the morning of the eighth day, I lay down before the old destrier housed in the stall adjacent to me. Alone, emaciated, addle minded, and desperate, I spread my legs before the destrier and offered her my sex.

With the peculiar instinct possessed by those who stand on the knife's edge of sanity, the dragonmaster guessed at the depths of my desperation that day; he appeared in the darkled stalls at noon, when I'd not expected him, to discover me on the stable floor, thighs venom tarred from the destrier's repeated feedings.

I believe I would have died that day, had he not come and interfered.

He tethered the destrier in her stall, then scrubbed my skin free of venom and forced a purgative down my throat. Foaming about the mouth, he railed at me, sounding for all the world as mad as I.

But the dragonmaster's grip on sanity was, I'm ashamed to admit, much stronger than mine at that dismal point in my life, for the very next morn, he brought a visitor down to the secret gloom beneath the domed pool, and that visitor announced, in baritone fury, that I was to imbibe venom no more.

"What've you become, blood-blood?" the giant with the waist-long, cleft beard roared as he loomed over me, stooped beneath the stable's low ceiling. Half of his pate was bald; the other half sported tufts of knotted black hair. Tussocks sprouted above each eye like windswept, cinder-black bush, and these furrowed at me in anger.

"Bleached and gaunt with toxin!" he roared, and the cobwebbed timbers loosed a film of dust upon us. "Servant to helplessness, maggot of despair, get to your feet and let me look upon you."

"Daronpu Gen," I whispered, dumbfounded and sprawled upon my featon chaff bed.

He windmilled his great, shaggy arms, his tattered and soiled tunic the snapping sail of a storm-gripped trawler. "What-what? It speaks, it moves, it lives. But does it obey? Get up, get up, let me look upon you, maggot!"

"Daronpu Gen," I repeated stupidly, and the giant ducked into my stall, enclosed my left forearm in an enormous hand, and swept me upright. I gaped at him as a gamut of emotion further befuddled my venom-addled mind.

Daronpu Gen: the eccentric Holy Warden who had disguised

me in an acolyte's tunic and scapular and hidden me in his decrepit temple in Clutch Re's Zone of the Dead. Daronpu Gen: the first other than myself to see my mother's haunt, the first to call me Dirwalan Babu, Skykeeper's Daughter. Daronpu Gen: the man who had shown me the scroll that stated that one such as myself could serve a bull as a dragonmaster apprentice.

His great, calloused hands cupped my cheeks. His waist-long cleft beard pressed against my chest and belly like a mat of desiccated weeds as he studied my eyes.

"You are missing, blood-blood," he rumbled. "Misplaced yourself in venom's deceptively beguiling swamps."

He released my head, turned a quarter to bellow over his shoulder, "She must be weaned off the poison, man, else we won't retrieve her from the noxious slough! Quicksand-sure, it'll suck her down."

"You tell me what I already know," the dragonmaster growled, his skeletal face scowling at me from behind the renegade daronpu. "All she cares for is the stuff. She's given up on life itself."

"You summon me from my secret lair, bring me to this pit of nihilism, and endanger my life only to convince me my journey is futile? She can be weaned off, I tell you! It's only a matter of knowing how best to counteract the craving in her soul."

Daronpu Gen looked back at me, hands still cupped about my head. "How shall I rid this tainted desire from your blood, hey-o? Tell me, now."

I looked away from him.

His grip upon my temples tightened; then he leaned suddenly into my face and pressed his savage forehead against mine. Rocking my head so that our foreheads rolled one across the other, he inhaled me into his lungs.

"I can taste the Skykeeper about you," he murmured. "A faded taste, a ghostly presence, and tangled about it, I taste your very soul."

Of a sudden, he pressed his lips against mine. His tongue twined round mine; revulsion shot through me. An obscure vortex flashed through my mind, a dizzying, blinding starburst display of light that I knew instantly to be his psyche.

He pulled away abruptly, rearing back and thwacking his head upon a rafter.

"So that's the way to be rid of it, blood-blood!" he cried, and he swiped the back of one rangy arm across his lips. "I've the answer now, Komikon! I'll mix the potion this very eve. And no venom must she receive. Not a drop of it."

"You think her will to live will be restored by a mere herbal?" The dragonmaster gave a vigorous tug on his chin braid. "Look at her! What magics do you know that can imbue the will to survive in one so determined to die?"

"You assume too much, man. I see no defeat in her eyes, just fear and a lost will."

"You speak foolishness."

"Do I, now?" Daronpu Gen patted my cheek and smiled. "What about it, Babu? Of these two ranting old men who stand before you, who do you think is correct, the Komikon or I? What choice would you make: a stab at life, or surcease found in venom?"

He'd asked me a similar question once before, upon finding me amongst the smoking ruins of the Zone of the Dead. *Life or death?* he'd demanded of me, as I'd lain paralyzed by agony from both the loss of Kiz-dan and her babe, and the terrible wound of a Cafar guard's sword. *Pain or ease?*

I'd chosen life then, spurred by the fantastical dream that one day I might kill Kratt, might have my own Clutch where a rishi babe would never be taken from its mother to serve Temple, where a rishi child would never watch her father murdered by a cruel bayen lord. A Clutch where a dragon would never be imprisoned, exploited, and abused through indifference.

My own bull dragon, my own dragon estate.

To kill Kratt.

Those, then, were what I'd once wanted. But now?

I'd come to understand that I was but a pawn in a game governed by others' needs. Kratt desired the answer to the bull riddle in his bid to become more than just Temple's overlord of a single Clutch. The dragonmaster sought the same answer, and was motivated by the belief that I was the prophesied Skykeeper's Daughter who would end the apartheid of the Djimbi and wrest Temple from the Emperor's hands. The Ranreeb wanted the answer to the bull riddle for Temple, for the wealth and power such an answer would confer, though he believed me to be no Dirwalan Babu, just a deviant who might provide him with the riddle's answer. But unlike Kratt, the Ranreeb knew that any woman could hear dragonsong during the rite; now that I'd escaped the Ranreeb's fortress, I was a threat that must be killed.

Yes, I may have been imprisoned in the viagand chambers, may have wanted to escape. But no freedom awaited me beyond its walls, either.

"I want surcease," I said, my legs folding beneath me. I curled onto my side and burrowed my head into featon chaff. "I want to be one with the dragon forever."

"It mumbles!" Daronpu Gen bellowed. "I hear it not!"

"She's chosen the venom; you heard her as well as I did," the dragonmaster spat, and I could envision his eyes rolling and his shoulders convulsing.

"She's lost, man, that's what I heard. Bogged down in toxic quagmire. Found and liberated, she'll choose otherwise."

"I've no time for metaphor. Arena draws nigh."

"Keep her off the venom. Give me a day or so, and I'll give her reason to survive Abbasin Shinchiwouk and continue the fight. Hey-o? Do that for a brother, would you?"

"The emancipation of our people lies there, in that stall! How can you be so sure—" the dragonmaster heatedly began, but the daronpu cut him off.

"Two days," he cried, and his voice echoed down the corridor as he departed. "I'll be back. Two days!"

He kept his word. He returned within two days.

But he was not alone.

I didn't recognize the young boy standing before him, didn't realize I should. In my febrile chill, I barely registered the rose color of his pleated tunic, the brand upon his forehead.

Daronpu Gen pushed the malnourished boy into my stall.

"I followed the Skykeeper's taste, hey-o," the daronpu said smugly. "Chased the traces of its flavor on the wind, wafting in feathered ribbons over the Clutch. Followed it to the Cafar, I did. Found this boy, outside his lady's room. Smuggled him out under the dead of night. Speak, boy, speak. Tell of your night terrors."

An asak-illyas, that's what the boy was. The hieratic branded onto his forehead by hot metal, his shorn head, and the rose color of his pleated tunic marked him as such. He'd been abused in his post as an indentured Temple eunuch trained to serve a bayen lady: bruises, scars, a missing finger, a lopped-off ear, and a haunted look in his eyes bespoke of cruelty enacted upon him, not discipline.

Darting glances this way and that about the stall, he stood before me, quivering with fright. Daronpu Gen placed his hands gently upon the boy's collarbone.

"Brave child, injured soul, you'll be harmed no further. I've a safe place where you'll grow hale and live long, away from all torment. Upon my life, I promise to take you there. But first you must speak, yes? Of the voice you hear whispering in the dark, of the unseen hands that molest your spirit. Speak."

"It comes to me," the boy said in a quavering voice, his whole twiggy frame shaking. "At night. I pray for Re's protection, but the bull doesn't hear me, and it always comes. It calls me son, but I'm no demon's child."

He began weeping, little ribs heaving.

"I taste it in my mouth. It invades me. I can't see, I can't speak, my legs try to move without me." The boy turned to Daronpu Gen and clutched his filthy robe. "Purify me; drive it out, please!"

My heart turned into a porcelain shard, a sharp, broken, brittle thing.

No.

It couldn't be.

I licked my lips.

"How old are you?" I croaked.

The boy didn't give an answer; I didn't require one. I could guess his age as well as his identity. Here stood my brother, born when I was nine, taken fresh from my mother's womb to Temple as reparation for a crime my mother had committed in her desperation to buy Waivia back.

Since my return from the viagand chambers to Clutch Re, with my blood so saturated still with venom, the haunt had turned her obsessive need to find Waivia upon the only other person besides me who shared the same blood as my sister. This little boy.

I rammed a fist into my mouth, aghast.

Why, if she could seek out her own blood, could the haunt not find Waivia by herself? *Why?*

"When did these visitations start, my boy?" Daronpu Gen murmured, patting the asak-illyas's shorn head.

"A clawful of nights ago," he sobbed.

Exactly the time I'd returned to Clutch Re.

"I'm no demon's son; please, drive it away!" the boy cried out.

The daronpu clucked soothingly and impaled me with his hoary eyes. "Can you guess whom he serves in Cafar Re?"

A feeling of dread presentiment filled me.

"Waikar Re Kratt's Wai-roidan yin. Don't you, boy? You serve

Kratt's First Claimed Woman. And when Kratt finds you alone, if he seeks to relieve a certain itch he oft feels, he hurts you. As he hurts many rishi in Cafar Re."

The boy's shoulders shook. The rangy giant knelt and enfolded him in his great arms.

"You're safe now, little flea. He'll not touch you again. Hey-o?"

I turned to the side and retched.

"Take him away," I gasped when the dry heaving stopped. "I don't want to see him. Take him, go."

"Not until you look the boy in the eye and tell him you'd rather die than alleviate his night-terror suffering. Because that's how it stands, blood-blood. You die in Arena, and this boy becomes the Skykeeper's channel."

"Not possible," I said, staring at the ground, at the flame-play of shadow cast from the daronpu's lantern.

"No, not possible. The prophecy speaks of a via, a girl child. A babu: daughter. But this boy is blood-bonded to you, the taste of him confirms it. If you succumb without fulfilling the Skykeeper's wish, this mite will be haunted by the Skykeeper till death."

With a throat filled with gravel, I asked, "And what do you think the Skykeeper wants, Daronpu Gen? Tell me what this obscure prophecy says."

"Nashe."

"Hatching," I said hoarsely, watching the boy shudder within the daronpu's arms. "The act of a dragon hatchling breaking free from its shell."

"It's metaphor, Babu. Everything in the Djimbi language is metaphor. Nashe translates in the Emperor's tongue as manumission."

"Manumission."

"Has maggot turned into mynah, that you parrot me so?" he roared. "Manumission, setting the enslaved free."

"You're Djimbi."

He grinned wickedly. "Not possible, hey-o! Not allowed into Temple, such blood-tainted curs. I am fa-pim, pure in spirit and body."

"Temple belongs to the Djimbi," the dragonmaster growled from the shadows. "The glory and dominion belong to us. Long before the Emperor turned it into the parody that it is today, the Temple of the Dragon existed in the jungles, for the Djimbi. Temple belongs to *us*."

"Yes, yes," the daronpu said, lifting a great arm and waving aside the dragonmaster's heated remark. "Now, Babu, you make a decision, what-what? Condemn this boy to lifelong torment, will you? Torment most useless, as he is not the prophesied one, is not the Dirwalan Babu, and therefore can never channel the Skykeeper's power as you might. That won't stop the frustrated Guardian from plaguing him, though, in its drive to unshackle the holy. Nashe, blood-blood! The Skykeeper demands Nashe!"

The Skykeeper demanded no such thing. The Skykeeper was my mother's haunt, and she wanted only to find Waivia.

Daronpu Gen spun the boy about so that he faced me. He was misery incarnate, that scrawny child. Tears shone on his cheeks like beads of aloe.

"Look upon this boy who has never known a mother's touch, look upon your brother and condemn him to a lifetime of torment, after a childhood of suffering Kratt's pleasures! Enfold his maimed hand in yours and reject him in preference for your base cravings and an escape into death."

"Stop," I gasped.

"Stand up! Approach! His hand awaits—"

"Stop it!"

"Answer, then."

Breathing heavily, I looked upon the terrified little boy.

"What's your name?" I said at last.

"I'm called Naji," he whispered through thin lips, and I shuddered.

"One Hundred. I am the one hundredth asak-illyas to serve in the current Roshu-Lupini's viayandor."

Viayandor: mansion for females. The bayen equivalent of a rishi women's barracks, where children and women resided apart from the men.

I shuddered again at how he'd been labelled: Naji. Vile coincidence that he and I, for a brief while, had shared the same name.

"Before you served Kratt's Wai-roidan yin, what was your name?" I asked quietly.

"I am Naji," he said tremulously, afraid of anger.

"He was fated at birth for his current post," the daronpu said. "He has always been called Naji—"

"He was *not* fated for such," I said hotly, throat tight with a flash-flood of unshed tears. "His name at birth was danku Re Darquel's Waikar, First Son of Clutch Re's master potter Darquel. And your mother's name was Kavarria. Darquel's Kavarria. She had to be dragged from Wabe Din Temple when she learned you'd been stolen from her breast and taken there. She loved you. Understand that."

Tears ran down the boy's cheeks. "Did you know her?"

I hesitated, then said grimly, wearily, "I know her."

"She's alive still?"

I could find no way to answer that hope except through evasive truth. "Her bones have long been exposed to sun and soil, her flesh consumed by animals."

He caught his breath and nodded with all the courage his difficult life had taught him to muster.

"Have you lost all your milk teeth?" I asked him. "Are you a man yet?"

His four-fingered hand drifted uncertainly to his mouth. "I don't have all of them. Some have been knocked out."

"You need your adult name, anyway," I said firmly. "I give it to you now: Ingalis Hadrun Alen. Do you know what this means?"

He shook his head, eyes wide.

"The will to be responsible to yourself. Go, Ingalis. You won't be tormented by either Kratt or night terrors anymore."

I looked at Daronpu Gen. "You go, too. You've done what you came to do. I'll start training tomorrow."

# EIGHTEEN

The next afternoon, the dragonmaster returned me by wagon to my stall in the apprentices' courtyard.

The coarse wooden bench beneath me creaked as the wagon rumbled over the ground. Wet dust stuck in red clods to the cartwheels, making the ride bumpy. Harnessed to the cart, a destrier pulled us forward, snorting plumes of steam from her nostrils. Her vitality was manifest in the glossiness of her rufous and ivy green scales, the fullness of her opalescent dewlaps, the impatience with which she pulled against her creaking leather harness. Her lizard-slitted eyes eagerly took everything in, even though she must have walked the stable domain many times in her service to Roshu-Lupini Re.

Her vibrancy was thrilling.

Frayed banks of fog hung suspended between damp red earth and the low, clouded sky. The Inbetween was drawing to an end. I'd been imprisoned in the viagand chambers throughout the Wet, the entire monsoon season.

A breeze ruffled my hair and dappled my skin with beads of mist. I clutched my pimpled arms. My hands looked frail, were gelid.

We entered a stable courtyard noisy with action. Hooked muzzle poles sliced through the air like scythes. Pitchforks clattered against flagstone. Banter, shouted orders, curses, and Egg's boarlike voice reverberated round the yard.

The nutlike smell of clean featon chaff wafted over me, as warm as fresh-cooked bread, mingled with the astringent pungency of crushed vines and the peppery bite of hoontip blooms, both chopped together as fodder. The leathery musk of dragon, laced by the citric tang of venom, hung over these odors like an aromatic benediction.

A surge of emotion rose like a monsoon river-flood within me at the familiarity of place and smell.

A clawful of veterans were leading nervy yearlings to the exercise field. In ragged stages, the veterans stopped and held their charges steady at our passage. I espied Eidon, flame haired and burly, standing as strong as a young bull beside his charge. My heart leapt and my throat tightened. I raised my hand in greeting.

He looked back at me, eyes hooded, face impassive. He didn't return my wave.

It was then that I noticed that backs were turning as stiff as pitchfork shafts as eyes fell upon me. Nostrils flared. The hands that held muzzle poles clenched tighter. Voices fell silent.

Tension spread from the veterans like ocean breakers, spumy, whitecapped, the ground almost palpably resonating from the outward-spreading rumble of silence.

The servitors busy grooming wing leather and scaled back stopped their work. One by one, their heads lifted from their labors. One by one, their expressions swooped through shock, consternation, and resentment, then turned grim and closed. I recognized Ringus atop one beast; his eyes dropped from mine and he flushed mightily.

The inductees mucking stalls and mixing straw and manure together in barrels to make fuel faggots stopped their work. They didn't even attempt to mask their astonishment, which rapidly turned into fear and dismay. A few exchanged horrified looks and hissed curt questions at each other, questions I couldn't hear above the snort of impatient dragon and the creak of axle and wood. But I could guess at them.

*"How?"*

*"Why?"*

Something hard rose from my cramped belly and snagged in my throat. My raised hand stiffly returned to my lap. I stared straight ahead. My vision blurred. From the fog only, I told myself.

Beside me, the dragonmaster grunted.

"You'll not eat with them, hey-o. Nor will you muck stalls or labor alongside them. I'll bring you your food each morn and eve, and you'll spend your every waking hour training alongside me. Understand?"

I gave a brief, stiff nod.

He pulled back on the reins. With a toss of her snout, the destrier shackled to our cart stopped before my stall. My hammock, cobwebbed and thick with dust and stray flakes of chaff, looked cold.

Two husky men stepped out of the shadows.

I reared back, shot a panicked looked at the dragonmaster.

"Cafar Re guards," he said. A superfluous remark; I could see what the men were by their steel-studded leather plastrons, their skirts of fine mail, their heavily tooled leather dirk sheaths snug against the sides of their shins, and the ornate sword scabbards slung low on their hips. The warrior cicatrices slashed across their faces made them look like glowering dragons.

Everything about the two guards exuded quiet, confident menace.

"What are they doing here?" I gasped.

"Protection."

"Against whom?"

The dragonmaster's eyes slid from mine and he spat to one side.

I swallowed. The hostile eyes of every apprentice bored into my back.

"Why?" I croaked.

"There's been a daronpu here most evenings during your absence," the dragonmaster said bitterly. "Preaching."

He gestured at me to alight. I hesitated, thoughts and emotions reeling.

"Get down, girl. I've business to attend elsewhere," he said impatiently. "You'd best sleep the day away, regain a little strength. I'll be back by nightfall with the potion Gen wants you to drink. And remember: Eat nothing but what I give you. Hear?"

I swallowed, hard.

"Yes, Komikon," I answered.

But I could not sleep, not with the shocking hostility of my fellow apprentices stabbing my spirit, not in the unnerving presence of those two Cafar guards, so reminiscent of the Retainers who'd stood day and night outside the door to the viagand chambers. I lay in my hammock, twining my fingers, thoughts whirling, and occasionally drifted into an exhausted doze, only to awaken a short time later with a heart-thundering jolt, certain that one of the guards had moved toward me with lascivious intent, regardless of their stoic immobility at the threshold of my stall.

When dusk finally came and the apprentices returned from their work, I watched many a thumbnail flick against an ear to ward off evil, watched many a mouth hack spittle on the ground while eyes flicked in my direction. Eidon strode by my stall without a sideways glance. Ringus slunk by like a whipped cur.

I stayed motionless in my stall, behind the unwanted barricade of the two Cafar guards.

The dragonmaster reappeared. Bald head damp with mist, he stalked into my stall and wordlessly shoved a tin box at me, then handed one each to the guards. From around his neck dangled a taut leather bladder and a gourd tied to a twine thong.

The tin box was warm, almost hot, upon my lap, and the savory scent of meat wafted forth. The lid had been stamped with impressions of eggs and featon sheaves. I cracked it open. Steam rushed forth from two thick slabs of paak, fresh from an oven

Be side them on a bed of twice-steamed grit nestled an aroosh, a slab of gharial meat baked in a thick, heavy, featon-flour pocket. A lime, three waxy red chilies, and a cruet of what I knew would be sesal paste filled the rest of the little tin box.

The Cafar guards began eating noisily.

I stared at the dragonmaster, unsettled by the luxury of the food before me.

"You need to build your strength as fast as possible, hey," he growled by way of explanation.

Looks were shot my way from the apprentices sprawled about the hovel. The rich, oily smell of baked gharial meat had wafted toward them, overpowering the soaked-grain smell of their tepid gruel.

"Here, drink this first," the dragonmaster said, uncorking the gourd that hung from his neck. He proffered it to me.

Daronpu Gen's potion.

I took it cautiously and sniffed; an earthy, herbal odor reminiscent of rotting fungi wafted forth. I lowered the gourd with a grimace.

"What is this?" I said gruffly.

"Make haste; the charm on it lasts a short while only."

"Charm?"

The dragonmaster glared at me and shot a look at the guards. "Lower your voice."

"But what is *in* it?"

He uttered a strangled cry, grabbed my head with one hand and the gourd with his other, and brought the two forcibly together. The edge of the gourd butted into my lower lip and drew blood.

"Abbasin Shinchiwouk is but a clawful of weeks away," he hissed. "Unless the Skykeeper appears the instant you step foot in Arena, you don't have a chance of surviving against Re in your current state, and I'll not see the emancipation of my people gored before my very eyes. Now, drink, girl, drink!"

I drank.

A starburst of luminescent blue showered down my throat, a visible taste, an effervescent color. A gamy odor tinged the potion, and I felt something within me yawn open, as if a fleshy cave had momentarily dilated wide.

I dropped the empty gourd, spluttering.

"The venom'll drain from your blood quicker, now," the dragonmaster said grimly, "and its retreat will be less harsh. Gen vows it."

From outside my stall, across the courtyard where the apprentices' hovel stood, a flash of emerald and purple silk caught my eyes. I straightened, squinting.

"Great Re," I breathed. "What's that?"

"What does it look like, girl?" the dragonmaster barked. "It's a daronpu."

I watched, jaw dropped, as the daronpu—resplendent in full pageantry dress—put a clackron mask to his face. The garishly painted mask was in the shape of a dragon's head, and the overlarge, flared mouth amplified the daronpu's voice as he began reciting from a scroll he held, unraveled, in one hand.

"Know this by these words that the offspring of the kwano lurk disguised everywhere," he boomed, while about his feet the apprentices sullenly slurped their thin gruel. "Ignorant let no one be who liveth in the Emperor's kingdoms during these woeful days. Midst the orchard of Fa's empire, the ceaseless fight against the One Serpent rages on. Wreathed in deception, crowned by duplicity, the suckling servants of the Sworn Adversary take many forms to violate the sacred order of Ranon ki Cinai. If thou wouldst view all closely, you would see that many a substance is not how it appears; such should bringeth dire affright to heart, liver, and brain."

"Ignore the fool," the dragonmaster spat. "Eat, eat. Gain your strength."

"Oh, Wai-Cinai, thou One Dragon of All, thou source of purity and strength, mercy show unto our poor, grieving breasts!" the daronpu continued to boom. "Reacheth down from your celestial realm and drive from our midst all that is unholy."

Several apprentices shot a brooding look my way.

With a clenched jaw, I bent over my food and doggedly ate.

The next day, after consuming another rich meal from the Komikon's tin box and quaffing another potion verdant with crushed herbs, I resumed my vebalu training alongside the dragonmaster. The two Cafar guards stood sentinel at the gymnasium's entrance.

The dragonmaster and I were alone in the outdoor ring, the ground churned into muddy furrows and ruts by bare feet throughout the Wet. I was dressed still in the viridescent bitoo the viagand eunuch had given me months ago. Using teeth and hands, I ripped the cowl off the garment and shortened its hem to my thighs. I then donned the worn rufous vebalu cape the dragonmaster held out to me. As I closed its rusted clasp above my left shoulder, the heavy chain lay nooselike just below my larynx. The feel of it was dreadfully familiar. I shivered and, for a brief moment, craved venom. I instantly could see my brother, Ingalis, standing before me, haunted eyes wide with terror; understand, I saw him not as a memory, but with dizzying clarity, as if he'd been plucked from Daronpu Gen's safe haven and plunked before me. At the same time, the strong, mushroomy taste of Gen's potion blossomed in my mouth.

Ah. So that would be the way of it. Each time I craved venom, I'd see the image of my wounded and terrified little brother, at the mercy of my mother's haunt.

Angry at Daronpu Gen, his charmed herbal, and my own lust for venom and dragons both, I ignored my desire for the dragons' fire and concentrated as best I could on the dragonmaster before me.

He handed me a bludgeon.

"So," he said, eyes riveted on mine, "you'll use the thing now, yes?"

I swallowed, remembered the looks of anger, hostility, and resentment upon the apprentices the day previous. Remembered, too, my vow to never strike one down in Arena, to never sacrifice a life to save my own.

"No," I croaked. "I won't use it. Not as you intend."

His eyes bulged. "By all that is sacred, have you no sense?"

"I made a vow. I intend to keep it."

"You'll not survive their hatred, girl, with your asinine vow! They've been poisoned against you; you'll have no ally but me in Arena!"

"I won't sacrifice an apprentice. I won't commit murder." But even as I said it, invidious doubt slithered through me. I was not as strong as I had been prior to being kidnapped, understand. Not anywhere near as strong.

"I order you to use it."

"No. Komikon."

"I'll whip the flesh from your back if you don't."

I cleared my throat, felt tears press at my eyes. "That will hardly improve my chances of surviving Arena. Komikon."

He stared at me for several moments, fists clenched, bandy legs braced, scarred chest heaving. He snatched his own bludgeon from the ground and thwacked it hard against my rump.

I fell to my knees with a cry.

"Get up, rishi whelp," the dragonmaster growled. "Get up and train."

I stared at the thick mud oozing claylike through my fingers, took a quavering breath, and clambered to my feet.

I trained hard that day, though nowhere near as hard as even the youngest inductee might. I spent too much time doubled over, hands braced against my thighs, wheezing like a hag with pleurisy. I was weak, appallingly so. Even my trademark technique with my cape seemed lost to me, for the speed and dexterity I'd employed prior to my kidnap by Temple were long gone.

By day's end, I trembled with exhaustion and dismay.

"I pray the Skykeeper appears swiftly at Arena," the dragonmaster said with a mixture of outrage and disgust as we left the gymnasium at dusk. "Or the hope of my people is dashed."

"Give me time," I begged.

"We don't *have* time."

"Give me more of Gen's potions."

"A lakeful of the stuff won't do you any good if you refuse to play by the rules!"

His words were too like the ones Dono had uttered, shortly after I'd joined the dragonmaster's apprenticeship: *You won't survive Arena, Zarq. Doesn't matter how hard you train, doesn't matter if the dragonmaster keeps Temple away from you. If you can't play the game by the rules, you won't make it.*

The dragonmaster turned to the Cafar guards. "Return her to her stall before I throttle her. I'll fetch your meals."

I could barely walk back to my stall, though once I came within view of the apprentices gathered outside their hovel, I bit my inner cheek and steeled myself to straighten my back and pick up my feet. They all turned and watched me, save for Ringus, busy at the cauldron, his back toward me.

At the threshold of my stall, I came up short. My hammock had been cut down and slashed to pieces.

I closed my eyes, overwhelmed.

Then I thought of Prelude, of its rotting wood walls covered with epitaphs. I'd slept upon its filthy, pebbled floor, had survived its vermin-infested isolation. I had no need of a hammock.

I entered my stall and collapsed upon the old featon chaff upon the flagstone, tamped down by time, dust, and the mud-caked feet that had carried into my stall the knife wielders who'd severed my hammock. Shivering, I waited for the return of the dragonmaster.

The next day went much as the first.

As did the day after that, and the day after that. With each passing day, my pitiful craving for venom decreased, though the resentment of the apprentices grew more barbed because of the inordinate amount of time the dragonmaster lavished on me.

Too often while I trained during the day, my stall was desecrated by dragon manure or renimgar offal, and when the dragonmaster lined all the apprentices outside the stable domain at dusk for a public whipping as punishment, he only increased their determined dislike of me.

I didn't know how to stop their spiraling rancor, didn't know how to end my alienation. A wild, hopeless desperation dogged me always, compounded by the fact that I could not seem to recover my sense of balance in vebalu, had apparently lost all quick reflexes. My energy, regardless of good food, charmed potions, and ample sleep, was always inadequate. The dragonmaster was right. With my stubborn refusal to use my goading tools as weapons against my fellow apprentices, I would never survive Arena unless the Skykeeper appeared the instant I stepped within the stony shadows of that great coliseum.

Then one morning, the dragonmaster was momentarily diverted to Isolation, to care for a feisty destrier with a stubborn abscess under one wing joint. He briskly sent me on to the vebalu course alone.

"Practice whipping targets till I join you," he ordered, stropping a blade in preparation of lancing the ill destrier's abscess. "Practice till you drop."

"Yes. Komikon."

Feeling like an old, old axle in a creaking cart, I headed toward the gymnasium, my ever-present guards a penumbra on either side of me.

I saw Ringus then, just ducking into a stall to groom a destrier.

Without thinking it through, I immediately detoured from my route to the gymnasium and cornered him.

Alarmed and trapped, Ringus looked wildly about. He held his grooming pole flat across his chest, as if it were a shield. Sensing his anxiety, the destrier beside him shifted, snorted, eyes dilating. The ebony claws at the end of her wings clicked together like wooden lathes.

I licked my lips, unsure of what to say, too aware of my desperate need for an ally, of the guards flanking me, of the other apprentices who might see me with Ringus and make the servitor suffer for it.

A light entered the stable then.

I cannot explain how or whence it came. Perhaps it was my fierce need, combined with whatever Djimbi magics I'd imbued from my mother as a child at breast. Perhaps it was the will of the Winged Infinite, touching me with supernatural light. Or perhaps it was merely a post withdrawal hallucination, for yes, it is true, I'd suffered many such light-drenched hallucinations since my stay in the viagand. But regardless of what is the truth—and I leave it for you to decide, according to your own beliefs and needs—this is what happened, and were Ringus alive today, I have no doubt that he would confirm my story.

A scintillating blue light filled the stall, bleaching flagstone and bedding chaff, stone wall and ceiling timber, erasing shadows and depth. It was as if we were all length and breadth, but lacked substance, as if we were a faded portrait painted in ghostly hues.

The destrier beside Ringus stilled. The tip of her forked tongue slid from between her ivy gums, quivering. Slowly, surely, she extended the full length of her tongue toward me. Not a speck of venom was upon it; it was as pink and clean as the petal of a rain-washed incarnadine lily. In the whitewash of that scintillating blue light, solely her tongue had color. Like a lover's fingers, her forked tongue caressed my cheeks, flickered over my lips, wrapped about my neck, and pulled me close.

I drifted the few steps to the destrier, didn't walk, but floated.

Her cat-slitted, amber eyes drew closer, closer, became my world. I closed my eyes.

Scaled lips pressed against mine. I breathed in the essence of dragon. Her mouth opened wide, wider, and serrated teeth and dagger-long fangs grazed my cheek bones, my chin.

My head was within the maw of a dragon.

Sunlight burst into the stall; I could see it as a coppery brilliance behind my closed lids. It exploded from every dust mote dancing in the air, as if each mote were a tiny, blazing sun, and the blue luminescence that had moments before blanched walls and floor alike twisted into a spiral and spun, slow and ponderous, about the dragon and I. An arm of the spiral brushed Ringus's grooming pole; the pole shattered into prisms of light. I was suspended in air, within a dragon, within coruscating radiance.

Then my feet touched the ground, the dragon withdrew her mouth, and I was staring, giddily, at a gawping servitor.

"I'm not evil, Ringus," I croaked. "I'm not your enemy. The grace of the One Dragon touches all who touch me."

As if entranced, Ringus nodded.

On the morning of my twenty-eighth day in the stable domain since my return, I awoke to a clear blue sky blazing with heat. The tart, sappy smell of ferns unfurling in the jungle lay thick upon the air. That distinctive fragrance heralded the arrival of the Season of Fire. Abbasin Shinchiwouk—Arena—was truly almost upon me.

I shuddered.

It was then, with a jolt, that I realized that I hadn't seen the haunt since it had vacated my body upon my return to Clutch Re.

Swiftly following that awareness was the realization that I hadn't experienced a single gutembra, had suffered no dream memories of Waivia, even though Ingalis, my brother, had long since been removed from Clutch Re and therefore the haunt's influence. To whom, then, had the haunt gone for help in search of my sister?

And what if the haunt didn't appear in Arena to save me?

I bolted upright.

I licked my lips, sticky from Daronpu Gen's elixir that I'd consumed the night before. The potion coated my palate like kaolin, that fine white powder used so often in the pottery clan in my youth.

She would appear, certainly. The Skykeeper had rescued me twice when my life had been endangered. It was only good fortune that the haunt hadn't yet resumed stalking me, yes? The last thing I needed was to be dogged by the haunt's obsessive will over seeking my dead sister, on top of all I was experiencing. I should thank Re for the respite. Surely.

But the thanks I tacitly sent to our great Clutch bull were ambivalent. For what *if* the haunt didn't appear in Arena . . . ?

Pulse skittering, I stiffly rose from my bed of chaff and stretched my cold, aching limbs. Without acknowledging the Cafar guards, I staggered across the courtyard, toward my lopsided latrine. Far above me, a bird skirled.

The haunt.

I looked up, quick, and squinted into the sky. The winged figure was too high; I couldn't ascertain what avian species it belonged to.

But it had to be the haunt. Had to be.

Teeth gritted, I continued to my latrine.

The Cafar guards followed me, clearing out their throats and noses with phlegmy hacks. While I awkwardly ducked into my latrine, my back bending as if made from brittle tin, the guards tended to their own bladders. As a silent trio, we returned to my stall and waited for the dragonmaster to appear.

Where he slept, I didn't know, nor where he ate or how he procured our food. But each morn, he appeared at the cusp of dawn, bearing his three little tin boxes punched with impressions of eggs and grain-laden featon stalks, and within those tin boxes there were always thick slabs of steaming paak, cruets filled with sesal paste, chunks of chili-salted gharial meat, and sometimes, little cork-bunged pots of hot jalen. I looked forward to that bayen dish most of all, for I found its rich yolk sauce, laced with mint and muay leaves, most fortifying.

Always while I and my guards ate such hearty fare in the privacy of my stall, my fellow apprentices slurped their tepid gruel from their cold wooden bowls. I felt their resentment build with each swallow.

That morning was no different. The dragonmaster appeared with the stamped tin boxes. I drank the charmed, marshy herbal from his gourd, then ate. The guards bolted down their food and swigged watered maska from the bladder the dragonmaster shared with them. As a group, we then started for the vebalu course as the rest of the apprentices labored about the stables.

Halfway cross the hovel courtyard, I abruptly stopped in my tracks.

There walked Dono, leading a yearling through the sandstone archway into the courtyard beyond.

My heart slammed to a halt, then pulsed in a flood-rush of emotion. On either side of me, the Cafar guards halted because I had.

The dragonmaster had been walking some ways ahead of us; oblivious to my stop, he continued on. He was muttering darkly to himself, scowling and shaking his bald head, hating that each apprentice we passed furtively made a warding sign in our wake. Whether it be inductee filling chinks in stall wall with mortar, servitor grooming scale, or veteran bolting a yearling's wings to lead the beast out for exercise, every single apprentice flicked both earlobes a clawful of times. From the periphery of our vision, we could see it, but each time the dragonmaster turned to catch an apprentice in the act, the apprentice would scratch nose, head, or neck, feigning irritation from louse or mosquito.

It wasn't until the dragonmaster was several stall lengths ahead of me that he noticed I no longer followed. With a dragonish bugle of frustration, he whirled about and waved clenched fists into the air.

"You can't be tired already! Walk, sorry rishi whelp, walk!"

I pointed at the line of veterans just starting to lead their wing-pinioned dragons out for exercise.

"What's he doing here?" I asked, my voice high. "What in the name of Re is he doing here?"

The dragonmaster followed my finger. He hunched his shoulders to his ears, stalked to my side, and opened his mouth to speak, but I cut him off.

"You've kept him here all this time! After what he did—"

"I banished him the moment I found out he informed Temple," the dragonmaster snarled. "Don't question my judgment; don't take me for the fool."

I stared into the dragonmaster's skull face. The mottled sage and brown skin covering his cheeks looked like ill-fitted, poorly cured leather.

"Then what's he doing here?" I whispered.

"The Ranreeb demands it."

I gaped.

"Did you expect much else?" the dragonmaster asked acidly. "Temple wants you dead, girl. Dead. And Dono is their assassin."

"How long was he banished for?"

"Today is his first back."

"So he's not been training, either."

The dragonmaster snorted. "Don't look to equalize his skill with yours."

I looked back at Dono. At that precise moment, he turned. The courtyard collapsed; it was as if we stood eye to eye. I caught my breath with the malevolence in his stare.

"He can't enter Arena alongside me," I said.

"The Ranreeb insists."

I tore my eyes from Dono's long-distance glare and stared

instead at the dragonmaster. He looked me full in the eye, and it was harrowing, that look, like gazing into a chasm that held a mirror faintly visible at bottom, a mirror reflecting my own face.

"Keep away from Dono in Arena. Whatever happens, however the bull attacks, be aware of where that veteran stands." He spat. "And for the love of your life, use your weapons the way they're meant to be used. Forget your asinine vow."

Fear made it impossible for me to reply.


Throughout that day, I trained hard, harder than I'd trained yet.

I sweated and ached, broke a great blister upon my palm from parrying with my poliar so vigorously. Just as dusk began to descend, for the first time since my return, I effectively applied my trademark technique with my cape against the dragonmaster.

I whipped my cape smoothly over my head, swirled it fast into a rope, and snapped it, chain end out, at the Komikon's testicles to fend him off. With a startled cry, the dragonmaster leapt back, badly stung. I acknowledged my triumph with a grim nod at the dragonmaster, who stood slightly stooped, cheeks suffusing red from the brutal sting against his manhood. He regained his poise with the swiftness that decades of discipline and training imparted.

"About time," he growled. He gestured at the bamboo bull. "Now leap over that, hey."

I flared my nostrils and stared at the bamboo bull, a hulking shadow in the oncoming dusk.

"Leap over that, I say," the dragonmaster ordered.

"Yes," I stiffly replied. "Komikon."

I put down my bludgeon and checked that my vebalu cape was secure about my neck. Taking several slow, deep breaths, I rocked to and fro from the balls of my feet to my heals, poised to break into a run toward the fake bull.

I could do it.

I'd leapt upon the back of a kuneus plenty of times in Convent

Tieron, using one of its closest forelegs as a springboard to launch myself atop the beast for grooming. I'd done so while debilitated from starvation, while plagued by the haunt's will. I could certainly mount the stationary bamboo structure before me now, however much taller it was than the senile bulls I'd once served.

What remained to be seen was whether I could flip myself over it as the dragonmaster had ordered, in the manner that I'd often seen Ringus and the other servitors do.

Taking a deep breath, I started toward the hide-covered bamboo.

I approached it at an easy run. Several body lengths before the foreleg, I shortened my stride and quickened my pace. I leapt onto the leg and used the momentum of my run to spring myself upward to the dorsum.

*Smack!* My hands landed on coarse hide and the structure shuddered, and I kept my arms straight as my legs swung up into the air from behind me. My feet were high above me for the briefest of moments while I did a handstand upon the dorsal ridge, and then, using the momentum of my vault, I flung myself into the air.

It was like flying, a soaring freedom of spirit and body. For an exhilarating moment, I was weightless. The air and I were one. I felt as if leathery wings would erupt from my shoulder blades.

Then I began falling.

Arms flailing.

*Thud.*

I landed hard upon my back, and my head slammed against the ground with stunning force. I think I blacked out for several moments, because the next thing I knew, my head was cradled in the dragonmaster's lap.

I felt viciously nauseous. The bamboo bull towered over me, undulating dizzily in my jarred vision. My head roared.

"Clutch Re's Calim Musadish has been scheduled for three weeks from now," the dragonmaster intoned above me, and his words sounded elongated and warped. "Three weeks, understand?"

Calim Musadish: Vale Ascension. The Temple-chosen day when a bull departed its Clutch for Arena.

Calim Musadish was always so well attended and the packed crowd in such a religious fervor upon seeing the holy splendor of Re revealed, that each year a clawful of young and elderly were trampled by the seething horde. Mother had refused to allow Waivia and me to attend a single Calim Musadish. Indeed, her graphic descriptions of how the unfortunate died under the feet of the frenzied pious instilled fear in all the women of my birth clan, and no children from Clutch Re's pottery guild had ever attended the spectacle during my youth.

The bitter irony was that I now would be not only attending but participating in that same ceremony.

"Tomorrow we practice on this bull some more, hey," the dragonmaster said grimly. "I'll have no repeat performance of today. Hear?"

I could but stare giddily at the sky and shiver at twilight's empurpled gloom.

# NINETEEN

That evening, Waikar Re Kratt visited the dragonmaster and me in my stall.

He appeared suddenly, flanked by his personal guards, whose sinuous facial cicatrices were as barbarous and frightening as those of the two Cafar guards standing sentinel at my stall's threshold. Outside the apprentices' hovel, the nightly appearing daronpu continued his reading of a Temple scroll, his clackron-amplified voice booming over the entire courtyard and not missing a beat upon Kratt's appearance.

The dragonmaster's spine snapped straight as Kratt strode into my stall. I inhaled sharply and choked on the chunk of meat I'd been eating. Sputtering and wheezing, I quickly rose from where I'd been crouched on my haunches, eating from my tin food box. I stepped back several paces, deeper into my stall, pulse racing.

Kratt stopped before the dragonmaster. His magnificent indigo cape came to a swirling rest about him. He held a scroll clutched in one fist.

Kratt studied the dragonmaster for long moments, as if he were looking upon a particularly intricate work of ceramic art that he highly detested. The sweet, cloying scent of ambergris filled the air.

"She's to enter Arena," he finally said, voice soft and toxic.

Confusion passed over the dragonmaster's face. "I know it."

"Today the Ashgon issued the Bill. Her name is on it."

The Ashgon: the titular head of the Malacarite branch of Ranon ki Cinai, and the sacred advisor to the Emperor. Every year, the Ashgon's Bill stated which apprentices, from what Clutch, would perform Abbasin Shinchiwouk. The number of times each apprentice would be required to enter Arena, and the hour at which each Clutch bull would perform, was also included on the document. Egg had lectured us at length about the Bill, stressing that the names a Clutch dragonmaster presented in advance to the Ashgon helped the Emperor's sacred advisor decide whom to include on his holy statement of reckoning.

The Bill, reprinted by the thousands, helped spectators lay wagers and Clutch overseers form alliances and increase their wealth and status during the eight days of Arena.

The dragonmaster now looked angry in his confusion. "So her name is on the Bill, despite my recommendations otherwise. We expected as much."

"Ah, but the Ashgon has given the Bill teeth, Komikon. Look for yourself." Kratt extended the hand that held the scroll.

The dragonmaster looked from the rolled parchment to Kratt, then back again. It was illegal for a Mottled Belly to know the hieratic arts, even a half-breed piebald like the Komikon.

Pursing his lips, he came to a decision, took the scroll, and moved outside a few feet, that the rising moon's light might help him read. I'd underestimated the breadth of both his skills and his courage.

"At the bottom," Kratt said. "Beside the Ashgon's seal."

The dragonmaster unrolled the scroll to its full length and with a mighty scowl read the paper.

He looked up. "It says here that a Clutch forfeits eight years of the right to perform Abbasin Shinchiwouk if a Bill-listed apprentice doesn't show."

"Yes, Komikon," Kratt drawled. "It does state such."

"Since when has this been the law?"

"Since the Ranreeb informed the Ashgon of my knowledge of a certain Temple fortress hidden in the jungle, I imagine. Since I kidnapped two of the women they'd imprisoned in that secret place."

The dragonmaster shook the Bill angrily and a muscle below his left eye began twitching. "Apprentices fall ill, get wounded. A fifth of the names on this won't appear at Arena because of either illness or desertion! It's always the way."

"And substitutes will be found for them."

The dragonmaster stared at Kratt, then swung his gaze upon me.

"But no substitute could ever be found for her, hey-o! The Ranreeb knows what she looks like, and her eyes bespeak years of venom use. No rishi has such eyes."

"Clever man," Kratt said quietly, acidly.

"The Ranreeb expects his assassin to be successful. He means not only to have the Dirwalan Babu murdered here, in these stables, but he means to ruin you as well in the process."

"For permitting the deviant to enter my stables, yes," Kratt murmured, and his voice dropped lower and his eyes turned upon me. My heart stilled. "For knowing about the rite, and guessing what knowledge I might glean from a woman who performs such."

"You'll station more guards here," the dragonmaster said. It came not as a request, but an announcement of fact.

"Yes." Still, Kratt's blue eyes impaled me. Sweat trickled down the insides of my arms. "More guards, to protect not only her, but every single apprentice within these walls. Eight years without entering Arena would ruin me, Komikon. No Clutch could survive such."

The dragonmaster cursed and spat on the ground.

"But I've really no fear of her dying while in my stables, have I?" Kratt murmured. He looked from where he'd been studying me to the dragonmaster. Steel entered his tone. "Because she's the Dirwalan Babu. Isn't she, Komikon? The Skykeeper's Daughter?"

"You know it," the dragonmaster replied shortly. "You've twice seen the bird appear in her defense."

"Yet it didn't rescue her from that fortress."

"She couldn't summon it in her state! There are boundaries, limits; the otherpowers of the Realm are structured by certain laws."

"Are they."

"Think you the Realm is a bottomless lode for any to pillage at will?"

"Or perhaps," Kratt drawled, and again he looked at me, "perhaps that bird is no Skykeeper. Perhaps this deviant is merely a demon disguised. As that faithful daronpu outside insinuates."

The voice of the daronpu in question rolled around the courtyard like the distant thunder of a fast-approaching storm.

"Perhaps certain advisors in Cafar Re are correct: This woman is not Celestial sent, but kwano hatched."

"She is the Dirwalan Babu, I tell you," the dragonmaster growled.

"Then why can she not understand dragonspeak any better than an ordinary woman, hmm?" Kratt's voice turned flinty. "Why does Caranku Bri of Lireh's Yenvia also reluctantly admit to having experienced dragon-tongue hallucinations while in the Ranreeb's fortress?"

"Jotan Bri," I gasped. I'd wondered all along what had become of Misutvia but had seen no way to get an answer. Now that I had one, I didn't like the answer whatsoever.

The bead on the end of the dragonmaster's chin braid quivered like an enraged hornet. "I've heard many a boy blather nonsense while in venom's grip. It means nothing."

"Does our Dirwalan Babu here understand dragonspeak better than they? Tell me, Komikon: How many times has she lain before your destrier since her return? How much have you learned about hatching bull eggs from this deviant?"

"I've not had her perform the rite; she needs to conserve her energy to survive Arena! After Abbasin Shinchiwouk, she can lay before the destrier day and night till we solve the dragons' riddle!"

"I see." Barely restrained fury was audible in Kratt's voice, was visible in his flushing cheeks. "So you don't believe she's the Dirwalan Babu, do you, old man? For if she were, you'd not fear she'd die in Arena because of how debilitated she is."

"I told you, the powers of the otherworld are governed by certain laws!"

"Laws that only you are privy to, it would appear." Kratt stabbed a finger in my direction. "Get her to lay with the destrier tonight. I'll renounce you if she dies without revealing the riddle's answer to me. Temple will have your head on a pike."

"But—"

"Do it," Kratt ordered in a tone that brooked no argument. "I can repair my relationship with the Ranreeb yet. I've not gone so far that I can't recover, having first tossed him a scapegoat for my temporary madness of permitting this dragonwhore into my stables."

"I'll not be your sacrifice!" the dragonmaster cried. "We'll have the answer, I tell you. She's the Dirwalan Babu; you've seen the Skykeeper!"

Kratt held up a hand to silence the dragonmaster. "See that you learn the dragons' secret, old man."

With a swirl of his cape, he stormed out.

For long moments, the dragonmaster and I stared at each other, both of our chests moving quickly, shallowly. I jumped when he broke the spell of stillness by striding over to me.

He gripped one of my biceps hard. His split nails dug into my skin.

"Stay here," he hissed into my face. "I'll be back at midnight."

"You'll take me to the destrier, as Kratt orders?" I was revolted by the ill-concealed eagerness in my voice, and I cringed at the sharp image of Ingalis that sprang before my eyes.

"Whore," the dragonmaster spat, and he released me, spun on his heel, and stalked out of the stall.

I crouched on my haunches and hugged myself to still my violent shivering.

It was not just my anticipation of once again experiencing the divine grace of dragonsong that rattled me, understand. It was the forces gathering against me, building to a frothing crest, that filled me with dread.

The rage of Temple. The resentment and hostility of my fellow apprentices. Kratt's determination to learn the dragons' secret. The dragonmaster's plans to free the Djimbi. The rapidly approaching date of Abbasin Shinchiwouk. My still-weak body. My stubborn determination to never strike an apprentice down to save myself.

And now, like a great, dragon-prowed ship cresting this formidable wave, was the knowledge that I *could* have my revenge against Kratt. I *could* ruin him, as I'd once vowed. Despite the storm-mass of forces gathering and colliding like a thunderhead about me, I saw a way that I could achieve that long-held ambition of mine. Instantly.

Kratt himself had inadvertently told me how to destroy him.

I could disappear.

The new law the Ashgon had woven into his Bill held the means to fulfilling my vow of vengeance against Kratt. *Eight years without entering Arena would ruin me, Komikon. No Clutch could survive such.*

If I didn't show up at Arena, if I somehow got past my guards and fled the stable domain forever, the Ashgon would refuse Kratt permission to enter Arena for eight years. With only unfertilized eggs being laid upon Clutch Re, his herd of egg layers would be decimated. He'd be financially ruined. His political alliances would crumble.

Why, then, did delight not rush through me? Instead of plotting escape, why was I wracking my brains to figure out how I might remain in these stables? Was I truly enslaved to venom? Was it solely for want of divine union with a dragon that I remained?

No.

I couldn't then put into words why I wanted to remain, but I can now.

Home.

I wanted a home.

Orphaned, outcast, and haunted, I craved a sense of belonging. I hungered for love and acceptance. The nine-year-old child who had watched her father murdered, who had been evicted by her clan, and who had been abandoned by her mother over a mad obsession now wept for want of a welcoming hearth.

And so, as darkness descended and the stars came out as hard and sharp as quartz and the chanting daronpu left the stable domain until his return on the morrow, I racked my brains to determine how I might stay in the stables, how I might again win the grudging respect of my peers. How I might secure for myself a place I might call home.

So enwrapped was I in desperate thought that I didn't notice the music until it eclipsed my mind like a finespun cloud that was both hirsute and silky. A green feeling slowly began pulsing through me, a raw, sappy feeling fluorescing with budtime, seedtime, dew, and youth. The stronger the sensation grew, the more it altered; I became buoyant, supernal, belonging to a higher world. I was lured and goaded by the sweetening infusion, a sound that both incited and soothed.

As I stared, eyes fogged, at flagstone, my flesh began pricking with latent memory. The sensation was akin to when one has sat too long in a still position, and then, upon moving, blood rushes painfully back into stifled limbs.

Djimbi chants. I was hearing Djimbi chants.

I felt a sting, then, down in my groin. Heat that titillated and seduced. Need that was suddenly incendiary.

Daronpu Gen loomed over me.

At once, the enchantment shriveled and I snapped back into the present.

Behind Gen, both my Cafar guards stood at the threshold of my stall, swaying, moaning, and lovingly handling themselves beneath their leather-and-mail skirts. Their eyes were closed, mouths slack.

Daronpu Gen shrugged. "Best Djimbi charm I know, what-what. It'll do; it'll do."

"Why are you here?" I gasped.

His expression turned dark. "Come to take you away. I don't like the way events are turning, not one bit." He flicked a mosquito from my shoulder. "Something is amiss; I can't see a clear picture."

"Amiss?" I croaked. My heart had begun pounding as fiercely as it had at Kratt's appearance.

"The prophecy, blood-blood," Daronpu Gen said. "I thought that it foretold your appearance in Arena: *Zafinar waskatan, bar i'shem efru ikral mildron safa dir palfent.* The Dirwalan Babu is present the day the efru mildron clash, on the field-soon-to-be-marked-by-talon-and-blood. But I think now that perhaps my interpretation of those words is wrong."

Efru mildron: those of great strength, intellect, and importance. Efru mildron: the colossals. I'd heard the phrase used by Djimbi before, when, during my stay in Convent Tieron, we onais had illicitly done trade with a passing tribe. The Mottled Bellies had used the phrase indiscriminately, applying it to both the senile bulls in our care and the ever-absent Temple wardens who had ruled Tieron life.

"Is that what dragonmaster apprentices are called then, in this prophecy?" I asked, struggling to grasp what he was saying. "Efru mildron?"

"I'd assumed the reference was to the bulls fighting."

"But bulls don't clash in Arena. Not with each other."

"No. They don't." His tangled eyebrows created sharp angles upon his brow. "As you can see, my interpretation of the passage is unclear. So you'll come with me now; it's no longer safe here for you. The Komikon has informed me that Kratt disbelieves you're the Dirwalan Babu, and Temple means to have your death."

I felt beads of sweat forming on my upper lip.

"So, Babu, we leave. You and your Skykeeper will wrest Temple from the Emperor's hands not at Arena, but at some other place and time, on some day yet to come."

I swallowed.

"No."

His eyes turned as large as plums. "What?"

I shook my head, barely trusted my voice. "I stay here."

Behind Daronpu Gen, someone emitted a strangled cry. I jumped, startled; the dragonmaster had appeared at the threshold of my stall, and he smacked his bald pate with both hands. "She's cracked! All is lost."

"What are you saying, Babu?" Daronpu Gen said quietly, his eyes boring into mine.

"I want to enter Arena."

"How so?"

I took a quavering breath, let it out on a flood of words. "I want you to lay a wager at Arena, a large one, a very large one. With Clutch Xxamer-Zu. The odds will be heavily against me, and if I survive against those odds, Clutch Xxamer-Zu will never be able to meet its debt. That estate Roshu is infamous for his reckless wagering; I want him to be forced to forfeit his entire estate to me."

"Madness," the dragonmaster spluttered, almost dancing in his outrage. "The crackbrained fool!"

"No," I whispered, and I felt a tear slide down one cheek. I was shaking badly by then, could scarce draw an even breath. "Kratt has Misutvia in his hands; by his own admission we know he's keeping her in Cafar Re. One of you must fly to the Caranku Bri of Lireh, the merchant guild clan in the coastal capital. Find Malaban Bri and tell him that you know where to find his sister, Jotan. Tell him you'll divulge the information only upon the agreement that he underwrites your wagers."

Daronpu Gen stared at me. "And then?"

I swiped a hand across my eyes. "Once the agreement is in writing, tell him that Jotan can be found in Cafar Re, but that he must arrive unannounced and with others, else Kratt may kill her rather than release her."

"If she's alive yet," Gen murmured. "He oft plays in the fields of algolagnia with unwilling partners."

"She's alive," I said with certainty. "He wants the secret to breeding bulls in captivity more than he wants that kind of pleasure from Misutvia. She's alive and well looked after."

Daronpu Gen conceded the point with a grimace and a nod.

"So it's true, then?" I asked him, voice quavering. "Any woman who lies before a dragon can hear the dragons' song?"

"Yes, yes, but only the Dirwalan Babu will understand the words!" the dragonmaster interjected, eyes rolling. "The prophecy says so."

Daronpu Gen nodded, a thoughtful look entering his eyes.

"Nashe. Freedom. Manumission. Only the Dirwalan Babu will answer the riddle that will lead to such," he murmured. He straightened, glowered at me. "You'll have to disappear from sight during Arena the moment you've performed shinchiwouk."

I nodded, and my teeth clattered together as I shuddered from the realization that he was agreeing to my wild plan.

"Can you arrange such?" I asked, voice small.

He sighed heavily, shook his head. "I don't know. Perhaps. This is such a risk you take, Babu. Such a risk."

"And all for what?" the dragonmaster hissed. He came at us as if he would tackle me in his outrage. "Look at you, girl! You're weak still from your imprisonment; you've not regained half your former strength and skills! You've no allies amongst the apprentices; Temple's poisoned them all against you. And make no mistake, Dono is slated to enter Arena alongside you, his sole intent to strike you down."

"These are poor odds, Babu," Daronpu Gen said gravely. "Your Skykeeper will be hard-pressed to come to your aid in time."

I shuddered mightily, felt another tear slide down one cheek.

" 'Advances are made,' " I whispered, " 'by those with at least a touch of irrational confidence in what they can do.' "

The line was famous, attributed to Zarq Car-Mano. My namesake.

The dragonmaster all but yanked his goatee braid from his chin in frustration. "Why take this mad risk? Why?"

"I want my own Clutch."

The dragonmaster snorted and threw his hands into the air. "She is mad, mad!"

Daronpu Gen rumbled in his throat like an unhappy cat. "Even if I place the wager, even if Roshu Xxamer-Zu forfeits his estate, Statute declares that only a Temple-sanctioned warrior or lord may hold a Clutch. In case you haven't noticed, Babu, I'm neither. The Ranreeb will whisk the Clutch from my hands the moment I win it."

"No," I whispered. "He won't."

"He most certainly will!" the dragonmaster shrieked. "You crackbrained fool, after all my scheming, it comes to this, to this idiocy—"

"Let the child speak, man," Daronpu Gen rumbled. "There's reason behind her risk, hey-o."

"You encourage this insanity? You let her commit this useless suicide?"

"I have faith!" the daronpu boomed, and a film of dust was loosed upon us from the stall's cobwebbed rafters. "I see in this girl a seed, pushed deep beneath sod; I await to see it push its way forth. Never forget that faith is the subtle chain that binds us to the Winged Infinite; I will not sever a single link in that chain until I'm sure I have a better one to put in its place, blood-blood!"

The two men regarded each other, passion joining and separating them.

At last, Daronpu Gen turned to me.

"Speak, Babu," he said. "Speak."

"This is what we must do," I slowly began, and I couldn't stop shivering; I was cold, so cold. "We find a Clutch lord who'll govern Xxamer-Zu for us. One who is above Temple reproof, one who is already suited perfectly to inherit a Clutch. One whose pride is chafed sorely that he has no Clutch himself, though he ought to; one who won't balk at governing a Clutch secretly owned by you."

The dragonmaster jerked like a doll caught in the teeth of a dog. "And where in the name of the Pure One are we going to find a lord who meets those requirements, hey? Where?"

I took a deep breath.

"Here, on Clutch Re," I said. "Kratt's half-brother. Rutkar Re Ghepp."

# TWENTY

Daronpu Gen journeyed to Lireh, the coastal capital, upon a winged destrier he later told me he'd stolen in the dead of night from Wai Bayen Temple, the principal temple on Clutch Re. He flew hard for seven days and, on the morning of the eighth, found audience with Malaban Bri of Lireh.

Seven days after that—flying as ruthlessly as the daronpu had done—Malaban Bri reached Clutch Re. Five dragons flew in a tight formation across Re valley that afternoon, outstretched wings shining like sheets of wild honey, ivy and rust scales glimmering like faceted jewels. They flew direct toward the Cafar.

Kratt, I learned many months later, wisely acted the gracious host and benevolent reuniter to Malaban and his sister. For his part, Malaban judiciously played along with Kratt's facade and aimed no accusations at him while under his roof.

But all this I learned later, as I said.

All I knew at the time was that I'd committed myself to a terrifying risk, and Calim Musadish was fast approaching.

Much preparation was taking place in the stables for the momentous departure. It would take almost a week for holy Re, our bull dragon, to fly to Fwendar ki Bol, the Village of the Eggs, where the great stadium of Arena stared up at the sky like a colossal, unblinking gray eye. As was customary, Re's flight would progress in manageable stages, with Re constantly surrounded by destriers to keep him on course.

Abbasin Shinchiwouk—Arena to most—was scheduled to begin a scant few days after Re's arrival in the Village of the Eggs. It was a mark of the Ranreeb's disfavor that Clutch Re's Calim Musadish had been scheduled so close to the beginning of Arena. Our mighty Re did not have much time to recover from his long flight before the important event, unlike on previous years, when our Clutch's Calim Musadish had occurred weeks prior to Arena, giving our bull plentiful time both to reach his destination and to recover from the journey.

While the servitors and inductees readied tents, cooking gear, vebalu weapons, and fodder for the trip, the veterans practiced removing Re from his quarters to the exercise field. The whole while I sweated frantically alongside the dragonmaster, dodging his bludgeon blows, parrying his poliar attacks, and practicing my trademark move with my vebalu cape.

I fretted terribly all the while.

I had no means of knowing whether Daronpu Gen had had the opportunity before his frenzied flight to the coast to speak with Rutkar Re Ghepp. Over and over in my mind I imagined the exchange between the two men: the daronpu clothed in the ragged, worn remains of his gown of office, delivering his tale of prophecy and perfidy while shaking his half-shorn head; and Ghepp, a sheltered, deliberate, pragmatic man, listening with open incredulity. He would have dismissed Daronpu Gen as a madman, no doubt.

Yet if Gen had phrased his words right, perhaps, just perhaps, he'd managed to penetrate Ghepp's skepticism and appeal to the part of the man that was always scheming to obtain what would have rightfully been his, save for the fierce affection his father had shown an ebani and the pride he'd had in the get she'd borne him.

So much depended upon how Kratt now played his dice, how effectively he wooed Temple while his father lay gaunt and unconscious at death's doorstep. That Kratt had abandoned me—that he no longer believed I was the Skykeeper's Daughter of an obscure prophecy—was a given. After his visit to the mock mobasanin and his subsequent inquisition of Misutvia, he thought he stood an excellent chance of obtaining the secret to breeding bulls in captivity without the mess of using a deranged dragonmaster and his deviant apprentice.

I could well imagine Kratt's discussions with Daron Re, could envisage the flurry of messages between him and the Ranreeb. Could imagine the Ranreeb, in turn, deliberating with the Ashgon himself how best to proceed with Kratt, a loaded cannon that, if loosed, could further damage the already tremor-marred Temple.

Would Temple assassinate him? I believed not.

Kratt had numerous allies throughout Malacar and had no doubt informed them that he knew how to unearth the bull's secret. All eyes were upon his fate. No, Temple would not assassinate him. Better to pull such an enemy under your wing and call him ally, at a time when your very foundation was cracking.

So I fretted and could scarce sleep at night for fear of what I'd committed myself to, and gear was packed, saddles were readied, and veterans practiced for the fast-approaching day when they'd fly the destriers out of the stable domain, alongside Waikar Re Kratt, his half-brother Ghepp, Daron Re, and a clawful or so of influential Re bayen lords.

And then, the day before Calim Musadish, something unexpected occurred. Unexpected, I say, only in that it caught everyone off guard, so inauspicious was the timing.

The news traveled fast, swept across our Clutch like a raging fire. A great wail rose up from Re valley and reverberated off the mountains. Dogs howled; dark clouds covered the sun; troops of monkeys in the sesal fields howled while wild cats shrieked like gutted pigs. Men beat their breasts and plastered their bodies in hot ash, and women remained in their barracks until nightfall, clutching their children close.

The father of Waikar Re Kratt and Rutkar Re Ghepp had died in his sleep, see. Roshu-Lupini Re was dead.

An heir for the estate needed to be announced.

The announcement was postponed.

Daron Re declared that his mental, spiritual, emotional, and physical faculties would dwell solely upon Calim Musadish, Vale Ascension. He would therefore not announce whom the Ashgon had chosen as Clutch Re's overlord until after Arena.

He would not announce it, understand, until after I'd died beneath the talons of Re, and the dragonmaster who'd succored me had suffered subsequent public evisceration and decapitation. Only then—after Kratt denounced me and recanted—only then would Temple set him on the overlord throne of Clutch Re.

My death was necessary, first.

This brought a fresh wave of alarm crashing down upon me, for if I didn't die in Arena and Kratt was therefore not presented the opportunity to publicly recant, Temple would give Clutch Re to his brother, Ghepp, to govern. Who then would rule Xxamer-Zu for me?

"This is madness, madness," the dragonmaster fumed, tearing out invisible clumps of hair from his bald head. "All is twisted and opaque!"

I longed for Daronpu Gen's stalwart faith, for the eccentric warden's steady presence. But he was gone, long gone, awaiting the day of Arena in the safety of Malaban Bri's mansion, on the coast of our nation.

He knew nothing of old Roshu-Lupini Re's death.

Calim Musadish.

Vale Ascension.

Though dawn had only just caressed the cinereous sky with an ochre-dipped brush, outside the stable domain's great sandstone walls the susurrus of the crowd was like a flood-swollen river. In-side the stables, dragons bugled, Egg and Ringus shouted orders, and servitors and inductees swarmed over the destriers, pinioning their wings with great brass bolts, grooming them, saddling them, muzzling and hobbling them.

In all the upheaval, only I stood still. Shackles hobbled my an-kles and bound my wrists. A chain ran through all four shackles, then up to the stout leather collar about my neck. Though I couldn't see the collar, I was keenly aware of the metal ring through which the chain ran beneath my chin, for every time I turned my head, the chain clanked through the steel and the sound reverber-ated against my throat.

Waikar Re Kratt had insisted that I be transported to Arena in such a manner. Clearly, he would succor me no more.

A guard clutched the end of my chain in one fist. I could not stop shuddering.

When every destrier chosen by the dragonmaster for the jour-ney to Arena was saddled, hobbled, muzzled, and wing-pinioned, the servitors led them toward the point of departure: the exercise field. The procession was chaotic as agitated dragons lashed tails, shied, tossed snouts, and bucked. Ringus led the haphazard pro-cession by sheer dint of will.

The guard tugged me forward, though he needn't have; I clearly knew we were leaving. Fettered and shuddering, I brought up the rear of the parade. My breath came erratically, too swiftly, inade-quate for my lungs.

We crossed through one courtyard, then the next. The dragons still in their stalls bugled and butted their domed crowns against gate and wall in agitation. Sight and sound collapsed and expanded around me. The air turned fulsome with the musk of impassioned dragon, the reek of steaming dung, and the sharp tang of venom.

We reached the exercise grounds.

There, in the center of the field, surrounded by every veteran in the dragonmaster's employ and fettered so thoroughly that his snout, wings, hind legs, and forelegs looked as if they were made primarily from metal bangle, stood Re.

I cried out at the size of him.

He was immense and beautiful and exuded raw power. Over sixteen feet high at shoulder, his massive tawny wings folded and bolted together across his dorsal ridge, the great bull dragon shimmered like a hillock of emeralds and amethysts. With every ripple of his muscled hindquarters, those purple and green scales shone as if each had captured the sun.

His head and neck were tethered, by many thick ropes, to one of the pillars sunken into the ground; his stooped neck imparted the impression that he was kowtowing. With his snout that low to the ground, his great opalescent dewlaps brushed the earth, glittering milky pink and blue despite the red dust. The majestic olfactory plumes arcing in iridescent feathered fronds over his domed head swiveled in the direction of the parade of female destriers entering the field, and his twiggy tail with diamond-shaped membrane at tip lashed to and fro like an enormous agitated snake.

Even though his snout was staunchly enclosed in a gem-encrusted muzzle, Re bugled.

The noise was pure fury. It blasted like a hurricane over my skin and blew my wits far from me.

A brief flurry of chaos broke out amongst the destriers at both sight and sound of the great bull. The ground reverberated under my feet. Clods of turf flew this way and that. Foam fell from snouts, whips cracked, hooks glinted in nares as snouts were caught and held steady. One inductee turned and ran back toward the hovel courtyard. Where he thought he might hide, I don't know. Certainly, there was no escape. If he even attempted to leave the stable domain on foot, the fevered crowd outside would rip him limb from limb for avoiding his Re-chosen destiny.

The destriers were battle beasts, trained to fly unflinchingly into a maelstrom of slashing talons and flapping wings; their training held them in good stead. After a brief commotion, they calmed, and Ringus was able to lead the procession forward a goodly ways, where it fractured so that each dragon was led to one of the great pillars sunken in the ground. One by one the destriers were tethered to the pillars.

While the inductees next strapped gear aboard the destriers, the dragonmaster wove among them, giving directions. Egg and Ringus left with the servitors to prepare more destriers for flight. Surrounded by veterans bearing whips, nare hooks, blow darts, and spare wing bolts, Re watched everything in shuddering agitation, his nostrils close to the earth, each breath blowing up clouds of dust.

I could not tear my eyes from him, was riveted by his wicked, curved talons. Each looked half the length of my forearm. Even a scratch by one would eviscerate me.

Dawn swelled with fly-buzzing warmth into noon. Waikar Re Kratt and those accompanying him on the flight to Arena arrived outside the sandstone walls, to much cheering from the crowd. I didn't know it was Kratt, of course, until a little sally port in the domain's great sandstone wall was opened at the end of the field. Although I stood far from him, I knew it was Kratt striding through the door. His hair gleamed like spun gold in the sunlight. He followed Daron Re, who first came through the sally port, his white cape as clean as a dove's breast, his tricornered hat topped by bobbing bull plumes.

Rutkar Re Ghepp ducked through the sally port third, his sable hair a stark contrast to Kratt's saffron locks. And, after a string of daronpuis and lords, a creature cowled, veiled, and gowned entirely in white came through the door.

A moan escaped my lips: an Auditor.

The Auditor scanned the vast field that teemed with action, and though I couldn't see his face beneath his cowled veil, I knew his eyes rested upon me. He came toward me, gliding over the rutted ground as if he were windblown through water.

When he reached me, he extended a chalk-whitened hand to my Cafar jailer. The guard handed him the end of my chain without touching the Temple executioner's hand, then stepped back several paces.

Cold spread up the metal links of the chain about my neck, I swear it did. I broke into a chill sweat and stared across the field, trying to ignore the massive scimitar scabbard hanging from the Auditor's waist.

Every destrier was finally ready, burdened with fodder, gear, or riding saddle. Every lord and Holy Warden who was blessed with the honor of accompanying Re on the momentous journey was present. Every dragonmaster apprentice in the stables stood on the field. Every one of the destriers in the stables was loaded and saddled.

Departure time.

Around me, my fellow apprentices began chanting the cinai komikon walan kolriks, the dragonmaster apprentice prayers for guardianship from Re. My lips moved of their own accord, my voice joining the intense drone as if I were entranced. United, our voices held all the strange power of a sand gale.

The apprentices began removing the hobbles and wingbolts from the destriers, clipping the empty brass shackles and bolts to the saddles.

The destriers knew flight was coming. While most stood taut and ready, hindquarters quivering, a few of the youngest shifted to and fro and impatiently beat the air with their wings, lunging against their tethers fastened to the pillars sunken in the field.

The lords approached the destriers, each talking to his beast and stroking its muzzled snout with familiar affection. It was then that I fully understood that, of course, the dragons did not belong to the dragonmaster. Not at all. These bayen men of influence and wealth were the masters of those fine beasts, many master of two or three, and Waikar Re Kratt, under the auspices of Temple, was the guardian of them all, including the great Re.

The lords mounted their destriers. The apprentices began to untether them.

There were fifty-four apprentices in the dragonmaster's stables, twenty-four of the latter being inductees, myself included. Holy Wardens mounted behind the bayen lords of highest status. Those lords of lesser status carried servitors behind them. One gorepotted lord looked unskilled in dragonflight. Indeed, he would fly seated behind a chosen veteran. Dono was thus favored. Some destriers had no lords to fly them; those would be flown by the veterans, some flying two to a beast.

Lastly, the lords of least standing were required to carry an inductee or two behind them. The dragonmaster would fly upon the great bull himself, alone. Waikar Re Kratt would fly his own destrier, an impressive beast caparisoned with a delicate metal lacework of ornamentation and jewels.

I was to fly behind the Auditor. No lord would carry a deviant.

Under the masked gaze of the Auditor, the Cafar guard unlocked my restraints so I could mount the destrier. Shuddering still, I placed my left hand on the saddle, my left foot in a stirrup, and swung up. Straddling the destrier, I assumed the flight position, laying forward along the destrier's dorsum. The saddle leather was smooth and sun hot beneath my thighs. I reached my shackled hands forward and grasped the saddle rungs on either side of the destrier's neck.

The saddle lurched as the Auditor climbed up behind me. I tensed, couldn't help it, and recoiled from his weight as he lay atop me, the touch of his gown drifting to either side of me like a shroud. Odd, how I rode in front while every other apprentice rode in the rear position. Perhaps it was unseemly for a woman to lay atop a man's back. Perhaps it was merely an extra measure to ensure my arrival at Arena, to prevent me from flinging myself from the dragon midflight and plunging to my death.

The dour Cafar guard secured my wrists and ankles to the saddle. The Auditor placed his albescent hands atop mine.

Everyone was mounted, save for ten of the veterans. Four of these began unbolting Re's wings. Two crouched ready at the hobbles between Re's rear legs; the remaining four stood stationed by the sunken pillar to which Re was tethered. The dragonmaster sat astride the great bull, all but his pate lost from sight by Re's great wings, folded across the beast's dorsum.

The tension in the air was bone piercing.

The last wingbolts came off. At the exact same moment, the veterans who were crouched by Re's hind legs unclasped his hobbles, and the four veterans stationed on the ground by the sunken pillar unclipped the tethers that held Re's snout low to the ground. All the veterans ran then, heads ducked, thigh muscles and arms pumping, sprinting as furiously as they could to get as far from Re as possible.

The bull raised his head from the ground. Shook it, great dewlaps flashing in the sunlight. He craned his neck to the sky, bugled, still muzzled, and unfurled his great wings.

A forty-foot wingspan, it was, but much larger it seemed upon the ground.

A great cry rose up around me, thrilling and blood foaming: The lords of Clutch Re were urging their dragons into flight. Above me, the Auditor likewise bellowed, and the excitement and power of the moment was as intoxicating and terrible as the first taste of venom.

We exploded into flight, the whole field of us, mighty Re in our midst.

Noise and wind and dust and the smell of dragon were all about me, and I closed my eyes and pressed into the saddle, gripping it with thigh and hand. Surging tumult beneath me as dragon muscles worked and flanks heaved and ribs sucked in and expelled air.

Then we were flying, the alleys below us packed with people, like a honeycomb with a swarm of bees.

The journey to Fwendar ki Bol quickly assumed a routine, and while each landing and takeoff was fraught with tension, the destriers over and over proved themselves worthy of Clutch Re's stable domain. They were stalwart, highly disciplined beasts, and although the occasional dragon was headstrong and nervy, the veterans and lords who flew such beasts controlled them with wondrous skill. Whenever one could not subdue his mount, the dragonmaster did so using skill, willpower, Djimbi curses, and vein-popping strength. I learned a new measure of respect for the bandy-legged piebald.

As for the great bull, he too behaved well, though the quivering power of him and his occasional outraged trumpeting imparted the impression that discipline played no part in his control, solely a constrained, waiting fury. At all times while in flight and on the ground, the bull was muzzled, and also hobbled and wing-pinioned while grounded, and for the duration of each night, he slept tethered by muzzled snout to a great pillar sunken in the ground. Each landing site sported such a pillar.

The flight path to Fwendar ki Bol had been mapped out a century and a half ago and used by every Clutch along the route every year since. Each landing field, annually slashed and burned free of sapling and vine, was situated by a river or lake. The apprentices erected a clawful of small canvas tents for the bayen lords and daronpuis to share every evening. Each morn, they dismantled the same. The rest of us slept upon ground, amongst the hobbled dragons.

As a woman, a condemned deviant, and an inductee, I was at all times avoided. Only the Auditor stood by my side, and he as silent as mist. I was given neither food nor drink the entire time, though the Auditor ate whatever an inductee brought him. Never once did the Auditor remove his long, enveloping garment from over his face, but instead he slipped food and water up under the white cloth to his mouth, through a slit barely visible amongst the folds, just below where I assumed his chin to be.

What I ate, I stole from our destrier's feed sack. What I drank, I sucked from river and lake, on all fours alongside the dragons, when the Auditor took me down for watering each evening.

By the time our cavalcade reached Fwendar ki Bol, I was weak, muddled, and nigh on incoherent from the stress of the journey and the lack of water and food.

Fwendar ki Bol, the Village of the Eggs, is situated a half day's easy flight from the outskirts of Liru, Malacar's capital city. Surrounded by sesal fields, orchards, and vineyards, the sprawling village is home to Malacar's nashvenirs, or hatching farms. Nashvenir Re is a splendid place, boasting a vineyard, a three-produce orchard, and a melon field, none of which I could appreciate because of my debilitated state.

Every Clutch of any consequence had a nashvenir, and those that did not rented a portion of a wealthier Clutch's hatching farm. It was in a nashvenir that each Clutch overseer stabled the bevy of wing-intact dragons annually bred to a bull in Arena. Those breeders, called exactly that in the Emperor's tongue, onahmes, were the dragons that laid fertilized eggs ninety-two days after being mounted in Arena. Their eggs were then transported in incubation wagons back to each overseer's Clutch, the unborn hatchlings within destined either for wing and tongue amputation and life in the brooder stables, or for service elsewhere upon each estate. A few lucky hatchlings kept their wings and tongues and joined a dragonmaster's stable.

Nashvenir Re stabled seventy onahmes. On average, each onahme laid a clutch of six fertilized eggs yearly. Save for a clawful that were sold and one or two that were kept to replenish the nashvenir ranks, the bulk of those 420 fertilized eggs were transported to Clutch Re, to restock and increase Re's egg-laying herd. Given the average forty-year life span of a dragon, and taking into account the small number of hatchlings that died unhatched in the incubation wagons, a well-stocked nashvenir ensured the continual prosperity of a skillfully managed Clutch.

Waikar Re Kratt, for all his many flaws, managed the egg-and-dragon portion of Clutch Re most skillfully.

On the far west side of the Fwendar ki Bol alluvial plains, Arena rose up like a strange monolith. There the bulls from each Clutch were stabled during Arena, in heavily guarded chambers underneath the huge coliseum. Outside, a labyrinth of taverns, inns, and elegant manors knelt about its base like subjects paying homage to a liege. Save for when Abbasin Shinchiwouk flooded the plains with hordes of bayen and rishi spectators, those manors and taverns stood empty except for the innkeepers' families, who worked in a nashvenir orchard or stable the rest of the year.

As an inductee, I stayed in neither manor nor inn. I stayed in the nashvenir Re stables, shackled to a manger, eating and drinking from the same trough of an onahme fated to be mated with the same bull that would kill me.

The Auditor stayed beside me always.

# TWENTY-ONE

The Bill the Ashgon had issued throughout Malacar listed which apprentices from each Clutch would enter Arena on what day, and which Clutch bull was performing at what time. My name, Clutch Re's Zarq-the-deviant, was on the Bill for two successive days.

To list my name for more than two days would have emphasized Temple's concern about me and suggested that I possessed the skills necessary to survive beyond the first day. Impossible, that. It was certain that such a deviant as myself would die the moment holy Re was loosed in Arena alongside me. His divine fury would slay me for my depravity and aberrance, and cleanse the nation of my presence.

But a second day was assigned me. Just in case.

These, then, were the wagering details for Clutch Re that year: Over the eight days of Abbasin Shinchiwouk, our bull would enter Arena alongside our dragonmaster once each day and mount ten to fifteen onahmes each time. (Kratt had sold his ten surplus breeding rights to the bull-less Clutches that annually paid to have their on-ahmes mounted by Re).

All of Clutch Re's twenty-four inductees were slated to enter Arena at least once over those eight days, as well as all eighteen servitors. Of the eighteen servitors, only twelve were expected to survive. Of the twenty-four inductees, only six.

Of Clutch Re's veterans that year, only Eidon, Dono, and four others were required to perform. The Ashgon had slated Dono to enter Arena twice, each time alongside me.

So.

Of the fifty-four Clutch Re apprentices present at Arena that year, only twenty-nine were expected to live through the event.

I was not one of them.

The long, unpaved road to Arena was crowded with rishi who could not afford entry into the great stadium, but who desired a glimpse of the apprentices who would compete. That year, they desired a look at me.

Rocks and rotten plums rained upon my cart, and the apprentices traveling with me covered their heads and ducked low. Beside me, the Auditor remained improbably still until a stinking turnip splattered soundly against his nape.

He didn't bellow rage or hurl invective. He rose slowly to his feet, withdrew his massive, wicked scimitar, and stood, swaying above me, as the cart trundled forward.

The threat was implicit. Any who fouled him with rock or produce would be decapitated. No one dared hurl missiles after that, for fear of missing me and striking the Auditor.

Our procession continued to Arena, Waikar Re Kratt far at the fore, magnificent upon his ostentatious beast, followed by his gaudy Holy Wardens and esteemed bayen lords.

The noise of the crowd was bewildering, the unbridled hatred in the faces screaming at me stunning. Perched upon tiled rooftop, hanging out window, leaning from balcony, packed tight along alley, faces both elegant and coarse shouted for my death. Fingers all sheathed in wooden or metal talons clacked angrily at me: *clitter-clack, clitter-clack!* The hailstorm was deafening. The shadow of Arena bathed us all in cool gloom.

Our procession turned a corner: The entrance of a gated tunnel leading into the stadium gawped at us. Waikar Re Kratt calmly rode his destrier beyond the guards at the entrance and led us down into Arena's dank depths.

I felt I was descending into the esophagus of a massive, primitive beast, and I swooned and wondered why I'd been so foolish to put myself in this position, wondered why I had not fled with Daronpu Gen when I'd had my chance.

"You perform shortly," the dragonmaster growled at me, his face a mottled half-moon in the gloom. The ground above us, the slick walls on either side of us, rumbled as if from a slight, ceaseless earthquake. The muted trumpeting of onahmes and the low, furious roar of bull dragons reverberated down the dank tunnels.

I could almost understand the braying dragons, in my fear. Could almost hear words, conversation, snatches of song.

"Are you listening to me?" the dragonmaster cried.

"Yes."

"Temple wants your death over and done with. Re is the first bull slated to enter Arena."

"You'll be there with me?" My head floated several feet above my shoulders.

"Yes."

"Who else?"

"Dono. Ringus. Three inductees."

My gaze wandered over the apprentices crouched about the tunnel floor, each rubbing grease over his limbs so that blows and whiplashes might slide off instead of breaking skin. Their lips moved as they muttered the komikonpu walan kolriks. Firelight from a single guttering torch played like demon tongues over their grease-slicked bodies.

"It'll be a blood bath," I murmured.

"Is the Skykeeper near?" the dragonmaster demanded. "Can you summon it yet?"

I countered his questions with my own. "How quickly can you arouse Re? How long must I last out there?"

"None of the chosen inductees will have presence of mind

enough to arouse the bull," he muttered. "And Dono'll be concerned only with striking you down."

"And Ringus?" I glanced at the effeminate servitor who had, so many months ago, witnessed the transfiguration of my mother's haunt from pigeon to specter. Who had, but weeks ago, witnessed the bizarre benediction I'd received from the destrier that had carefully placed my head in her maw.

"You need to summon the Dirwalan, understand?" the dragonmaster growled. "Summon your Skykeeper, girl, and use your damn bludgeon to strike others down!"

"I won't . . . I can't . . ." The words were lodged in my throat, my vow withering under the onslaught of fear.

The dragonmaster grabbed my hair and pulled my face right up against his.

"Kill any apprentice that comes near you. Or you'll die."

"It's time."

Ringus stood beside me, his lean body shining with not just grease but a thin film of sweat, from where he'd spent every moment since our arrival in the dark bowels of Arena practicing with whip and poliar and readying his muscles for combat.

I pushed away from the wall I was leaning against, the bludgeon and vebalu cape I'd been assigned at my feet. I stiffly bent to pick up my cape, muscles gone suddenly rigid from fear. The rusted clasp had been badly bent by its previous wearer; the hook snagged out at an angle, sharp and curved as a miniature scimitar. With difficulty, I snapped the rusted clasp closed over one shoulder, felt the weight of the chain heavy against my throat.

Ringus still stood before me, nervous, uncertain. He tossed a look into the pockets of dark behind him, lit here and there with inadequate, guttering torchlight.

"You remember what you saw the other week, hey," I said hoarsely, my eyes on his. "Remember how the destiny wheel spun, before my kidnap. I'm not your enemy, Ringus. And the grace of the One Dragon touches all who touch me."

His narrow larynx punched up and down and he licked his slim, sweet lips. With a barely perceptible bob of his head, he turned and walked away from me.

I picked up my bludgeon. It felt much, much heavier than any bludgeon I'd ever held before. My hands felt clammy. Teeth chattering, I wended my way toward the dragonmaster, who stood beside Dono and three other inductees. At my passage, the apprentices sprawled about the ground hissed like snakes and one voice—lovely, low, belonging to Eidon—began uttering the Gyin-gyin.

The dragonmaster looked at me, blood-marbled eyes glistening.

"Don't fail me, Babu," he growled.

With the dragonmaster at the fore, we then started up the dark tunnel, to the great dusty bowl of Abbasin Shinchiwouk. The elegiac sound of apprentices muttering the walan kolriks followed in our wake.

The three chosen inductees moved in stiff-legged terror. One wept silently, eyes protruding like those of a dead fish. One looked angry, held his poliar tightly, shivering. The third was being tugged up the tunnel by a rope the dragonmaster had fixed about his neck; I recognized him as the inductee who'd fled the exercise field upon first sight of Re. He began calling for his mother in a breathless whisper, over and over.

All of the three inductees were younger than nine years old.

Strike one of them down to save my own life? Watch Re rip their guts from their small, smooth bellies? Never. I would never stoop to such.

From where he walked alongside the dragonmaster, each footfall landing just slightly ahead of the Komikon's, Dono looked at me. There was so much anger in that narrow, unshaven face, so much determination and bloodlust, that my footsteps faltered.

I wanted to say something to him, wanted to remind him of how we'd swung together on the same vine, as children, in the warmth of a summer twilight. We'd both come bawling from the wombs of separate women within the space of a week; we'd both nursed from the same breasts.

But my voice wouldn't come, dammed by the fear freezing my blood and the fury raging through his.

To the great rolling, quavering sound of water gongs struck by the plethora of monks in the Arena tiers, Cinai Komikon Re led Dono, Ringus, three twiggy-limbed boys, and me through a guarded gate and onto the stadium grounds.

The sunlight after the tunnel was overbright. The lot of us came to a stop, blinded. At the sight of us, a low roar started up from the tiers of Malacarites packing the stadium. The eerie noise swelled, just like the gale that rips over a jungle canopy before a hurricane tears leaf and frond asunder. The crowd moved as it roared its disapproval; the tiers rippled as if alive. Awed and terrified, I craned my neck up, up, as the *clitter-clack* of more than two hundred thousand finger sheaths beat a hail of outrage upon my ears.

The amphitheater was roofless, but instead of a bowl of blue sky gazing down at me, huge arcing columns extended like protruding ribs toward Arena's aerial middle. The massive, tapering spars did not meet at center, for no feat of Malacarite architectural engineering could yet make such possible. But to create the illusion of a roof, silver netting had been strung from rib to rib, festooned with objects that glittered and twirled, catching the sun rays, sending prisms and blinding diamonds of light dancing over the crowd below. Faceted mirrors, bells of hammered gold, and glass baubles encrusted with jewels glittered in the sunlight, though I could discern no individual shapes from the silver netting's great height, only knew by stories I'd heard as a child what the objects were.

I was looking at the renowned Fa-Tigris Wamanarras, the Emperor's Ceiling of the Firmament, each silver link and ornament

polished and strung annually for Abbasin Shinchiwouk. The dazzling chandelier display looked impenetrable to a dragon's eye, and
only once in the history of Ranon ki Cinai had a bull attempted to
perforate it and escape.

Far below the ceiling coiled the great ring of spectator tiers.
Though I knew it not then, each tier jutted out somewhat. The
subsequent concavity beneath the overhanging ledges, behind the
knees of every seated or standing spectator, was called the iyamunas, the grottos. Whenever a bull launched himself into flight, either during shinchiwouk or when Arena reverberated with the
wing beats and lust-bellows of the loosed onahmes, most spectators crouched into the iyamunas. Much infamous behavior took
place then, consensual or otherwise, as thigh was pressed against
thigh and breast against chest, while dragons swooped overhead in
musky passion and a bull mounted whatever onahme landed upon
the ground.

Those who chose through bravado or dignity to forgo the iyamunas ran the risk of being splattered by a cascade of onahme
guano. Guano boys darted hither and yon among the stands with
great baskets on their backs and shovels in their hands, the inebri-
ated spectators either cursing or throwing coin at them.

Situated at regular intervals throughout the tiers stood canopied
balconies, each emblazoned with a Clutch insignia. Daronpuis,
bayen women, skilled ebanis, Clutch overlords, and tables groaning with wine flagons, wagering ledgers, fruits, cakes, and nuts
crowded such balconies. On some, orgies would ensue after each
shinchiwouk, the spectators intoxicated by wine, the scent of
dragon musk, the spectacle of spilled blood, and the sight of a
great bull pumping atop one onahame after another.

My dazzled eyes skittered along the tiers and stopped at a heavily garlanded balcony topped by a magnificent purple canopy
bearing the cursive, elaborate insignia of Ranon ki Cinai. Ah. The
balcony of the Ashgon. From where I stood, I saw the great man as

nothing but a blurry plumed hat and mound of embroidered cloth sitting upon a great crimson throne. The gore-bellied man beside him was the Ranreeb of the Jungle Crown. I felt sure of it.

The Ashgon ponderously raised a hand. The monks throughout the stadium stopped striking their water gongs. The crowd fell silent. The air grew taut with expectation. My mouth went dry. My heart hammered even faster.

"Fan out," the dragonmaster cried, and we apprentices began moving, placing distance between us. I moved as if in a dream, couldn't feel my feet or legs beneath me. Perhaps I floated.

Two of the inductees stood together, paralyzed with fear.

Dono stationed himself to my far left, legs braced in a half crouch, facing halfway between me and the massive iron gate that held Re out of the stadium bowl. The dragonmaster stood crouched in his simian stance between myself and Dono. Ringus stood a goodly distance to my right.

Time stretched, sound elongated. I became aware of the dust under my bare feet: hot, gritty. A fly buzzed about my head.

The Ashgon lowered his hand.

A pause. Then the squeal and clank of rusty cogs reverberated through Arena as the great iron gates that separated Re from the stadium bowl were winched up. The crowd murmured, moved, rustled like a wind through a grove of trees.

Behind the series of gates, mighty Re bellowed.

His roar was my heart, thundering wild in my chest. I could not breathe, could not move, could not think as his blast of outrage distorted reason.

His battle cry stopped. It felt as if my heart, too, ceased.

The onahmes visible behind a gate adjacent to him bugled in response. A cloying wave of musk filled the air.

The iron gate in front of Re winched higher. Dono hefted his poliar and looked at me.

At that moment Re lunged forward.

My heart convulsed; my fingers went slack. The dragonmaster sprinted toward Re, yelling insanely. The crowd surged to its feet with a great cry.

Re altered his charge and swung toward the bellowing dragonmaster. Dono charged toward me.

"Mother!" I tried to yell, but no voice came from my throat, no power erupted from within me, and no massive otherworld form crashed through the Emperor's Ceiling.

"Mother!" I screamed again, but still she did not come, she did not appear, she stayed away.

No. No. It was not possible, she couldn't abandon me again, she would not, she could not . . .

She had.

I turned and ran.

There was nowhere to run to.

I slammed into the high coliseum wall, scrabbled ineffectually at it, bludgeon falling to my feet. Ten feet above me, leaning over the rail of the first tier, rishi spectators hurled insult, rock, and rotted food at me. The onslaught hailed down upon my head and shoulders. With a cry, I staggered away from the wall and sloppily turned about.

I saw, in the periphery of my vision, the dragonmaster cracking his whip at Re while Ringus darted toward the great beast's testes. And I saw, direct in front of me, Dono, fast approaching.

My vision collapsed to encompass only Dono.

He slowed to a stop a short ways from me and adjusted his grip on his poliar. My body moved by rote: I back-stepped, took off my vebalu cape, and spun it into a rope, chain-end down.

As if we were wary partners in some primitive dance, we began circling each other.

"You're my milk-brother, Dono," I said hoarsely, mouth dry. "You don't want to do this."

"Dragonwhore. Deviant."

"Don't be Temple's assassin. Don't sell yourself to the Emperor."

"You corrupted me once, Zarq. You won't do it again."

"Corrupted you!" I cried. "Look to Temple for corruption, not me."

"Demon's spawn. Djimbi get."

And then, just like in my childhood, just as always throughout my youth, I couldn't hold my tongue when I should have, couldn't dam the anger and indignation flood-swelling within me.

"Ebani-basa Coldekolkar," I shot back.

Ebani-basa Coldekolkar: Womb-Ripping First Son of a Many-Men Pleasurer. It was Dono's inglorious, long-buried birth name, a name replete with a childhood filled with humiliation and mockery. It was a name he'd almost killed himself to get rid of.

With a roar of outrage, he charged at me.

I sidestepped his charge. Misjudged. His poliar caught me on my hip, sent me spinning round with a blast of pain. The crowd roared. The pain turned my head airy and fuddled.

The ground reverberated beneath me. From one corner of my eye I realized, shocked, that Re was close, engaged in combat with the dragonmaster and Ringus, his snout darting forward, his venom-coated tongue snapping forth.

How big he was, how muscled and fast! He exuded heat and fury. His great scaled hindquarters were swinging toward me, talons shredding up clouds of dust. The dragonmaster danced about him, wielding his whip, while Ringus darted in and out between the bull's hindlegs.

The two inductees who'd stood as if paralyzed shrieked as Re's hindquarters loomed suddenly closer. They both dropped their weapons and fled, blindly.

The panicked movement caught Re's eye. With breathtaking speed, he spun round, nearly trampling Ringus, knocking the dragonmaster into the dust with his furiously lashing thin tail. Re's neck snaked forward, his tongue shot forth: *Smack!* He hit one of the fleeing inductees square upon the back. The stricken inductee sailed through the air and landed hard facedown, skidding upon belly and chin through dust. Re's snout shot toward him, his jaws opened, and he picked the fallen little boy up in his mouth. A gurgled scream. A blur as Re shook him. A foreleg talon slashed up toward snout. The ground turned red with blood.

The crowd roared anew.

Dono smashed his poliar against my ribs and I crumpled.

Blinding pain white-hot through my torso. My head turned buoyant and cotton clouded.

Dono came at me, poliar raised like an axe above his head. Fear injected adrenaline through my veins and I scrambled for my cape and snapped it wildly at him as he brought his poliar smashing down to my face. I rolled. His poliar slammed into dirt. I felt the chain hook-clasp of my cape catch on something, and as I rolled, the clasp tugged reluctantly along the rolled rope of my cape.

Dono screamed.

The clasp had snagged upon his left eyelid.

He clawed at his face, ripped the thing out of his lid. I stared in horror as blood poured over his cheek from his self-shredded eyelid. Behind me, Re bellowed, close, too close. Still on my back in the dust, I turned, looked wildly over one shoulder. One of Re's great clawed feet scored the ground a hand's breadth away from me, and the ground shook.

I screamed shrilly.

Confusion, clouds of dust, a mountain of heaving belly scales above me.

Through the clouds of dust, a figure. Ringus.

"Get out, get out," he screamed, and as I struggled to stand, Re shifted again, lightning fast, and I saw two slitted, amber red eyes appear suddenly above me, and then Ringus was snatched up in Re's maw.

Re reared up on his hind legs. In typical dragon fashion, he used the sharp, hooked talons of his forelegs to eviscerate the prey in his mouth.

I staggered away, terrified, half blind with the pain that radiated outward in crippling waves from where Dono had smashed his poliar against my ribs.

I heard Egg's voice in my head then:

*"If you've been hurt bad in Arena an' Re is chargin' at you, your only hope of survivin' is pundar. You drape your cape over yourself, drop to the ground, keep your mouth shut, an' don't move."*

But I had no cape.

I espied one of the inductees, standing terrified near the very gated entrance we'd come through, a clawful of feet away from me. I launched myself at him, tackled him about the midriff. We both went down hard.

Clapping one hand over his mouth, I wrenched the cape from his neck.

And covered us both.

"Stay still!" I hissed into his ear. "Pundar, pundar!"

Quivering mightily, the terrified young boy obeyed.

The ground reverberated beneath us as Re's great feet slammed into earth, growing closer, closer. I held my breath, closed my eyes, fought the shrieking urge to run, run, run.

A mighty, bone-rattling roar from the bull.

Beneath me, the inductee screamed shrilly.

I waited, tears of dread rolling freely down my cheeks, for the snap of Re's teeth upon my spine.

But it didn't come. No.

Only a dusty gale of wind, whooshing over us in violent, rhythmic gusts. Our cape was blown away.

Exposed and helpless, I squinted through the billowing dust. Mighty Re stood in the center of the stadium, the dragonmaster bellowing at him.

The great bull had spread his massive wings and was beating the air. Along the coliseum's lowest tiers, canopies shuddered and veils and bitoos flapped like flags.

I saw it then. Re's erection. His great, forked phallus glistened a red-mottled pink in the sun's light.

Relief and incredulity rushed over me: Ringus and the dragon-master had succeeded. Re was ready for mating.

As the iron gates holding back the onahmes were rapidly winched open to the cheers of the crowd, I staggered upright and hauled the bawling inductee to his feet. I leaned heavily on him, as if he were a crutch, and we returned to the tunnel from which we'd emerged beneath Arena, a lifetime and yet only moments before.

# TWENTY-TWO

I begged the dragonmaster for venom that night as the pain from my smashed ribs rolled up and down my torso in agonizing waves, as Eidon bellowed again and again for my head, for having caused the death of his lover. I craved venom not just to end the pain, understand, but to erase the horrific image of a young boy being ripped apart, of Ringus's guts dangling in glistening loops above me. I needed venom to obliterate the fear inspired by the certainty that such would be my fate on the morrow.

The Komikon denied it to me.

"Think you I can repeat today's performance?" he bellowed. "None but Ringus could work the bull so swiftly alongside me! Tomorrow you go in with dragonbait at your side: a maimed veteran who would kill you, and four lackluster inductees."

"Please, I need venom."

"You splayfooted crookback!" the dragonmaster screamed, causing the onahmes stabled about us to snort and shift in agitation. "You yolk-brained screw! Summon the Dirwalan; summon your bird!"

"I can't!" I roared back, and was at once limp and sweat-slicked by the pain that laced across my ribs. "She won't come to me, understand? She's abandoned me; I called for her, but she didn't come . . ." My voice choked off into a series of rib-tearing sobs.

I was shattered. I was forsaken. My mother had not come.

"Give me some venom, please!" I wailed, and I think the

dragonmaster would have fled then, either to find me an analgesic potion or because he realized that all was truly lost and his public execution was now a certainty.

But he couldn't leave.

Not just one Auditor stood in my stall now, see. The onahme that had been stabled there had been relocated; four Auditors, all of them tall and enveloped from crown to toe in white, stood in her place—guarding both the dragonmaster and me, that on the morrow, we both could be publicly eviscerated by Re.

I knew Temple would not make the mistake the day following of allowing either of us to survive.

Dawn again, and I could barely move. Heedless of my pain, the Auditors led me, shackled once more, to the carts waiting to transport us to Arena.

The dragonmaster, too, was shackled about wrist and ankle, though he moved not in stiff, silent agony, but flung himself against his chains, twisting, snarling, utterly wild. It had taken seven brawny nashvenir stablemen to fetter him earlier, upon Waikar Re Kratt's orders. All of the seven bore bruises, bite marks, and gashes from the brawl, if not broken bones.

Screaming invective and Djimbi curses both, the dragonmaster was tethered by three of the Auditors to the back of the last cart in the procession. He would be forced to walk the distance to Arena.

*Clank.*

The chains about my own wrists were likewise fettered to the back of the cart. I would be forced to walk the distance, too.

I would not make it. If I didn't faint from pain, I would be stoned to death by the crowds en route. A dense numbness descended upon me, so complete that when my eyes fell upon Dono, whose left eye was grossly swollen and bruised, I felt nothing. Nothing.

The carts creaked forward, trundling down the long, tree-shaded avenue of Nashvenir Re. Halfway down the avenue, Waikar

Re Kratt's daronpuis and lords waited upon their wing-pinioned destriers, glutted with the certainty that Kratt's folly over me would
soon be ended, that his unfathomable mistake in allowing me to
live this long would soon be corrected.

Waikar Re Kratt sat at the fore of the procession, indifferent and
imposing upon his magnificent beast. He lifted his reins and started
the slow, stately walk for Arena.

I fell. I was hauled upright. I fell again. An Auditor stood me upright a second time, but the ground would not stay beneath my
feet. I crumpled from the pain in my ribs.

Kratt rode down the length of our parade and studied me from
atop his bejeweled dragon, his golden hair a dazzling crown.
"Throw her in the wagon," he said. "We waste time."

And so I was not forced to walk to Arena.


The thoroughfare was choked with humanity, even more so than
on the day previous. There were hawkers selling finger sheaths and
sugary biscuits, and kiyu komikons parading their strings of enslaved girls. Half-breed men in ragged pantaloons sold roasted
coranuts to elegant children herded by nursemaids, while scrawny-
limbed youths danced slapfoot on top of wooden crates, their begging bowls cupped in their palms. Ornate litters borne upon the
shoulders of grim piebald servants wove like drunken boats above
the heads of merchants dressed in frock coats and above bearded,
blue-eyed Xxelteker sailors wearing their trademark animal-skin
hats. Thieves and gambling-den proprietors rubbed shoulders with
gaudy bayen men in shiny byssus, while lanrak paras, soldiers outside of army—or mercenaries, as some would call them—armed
with half pikes and sabers, flanked the entrances to the inns and
taverns they'd been hired to keep free of ruffians. Music, laughter,
shrieks, and guffaws spilled out from the inns on clouds of blue
pipe smoke.

As our retinue crawled along the thoroughfare and into the

shadow of Arena, those who had lined the streets to hurl invective and rock at me were jostled by the self-absorbed mayhem choking every avenue, door frame, and verandah. Free from any such hindrance, bayen women with hair coiffed into bizarre topknots leaned from the windows of some of the finer inns to hiss and clatter their silver fingersheaths at me. One went so far as to hurl her chamber pot in my direction in her righteous rage. Urine and excrement rained upon the crowd; outraged bellows exploded from the street. A riot seemed imminent.

I felt caged and vulnerable and half-wild with fear in the back of the cart, and as we lurched through another pothole and pain lanced across my ribs, my bladder threatened to loose. Shackled to the back of the cart, flanked by the walking statues of white cloth that were the Auditors, the dragonmaster bucked against his chains, shrieking and foaming at the mouth. A bold bayen youth, clothes as black as a cat, darted forward and clubbed the dragonmaster across the back with a stool. The dragonmaster staggered, fell, was dragged several feet by his chains before one of the Auditors hauled him unceremoniously upright.

The crowd roared its approval and pelted us with rocks and rotten fruit.

The apprentices covered their heads and crouched small and low in our carts, and at the fore of our parade, I saw several of Kratt's chancellors bellow indignantly at those who'd inadvertently struck them. The dragon pulling our cart tossed her head and rolled her eyes, and several of the destriers upon which were seated Clutch Re lords pranced nervously.

We turned a corner, came to a ragged halt before one of the dank tunnel entrances leading underground into Arena—the same tunnel we'd entered the day before. The guards within winched the gates open; something crowd-sent glanced off my right ear and sent my vision reeling.

As my eyes cleared, I found myself staring into the red face of a portly man standing atop a crate, an arm's length from where I sat. He held a handbill in one hand and was shouting for all to hear, spittle flying from his lips:

"At midnight precisely, come see the extraordinary fight of furious animals! For the first fight, we offer you a Xxelteker steer, attacked and subdued by six of the strongest dogs of the country. Our second fight will pit a wild she-cat against a Northern Bear, and if the she-cat is not vanquished, several pieces of fireworks will be tied to her tail, which will produce a very entertaining amusement indeed. Purchase your admittance tickets, all!"

And then the cart I was in lurched forward, and we were rolling into the clammy gloom beneath Arena.

Two boys in loincloths stood to one side of the tunnel guards, dipping tarred torches into a metal barrel of glowing faggots and handing the lit torches to those Clutch Re lords who asked for them as they rode past. Eidon took a torch. Two of the four Auditors flanking the dragonmaster also took a torch each.

We descended into the web of stone tunnels. The air reeked of urine and dragon dung, of old sweat and torch smoke. It was hard to inhale.

I started shivering, could not stop. With each shudder, the chains shackling my wrists rattled, and pain flared across my broken ribs. Those about me did not look human, had been reduced to undulating silhouettes in the torchlight. I looked instead at the shadows oozing over the uneven stone walls.

Our cart stopped. Under the barked orders of the veterans, the apprentices clambered out.

One of the Auditors half lifted me down, his hands tight around my biceps. I swayed for a moment as my feet touched the cold floor, the heavy chain fettering my wrists slapping against my belly. Above and around us, the huge stones of Arena reverberated with the coliseum noise of dragon and spectator.

Within the tunnel, the apprentices pooled into niches and

against the wall. All but the veterans were subdued and moved uncertainly. Some of the apprentices began chanting the komikonpu walan kolriks, their breathless whispers whisking down the tunnel like the breath of ghosts. Eidon slotted his torch into a wall sconce, and he and another veteran began feinting and lunging with poliars, warming up their muscles. Eidon moved with vicious certainty; his weapon sliced through the air like a dragon's claw. Dono crouched on his haunches to one side, a shadow hunched over a poliar. A sliver of something gleamed against one of his thighs. It looked like a dagger.

Kratt and his retinue of fine lords continued through the labyrinth, the creak of axles and saddle leather echoing eerily down the tunnel long after they'd disappeared from sight. They would be taking one of the many tunnels leading to the underground stables, whence they'd go to a stairwell and ascend into the brilliant glare of Arena's spectator stands.

I closed my eyes and held my elbows tucked into myself, as if by letting go, I'd lose what vestiges of courage I may have had left to me.

I felt small and impotent and exposed, and I was very, very cold.

"Mo Fa Cinai, wabaten ris balu," I gasped between chattering teeth. Purest Dragon, become my strength.

The slap of feet and the uneven breaths of someone approaching at a run intruded upon the grim silence. The veterans practicing with poliar paused; we all looked toward the sound. A shadow appeared, then materialized under the torchlight as a scrawny rishi boy.

"Summons for the first shinchiwouk participants for Clutch Re!" he panted. "These being: Zarq-the-deviant, danku Re's Dono, arbiyesku Re's Kaban—"

My head turned diaphanous and filled with a roaring sound and I remembered, too late, that I needed to empty my bladder.

The two Auditors on either side of me started forward. I shuddered violently, cringed back into the shadow.

"Wait, it's too soon," I gasped. "We just arrived; I haven't been assigned a vebalu weapon—"

One of my biceps was clutched in a hard grip and I was jerked forward.

Dono rose from his crouch and came toward me. In the dark, his damaged eye protruded from under his swollen, ripped eyelid like a rotting plum. Hatred spilled off him like smoke from the torches. As well as a poliar in one hand, he carried a coiled whip tied loosely to his loincloth sash, and tucked within that sash, a dirk. The ivory and gold handle clearly designated the blade as bayen.

Not a vebalu weapon, that. He'd been given it by some Clutch Re lord intent on my death.

I looked wildly about. "Where's my vebalu cape? Where's my weapon? I can't go into Arena empty-handed!"

"Shut up, whore," Dono rasped, and his voice was so warped with loathing, it was unrecognizable.

Beside me, the dragonmaster went into a fresh paroxysm of mad rage. He was still fettered about the wrist, like I was, and, too, was hobbled about the ankles. But that didn't stop him from flailing about, jaws snapping like those of a cur. The man was clearly functioning on the might of the deranged.

"Unhand me, you Temple harlots!" he shrieked. "Unchain me; give me my whip!"

From the shadows, Egg began gathering up the four apprentices listed, alongside the names of Dono and me, on the Ashgon's Bill. All four wept. One cowered down against a wall.

"Please, Egg, please," he sobbed, looking up at Egg as if Egg were an older brother who had the power to free the inductee from his fate. "Don't make me go."

"Get on your feet!" Egg roared, and when the boy continued to cower, looking up at him imploringly, Egg clouted him over the head. "Do what I taught you an' you'll be a servitor when we get back. Now, get up!"

The boy covered his head and sobbed. Egg picked him up and stood him upright; the boy sagged groundward. With a curse, Egg threw him over one shoulder and stomped over to us, the boy's vebalu cape swishing in front of his chest like a Temple scapular. The boy sobbed against the back of Egg's neck and pleaded, over and over, to be let go.

The other three inductees assigned shinchiwouk duty alongside Dono and me hefted their vebalu weapons and looked glaze-eyed with fear.

"I'll carry him up," Egg growled to no one in particular, and with that, the Auditors started up the tunnel, pulling the shackled and struggling dragonmaster by a chain, leading me by another.

Mo Fa Cinai wabaten ris balu, I thought, and somehow, that desperate prayer became mingled with the sobbing boy's pleas, so that as we wound our way up the murky tunnel, I was no longer asking the Winged Infinite for strength, but to let me go, to please let me go.

Ahead: daylight.

Susurrus of two hundred thousand people gathered for bloodshed and merriment.

Fresh air, redolent with the dusty smell of sunbaked earth and the sweet pungency of fertile onahmes waiting to be bred to a bull.

We reached the rusted gates; beyond them, the dusty coliseum bowl. My eyes watered in the harsh light.

Egg tried to lift the boy down; the boy clung to Egg's neck and wrapped his legs tight about Egg's bulky girth. Egg reached up, grabbed a fistful of the boy's hair, and peeled the terrified inductee headfirst off himself.

"Please, Egg, don't make me go!"

I turned away, fought my body's urge to retch.

The guards standing on the inside of the gate briskly went about their task of checking everyone's vebalu weapons and capes, to make sure they were standard issue. They ignored Dono.

"He has a dirk!" I cried. "That's illegal!"

One of the guards leaned toward me, his breath reeking of maska spirits. His sinuous facial cicatrices looked blue in the backlight of the coliseum bowl. He was missing a front tooth.

"I'd use the thing on you myself, if I had the choice," he growled. I fell silent.

"Unchain me, lest the wrath of the Realm descend upon you!" the dragonmaster cried. "You sluts of demons, unchain me!"

One of the guards unlatched the gate, swung it open on rusty hinges, and stepped aside. The Auditors shoved me through, then the dragonmaster. The hobbles about the dragonmaster's ankles were not removed; neither were the shackles about his wrists, nor the shackles about mine.

We stumbled, blinded by sunlight, onto the stadium's dusty bowl. At once, it was as if a simoom blasted through Arena; the roar of the crowd was as hot and fierce as a desert gale.

*Clitter-clack, clitter-clack!* The hailstorm of thousands of finger sheaths drumming against Arena's tiers deafened us. One of the inductees instinctively covered his head, as if the noise were a rain of rocks. I staggered away from Dono, away, away.

But not so far away that I would be picked off by the bull, should he charge in the direction of us apprentices. Which he would.

I came to a stop, breathing rapidly, unevenly, stabbed by pain from my broken ribs with each breath. Like the day previous, I felt my eyes drawn to the dazzling chandelier display of the Emperor's Ceiling.

How can such beauty, I vaguely wondered, be created and appreciated by those who can also be incited to lust by the deaths of children?

My gaze drifted down, as light as dust, fogged by pain and fear, to the balconies of the overlords. I found Clutch Re's balcony, the crimson pennants that flapped above its tasseled canopy emblazoned with the elegant purple hieratics of Cafar Re. Cafar Re. The Bastion of Tears.

And there, weaving between the lush-limbed ebanis upon that balcony, dressed in a gauzy bitoo of palest blue, walked a figure that riveted my blurred gaze. The feline way she moved, the wild fall of her tawny hair, the swell of her bosom and the distinctive roll of her hips . . .

I swear to this day that despite the distance, despite my debilitated state, despite the dazzling prisms thrown by a million faceted mirrors high above, I knew at once exactly who she was.

My sister.

Danku Re Darquel's Waivia.

I stared, ears roaring. I did not hear the crowd fall silent as the Ashgon raised his hand. Did not hear the clank of iron gates winched open. Did not hear the bellow of Re as he came charging from his holding stall, nor the answering roar of the crowd. All I heard was the rush of blood in my ears. All I saw was that figure, no more than a distant smudge, standing beside Waikar Re Kratt, her closeness to him declaring that she was his Wai-ebani Bayen. First Pleasurer of an Aristocrat.

That had always been her ambition, see. To serve as pleasurer to Roshu-Lupini Re's First Son.

So that was why mother's haunt hadn't returned to me: She'd had no need. She'd found someone I'd long believed dead. She'd found my sister.

I swooned.

It was that swoon that saved me.

As I melted groundward, Dono—already running toward me with his dirk raised—struck. Instead of striking me, he struck air, though so close was his blow, so much power was there in his strike, that to the crowd it must have looked as if his blade buried deep into my neck, for the spectators rose as one to their feet with great cheers. As it was, his blade only nicked me as I fell.

Carried forward by the momentum of his strike, Dono tripped over my prone form and went sprawling. The dragonmaster leapt over me, his mottled green and brown form appearing briefly to my befuddled mind as a gazelle, though that couldn't have been true, for he was hobbled. He fell upon Dono. While he used the chain binding his shackled wrists as a garrote around Dono's throat, while the two rolled in the dust to the wild roars of the crowd, the ground beneath me shook as Re charged toward us.

The inductees ran in different directions, screaming. Re abruptly veered after them.

I only saw all this from the corner of one eye, understand, for I lay upon my back staring at the glittering display far above my head, my senses shredded, my body detached, thinking: My mother *did* abandon me, just as she did when I was nine. For Waivia. Again.

Why? What had I ever done as a child that had made my mother give her love so unfailingly to Waivia but not to me?

Those scintillating mirrors high above . . . how hypnotic they were, how beguiling. Like the flecks of quartz I'd been so entranced by on the roof of my little burrow in the viagand chambers, not all that long ago. Like the thousands of stars that had glittered in the night sky, the first time my mother openly defied Temple by hiding glazes and clays in the jungle instead of giving them away on Sa Gikiro, almost a decade ago.

I experienced a grunu-engros, then, there on my back, staring at those scintillating reflections while a great bull mauled a young boy. I had a dragon-spirit moment, that illusory feeling of having already experienced a similar situation that is a portent of one's life yet to come.

And I remembered.

I remembered what I'd envisaged while lying in venom torpor in my burrow in the viagand chambers, staring at flecks of quartz and feldspar in stone. I remembered that I had experienced being a bull.

Not once, not twice, but thrice while under the spell of venom, while listening to dragonsong, I had fought in shinchiwouk as a dragon, until even in sleep my limbs had twitched with the re-membered feints and lunges of dragon combat.

I knew then that I could survive Arena. Without the protection of my mother's haunt, without even the certainty that I'd once been loved by my mother, I knew I could survive.

How?

Because I could think like Re, could predict each of his move-ments before he acted.

With this heady rush of hope, adrenaline coursed through my body, and the combination of hope and adrenaline was as momen-tarily powerful as venom infused direct into my muscles, my nerves, my sinews and flesh.

In stiff, jerky stages, I rose to my feet.

Breathing heavily, fingers tingling with a flood-rush of blood, I looked for Dono's dropped poliar. I found it close by, not far from where the dragonmaster was straddled across Dono's back, chain tight against Dono's throat. I bent toward the poliar; pain like a bolt of lightning blasted white-hot through me. Vision blurred, I groped for the poliar, found its smooth, dust-coated shaft. I hefted the poliar's weight in both my shackled hands and straightened with a sharp intake of breath.

Slowly, I turned about.

Half the stadium's length away, mighty Re had quit worrying the disjointed form of one of the inductees and was just raising his head from the corpse. Our eyes met. The ground between us con-tracted.

I lifted my poliar into the air. Inflating my lungs, I bellowed out a challenge.

All the fury, fear, and pain I felt, from all I'd witnessed that day and all the days of my life, rushed into my bellow. The sound that came out swelled, became enormous, was hoarse and primal and puissant. It was not human, that sound; it was misery and hope in-carnate, clashing and exploding with all the force of a thunderstorm. Amplified tenfold by the coliseum, the war cry boomed and echoed round tier after tier, and I swear even the pennants and tents upon the bayen platforms shuddered under its boom.

Re reared up on his hind legs and shook his head, massive dewlaps swinging, and blasted the stadium with an answering roar. He crouched. Sprang into the air, wings slightly outspread, neck and snout pointed skyward, torso exposed, hind legs braced for landing.

A vulnerable, upright position, that, belly and testes fully exposed, unfurled wings unprotected. A lifetime of captivity had turned Re guileless, had deprived him of the learned skills of shinchiwouk survival in the wild, had dulled his dragonsong memories. Bloodlust, combined with his predictable, repetitive experiences in Arena, had blinded him to the danger of unfurling his wings while in battle.

Not so me.

By means of the dragons' ancestral memories that I'd experienced in the viagand chambers, I'd fought with my wings unfurled as a hatchling bull, my infant bones mere flexible cartilage. By dragonmemory, I'd learned to never unfurl my wings in grounded combat, lest they be broken by an opponent.

And from dragonsong, I had the memory of being a captive destrier, of being trained to go for the vulnerable wings of my opponent in battle flight and shred membrane from wing spar and fracture wrist bone with a clawed, well-aimed kick.

I had no claws; I was not dragon. But I did have Dono's poliar.

I stumbled toward Re as he launch-glided toward me, his neck outstretched, his hind legs forward-braced for landing, his wings unfurled. With each of my footfalls, ice-shards of pain slashed across my torso; it felt as if the shredded end of one of my broken ribs was lacerating my guts from within. I gripped the poliar tighter, concentrated on moving forward, on not tripping over dust and rock, concentrated on those amber wings unfurling in the air like the sails of some great ship.

I did not stop outside the range of a tongue lashing as the dragonmaster had during his mad charge toward Re on the day previous. I continued forward, the leathery stink of Re about me, his bulk looming over me, his purple and green scales brilliant. Dust billowed everywhere, choking me, and now I was running half-blind, blinking rapidly.

Too late Re realized my intentions. Too late instinct and dragon-memory punched through the battle lust blazing through him. As his hind legs hit the ground, great talons scoring the earth and billowing up more dust, he tried to draw his wings in, tried to swing his ponderous bulk sideways from me.

Dust thick and smothering about me. Noise and confusion, flash of brilliant scales. Wing leather the color of sunlit amber before me, the ebony wing-tip claws curling in on themselves.

I slammed my poliar down hard against the pteroid bone, the peculiar wrist a third of the way along a dragon's wing. Re roared anew, and I screamed, too, from the pain of my violent movement, and let go my poliar. Re swung about and dropped down on all fours, his injured wing dragging.

I darted in, then, moving in a lopsided, pain-drunken lurch, and began the loathsome work of a dragonwhore.

*You have to make the thing move, hey! And don't spend so long under there, you think Re's gonna be standin' still while you're doin' that? You have to get in an' out, in an' out, else you'll get trampled!*

Egg's voice boomed through my head as talons shifted about on either side of me, as Re's belly brushed the top of my stooped back. The stink of him was unforgettable: manure and musk, regurgitated crop food and semen, hot leather and licorice-and-lime venom. The stench was bawdy, earthy, savage.

I spread my arms as best I could and embraced his stinking

scrotal sac and rubbed my body against his leathery warmth. Red sheets of pain washed over me; I think I screamed.

A trembling, muscled hind leg slammed down on the ground a hand's breadth from my right foot. The force of that impact upon the ground seemed to momentarily bounce me; the back of my stooped head struck his bulging testes hard and my neck made a horrible, gritty sound from the collision and I was dizzy and disoriented.

A leathery knee slammed against me, and some wild animal shrieked in pain, and all was dust and the flash of talons, and then, abruptly, the towering mass I was stooped beneath spun away from me as Re heaved his massive form about, and I stood exposed and confused before him.

He roared: A gale of warm air redolent with the smell of venom blasted into my face. Venom misted over me; it peppered my skin with minute droplets that seemed to incandesce before burning into my marrow.

A huge maw with great fangs opened before me.

"Hey-o, bull, hey-o!" The hoarse, wild cry of the dragonmaster, followed by the crack of his bullwhip, right against Re's snout. The maw pulled back from me; whip snapped against muzzle, hard, again. With a furious roar, Re swung his snout toward the dragonmaster, who stood hobbled and wrist-shackled, Dono's whip in both hands.

Re would kill us both if the onahmes weren't released soon.

Sucking in a dust-gritty breath, I ducked back under the enraged bull's belly.

In and out, in and out. My world collapsed and became only the leathery reek of dragon hide, the sour musk of scaled scrotum, the grit and choke of dust, the flash of claw and thud of belly against shoulder, back, and head. I embraced those foul testes, was shoved and battered, jarred and bruised, and again I embraced the bull. If not for that spray of venom that had misted over me, I would have been incapable of it, but the rasp of broken bone within my rib cage and the violent slam of leathery, scaled muscle against my body was bearable because of the dragon's poison.

From the corner of one eye, through a cloud of dust, I saw Re's venomous tongue meet its mark upon the dragonmaster's chest. *Slam!* The dragonmaster sailed through the air and landed hard, *thud,* flat on his back in the dust.

But instead of lunging forward to scoop the fallen Komikon into his mouth, Re reared up on his hind legs, neck craned to the sky, and suddenly I stood exposed again, right at the very feet of this fanged tower of might. His great dewlaps inflated above me like opalescent sails, and he trumpeted. His lusty cry vibrated right through me; for a moment, I heard dragonsong.

And then something wet and hot shoved me in the chest, and I was staring direct at the red-mottled pink of Re's forked phallus. I staggered back, revolted, then turned and loped away from him, stumbling as the ground reverberated from his triumphant bugle.

I had succeeded. I'd aroused the bull.

The iron gates to the holding corral of the trumpeting, pheromone-fragrant onahmes were winched open. I looked blearily about, trying to orient myself, saw the apprentices' tunnel door I'd come through, then staggered toward it.

Pain turned my vision blotchy. I lurched, wheezing, eyes locked upon that dank tunnel. Behind me, the onahmes flooded the stadium, the flood-rush of their wings a tempest. The inhuman roaring of the crowd warped further.

Something struck my shoulder, a rock, a sandal, I don't know what. I stumbled. Something else struck me, and a third thing. I fell to my knees. Swaying, I stared drunkenly at the tunnel exit, still so far away. White figures floated from its depths.

Auditors.

I tried to get to my feet. My legs would not obey me and pain from my ribs exploded throughout my body. I fell forward, onto my hands. Head hanging, I sucked in air that was too hot, too cruel for my lungs. A hail of objects bounced off my back.

White before me: the hem of a gown.

I raised my head, followed the gown up, up, to where the veil-mask of an Auditor wavered and swooped. Beside the faceless creature stood another. One of them held an axe. I thought, for a moment, that he held it backward, so the sharp end pointed not at me, but at the sky. But then the axe came crashing toward my neck, and I knew no more.

Blackness.

Through the blackness, a roar. The blood-fevered roar of a crowd.

Ah, I thought. I've heard stories of how the decapitated experience sound and vision for several heartbeats after the head has left the shoulders.

The two Auditors picked up my corpse and dragged me, head dangling upon my chest from half-severed neck, across the talon-scored Arena ground to the tunnel.

I foggily remembered how Prinrut had been dragged out of my life in the viagand chambers, remembered how her bare feet had rasped along the ground even as mine did now.

Blackness again.

Then light.

Firelight, guttering from a torch. I looked about me blearily, confused, aching, nauseous.

I was in the dank gloom of an Arena tunnel. The muted bellows of the crowd outside swelled and ebbed, and onahmes bugled. Two Auditors lay upon the tunnel floor, the necks of their white gowns rapidly turning red. Beside them, two Arena guards, eyes glazed, blood flowing heavily from slashed jugular veins; I recognized the sinuous cicatrices and the gap-toothed grimace of one of the guards.

Bleerily, I looked up.

Before me, draped limp between two standing Auditors, hung the dragonmaster, the welt of venom across his chest as thick and long as my arm. He was slur-muttering, saliva hanging from his slack lips in ropes, head lolling. He jerked rigid and his eyes snapped wide.

"They demand Nashe," he shrieked; then his head dropped against his chest again. He began to convulse.

"Get it off him, blood-blood," one of the Auditors barked, and he tore off the hem of his gown, wrapped it swiftly about one hand, then quickly scraped the tarry toxin from the convulsing dragonmaster's chest.

"That'll do. He's survived worse. Pick up the girl again and let's be off, quick. We've not got much time."

I stared at the Auditor as he shook the venom-thick swathing from his broad hand. It was not chalked white, that hand.

And I was not dead, my neck not a bleeding stump.

The Auditor bent over me. I cried out as he and his twin lifted me upright.

"Conscious already? After the blow I gave you? Great Dragon, Babu, you've got steel for muscles!"

"Daronpu Gen," I gasped.

"Don't say the name aloud, girl. Not till we're elsewhere."

"You came for me."

"'Course I did. Sorry about that clout with the axe. Had to make it look real, hey-o." He touched the back of my neck gently. "Don't think I hit you too hard. But you'll have a throbbing head for days anyways, I'd wager."

Wager.

I remembered then.

"Xxamer-Zu?" I gasped.

"All yours, girl. All yours. Malaban Bri came through, as did Ghepp, in the end. I imagine Ghepp's collecting his land deed from Roshu Xxamer-Zu even as we speak."

I closed my eyes. Swallowed. Swooped in and out of consciousness, the pain in my broken ribs like serrated knives, the nauseating throbbing where Gen had struck me with the dull end of his axe immense.

I had done it. Without the haunt's powers, I'd survived Arena. *And* I'd secured myself a Clutch.

"Give me a little venom from that swathing," I begged. "Please."

Daronpu Gen hesitated. Grunted. "A little only, for the pain. A little only."

The burn of it in my mouth was the fire of the Realm. It coursed through me, made me mighty with dragon strength, with otherworld hope.

I remembered my mother's haunt, remembered seeing Waivia upon the Cafar Re balcony of Arena.

How had my mother's haunt found my sister? And why hadn't she found her years earlier?

I didn't know.

Nor, too, did I know what the bizarre reunion between mother and daughter would herald for the future. That my sister was the Wai-ebani of Waikar Re Kratt—a man driven by a need for power and causing pain in others—and that Waivia now had access to the powers of the haunt, boded ill for Clutch Re. But Waivia wouldn't stand by the sadistic lord's side with the might of the Skykeeper behind her. Surely.

And even if she did, it wouldn't affect me, living safely and anonymously in Clutch Xxamer-Zu.

Surely.

With a weary sigh, I nodded at Daronpu Gen.

"Let's go to Xxamer-Zu, then," I said. "Let's go home."

# ABOUT THE AUTHOR

**Janine Cross** has published short fiction in various Canadian magazines and was nominated for an Aurora Award in 2002. Her nonspeculative fiction has appeared in newspapers and a local anthology, *Shorelines*. She has also published a literary novel.